THE PARADISE TREE

The circle of light   e
to resist the weigh   s
if they had put up

*"Behold the Ang   r
world. I am Abad   y
prey!"* The deep

The physical form was only a shell which had been filled
now by something never meant to be made manifest in this
world. He stood in the midst of his shattered circle on the
top of his tower, urging on the forces which boiled in the
air above the city like a hunter his hounds.

*"Lilith, I command thee! Night Walker, Demon Queen!
Summon thy minions! Speed to destroy those who would
oppose my will!"*

Other books by Diana L. Paxson

BRISINGAMEN
WHITE MARE, RED STALLION

Diana L. Paxson
The PARADISE TREE

ACE BOOKS, NEW YORK

Acknowledgements

This is a work of fiction. The Paradise drug does not exist, and although I hope that my characters have the internal truth that all novelists strive for, none of them represents any real person who has ever been associated with the University of California or the neo-pagan community in the Bay Area. However I would like to acknowledge my debt to those who helped me make their personalities, actions and settings as convincing as possible.

My first thanks go to Mary Mason, Renaissance woman, who worked out the structure and effects of the Paradise drug. I would like to credit David Oster of Mosaic Codes for explaining the more esoteric aspects of programming and computer games. He has first dibs on designing the "Forbidden City" game when the state of the art catches up with us.

My gratitude also goes to Dr. Frederic Hollander of crystallography at the University of California for general background and guidance through the labyrinth of the department, and to Chris Noren of chemistry, who illuminated the mysteries of gene splicing and tried to correct my mistakes in procedure. Where I have got it right, the credit is due to them, my errors are my own. I am indebted also to D. Hudson Frew for sharing his research on ley lines on the campus of the University of California. Michael Masley can be found playing the bowhammered cymbalom on Telegraph Avenue on sunny weekend afternoons.

The Berkeley of Del Eden is on a slightly different timeline than our own. In our world, Macintosh has not yet developed a computer with all the capabilities of Ruth's machine, though that is changing fast, nor is there a permanent space station in the skies. All the commercial spaces in the building where Eden Books is located are currently otherwise occupied. Aside from that, everything is pretty much as I have described it.

The Queen of Angels exhibit never went on tour; however, it exists, and is more wonderful than my description can convey. I saw it originally at the Exposition Hall and the Archangels are *now* in the Duquette Pavillion of Saint Francis in San Francisco. I would like to thank Ray Bradbury for permission to quote from his narration to the exhibit. Security on the Campanile is better than described, and the spiral fire escape at the Claremont has been taken down, but both towers are quite real.

Most of the quotes that serve as chapter headings are also quoted in Volume 13 of the *Collected Works of C. G. Jung— Alchemical Studies*. My apologies to the memory of Master Therion for distorting certain selections from a ritual that, taken in its entirety and in the proper spirit, should be both impressive and effective. It must be remembered that evil is not capable of true creativity, but can only pervert the original work of others.

In that understanding, and in hopes that my work has built on the creation of others rather than perverting it, I would also like to acknowledge my debt to Dion Fortune, Charles Williams, and John Buchan.

Diana L. Paxson,
Spring Equinox, 1986

To Kelson
Priest of Tiphareth

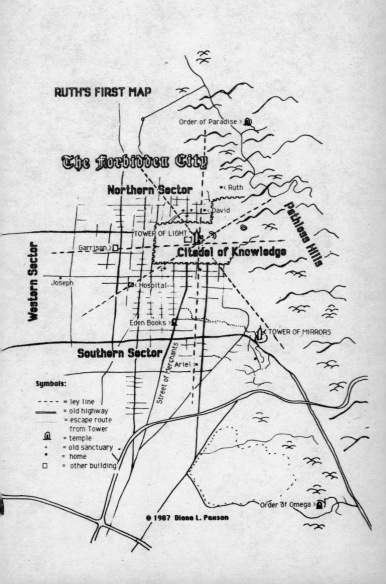

RUTH'S FIRST MAP

Order of Paradise >

The Forbidden City

Northern Sector

• Ruth

David

TOWER OF LIGHT

Citadel of Knowledge

Pathless Hills

Garrison

Joseph

Hospital

Eden Books >

TOWER OF MIRRORS

Southern Sector

Ariel >

Western Sector

Street of Merchants

Symbols:

- - - = ley line
———— = old highway
········ = escape route from Tower
⌂ = temple
+ = old sanctuary
• = home
□ = other building

© 1987 Diana L. Paxson

Order of Omega >

Prologue

The Void was empty, yet in that emptiness all things were implied.

The Void was Darkness, yet that darkness glowed with potential Light.

It was everywhere and nowhere, uncreated and eternal, a nothingness so full there was no room for creation, until for the least moment it contracted, like a man drawing breath to sneeze, and expanding again thrust immanence into manifestation—pure Light prismed through myriad refractions until all the colors glowed against a Night their presence had made visible.

White light shone—blinding, had there been anyone to see—and was filtered to a softer silver by a vibration that set waves of light and sound in motion, seeking balance and harmony.

In a sphere of warm darkness manifest power took on substance, and the vibration organized it into the patterns of form. From force and form all the other spheres were born: focused lenses, crystals vibrating each to its own frequency of light and sound, until in the Void grew a Tree of Light.

But where force and form first met, consciousness emerged, knowing and self-known, enabling all the others to know themselves. That point became a meeting place where energies, perceiving their differences, developed individuality.

They were gods, they were angels, they were the Regents of the spheres. And four become mightiest among them: Raphael, Gabriel, Uriel, and Mikael, greatest of them all.

In that realm life flourished as in a garden, and the fruit of knowledge hung from its trees.

1

But the Source of the first emanations continued to seek experience, even unto manifestation and physical form. And this new creation was opposed by the Regent of the sphere of Knowledge, and there was War in Heaven.

Then was the plan of creation altered, and the knowledge of the spirit sundered from the knowledge of the flesh. The Regent of Knowledge was cast out, and outside of the first pattern, the new sphere was formed yet in its gardens the conflict was played out again and again. A great gulf stretched where the sphere of Knowledge had been.

That gulf is the Abyss, and there dwell demons. But on the other side is the garden of the spirit, and there the Tree of Life still grows.

Those who snatch at the fruit of the Tree like thieves or children are the demons' prey, but they who come by that path which is as narrow as the edge of a sword, taste Knowledge as their natural food, and to them is given the freedom of all worlds.

In the day when all souls shall eat of that fruit, the earthly and the heavenly spheres shall be united once more, and the Plan of Creation shall be fulfilled . . .

1.

Let him take care to recognize and guard against the deceptions of the devil, who often insinuates himself into chemical operations, that he may hold up the laborants with vain and useless things to the neglect of the works of nature ...

Theobald De Hoghelande,
De Alchemiae Difficultatibus.

The telephone rang like a siren, insistent and shrill.

Ruth Racusak hardly heard it. Her eyes were still following the metamorphosis of the image on the computer screen as she moved the light pen across the digitizing pad. The acid-rock music she had synthesized for the northern sector of the "city" pounded in the background as the point of view moved along the street. So far this sequence was working perfectly. The buildings, created by applying her own algorithm for simulated texture mapping to photos of real structures that had been digitized by the scanner, looked realistic, and the shadows shifted convincingly as she "moved."

Now she came to a corner. Ruth moved the light pen across its pad, checking, then retraced her route and moved left. Somewhere before she came to the end of the block, something was going to happen—she moved the pen more slowly, then dropped it as the screen flickered and the image shattered into slanting bands of light. The music disintegrated into an ear-destroying high-pitched whine. Swearing, Ruth jabbed at

3

the interrupt switch at the back of the computer.

She sat back as the screen cleared and the sound stopped, and becoming aware of the telephone at last, reached for it.

"Look, Ruth—I thought we had agreed that you—"

Ruth held the receiver away from her ear, grimacing. The voice of her ex-husband receded into an irregular murmur in which she could distinguish the name of their son, and she sighed.

"Leonard, I'll be happy to take Martin two weekends next month—*every* weekend if you want me to." Ruth angled the mouthpiece so that her ear was still distanced. One-handedly, she pulled the masses of her wiry dark-auburn hair back from her face, twisted them into a knot at the nape of her neck and thrust a pencil through the coil to hold it there. Leonard was still talking.

"But I've got to have this time free," Ruth interrupted him. "I told you I have a deadline—the Star Wares people want the prototype of the Forbidden City game by July so we can revise it and get it into production for Christmas. I have less than six months to get this done, and I'm just beginning to get it together."

She felt her heartbeat speed up and gripped the telephone receiver harder, just thinking about it. When the Star Wares people had seen her graphics for the Career Education program at the West Coast Computer Fair and started talking game design, it had seemed like the chance of a lifetime. Now she wondered if it was going to be the crash of a lifetime, instead. She *had* to concentrate now—once she was into it, she could cope with distractions.

"It'll be Sissy who has to take care of Martin anyway, not you, so what's your problem? I thought Sissy adored him . . ."

As Leonard began indignantly to defend his new wife, Ruth felt the old guilt cramping in her belly. What if Sissy really couldn't handle Martin? What kind of mother was she to let another woman raise her child?

"Ruthie, it isn't that Sissy can't take care of the boy, it's the principle of the thing." Leonard's voice boomed in her ear as she inadvertently brought the receiver closer. "You have to stick by your responsibilities. But sticking with things always has been your problem, hasn't it—I'm not surprised to hear your project is in trouble! I knew you were frigid, but I thought you had some feeling for your child. But

I suppose we could always renegotiate the custody agreement if making a home for your son two weekends a month and a few weeks in the summer is too much for you . . ."

"You wouldn't—all right, Martin can come here this weekend! Leonard, you know how I feel—" appalled, she heard her own voice sharpen hysterically and bit off the words.

"No, no—" His voice had recovered a lawyer's blandness. "We can manage just fine. I just wanted to make sure you understood . . ."

Ruth's fingers clenched the receiver. She had reacted—Leonard had punished her, and now he would be satisfied. It really had nothing to do with Martin at all.

"Yes, I understand . . . I'll take him, Leonard, okay?" Very carefully, she set the receiver down.

The blank gray face of the monitor made a dull mirror. Dim and distorted, she could see a face plump enough not to show the lines that the past ten years had etched there, and haunted dark eyes.

Resisting the temptation to bring up the program again and try to figure out what had gone wrong, Ruth unfolded herself from the computer chair. Slowly she felt her fury drain away. The Vangelis tape she had put on when she started had run out even before she started on the music sequences, and the wall clock was ticking out half-past noon.

My blood sugar level must be lapping my toenails, she thought morosely. *I bet I did something really stupid, like a typo in the code . . . I should be grateful to Leonard for breaking me out of the trance*. Maybe true hackers could produce pages of precision code on minimal food and sleep, but Ruth had learned long ago that she made silly mistakes if she tried it.

Last week's vow to eat a good breakfast every day seemed to have gone the way of her decision to jog every evening, to lose the fifteen pounds she had gained during the divorce, to give up coffee. But by the time that thought came to her she was standing in front of the coffee maker in her kitchenette. Smiling in self-mockery, Ruth dumped a spoonful of Mr. Peet's best Blue Mountain into the filter cone and put the kettle on the stove.

As she savored the rich scent of brewing coffee, she reflected that she might as well give up on breakfasts. When she was married to Leonard and writing accounting-data-entry and financial-page-layout software for the bank, she had been too busy getting her husband and son off to office or babysitter or school and herself across the bay to San Francisco to think about eating. In those days she had made do with the aluminum caffeinide they served at the office and, too often, with pastry from the machine.

She had had her caffein-consciousness raised from instant to custom-ground imported coffees when she had started writing educational software for the Ecology Education program at Instructional Training Systems. After that she had developed a graphic language for a preschool program, and finally, when she started working as a free-lancer and discovered a really elegant algorithm for doing realistic graphics by simulated ray tracing, the Career Education game that had impressed Star Wares.

At least having the computer in the big loft that was also her bedroom saved her from institutional coffee. The beauty of programming was that you could do most of the work at home, which made it more comfortable, but not, unfortunately, any easier.

Ruth looked around with a sigh. Steam from the coffee maker swirled white in the intermittent sunlight that filtered past the plants in the window and glowed warmly on the redwood paneling. The lower level of the loft made a comfortable book-lined living room, with a futon couch and easy chair, and hand-woven rugs on the wax-finished boards of the floor. Next to the bath was a small room where Martin slept when he came to stay. The house was not quite a Maybeck, or even one of Julia Morgan's designs, but it had a homey elegance typical of the Berkeley tradition.

Cut with a little cream and a half-spoonful of raw sugar, the coffee was hot and comforting. Ruth padded over to the big chair and eased down, putting her feet on the redwood coffee table. *Woman, you've got it made—you have creative work and a chance to make it really big in your profession, freedom, a nice place to live, friends—so why aren't you happy?*

Logic could find no reason for this nagging feeling that something was wrong. All her personal problems were in the past and, except when her programs crashed, she had no reason to complain.

She took a deep breath and worked her head back and

forth, trying to loosen her neck muscles. If she could somehow attain the detachment that came to her when she was programming without having to face the computer, maybe she could relax. *Let your mind go blank, as blank as the screen—* she told herself.

The telephone rang.

Ruth jerked and spilled her coffee. Swearing, she tried to mop up the liquid with a dishtowel with one hand, and reached for the extension with the other.

"Ruth? Is that you?" The voice on the other end of the line had a breathless quality, as if the speaker had been running. Ariel Ashton had always sounded that way. Her name on the college records was Alexandra, but after her triumphant performance in a school production of *The Tempest,* she had been unanimously rechristened.

Images flickered on the screen of Ruth's memory—Ariel rushing into the dorm room they had shared at Mills College with her tawny hair flying and gray eyes wide—always in a hurry, always eager for new experience, dragging Ruth out of her books and blue jeans and into dresses and concerts and for the first time in her life, just having fun. They had both graduated, married, divorced, and gone their ways. But they had remained in the San Francisco Bay Area, and they had stayed friends. For a moment, the fifteen years that had passed since Mills fell away.

"Yes, Ariel," Ruth's gaze sought the empty computer screen as if for reassurance, and she grimaced. "Who else would it be?"

"I'm sorry, you sound upset—did I call too early?"

"No, I've been up for hours, unfortunately. It's not you— the program I'm working on just blew." She glanced at the clouding sky outside, and shivered.

"I'm sorry." Ariel repeated herself, and Ruth wondered if she had really heard. "Ruth, I have to talk to you!"

"So you're talking—" Ruth stopped short, knowing that Ariel would only be hurt if she understood the sarcasm, and there was no reason for Ruth to hit out at her. "Don't mind me, I just had another fight with Leonard."

"I need to see you—" said Ariel.

Ruth bit her lip, thinking. With Ariel, it was always right now. She recognized the edge of excitement in her friend's voice and wondered what rainbow she was chasing now. She ought to say no. She didn't have the time to hold Ariel's hand right now. And then she remembered how Leonard had taunted her with running out on her obligations. If that was true then she had no right to put off Ariel, to whom she had owed her life, probably, and certainly her sanity, long ago.

"I have to go shopping tomorrow," was what came out. "Can I meet you somewhere?"

"I suppose so—how about at Petrouchka?" asked Ariel. "We could have lunch there."

"Can you at least tell me what it's all about, so I can listen intelligently?"

Ariel laughed softly. "I have a new Teacher." Ruth could hear the capital letter. "His name is Joseph Roman." Ruth sighed, knowing that Ariel was incapable of being any more explicit now.

"All right, I'll be there at one." She hung up and sat staring. Flickers of light still danced across her inner vision, and she realized that she had been gazing at the terminal for too long. How long? She had slipped the discs into the Mac after her second cup of coffee, just to get a start before she ate breakfast.

Perhaps Ariel's phone call had triggered a memory of the dream she had been having just before she woke that morning. She had been walking through a city, and it seemed to her that Ariel had been there too, and then the streets had gone all dark and threatening, and Ariel had disappeared. Ruth had a vague impression of running wildly, tripping over strewn garbage and blowing papers, calling for her friend.

But it was ridiculous to let that bother her. It was obviously an anxiety dream caused by her troubles with the game program. She would be happy, Ruth told herself, when she got it working. Or maybe when she found out what was bothering Ariel. Or perhaps, she thought as she reconsidered the state of her stomach, when she had put something more substantial than coffee inside.

From outside, Ruth could hear the steady scrape of a shovel going into the ground. She set down the coffee and went to the window. Tom Halpern was working in the yard below, highlighted against the redwood fence and the pine trees that hid the houses further up the hill. For a moment she simply watched him, enjoying the easy grace with which he worked. The weak sun of January was burning through the clouds, and he had rolled up the sleeves of the Yukon jersey he wore. She could see the play of muscle in his tanned forearms. An inhibition so ingrained that it never reached her awareness shut off her physical response to his masculinity, but she was conscious of his strength, and felt obscurely reassured.

Tom lived on the second floor of the big, brown-shingled house that Ruth joint-owned with him and a young lawyer and Lorraine, who lived with her two small children on the first floor. They were a sort of cross between a family and neighbors. In general, they all took care of their own parts of the house, but Tom was a landscape gardener and they had happily turned the yard over to him.

"Tom!" she called suddenly, leaning out of the window. "Have you had lunch yet?"

He straightened and grinned up at her. "What are you offering?"

Ruth did a quick review of the contents of her refrigerator. "Coffee, grilled cheese on black bread, and salad if you've got something left in the garden to liven up last week's lettuce."

"Sounds good—" Tom pulled a faded bandanna from his back pocket and wiped his face with it. "Let me just finish getting this apple tree in before the roots dry."

He knelt to ease the little tree tenderly into the hole he had dug for it. Ruth realized that she was still wearing the faded nightgown she had slept in, and concerned less with modesty than with esthetics, stripped it off and pulled on a sweatshirt and jeans.

By the time Tom trudged up the stairs with a basket of miscellaneous greenery, Ruth had shoveled the pile of *MacUser, Dr. Dobb's,* and the other computer magazines off the second chair, cleared the printouts and old coffee cups from the table, and thrown a fresh cloth over it. As she had hidden the kitchen's clutter, her reactions to the morning's phone calls had been tidied away in the mental file where she kept her pain.

For a moment she fingered the worn linen of the tablecloth, tracing the pattern of drawn-work around the edge. It had been her grandmother's—one of the few things Ruth had inherited from her. A flicker of memory brought her the image of linen and silver glowing gently as her grandmother lit the Sabbath candles, holding the taper and smiling like a priestess of some ancient rite. Ruth had been eight years old, but she could still remember the sense of security she had felt in the ritual.

It had been one of the few times she had seen her mother's old home. Her grandfather must have been away on business, or they would never have gone. Ruth could still remember her mother's defiance, and the strain of that evening, even though the old woman had clearly been delighted to see her grandchild. But her mother could not forget that she had been disowned for marrying a gentile, and some obscure sense of loyalty had prevented Ruth from trying to learn more about her grandparents or their heritage.

"Where do you want me to put this stuff?" Tom's voice—deep, with a hesitance that partly disguised its power—startled her back to the present. He was standing in the doorway, wiping his yellow rubber boots on the mat. "The garden herbs haven't come up yet," he added as he came inside, "but I've got new violet and dandelion leaves, mustard greens and some fresh chickweed and dock and a few new shoots from the blackberries . . ."

"Weeds?" Ruth looked up at him dubiously, taking the green basketful and setting it on the drainboard.

"I prefer to call them spring salad," Tom grinned back at her. "Don't worry—I've eaten them all myself. Almost any of the seed-bearing plants are edible if the taste is good and you pick them in the spring before they flower."

Ruth grimaced, but she supposed she had better take his word for it. Making up for wasted time, she tore up lettuce, washed the leaves Tom had brought her and chopped them with swift, efficient strokes. He knew her kitchen well enough to set out the stoneware plates and bowls, and soon they were eating.

"You know, this stuff is pretty good," said Ruth finally. There was a tangy life to the wild greens that added a whole new dimension to the tired lettuce leaves. "Why don't the restaurants make salads this way?"

Tom smiled. He was not a man who laughed aloud often, but his smile warmed like a hearth fire. "Too much work to gather them, probably. They have to be really fresh, and they're only tender enough at the beginning of the year. You want to start a new business supplying them?"

Ruth shook her head. "Don't remind me. I've got enough work already."

"What are you doing now?"

She shrugged. "The Forbidden City game, still. Didn't I tell you about that? The computer-game market has been in a slump for the past few years, but now that a Mac with color screen and coordinated synthesizer is affordable, you can develop interactive home games that won't bore people who are used to TV."

At least, thought Ruth, *if I can ever get this damn program written there will be.* It had all seemed so easy when she was talking to the president of Star Wares. They had even flown her to their place near Lake Tahoe to discuss it. But she should have remembered that any programming task always takes at least twice as long as it says in the plan.

"Yeah, I think you did say something. Everyone who ever wanted to play D&D but can't find anyone to run a game will be after it."

"I hope so. The graphics should be realistic enough to be convincing, and I'm setting it up so that more than one player can participate through a computer net and they can cooperate in the problem solving. The problem I'm having is where to find the conflict. I don't want the players to fight each other, but I'm having a hard time making the usual D&D cast of mindless demons and other baddies interesting. And I'm not really sure what they ought to be looking for. What is real Evil, anyway? And what's a really worthwhile goal?" She stopped short, looking at him suspiciously. "I've given you this rap before, haven't I?"

"Yeah—" the weathered lines around his eyes deepened as he smiled again. "But you need to talk it out. I've got to get back to the garden and finish covering the roots of that apple tree I'm putting in before they dry out. The people I'm working for right now wanted to get rid of the tree and I thought it would be nice to have it here, but I can't let the other stuff go too long. Still, I'd like to come up tomorrow and hear more," he added apologetically, as if he were afraid she might misunderstand.

Ruth smiled reassuringly. "Maybe for dinner? The thing is, I promised Ariel I'd have lunch with her tomorrow. She has some new guru she wants to tell me about."

"She's that elegant friend of yours who comes over sometimes? I'm afraid to say anything when she starts talking about her spiritual studies for fear I'll hurt her feelings."

"I suppose she does seem rather delicate," Ruth shook her head. "And heaven knows she's had a lot of enthusiasms. First there was EST and then transcendental meditation. Then she went after every-*ishi* in a Cadillac that drives by. I don't understand it—she's really bright, you know—she had scholarships all the way through school. Whatever she's looking for, I wish she'd find it so we could both relax!"

"Why does it matter to you?" he asked then.

"It shouldn't, should it—but we've been so close, for so long! And besides, I owe her." Ruth's throat closed. There had been a time, in college, when she had needed Ariel as the other woman had never yet needed her. But though she felt more at home with Tom than she did with any other man she knew, she was not yet ready to let him share that memory.

He nodded, too polite to press her, and picked up his blue jacket. In a few moments she heard the scrape of the shovel once more as he finished covering the roots of the apple tree.

Ruth sighed, took the telephone off the hook, and turned the computer back on.

A telephone rang insistently downstairs, distracting him. Joseph Roman frowned, finished totalling up the donations from the last meeting of the Order of Paradise, and frowned again. Income was down another ten percent from the meeting before. It was going to be hard to pay the rent on the house if this went on. He stood up, straightening the hooded robe of white velvet that one of his more enthusiastic students had given him, and moved across the worn carpet to the shrine that hung on the wall.

A votive lamp was always kept burning on the shelf below it, but a little curtain of black velvet hid the shrine. Carefully, he drew the cloth aside. The picture inside was rather crudely drawn in crayon, but the intense dark eyes, the jutting nose and the sleek, wavy black hair were recognizably Joseph's own. The head was framed by a flaming halo of multicolored light.

Joseph lifted his hands in salutation.

"Angel who spoke to me from the mirror, help me now! I have waited too long and worked too hard to fail! Where there has been darkness I will bring enlightenment; where there has been confusion, I will bring clarity; where there has been fear of love, I will bring joy! I am the Chosen of the Most High—I must fulfill my destiny!"

Still staring at the picture, he projected upon it his memory of the Light that had blazed around him in his first vision, the experience that had started him upon this Path, straining for the ecstacy that had possessed him then. A knock on the door broke his concentration.

"What is it?" he asked sharply. His hand was trembling as he drew the cloth over the picture again.

"Master Joseph, Mrs. Winslow is on the phone. I can tell her that you are meditating . . ." The answer was an apologetic whisper. It was not Laurel's voice. Joseph thought it must be the new girl who had moved in. He could not remember her name, but she had lovely breasts that he was hoping to know better soon.

"No, I'll take the call here," he said more gently. He went back to his desk and picked up the phone.

"Master Joseph?" Joanna de Laurent Winslow's expressive contralto still had most of the power with which she had dominated the stage before she had made a prudent marriage and retired, still in possession of her astounding good looks. She was a wealthy widow now.

"Joanna, my child, I am delighted to hear from you—" Joseph began.

"Oh." Mrs. Winslow sounded a little disappointed. "Well, actually, I was calling to let you know I may not be at the next meeting of the Order."

"I'm sorry to hear that. Is there anything wrong?" Joseph fought to keep his voice untroubled. Mrs. Winslow was the only one of his students who really had money, and her dramatic training had made her a natural at ritual. To lose his best priestess and his best patron at once would be a major disaster.

"Oh, well, not really. But I've been invited away for the weekend, and in the past few meetings we have gone over the same material I covered when I began studying with you, so I thought . . ."

"I understand—it is hard sometimes for those who have advanced upon the Path to restrain their steps so that the Once-Born can keep pace with them. But Joanna, you set such a wonderful example!" Joseph said compellingly.

Mrs. Winslow gave a little trill of laughter. "Do you really think so? I know I should be patient, but lately it's been very hard for me to keep my mind on the meditations. I keep feeling that there must be something more!"

"Ah, but Joanna, there will be!" Joseph exclaimed. "You are ready now for the next level. At the next meeting I was planning—well, I must not tell you that if you will not be there."

"The next level? What do you mean?"

Joseph could hear the awe in her voice, and smiled. "I have already said too much—I should not speak of it over the telephone. But come to the next meeting, and you will understand."

But when Mrs. Winslow had agreed to be there and clicked off the line, Joseph stood still with the receiver in his hand, realizing that he had no idea what he was going to do.

The Campanile at the University of California was tolling midnight with long slow strokes of the chimes. In the stillness of the lab on the fourth floor of Hildebrand Hall, it seemed to David Mason as if he could feel the sound waves pulsing through his flesh. He paused, the Gilson pipette poised in midair, suddenly vividly aware of himself—scruffy brown beard, coffee-stained T-shirt labeled "Better Living Through Chemistry" and all—and his surroundings.

A few other grad students were working down the hall or on the floors below, but alone in the lab, David was as isolated as an alchemist working in his tower. His eyes moved along the familiar clutter of flasks and beakers on the tattered plastic that covered the counter, and the interlace of pipes above it, seeking the incubator where his latest batch of *E. coli* was happily reproducing. The orange light glowed reassuringly below the temperature dial. He had innoculated the vats with *E. coli* when he came in that afternoon. Now there was almost enough of the bacteria to spin down and analyze. And then—then he would see.

David finished filling the tubes, racked and placed them in the refrigerator, and after giving the instrumentation a final check, washed his hands and headed for the coffee maker in the crowded office he shared with the other grads in Professor Langdon's research group. The coffee was hot and reviving. He would have to add his vote in favor of Mr. Peet's to the tally on the blackboard in the lounge. With a sigh of satisfaction, David sat down at his battered, gray metal desk.

Half-hidden by the books on the shelves above it, a postcard of a Renaissance painting of an alchemist had been taped to the wall, and serving as a makeshift bookend was a three-dimensional model of the symbol the Kabbalists called the Tree of Life, which he had put together out of knobs and rods from an old kit for modeling molecules. He enjoyed the similarity in the symbolic languages by which ancient Kabbalists and modern scientists represented their invisible realities. He got an even greater kick out of the fact that although he had kept the model on his shelf for years, no one had ever asked him about it.

Still grinning, he pulled open the bottom drawer of the desk, took out his lab book and began to make notes. But he found it hard to concentrate. If the batch that he now had working proved out, he was going to be concealing something a lot more important than a model under the guise of straightforward research.

Professor Frederic Langdon's project was to engineer a stable form of *delta 9 tetrahydrocannabinol,* or THC—the psychoactive chemical in marijuana. NIH was interested in developing a controllable drug for alleviating the discomfort of victims of cancer and other diseases, a mild, and legal, euphoric and relaxant whose dosage and effects could be predicted. Langdon's early work had involved getting bacteria to express plant metabolites, and although it might have been simpler to try and synthesize the chemical, achieving the same result through genetic engineering would provide useful support for his major research.

David Mason had other plans.

On some people, and David was one of them, cannabis had no effect at all. After a time, the frustration of working on a project whose results he could never appreciate had become too much for him. He had taken the research just a little farther—tinkered with the enzymes on the synthetic pathway to THC in the still hours of the long nights when there was no one to ask questions, until he had persuaded them to change Δ9 into *11 hydroxyTHC*, which was the active chemical into which, in most people, the liver changed THC. The ancient alchemists had labored to transform the human soul through the disciplines of mystical chemistry. It seemed to David that he had found a surer way, the recipe for a stable, non-addictive and non-damaging drug that would produce the perfect high.

But first he had to refine his procedures until they were dependable, and he could produce a sufficient quantity of the appropriate *E.coli* for testing. But he was going to do it—he could sense the elegance of the procedure almost as he had tasted the coffee. He took a last appreciative sip and set the cup down.

As David started back to the lab, he found that he was whistling an old tune—he had to search back to his childhood to identify it. But when he remembered the name at last he smiled. Still whistling ''White Rabbit,'' David went into the back room to check the incubator.

Dimly in the distance, Del Eden could hear the Campanile striking the hour. It was a week night, and outside the bookstore and the apartment behind it, Telegraph Avenue slept. But at her age, Del found that she needed only a few hours sleep, and although business in the store sometimes forced her to skip the salutations at noon and sunset, she was refreshed by the peace at midnight and at dawn.

Del had taken off the sensible skirt and sweater she wore in the store, and stood now in a plain, dark-blue caftan, brushing her short, silver hair. Everything had been put away, and the sheen of rubbed wood and polished brass gleamed in the light of the votive candle on her altar. Only her quilt remained to be unrolled upon the open futon.

She put the brush back in its drawer and turned to face her altar, a small table in the eastern corner of the room, where the elements were honored by incense, candle, chalice and a small pot of rosemary. She lifted her hands and, turning clockwise, inscribed a pentagram in the air and vibrated the appropriate God-name for each direction. Then she turned to face the east again and lifted her hands.

''Before me, Raphael, behind me, Gabriel, at my right hand, Mikael, at my left hand, Auriel,'' Del Eden intoned, sensing the approach of the Archangels as she invoked them, like a scent, like the striding chords of an organ, like a storm of bright wings. For a moment she stood in silence, refining her awareness of those mighty Presences, then she stretched out her hands toward the floor.

"All Hail to Thee, Khepera, in Thy passage through the underworld.

I pray Thee to put my faults behind Thee;

grant Thou that I may be with the shining ones!''

Dimly, Del perceived the image of the sacred scarab beetle rolling the golden orb of the sun through the dark places of the world, and added to her invocation a prayer for those who walk in shadow.

Then, in a single, swift movement, she lowered herself into the lotus position on the futon. Muscles kept supple by years of yoga moved easily and she sat up straighter, taking the first deep breath toward that inner stillness that was her gate to the other world. For a few moments she hovered between states of consciousness, and on that threshold she was open to the emotions of all those around her.

Through the shield of the Archangels' protections, Del Eden sensed joy and terror, hope and fear. Without knowing it, she was aware of Ruth Racusak, sobbing in her sleep, and of David Mason's disappointment as he realized that his latest batch of bacteria had failed, and with almost enough force to break her concentration, she perceived Joseph Roman's desperate invocation to his own self-imaged Power. But the strength of the Archangels warded her, and in a few moments she had lost awareness of herself and all else but the white light that pulsed through her as she vibrated the Divine Name.

2.

Now does my project gather to a head:
My charms crack not; my spirits obey;
and time
Goes upright with his carriage.

Shakespeare, *Tempest*, V: i

Ruth paused a moment in the doorway of the cafe, blinking to let her eyes adjust to dark wood and the intricacies of Russian folk art after the brightness outside. The boutiques and shops that flourished in the area around College and Ashby seemed to change with the seasons, but Petrouchka had been there for over ten years now, and Ruth and Ariel qualified as regulars.

A quick survey located Ariel, who was wearing a loose muslin tunic-top over a flowing skirt of the same material. Both garments had been dyed with the delicacy of a classic kimono in subtle shadings of rose through mauve, and the handwoven shawl draped around her shoulders echoed the same colors, so that she looked like a very expensive, up-dated flower child. The same swift inventory showed Ruth that Ariel had twisted her tawny hair into a knot at the back of her head, skewered with delicate lacquer and cloisonne pins. But wisps of her soft bangs and side hair escaped in an artfully haphazard profusion to soften the severity of the line.

Feeling suddenly grubby, Ruth tried to loosen her own hair from its twist around the elastic, grateful that she had remembered to remove the pencil that usually knotted it there, and sat down at the table. Ariel already had a cup of tea. A little notebook lay open before her.

"Sorry I'm late. Half of Berkeley decided to do its shopping today, and I feel like something from the bottom of a garbage can."

Ariel frowned faintly at the metaphor, and Ruth realized that she had unconsciously wanted to shock her. She remembered how Tom had described Ariel, and flushed faintly, understanding that her words had been a kind of defense against the delicate beauty of the woman across the table.

"You don't need to apologize, I was writing up my dreams for this week and lost track of the time." Ariel did not appear to have noticed Ruth's embarrassment. With a flourish, she crossed the last *t* and closed the notebook.

Wondering if she was being subjected to some kind of psychic one-upsmanship, Ruth raised an eyebrow. "Your dreams?"

Ariel's eyes brightened, and Ruth felt a sinking sensation. Whatever the new enthusiasm was, Ariel had it bad. Ruth recognized the signs.

"That's why I wanted to talk to you—" said her friend. "I've found a wonderful teacher, and I'm finally learning how to be free! That's your problem, Ruth—you're too involved with the flesh and the world, you're stuck on the material plane."

And what about the Devil? Ruth wondered wryly. Ariel might be right about the world, but it was the intellect, not the flesh, that preoccupied her now. What she needed was a computer wizard, not a New Age guru.

"Who is this paragon?" she asked aloud.

"His name is Joseph Roman! Master Joseph—" Ariel stopped as the waiter came to take their orders.

"What is this group called?" asked Ruth carefully.

"The Order of Paradise—it's like a prayer circle. He's helping us to dig deep down and establish communication with our Higher Selves!"

Ruth blinked at the metaphoric contradiction, but managed not to laugh. The odd phrasing was a typically Ariel mixture of mirroring and idealism. Ruth remembered that she had been like that in school, responding to each new professor with a genuine and flattering enthusiasm, coupled with intuitive leaps of the imagination that were close enough to brilliance to get her good grades. And Ruth supposed that the professors had been as vulnerable as she was to the enchantment of Ariel's smile.

The waiter arrived with soup for Ariel and the *blinchiki syrom* that Ruth had been unable to resist. She pulled herself back to the present.

"Just how is he doing this?"

"Well—" for a moment Ariel looked a little unsure. "Master Joseph believes in using all the resources of modern research for the work of enlightenment. He combines Neuro-Linguistic Programming, and some guided trance work, dream interpretation, ritual, a lot of things. He has traveled all over the world, studying. He used to teach at Esalen!"

"Ah, the New Age Jerusalem!" said Ruth, wondering why everyone seemed to feel that constituted some kind of imprimatur. "Haven't you studied all that stuff before?"

"Yes, but he's pulling it all together for me, and he *knows* things." Ariel leaned forward earnestly, and the light behind her aureoled her fair hair. "Simply by looking at me he could tell that my sensitivity had made life hard for me, and he said that I needed to develop my psychic abilities in order to free myself from the physical world. He knew I had been divorced without being told."

Ruth sighed. These days, the chances that any good-looking woman over thirty who did not wear a wedding ring had been through at least one marriage were a virtual certainty. Ruth had thought she knew her friend's life history in exhausting detail, and she wondered what sins could possibly be weighing on Ariel's soul.

"And how much is he charging to teach you all these things you already knew?" she asked tiredly.

"Oh he doesn't charge money for serving the Light, but of course we contribute to support his work—"

"And how much have you been contributing?" Ruth insisted.

Flushing a little, Ariel told her.

Ruth whistled. "Are you paying for that out of your alimony? I should have married an advertising man instead of a struggling lawyer!"

"Now that's not fair!" Ariel glared at her. "The Bible says, *'The laborer is worthy of his hire!'* Why do you always try to pick things to pieces? This isn't one of your programs, you know! Some things are subjective, and to understand them you have to use your intuition.'' Ariel took a deep breath, and her perfect features recovered their serenity. Her blue eyes grew luminous, like a questing knight sighting the Holy Grail.

Ruth opened her mouth to explain that good programming required at least as much intuition as any other creative act, but she knew it was pointless. Ariel classed computer programming with nuclear physics and gene splicing, and when Ruth tried to explain her work, usually responded with a pitying stare.

"It's not just what Master Joseph says, but how he says it. When he is talking, I almost understand the pattern behind everything. Beauty exists! Purity and Perfection exist! If I could only understand *why* all these things have happened to me I could get free of what's weighing me down and reach them. Don't you feel that too?''

Ruth stared down at her *blinchiki* without really seeing it, automatically mixing the sour cream and black cherry sauce together and spreading them over the crepe. Pattern—that was the essence of programming, but the computer could only provide those answers that someone had put into it.

"What can I say?'' she answered finally. "Isn't that what everyone wants to know? Half the time I'm sure there is no God, and the other half I hope there is, because I've got a little list of questions I want to ask Him!''

"Well, then, why don't you come to the meeting with me? Nobody would expect you to make an offering the first time.''

This Master Joseph must really be recruiting, thought Ruth; then she saw Ariel's eyes on her, wide and blue with that lost expression that she had never been able to withstand, and forced a smile.

"But I'm not even a Christian!''

Ariel shook her head indulgently. "What does that have to do with it? The Light of the World is for everyone!''

"Ariel, I can't. I should be home at the computer now instead of hanging out here,'' Ruth looked down at her plate and pushed it away, "pigging out. I've run into some problems with the game I'm developing, and I shouldn't go anywhere until I've figured out what's wrong.''

That was putting it mildly. When she started, it had seemed that sophisticated graphics and clear instructions would carry the game. But now she knew that the problem was fundamental—not simply a matter of getting the code to work, but figuring out the real purpose of the game.

"Well, that's just why you should come with me!" Ariel smiled radiantly. "Joseph can help you! He's gotten lots of people over mental blocks like yours."

Ruth repressed a shudder. She laid no claims to enlightenment, but she had always managed her own mental health without assistance. No, not quite always, she thought suddenly. There had been that time in college. Ariel had saved her then. She looked up at the other woman.

Ariel had not noticed her silence. She was gazing at the picture of Barishnikov in mid-jeté that hung on the wall of the restaurant as if her spirit, like his body, had overcome the limitations of gravity. Ruth shuddered again, and abruptly found herself wondering how this teacher had made such an impression. For Ariel, each new love was forever, and each guru was the One True Way, but she could not remember having ever before seen her friend so enraptured. She felt the cold touch of apprehension.

"All right, I'll go with you," she said suddenly. "When is the meeting, and where?"

Ariel's attention focused suddenly, and her smile made Ruth's throat tighten. It took so little to make some people happy—surely she could endure one evening of boredom for Ariel's sake, and perhaps she would find some way to extract her from a situation she liked less and less the more she learned.

When they came out of the restaurant it was raining, a thin, misty drizzle that veiled the hills. Ruth drove home through a world of blurred outlines and familiar shapes grown strange.

It looks like a night for magic, thought David Mason as he crossed the bridge. *Maybe this time the bugs will do their thing!* Mist lay heavy on the campus, conjuring away the solid buildings and haloing the lights along the paths with a ghostly glow. The pine trees in the ravine below Hildebrand Hall were jeweled with silver. Then a few of those glimmering droplets fell down his neck, and grimacing, David pulled up his collar and sprinted up the stairs.

He passed the chem library on the first floor and pressed the button for the elevator, just as the campus security guard was going by. David didn't know the man's name, but they had got to the point of exchanging waves and an occasional greeting. Like the tolling of the carillon in Sather Tower, the guard's rounds measured out the watches of the night, almost as dependable as the instruments in the lab.

Someone had put up a new Far Side cartoon beside the door. David stopped for a moment to appreciate it—laughter was not always the appropriate word for one's reaction to Gary Larson's peculiar art form—and went on in.

The beaker holding his last batch of *E. coli* was still in the refrigerator, anonymously labeled with the code that referred to his other lab book, the one Dr. Langdon had never seen. David had grown the culture the day before, but by the time it was ready the other students had begun to come in, and he did not want questions.

But now the lab was his own. Whistling softly between his teeth, David took the beaker to the rotor, positioned it carefully, set the timer and turned the dial.

While he was waiting for the mass to spin down, he felt in the pocket of his jacket for the mail he had picked up on his way out of the apartment. He did not expect any surprises. The electric bill was small, even at this season—David only went there to change clothes and sleep. He could not remember the last time he had cooked a real meal in his tiny kitchen, and he wondered sometimes what he would find if he analyzed some of the molds in his refrigerator.

But the apartment did not matter. It was hardly worthwhile even paying rent on the place. David's life was here. Perhaps when he had his degree and a job somewhere he would find himself with a house and a wife—all the usual things—but it was hard to imagine. He had not gone into molecular biology to acquire what any business major could get with a lot less time and trouble.

The other grads talked about things like that sometimes, when they were complaining about the present workload. But the others also argued about what kind of beer to get for the keg in the Commons, and played cards while waiting for experiments to run. The sense of community that seemed to come so easily to them was to David a mystery. He had learned enough of the social formulae to get by, observing and analyzing human interactions with the same careful patience he brought to chemistry. But his fellow researchers sensed somehow that his heart was not in it, and generally left him alone.

The indicator signaled completion and, with a sureness trained by repetition, David resuspended the mass of yellowish-brown goop and then transferred it to a Denar thermos, where immersion in liquid nitrogen would burst the cell walls so that he could analyze what was inside. He checked his watch and began to sort through the rest of his mail.

Several ads and pleas for contributions went into the waste-basket. He took a little more time to look through the cata-logue of scientific equipment, wondering just how much it would cost to set up a lab on his own, maybe on top of a mountain somewhere, with a view of blue-hazed ridges to contemplate while he was waiting for experiments to run. And there would be no forms to fill out, no need to waste time writing progress reports and justifications, or wait for authorization—just the enthralling exploration of the secrets of the cell. At the end of it all he sensed there must be one single, overwhelming truth, and when he understood that, it would not matter about his difficulties with people, for he would understand everything.

At the bottom of the pile was an envelope addressed in his mother's careful writing. Frowning, David set it down on the counter and went back to his bench.

Now the cells looked like viscous goo. Before he could test for the THC he would have to perform centrifugation to separate the soluble chemicals from the rest of the cellular material. He scooped the glob of lysate into a centrifuge tube and set it to spin down.

Still watching the centrifuge, David reached for his moth-er's letter.

She complained that he hadn't written home. She had tried to call, but no one ever answered at his apartment. Was he still living there? Was he getting enough to eat? David skimmed the cramped writing, wondering if there were anything here he hadn't read a hundred times before. His sister was expect-ing again—her third child—but of course Lucy's children could not continue the family name. His father's heart condi-tion was getting worse but he continued to spend long hours at the office. It was a pity there was no one to take over part of his workload—if he didn't let up, he was going to drop dead at the office one of these days.

David resisted the impulse to crumple up the paper and throw it across the room. His mother never came out and accused him directly, but her meaning was clear. He should come home, get married, go to work for the paper company with his father. She had never understood him; even now she would not understand what he was doing here. If he could have turned himself into the kind of son she wanted, David would have done it, but he did not know how. Yet even though he had no interest in the family business, David recognized abruptly that he was like his father in one thing—if he couldn't do his work he would just as soon die.

With deliberate control, David folded the letter, put it back inside the envelope and slipped it into his pocket with the bills.

The centrifugation was almost finished, and David could feel his heartbeat speeding as he realized that soon he would know if the *E. coli* had bred true. He had gotten the right formula, but he needed to turn enough bacteria into little chemical factories to manufacture it in sufficient quantity to use. David had been with friends who were smoking grass. He had seen the euphoria, the relaxation, seen the barriers go down. Perhaps this stuff would work for him. It seemed like an elegant solution to his problems—to learn to relate to other people by doing the work he loved.

Taking a deep breath to steady himself, he transferred the spun down mass to the spectrophotometer cuvette.

"Come on now, babies, show me what you're made of—" he whispered as it moved down the tube. And slowly, subtly, he saw it change, and knew that it was going to be all right.

"Hey Mom, can we stop at the science-fiction store? See— there's a parking place right in front!" Martin tugged at Ruth's elbow. She braked as the car ahead of her slowed for a turn and saw Dark Carnival's carved dragon sign. Her work was going a little better, and now she was glad that she had agreed to take her son for the weekend after all, even though she always seemed to end up buying him things.

"Is your homework all done?" Ruth glanced at him out of the corner of her eye and saw him nod.

"Yeah, it's finished—but Mom, why'd you have to pro- gram a dialogue box that asks me that same question into the new maze game you gave me? It came on when I was showing Larry the game and it was awfully embarrassing!''

Ruth suppressed a grin. ''You'll get worse than that if you hang out with hackers, my child, so you might as well get used to it! But I wish you'd told me you've run out of stuff to read when we were up by the University. Other Change of Hobbit is right there—'' She shook her head in wonder. Martin had brought two bags with him for the weekend, the larger of which was weighted with books and material for gaming.

When Ruth had been his age, she had been in one scrape after another, trying to win the respect of the neighborhood boys. Remembering some of the things they had done, she supposed she should be grateful that Martin was such a bookworm.

''I haven't run out yet, but I will by tomorrow,'' he said cheerfully. ''I didn't think about it before! If you won't let me play that game you're writing, I have to have something to do!'' Martin tested all of Ruth's educational programs, and although he was probably more sophisticated than the average student, he was good at picking out gaps and inconsistencies.

''All right—'' she answered a little abstractedly. Next to the store Martin was pointing at she had noticed another sign, one that showed Eve plucking the apple from the Tree of Knowledge. ''You go on in,'' she went on as she pulled into the parking place. ''I'll be next door.''

Martin dashed off as soon as the car halted, but Ruth found her steps slowing. ''Eden Books,'' said the sign above her; ''Occult and Metaphysical Literature.'' Ever since her lunch with Ariel, Ruth had been wishing she had access to some equivalent of a medical directory in which one could look up occult practitioners. Perhaps they would know something about Master Joseph Roman and the Order of Paradise here.

A silver-haired woman—Mrs. Eden, presumably—was leaning over the counter, considering an arrangement of carved sticks that the striking blonde girl on the other side of it had laid down. Blonde *woman*—Ruth revised her estimate as she noticed the toddler in the stroller beside her. The child was beautiful, too—fair as her mother, with blue eyes that seemed uncomfortably wise.

Together, the two of them looked like prototypes for the super-race, thought Ruth wryly, mentally comparing the little girl's aureole of blonde hair and angelic smile to Martin's brown cowlick and crooked grin. Not that she would trade him, of course, but sometimes she wished she could have had a pretty little girl to name after Ariel.

Ruth began to browse along the shelves, waiting for the conversation to end. She passed the section on Oriental religions—from what Ariel had said, Master Joseph was using a mixture of half-digested New Age philosophy and some kind of ceremonial—and began leafing through books from the shelves on European magic. The conversation at the counter came to her in fragments, confusing as the shoptalk of any unfamiliar profession.

"Yes, I can see how the runes lie on the Tree—" Mrs. Eden was saying now, "but Karen, you must realize the two systems will never fit exactly. Heimdall with his horn goes in Yesod and Freyja belongs with Aphrodite in Netzach, certainly, but where are you going to place Odin?"

"Does he have to be confined to one sphere?" the younger woman asked. "He has aspects in several, even in Tiphareth, but I would put him mostly in Chokmah and Hod." She grinned suddenly. "Especially now. Did I tell you? Northpoint Press has just accepted Michael's book of poetry."

As if the shift from esoteric to social conversation had broken the storekeeper's concentration, she looked up and seemed to see Ruth for the first time.

"Can I help you?" she asked quietly. Meeting the woman's luminous gaze, Ruth felt suddenly self-conscious.

"I don't know," she said helplessly. "A friend of mine is studying with a—I guess you'd call him a spiritual teacher—and I wondered if you could tell me anything about him. He's called Joseph Roman."

"I have met him," Mrs. Eden said after a moment's consideration. "He seems to be sincere."

"Oh come on, Del—" said Karen. "Is that all you're going to say?"

"That is all I *know*," Del Eden said without expression.

"Well, I suppose he respected *you* too much to try anything. I was eight months pregnant when he made a pass at me." Karen grinned, and Ruth found it suddenly easy to understand why any man, and a good many women, would desire that blonde vitality.

"First I couldn't get him to take *no* for an answer," Karen went on, "and then I had to keep Michael from killing him. Come to think of it, last time I saw him he was very respectful to me, too." They all laughed.

"Well, my friend is the spiritual type. If he's tried to seduce her, she hasn't noticed it," said Ruth finally. "Aside from that, is there anything wrong with him?"

"His scholarship is pretty good, and he has a flair for the dramatic. I find it hard to take him seriously, but aside from his conviction that he's God's gift to women, I don't know that he's done any harm—" Karen answered her.

"Dion Fortune once divided magical fraternities into the white, the black, and the fatuous—" said Del Eden with a smile. "I'm afraid that these days the fatuous fraternities are in the majority, but usually the only harm done to the people involved is a loss of time and money. Joseph Roman likes money, but I think he is mainly after adulation. And even a dirty window can let a little light through."

The shop door banged shut as Martin came in, startling the large golden cat who had been sleeping in the window into affronted motion. "Hey, Mom—they've got a new book on the Space Station, and there's a D&D module I need . . ."

"All right, just a minute—" Ruth agreed, with a moment's passing wonder at finding herself in a setting where magic and orbital space stations were considered equally real. "Thank you for your help—" she said to Karen and Del.

"I just wish we could have told you more," said Karen.

Ruth nodded, but as she followed Martin out the door she glanced back at Del Eden's closed face, and wondered what it was that the older woman had been unwilling to say.

Long ago, Joseph had mastered the trick of seeming to look at one thing while his attention was actually on another. Just now, he was admiring the legs of the girl going by outside the window of the *Mediterraneum*, while continuing to listen attentively to the young man on the other side of the table.

The rain had let up and the day was hazy but clear. On a Sunday afternoon Telegraph Avenue was a colorful kaleidoscope of people in scarves and down jackets and street merchants showing their wares. The *Mediterraneum* was full of late risers having brunch. Joseph had come here to decide what to do about the Order of Paradise. Finding David Mason had been a welcome way of putting off dealing with it.

"You showed considerable potential." Joseph turned the full force of his gaze on his companion as the girl passed out of view. "I was very sorry when you had to leave the study group, David, but of course I understand the importance of your work . . ."

Watching David Mason's face, Joseph saw swift color come and go above the straggling beard. David picked up his espresso and took a hasty sip. "We were starting a new project—" he mumbled. "I didn't have the time."

"Why are you embarrassed?" Joseph asked softly. "Your work *is* important. To create life is godlike. No sorcerer could do more . . ."

Finding himself behind David in the line for coffee, it had been automatic for Joseph to try and reestablish the influence he had exercised when the younger man had been in one of his study groups the year before. He would have preferred female company, but anything was better than sitting alone and racking his brains for some way to deliver what he had promised to Joanna de Laurent Winslow.

But his studies had taught him to read people with some accuracy; now, he sensed in David an aura of excitement barely held in check, and a well-honed instinct pricked him to find out why.

"We don't create life—just—make the cells do things a different way." David was fingering something in the pocket of his jacket like a man with a lucky charm. Joseph wondered what it could be. The approaching sound of drums and cymbals outside swelled to a deafening climax as the daily Hari Krishna procession danced by, pale orange and yellow draperies glimmering like ambulant flowers in the pale sunlight.

"You used to be curious about alchemy—" Joseph went on. "Have you learned anything more? Chemistry is a Path like any other, and you did not seem to me to be a man who would give up the quest."

"I haven't!" David's eyes glowed suddenly. Joseph could see him struggling for words, and stilled, expanding his own awareness like a hunter waiting by a water hole.

"You are the heir of the alchemists. You have great abilities," Joseph said soothingly, "you can do great things . . ."

"Yes, I can!" came the surprising answer. "I've done more than they ever thought of when they started the project, but I don't dare let anyone know."

Joseph felt the tickle along his nerves that told him his powers had not deserted him after all. The Pattern was arranging itself to bring him what he needed. It was like the moment in a seduction when the woman is still protesting but you know she is going to yield. He had only to recognize it, and stretch out his hand.

"They don't understand you—how could they? They're only after money and promotions, not Truth—" he went on in the same smooth tone. "But you can tell the truth to me . . ."

"The truth?" David looked into his coffee cup as if he found it easier to talk to his reflection there. "The truth is that I didn't leave your class because of my work. It was because they all seemed to know each other, to know how to get along. I didn't belong."

"You know things they will never understand," whispered Joseph. "But you can tell me!"

"But now I *will* understand—" David went on as if he had not heard. "I could never go out drinking because booze makes me sick, and my body doesn't react to grass. But I've got something that will work now!" He patted his pocket and favored Joseph with a conspiratorial smile.

Joseph looked at him sharply, noting the reddened eyes and the leap of a pulsebeat in David's throat. "Have you discovered a new drug, then?"

"THC—" David grinned glassily. "*Super* THC, that nobody could ever figure out how to make stable before. I took some, just a little, so I know it's safe—'n see, here I'm talking to you and I'm not nervous at all!"

"That's a wonderful thing, David, a real Paradise drug," said Joseph admiringly. "You really are a wizard. But what if you only feel this way because you expected to? It's not really a fair test with only one subject, is it now?"

David looked up at him with a sudden frown. "That's true—it's not scientific—but I can't tell anyone . . ." He reached for his water glass and drank thirstily.

"You've told me—" Joseph said, smiling. "Why not let me try some, too?" Forcing himself to remain relaxed, Joseph concentrated on projecting good will.

"Yeah . . ." David said slowly at last. "Why not—you're my friend . . ." He fumbled in the pocket of his jacket and pulled out a small glass jar half filled with a pale golden powder. "You dissolve it, you see—up to a gram in ten millimeters of water.'' He started to pull off the top of the vial.

"No, no—this water isn't pure enough, and I wouldn't want to do it here—someone might see.'' Joseph covered David's hand with his own, and eased the glass away from his unresisting fingers. "I'll take it home, test it properly, and let you know . . .'' The vial was in the pocket of Joseph's cashmere coat now.

"Yeah, okay,'' said David sunnily. "I've got more at the lab. I'm an alchemist, y'see.''

"Yes, you certainly are,'' echoed Joseph, *and the answer to a magician's prayer,* he continued silently. Keeping his eyes on David, he eased back his chair and got to his feet. But David was looking around him as if he had never seen human beings before, and smiling.

Smiling himself, with a triumph he could no longer deny, Joseph Roman moved swiftly through the door.

Afternoon sunlight slanted through the windows and paled the computer screen. Ruth brightened it and made a slight adjustment in the text before her. She had dropped Martin off at his father's early, and if Leonard wanted to complain about that, it was just too bad. She had promised to go to that damned Consciousness group with Ariel in the evening, and she had only this afternoon to spend with the computer if she wanted to get anything done this weekend at all.

Ruth stared at what she had just typed in, wondering if it would fit with the rest, and realized that she needed to look at the entire beginning sequence again.

Sighing, she shifted applications and activated the four-foot high remote screen across the room. A full-page graphic of a shining tower appeared, enhanced so that its original incarnation as a picture of the Campanile could hardly be discerned. Synthesized trumpets blared, and the legend "Forbidden City" was emblazoned across it, followed by her copyright.

After a moment a new splash appeared on the screen, which took the form of a scroll with Gothic lettering—

In the Final Conflict, the great centers of civilization were abandoned. But in the chaos that followed, Knowledge became a prize worth more than gold or jewels. The cities had become dangerous, inhabited by mutated creatures more deadly than the demons of old.

But it was in the cities that the ancient centers of learning were to be found.

Now humankind has grave need of the scrolls still stored in the Forbidden City. You have volunteered to seek them, along with any companions who choose to join you. You know that there will be many dangers, and enemies may be concealed around any corner or behind any door. There are those who are determined that the ancient knowledge shall not be revealed. But know also that friends may unexpectedly come to your aid, and there are forces that work for good that will help you.

If you have the courage, scroll onward, and let the adventure begin!

3.

O they rade on and further on,
Until they came to a garden tree;
'Light down, light down, ye ladie free,
And I'll pull of that fruit for thee.'

'O no, O no, True Thomas,' she says,
'That fruit maun not be touched by thee,
For all the plagues that are in hell,
Light on the fruit of this countrie.'

"Thomas the Rhymer" traditional
Border ballad

The day had been bright, but fog was rising over the Bay as
Ariel maneuvered her little Fiat through the early winter
evening into the Berkeley hills. Looking through the back
window, Ruth saw the air thickening, veiling the water, cold
gray below, but shining like opalescent foam above in the light
of the setting sun. She shivered unaccountably—for a moment it had seemed as if the world were dissolving back into
the primal flux, like the images on her computer screen.

"Are you sure you know how to get to Grizzly Peak?" she
asked. "All these streets look alike, and none of them seem
to go where you'd expect them to."

Ariel laughed. "Who, me? Lost?" Ruth gave her a quick,
considering glance. Today Ariel was wearing the colors of
a very early daffodil, with an intricately knitted, shaded
yellow pullover atop a cream silk shirt and pants of matching
wool. The ensemble was pulled together by a Japanese

print silk scarf in corresponding colors that half-covered her hair.

"Yes," said Ruth. "I still remember the time you drove me and Jodie Chavez and Linda Adams to a party at Stanford and we ended up in Santa Cruz." She was wearing a scarf, too—a maroon wool paisley that had seemed quite smart until she got a good look at Ariel's glory.

"That's not fair," said Ariel. She braked suddenly, and Ruth held her breath as they made a sharp right turn and the little car darted up the hill like a hummingbird. "It was dark, and the map was wrong."

"Well, it was certainly the wrong map," Ruth agreed.

"Anyway, Santa Cruz was a lot more fun than that party would have been." Ariel went on. "Remember how we walked on the beach and then got hot dogs and beer and spent the night singing in the front seat of the car?"

Ruth blinked back a sudden stinging in her eyes at the memory of women's voices soaring, with the sound of the surf for accompaniment. In the darkness there had been no differences between them—honor student or socialite, rich or poor—and Ruth had found herself able to sing out for the first time, one of the gang.

Ariel had a gift for combining the oddest groups of people and leading them into adventures, Ruth thought then. If they had had more adventures and gone to fewer parties, she might never have met Jeffrey. But that memory was like the rattle of a doorknob on a door that must stay closed, and she shut it away.

They passed the entrance to Tilden Park, dipped down on another street, and pulled up. As Ariel maneuvered the little car into a parking place, Ruth told herself to stop worrying, for this was certainly one of the most respectable, even affluent, parts of Berkeley, a street of fifties ranch- and hacienda-style homes that took full advantage of the spectacular view of the bay, with manicured yards and Volvos and Mercedes parked in the drives. In such a setting, her fantasies of arcane rites and sinister gurus seemed ridiculous.

"You must be the friend Ms. Ashton told us about—I'm Laurel, and I'm *so* glad to *see* you here!"

Ruth stiffened as the woman who opened the door to them clasped her hand. Laurel was wearing a voluminous black caftan with Morrocan gold embroidery around the neck and hem, which suggested a more dramatic personality than Ruth could read on the other woman's plain round face and wispy brown hair.

"Thank you." She eased her fingers from the grip of Laurel's pudgy hand. "Is this your house? It's beautiful!" Mentally, she priced the ceramic tile on the hall floor and the woven hanging on the wall.

"Oh *no*—" Laurel blushed rosily. "George and Ellie Makarios have *generously* offered us their home for the meetings of the Order. But I've had the privilege of assisting Master Joseph for three years, and I'm always so *happy* to welcome new people to his classes!"

Considering how much Master Joseph's students were contributing, Ruth could believe it, but as she noted the glow in Laurel's eyes, she decided that the girl was either genuinely enthusiastic, or an excellent actress. Curious about the object of all this devotion, she followed Ariel into the living room.

"Master Joseph—this is my friend Ruth Racusak!" Ariel grasped Ruth's arm and pulled her forward.

Ruth allowed herself to be piloted toward a young man with smooth dark hair and very bright black eyes, who was seated on a white shantung cushion next to a low table on which were set two candles and a basket draped with a white silk cloth. Or perhaps he was not so young—Ruth noted lines around his eyes and a glint of silver in the dark hair. He was wearing an ornate silver cross over a cassock in cream-colored linen, belted with a white silk cord.

"Ariel has spoken well of you." Master Joseph's voice was very good, a light baritone with a kind of caress in it. His eyes moved up and down her body in automatic calculation, and Ruth was abruptly glad she had worn a loose tunic top. She smiled tightly, wondering just what her friend had told him, and remembering what the woman at the bookstore had told her.

"Ariel's said a lot about you, too. She has quite a gift for describing people, wouldn't you agree?"

For a moment the black eyes seemed to go a little blank; then, an excellent set of teeth flashed as Joseph Roman smiled.

"Perhaps," he answered, "but then, we know so little about each other, after all. Only the Divine light can illuminate the shadows of the human heart."

But according to Ariel, Master Joseph could read the secrets of the soul. Ruth wondered if this charming diffidence had been calculated to disarm her. Her hostility must be fairly obvious.

She laughed. "I'm looking forward to learning more."

Joseph's eyes sparkled suddenly. "You will—I can assure you of that much, Ms. Racusak. You will."

His attention shifted as an auburn-haired woman, with the kind of carefully tended beauty that can hold age at bay, made her entrance, and Ruth had the sense that the audience was at an end. Already the woman was sweeping past her, burbling something about some powerful businessman she knew whom Master Joseph simply *must* meet soon. Only the name was odd enough to claim a moment of Ruth's attention— Luciano Abaddon. Then, suppressing an impulse to respond to her dismissal with a genuflection, she stepped aside.

"What's the procedure?" she asked Ariel. The room was almost full now. The students seemed to be mostly professional people in expensively casual clothes, couples or single women with the strained look of naturally plump people imprisoned in bodies thinned by diet or exercise.

"Almost everyone's here. We should be starting soon." As Ariel answered, Laurel came into the room and started rearranging cushions and chairs. Then she settled herself on a cushion slightly lower than Master Joseph's on the other side of the low table.

"My friends, it is time to be seated now—" Joseph seemed to speak softly, but his voice penetrated the conversations around him effortlessly. Ruth felt her skin twitch and knew a swift spurt of anger.

It's the voice, she told herself. *But that's no reason to react like a trained dog!* Still frowning, she arranged herself cross-legged on a cushion beside Ariel.

"Soror Joanna, take your seat at my right hand—" he gestured to the dramatic-looking woman with the auburn hair, who smiled radiantly and lowered herself to a sitting position on the cushion beside him with a rustling of blue silk robes.

"Frater Rodrigo, let the portal be closed!" Joseph Roman's rich voice rolled out suddenly, startling everyone to complete attention.

A stout man wearing a loose black robe over his clothes took up a position by the door, holding a long, intriguingly carved staff. Lifting the staff, he brought it down against the floor.

"All ye who are unclean depart from here—" he proclaimed in a gravelly voice.

"We are the pure in heart!" came a ragged chorus of replies.

The warden thunked the staff down again.

"All ye who have not kept faith depart from here!"

"We will be faithful unto death!" The response was clearer now, and Ruth shivered as the thudding staff heralded the third demand.

"All ye who have not been Chosen, depart from here!"

Ruth jerked, and only the grip of Ariel's hand kept her from instinctive flight as the group chanted with a single voice its reply—

"We are the Elect of God, and here we stay!"

The warden turned and locked the door, then laid his staff across the threshold and sat down.

Ruth stared at Ariel, and then at Master Joseph, who was watching them all with a bridled eagerness that disturbed her even while her intellect assured her there was no way he could do her any harm.

"My brothers and my sisters—" The guru's voice was softer now, but even more resonant. "Hear me! You have been homeless, but in the house of holiness you shall find rest. You have been sinners, but the radiance of the Most High shall burn all your sin away. You have been wounded, but by the love of the Enlightened One you shall be healed. You have wandered in darkness, without goal or guide, but I shall show you the Way!"

He struck a match and lit the white tapers on the table beside him. Ruth shut her eyes tightly against the betraying tears, grasping at her distrust of the man in an attempt to counteract the power of his words. It was true—she had never truly felt at home anywhere, and the promise he was offering was almost too much to bear. Joseph Roman might be a fraud, but his message had a core of immortal truth in it. No wonder all these people were sitting with rapt faces, watching him.

"The Light is Love, and Love is the Light of the World. Love each other and the Light will bless you. You are the blessed of the Lord, the children of Light. You can do no evil, you are free of darkness. The holy angels are gathering now, with a shimmer of bright wings. Let your heart see the brightness around you; let your heart glow with Love . . .''

Ruth felt a warm tide of emotion wash over her, comforting, almost complacent in its assurance of being chosen and saved. He was talking about the angels again now, and she had a sudden incongruous memory of the angel chorus in *Hansel and Gretel.* In that moment of humor she recovered her detachment, and the warmth disappeared. Had they all suddenly become enlightened just because Joseph Roman said so? Love had to be worked at—she knew. If she had been better at the job, she and Leonard might still be married, though it was a moot point whether she would have been any better off.

''Let the strains and distractions of the week just past rise to the surface of your minds—rise to the surface, and float away—.'' Master Joseph's voice deepened, grew smoother. ''Breathe deeply, regularly, in . . . and out . . . in . . . and out . . .''

Ruth could feel the change in the people around her; small movements of bodies settling into more comfortable positions, sighs that became deep breathing as they were caught by the rhythm of instruction. It was a hypnotist's voice, and a hypnotist's technique. But there was nothing wrong with that, in itself. She had taken classes in self-induced trance a few years before, when she was having trouble sleeping. She tried not to fight it, knowing she would learn nothing if she allowed her suspicions to rule her.

She glanced at Ariel, whose face had gone empty and still, saw the same lack of expression on the faces of those around her. They were not in deep trance yet, only waiting, open to whatever their leader might say.

''In our past meetings I have guided you to the Gates of Paradise. This is the Hidden World, which is as close to our own as sunlight to shadow, but how few understand its mysteries!'' Master Joseph leaned forward on his cushion, his dark eyes fixing each one in turn. Except for the sound of his voice and the gentle, regular breathing of those who listened to him, there was silence in the room.

''He who wanders at will in that realm possesses power over all external things, for they are only shades of what lies within. This is the Garden in which the Tree of Knowledge grows—but men have feared to taste its fruit, and posted great signs of warning round about. Knowledge is Power, and they are afraid. Are you afraid?'' Once more the dark gaze swept the circle, and Ruth shivered as a rapt murmur answered him.

"Listen to me, and I will give you the key to the Garden! I will give you the fruit of the Tree to eat if you will follow me.''

Ruth shook her head, sensing a paradox here. If knowledge brought power, then surely each soul should be its own guide.

"Ordinary men fear this knowledge, but you are the chosen ones, a sacred generation who will inherit the world. Listen to me! I know the secret words and the hidden ways! I will guide you to the feast of Power!''

On the faces of those around her, Ruth saw a kind of avid eagerness that made her feel as if someone had scraped a fingernail across her soul. These were ordinary men and women, but this was not an ordinary desire.

And yet she had no words to say what was wrong with it. There was only a feeling in her bones, as if Master Joseph were breaking some taboo of whose nature her lack of formal religious training denied her knowledge. The image of her grandmother lighting the Sabbath candles flickered into her mind, and she clung to it.

Movement focused her attention. With a swift flick, Master Joseph pulled away the white cloth to reveal a silver platter upon which apple slices lay. He gestured, and Laurel left her place and knelt before him.

"Behold the fruit of Paradise! Eat of it, and you will know ecstasy!''

Laurel took the platter and carried it around the circle, offering the apple slices to each one. Ruth watched her, wondering.

It was only apples—a symbolic meal like the communion in her father's church, though she had to admit that Joseph Roman's preliminaries were more impressive. If more rabbis and ministers had his charisma, the synagogues and churches would probably be better attended. Was it Master Joseph's portentous build-up or the intent look with which he watched Laurel move around the circle that made her so twitchy?

Laurel paused before her, smiling encouragingly, and held out the tray. The white flesh of the fruit was already browning a little, as if the slices had sat too long after having been cut, but they looked wholesome. She took one and bit into it as Laurel offered the apples to Ariel.

The apple had an odd, sweet taste, as if it had been dipped in honey. Ruth chewed thoughtfully, wondering what was supposed to happen now. Ariel had told her that the usual procedure was for the guru to lead them in meditation and then they would do some singing. Abruptly she realized that Master Joseph was talking again.

"Lord of Might, listen, and hear our prayer. Open our ears that we may hear! Open our eyes that we may see!" his eyes glittered. "Are you pure in heart? Sinners will be cast into the outer darkness, but the pure will enter into Paradise."

Ruth's eyes blurred. She blinked, momentarily dizzied, striving to focus on Master Joseph's bright eyes. In the flickering light they had a beady quality that reminded her of some animal, a rat, maybe, watching from the shadows of an alleyway. What was wrong with the lights, anyway? She looked up at the expensive ceiling fixture and saw it glowing steadily, but light and shadow flickered in time to her racing pulse as soon as she looked away.

"Oh Lord, Lord—take me! Fill me with your holy power!" cried Laurel. She swayed back and forth, her wispy hair falling over her face.

"Power!" echoed Master Joseph. "Give us power!"

"Power, power, give us the power!" came the response from around the circle in voices that had grown guttural or shrill. Ruth saw faces flushed with excitement, eyes glittering, expensive coiffures coming undone. She grimaced with distaste, and rubbed at her forehead, finding it oddly numb.

Power for what? she wondered. *If you're not specific, you'll get gibberish! Garbage in, garbage out—gigo . . .* That was programmer's thinking, she realized, but was a computer so different from the brain? Her head buzzed, and she shook it, wishing she could blink with her ears. The chanting of the people around her came distorted through the internal sound, as if she were hearing it through a screen.

Across the circle, a man began to giggle softly. Master Joseph was watching him, watching them all. What was he waiting for? But his pale face was as flushed as those of the others—as hers must be too, Ruth realized as she put her hands to her cheeks and felt the heat there. Could a group hallucination produce these physical symptoms? Could even a very clever hypnotist achieve such a uniform response? Dry-mouthed, she swallowed, and tasted the sweetness of the apple again.

"The pure in heart will enter into Paradise—" chanted Master Joseph. "Soon the doors will swing open! Do you see the doors?"

"Yes, I see them! I see them!" answered Laurel.

Ariel gave a little gasp, and Ruth heard her whisper, "Gates of horn and ivory, and pearl!" And as she spoke Ruth saw gates too, opening in the recesses of her mind.

They looked like the doors of her walk-in closet at home, but they opened onto a glimmering brightness, like the shimmer of sunlight on the sea. A wave of dizziness shook her, and the analytical part of Ruth's personality—the programmer's mind—recoiled, detached itself, and stepped aside.

—*This is more than hypnotism*—said that other self,—*he has given you a drug of some kind*—

It was true; the feeling self understood that it was true, but the radiance drew her. Awareness flowed forward, inward, downward, and consciousness drowned in that silver sea.

For a time it was pleasant simply to float there, bathed in cool light. Images flickered past like snapshots of memory—morning sunshine slanting across her kitchen, Ariel writing in her diary at the cafe, her son Martin playing with his dog, a dress she had admired in a shop window, the Campanile at the University shining like an elven tower in the morning sun, the play of muscle in Tom Halpern's back as he worked in the garden . . .

The parade continued like an ineptly edited film. The pictures that presented themselves to Ruth's awareness were from an older level now—she reexperienced the strangeness of her first night alone in the loft, remembered counting the tiles on the ceiling of the hospital waiting room while they pumped out Martin's stomach after he had drunk the cleaning solution when he was three, saw the uncomprehending hurt on Ariel's face as she described how her husband had walked out on her, saw once more the look of complacence on Leonard's face at their own wedding reception.

The older the memories that Ruth relived, the more vivid and painful they seemed to be, as if only those things that had moved her strongly had been retained. And although there were some moments, like her graduation day, that glowed like Dorothy's arrival in Oz, the farther back Ruth went, the worse it became. And she could not control it. The images appeared and disappeared at their own will, and she relived each experience more fully than the last.

And then suddenly she was at the fraternity party again, feeling the pleasure of Jeff's arm around her and the bite of the Scotch he was feeding her, the way he laughed when she couldn't stand up, how they all laughed, pulling at her clothing, and then the pain and the weight of their bodies thrusting against her again and again until they were done.

Through the haze of alcohol the bestial faces wavered, fleshy faces distorting monstrously. The lovely silver light had darkened; the men were shadows, from shadow, their features lit by a sourceless, lurid glow. Even their shapes had grown inhuman now. Fanged, humped, furred, they fell upon her, and she fought to move nerveless limbs.

Fear focused, became hatred, a passion of betrayed fury that had lain within her, unrecognized and unreconciled all these years, like the molten magma at the heart of a volcano. Her lips did not move, but she screamed like a she-wolf, and felt the fire within her explode. Her body changed; she was some creature all whipcord muscle, armed with fangs and claws, less human even than her foes. With an animal's ferocity she attacked them, and screeched triumph at the sweet taste of blood, and her talons ripped flesh from bone. The men were beasts, but she was a monster, fueled by a primal power that exploded up from depths she had not even known were there.

Exultantly she raged until their flesh lay in fragments around her, all but the last. As her claws ripped away his face she saw that it was Jeff's face, and his eyes were the eyes of a man.

Silence. Silence rang in her ears. Nothing moved in the shadows. She licked blood from her lips and looked around her, but the cityscape around her was a dim maze. The dark fire still pulsed hungrily within her. Someone—she could no longer remember his name—someone had promised her power. Now it was hers. Whatever she wanted, she could take; whoever she hated, she could kill.

She stalked down empty streets and past decaying houses, seeking her prey. The distant light at the top of the Campanile stabbed the gloom like an evil eye. In the distance she glimpsed other figures, as misshapen as she supposed she herself must be, wandering aimlessly or purposefully, in search of their own victims. She passed one beast that looked at her with Ariel's eyes, but that meant nothing to her now. She was going to destroy her father—a cold, constrained man who had never given her more than a monosyllable of praise no matter how she tried to please him. Or perhaps she should seek Leonard, who had left her body unsatisfied while he caged her soul.

Or else Martin, whose birth had condemned her to remain in that prison for ten long years—abruptly the image of his babyhood was before her, petulance shattering into squalling as he saw the horror that she had become. The sound of it was infuriating. She remembered a time when she had almost thrown him through the window in her despair. Then she should have done it, now she *could* do it—she reached for him.

But as she touched his flesh, different emotions flooded her fury like cold water on coals. Some Other who was still alive within her screamed, *No, no, no!*

And then there were no images at all, only a dreadful swirling that sucked her down into a darkness deeper than she had yet known.

A figure robed in black precipitated from the gloom around her; draperies fluttered like inky wings; from beneath a deep hood, eyes gleamed mockingly. *"Let go,"* it told her. *"Let the Shadow swallow you completely, and then there will be no pain."*

She faced the figure, swaying. Though she had fallen forever, somehow she had landed on some kind of a bridge. It was impossibly narrow. It would be so easy to let herself fall and follow that seductive whisper into oblivion. Too easy. She fought for balance, something, not guilt, but some habitual stubbornness, stirring within her. *Not that way!*

The shadows shimmered, and for a moment she saw imprinted on the darkness a towering winged form that brandished a flaming sword. Then the contrasts blended into a dim light like a rainy afternoon.

If she would not seek escape in annihilation, how was she to get out of here? She looked around her. She was on a height, and gray distance stretched away below her, punctuated by odd, dully colored shapes like a landscape by Paul Klee. After a time she realized that she was looking down at the rooftops of a city. They mutated as she looked at them, shading from color to color, shapes shifting with a kind of monotonous irregularity. Strangely, she found this universe of geometric abstraction familiar. She had seen these shapes, and these transformations, somewhere before.

Involuntarily her fingers twitched as if she were playing an invisible keyboard, and stimulated by the movement, her mind shifted levels, and she understood that this was a map like the one in her game—a symbolic representation of reality. And if these were symbols, then she knew how to manipulate them. A choice here—to extend or contract, to move forward or back—yes/no and yes/no again and again in a sequence of decisions that would bring her back out of the maze.

Out—to get out of here she must find a Gate. The word triggered access to other knowledge; a series of gates would take her home. And abruptly a gate stood before her, a massive thing that seemed to have been cast from dull gold. Ruth took a deep breath, and went through.

Sunlight blazed blindingly. The light was like the desert at noonday, an imperious splendor that made the unshielded spirit cower. She held her hands over her eyes, feeling unclean before this uncompromising clarity. It was not evil as the darkness had been, but in its way it was just as dangerous to her naked humanity. She had to find a way out of here.

Colors shifted and swirled through her vision—a radiant green that was also the overwhelming moist sensual perfume of the jungle in full bloom, alternating with a crisp wind and a hard carnelian glow. But that was not what she wanted, either. Her last memory before the nightmares had been of a serenely silver sea. She forced herself to remember the gate of gold through which she had entered, and to alter its color to silver, and when the change was clear in her inner vision, she crawled forward.

Cool light cradled her. After a time, she opened her eyes. She floated in a sea of moonlight. Above her, a moon-rainbow glimmered across purple distances. Something glowed where it ended, and she had a sense of a watchful Presence waiting there. But she had no time to wonder what it might be—she was aware of a twitching discomfort, as if her human body were pulling her back, but she sensed that it was important that her mind make the journey in an orderly fashion, too.

She needed another gateway. Searching, she found three of them. The one above her was bright but unbelievably small. The one at her feet gaped like the maw of darkness that had dragged her down before. But in front of her was a wooden gate, achingly like the redwood gate that Tom had built for the garden at home. She remembered the smell of new-turned earth, and the warmth of sunlight. The memory drew her forward and through.

Images whirled around her, but she denied them. Before her she saw her closet doors. She was moving faster now, faster still, falling up, toward them. Sight and sound and taste collapsed into one in a confusion of senses; awareness swam upward through random pain that subsided to a dull aching of stiffened limbs as Ruth's mind meshed fully with her body at last.

The sky beyond the windows was the dull gray of the hour just before dawn. Inside, the candle had burned down and spilled white wax across the silk cloth of the table altar, but otherwise, very little seemed to have changed in the room. Cramped muscles complained as Ruth sat up. Her tongue was like a piece of felt in her dry mouth, and there was an odd internal tenderness in her head, but otherwise she felt no worse than she might have expected to, after spending the night huddled on someone's living room floor.

Nor worse physically, at any rate. Ruth's memory still pulsed with flickers of aftervision, as if she had just awakened from a nightmare. But if she had been dreaming, the dreams had lasted all night long, and she had an unhappy conviction that they were not going to fade away.

Levering herself to her feet, she stumbled past the others and down the hall to the bathroom, where she emptied her bladder and then drank thirstily. The mirrored wall showed her a face haggard and red-eyed. Shuddering, Ruth bathed it in cold water and tried to smooth her tangled hair. Then she went back into the living room.

Two of the others were stirring now, and as she looked around her Ruth realized that many of those who had been in the circle were already gone. From the kitchen she heard a woman's laughter.

Maybe I was the only one who had a bad trip, she thought muzzily, *whatever it was . . . I wonder how Ariel—*

Her gaze went back to where she had lain, seeking her friend, and saw her, not asleep, but mute and trembling, curled in fetal position on the carpeted floor.

The clouds were beginning to grudgingly admit a faint gray light as David Mason trudged up the hill. There was only one bus line through this part of Berkeley, and it did not start running for another hour. With no money for a taxi, he had been forced to hike up from Shattuck Avenue. And what if the information he had been given was wrong, and Master Joseph was not here after all?

The raw air scraped his laboring lungs, and David could feel his leg muscles trembling with strain. He was out of shape. A daily walk across campus to his apartment on the Northside had never prepared him to climb the Berkeley hills. But Joseph Roman had to be here. He had to find him and get the drug back again.

It had taken David so long to understand what had happened! He had taken .25 milligrams of the 11 THC that morning—it seemed much longer than twenty-four hours ago. It was a minimum dose, and he had to admit it had done what he hoped it would do. But he had no experience with drugs from which to predict his own reactions. He knew now that he should never have left his room.

He should have never gone out, never have gone into *The Mediterraneum*, never spoken to Joseph Roman—the reiteration of those "nevers" lacerated David's soul. How, even stoned, could he have allowed Joseph to take the drug away?

He paused by a street lamp to peer at the grubby scrap of paper on which he had scrawled the address, then looked at the houses, trying to find a number on one of them. Headlights swept down the street. David glimpsed a patrol car and, heart pounding, forced his legs into a slow jog, hoping they would think him just an early runner bundled up against the chill. Surely he looked harmless enough, with his soft, irregular beard and the padded jacket disguising a slight pudginess around his middle that came from lack of exercise. The police car turned the corner and swept down the hill, and David realized with relief that it was probably going to the scene of the accident he had seen at the bottom.

Perhaps he should have called the cops in the first place, but there was no way Joseph was going to keep silent about where he had gotten the drug if they hauled him in. *11 hydroxy THC* was too new to be illegal, but if Professor Langdon found out that he had made it, and having made it, had let it out of his hands, David would never work in biochemistry again.

Maybe he could get the stuff back from Master Joseph. Maybe nothing had gone wrong. *And maybe,* said a sarcastic commentator within him, *your next project will be to genetically engineer pigs with wings!*

By the time David had come down enough to remember what he had done with the little vial of powder, darkness was falling. By the time he got to the house where Joseph Roman lived, the guru was gone, and the subdued girl who answered the door flatly refused to give David the address of the meeting. It was pure luck, he supposed, that he had run into a guy from the class he had been in who had also been in the Order of Paradise for a little while, and knew where the group was meeting now.

But that had been after midnight, and now it was daybreak. David peered at the street numbers again.

Ahead he saw one house whose windows were still lighted. As he hurried forward, the door opened and several people came out. David heard one of them giggle softly, and then, just as suddenly, moan.

"Do you think it was LSD?" came a woman's voice as they got into one of the cars.

"Master Joseph swore by the Light that it wasn't. I do not believe he would lie to us," another woman answered.

David paused, hoping they would not notice him. He had been afraid that Joseph would use the drug and tell everyone where he got it. Now, years of scientific conditioning set his stomach to churning as he realized that the guru had done something worse—Master Joseph had given the drug to his students without telling them what it was!

Too shocked to worry about being recognized, David found a last fund of energy somewhere to carry him through the open front door.

Several people lay curled on the deep pile of the rug. For one heartstopping moment David was afraid they were dead. Then he realized they were simply sleeping off the results of their tripping. Others were rousing now, trying to pull themselves together for the drive home. Perhaps it wasn't such a disaster after all, thought David as he pushed past them. But he didn't like the looks of the blonde woman who stared into space from her place on the sofa, or the anger in the face of the dark-haired one who was trying to get her to move.

He found Joseph Roman in the kitchen, drinking tea with a woman who retained a certain theatrical beauty even with shadowed eyes and tangles in her mane of auburn hair. Joseph, still suspiciously bright-eyed for this hour, stood up rather suddenly when he saw David in the doorway, but after a moment his face changed and he gave a quick hoot of laughter.

"Where is it? What have you done?" David said hoarsely. He could not bring himself to say more.

Joseph raised one dark eyebrow. "My dear boy, to your scientific mind, it must be obvious where it is now and what I have done. I have shown them Paradise." He seemed to still be high from the drug and, clearly, the ambiguity of their conversation was amusing him.

Paradise . . . David swallowed, remembering that was what Joseph had called the drug before. "You stole it from me—"

Master Joseph shook his head. "No. You gave it to me."

David stared at him, knowing that was not the truth even if it was no lie. "Not for this—" he began desperately, but the woman, who had been listening without understanding, tugged at the guru's arm.

"What is he talking about, Joe honey? I want to know."

"Shall I tell her?" Master Joseph grinned, challenging him.

David remembered the cop car and abruptly understood the threat that the other man was not putting into words. Anyway, whether it was Paradise or Hell, the stuff was gone now. There was nothing he could do.

Slowly, accepting his defeat, David shook his head.

4.

The reflection of the Sophia who dwells above, compelled by necessity, departed with suffering from the Pleroma into the darkness and empty spaces of the void. Separated from the light of the Pleroma, she was without form or figure, like an untimely birth, because she comprehended nothing.

Irenaeus, *Adversus Haereses*

Ruth stood up as the doctor came down the hall, then blinked at the momentary twinge of vision that sent refracted rainbows from the indirect lighting across the mottled carpet of the floor. She wondered how long this was going to go on. She had felt weak and shaky since she awakened, as if she were recovering from the flu, but a few visual distractions could be managed.

Ariel had not been so lucky.

The doctor ran her fingers through her already rumpled iron-gray afro, then looked down at her clipboard again. "Ms. Racusak?" Ruth nodded, and still talking, the woman led her around the curve of the hall toward the door. All the corners at Herrick were curved, with matching furniture, painted in warm colors above beige enamel. But it still smelled like a hospital.

"I want to thank you for coming down." The woman gestured Ruth to a chair on the other side of the big desk, that was cluttered with papers and photographs. The framed certificates on the wall proclaimed that Dr. Roslyn Henry had all the appropriate qualifications. Including psychiatry.

"Frankly, there are a few things—a lot of things, actually—about Ms. Ashton's case that have me puzzled." Dr. Henry shuffled her papers again with slim brown fingers, then looked up and caught Ruth's gaze. "I'm hoping that you can help."

Ruth nodded again. She had managed to get Ariel into the car and drive her home, still shocked and staring at whatever it was she had seen. But she seemed to be recovering. When Ruth had said good night instead of good morning, Ariel had managed to smile. Then Ruth had gone home herself, but it seemed to her she had barely managed to fall asleep when Ariel's neighbor called to say they'd found her trying to slash her wrists with a dull kitchen knife and the police ambulance had taken her away.

"Is she going to be okay?" Ruth's voice came hoarsely and she swallowed, trying to ease the tightness in her throat.

"Frankly, Ms. Racusak, at this point we can't say. It would help if we knew whether your friend's disorder is mental or physical!"

"But can't you tell?" asked Ruth. "Aren't there tests you can do?"

"Ms. Ashton was hallucinating when they brought her in," Dr. Henry's tone sharpened. "Naturally we suspected drugs—an O.D. or a bad trip of some kind. But the results are negative for LSD or any of the alkaloids. We tried Thorazine anyway, but the effect was minimal. We've got her sedated with Demerol now, but I suspect that's only suppressed the problem. At least she won't do herself any more damage this way.

"Her neighbor said you brought her home this morning after having been out all night," the doctor went on. "Do you want to tell me about it now?" There was a pause while Ruth stared at her. "Or do you want me to get it from the police report after you've talked to them?" the doctor went on.

Ruth rubbed her eyes tiredly. "Look, Dr. Henry, you don't need to threaten me. It could just as easily be me lying in there, and Ariel—Alexandra, that is, was the only one involved that I even know. I haven't been to the kind of party you're talking about since I was in school. I was just surprised about the tests. I thought it must have been LSD."

"Didn't you know what you were taking?" Dr. Henry interrupted tartly.

Ruth straightened and looked at her. "You don't understand. This was supposed to be a sort of consciousness-raising session. All we *took* were apple slices. It wasn't until I started feeling the buzz that I thought we might have been drugged somehow."

Dr. Henry sighed. "The police will want to know where you were, especially since your friend tried suicide. But if we can't prove an illegal drug was involved there's not much they can do."

"It was up in the hills. I don't remember the address, but I think the slip of paper Ariel wrote it on is still in her car. She persuaded me to come with her to this group she's been studying with. But she didn't say anything about drugs. Ariel hasn't been into drugs for years." Ruth shivered suddenly.

"Do you mind if we take a blood sample from you?" the doctor asked her then. "This might be something new. Maybe we can analyze it if we have two examples to compare, even though the effects were different for the two of you."

The random texture of the carpeting blurred and swam beneath Ruth's fixed gaze. *Not that different,* she thought dimly, trying to recollect images that were receding like the horrors of a nightmare. Even the attempt to remember how she had gotten free of it set her heart pounding with fear. She closed her eyes, frowning. *Pull yourself together, or they'll have you strapped into bed beside Ariel!*

Ruth drew a long sigh. "Go ahead, if you think it might help her. But I want to see Ariel now."

Dr. Henry shrugged. "Why not? We had her in the locked ward at first, but she's sedated and quiet now, so we've put her on the regular wing. Maybe she will sense that you're there. It certainly can't do any harm!"

Or any good, either, Ruth finished the doctor's sentence silently as she stood beside her friend's bed in the open psychiatric ward. Nearby, she could hear the constant muttering of one of the other patients, but the curtains had been partially drawn around Ariel's bed, and all she could see through the opening was the window, and a budding branch of a sycamore tree against the pale sky.

Ariel's wrists were bandaged and restraints held her arms; an I.V. was inserted in the big vein in the crook of her elbow.

Ruth understood that was standard practice, but it was still a shock to see her that way, with the helplessness of youth and the fragility of age.

She tried to pretend that the other woman was only asleep, but when they were in college Ariel had been an early riser, even when she'd been out late the night before, while Ruth slept in. Ruth could not recall when she had seen her friend asleep during the day. Ariel had been like a butterfly, always in motion, lighting the world through which she passed with gossamer charm.

But this was no restful slumber. Even as Ruth watched, she saw her friend's face twitch, heard the whisper of a frightened moan. For a moment Ariel seemed to fight the restraints that held her, then she subsided again. The fair hair was lank on the pillow, showing darker at the roots, and without the artistic make-up, her skin looked worn. It was a face reduced to its basic humanity, and Ruth realized that through all the years of admiration and resentment and exasperated affection, she had never really accepted that her friend was only a human being, as vulnerable in her own ways as Ruth had ever been.

She would be so ashamed to be seen this way! It was the fullest confirmation of her friend's distress that Ariel should lie here like a travesty of the work of art she had always tried to show the world.

The memories that had been stirred up by her vision of the night before resonated suddenly, and Ruth found herself wondering what *she* had looked like, huddled in her bed after being raped all those years ago. She had wanted to die then, when the stupor of the alcohol had worn off and she had understood what had happened to her, and it was Ariel, elegant, fastidious Ariel, who had held her and nursed her until she could face the world once more.

Carefully, as if she feared to disturb her, Ruth reached down to stroke her friend's hair. The other woman quieted a little then, and Ruth bent over the hospital bed and kissed her on the brow. Faintly, above the hospital smells, she caught the scent of Ariel's favorite lilac perfume.

"Ariel, it's all right, it's Ruth—I'm here, and I won't let anything happen to you. Rest, love, and hang on, and I'll help you somehow," she whispered, and knew, though she had no idea how she was going to fulfill it, that she had made a vow.

As she straightened, Ruth turned toward the light coming through the parting of the curtain, and suddenly she was dazzled by a blaze of gold like the unfolding of mighty wings.

"Do you have a warrant?" Laurel's voice came faint and frightened from the floor below. Joseph took a swift step to his window and saw, through the latticed branches of the sycamore tree, the police car drawn up in front of the house. Adrenaline shocked along his arms, and he stood shivering, cursing himself for not having left town yesterday, immediately after the ritual. But they didn't have anything on him—they *couldn't* have.

"I just need to ask him some questions, Miss—" the deep voice had a faint Midwestern twang. "Is he here?"

"I'm not sure—" Laurel faltered, unconvincingly. "Let me go see—"

Joseph heard her steps on the staircase and thought furiously. He could refuse to see the officer, but then they might think he had something to hide. Better to confront him, Joseph decided then. His lips twitched. If he could not convince a college-town policeman of his innocence, he deserved to be taken in.

Joseph forced his breathing to slow, stripped off the white robe, and pulled a clean shirt from the drawer. He could hear Laurel pause outside the door.

"Invite our guest in and offer him coffee or tea," he said before she could speak. "Tell him I will be right down."

A few moments later, dressed in a white turtleneck and a corduroy suit in soft beige, Joseph Roman descended the creaking stairs. The antique silver cross he had put on winked richly as he came into the living room.

"I'm Patrolman Zabrowski from Special Investigations. You're Joseph Roman?" The officer, a big man whose thickening middle still covered muscle, got to his feet and flashed his ID. Joseph took swift note of the contradicting weariness around the man's eyes and smiled.

"Reverend Roman," he corrected. "Yes, I am." He gestured hospitably, sat down, and smiled again as the officer automatically seated himself at the other end of the sofa. "I hope you have not made a special trip out to see me. I could quite easily have come in to the station when I was downtown."

"I was in the area—" the officer said, obviously taken off-balance by all this sweet cooperation.

"And how can I help you?" Joseph bent forward so that the lamp would catch the worked silver of his cross and saw the officer's eyes follow the little flicker of light.

"We've had reports that last Sunday evening you presided over a—meeting—" Joseph noted the quick editing, "at which drugs were used. One woman is still in the hospital, and there was an accident, possibly related, which we are investigating." The patrolman glanced down at his clipboard and then back at Joseph.

"Drugs?" Joseph edged his voice with indignation. "What kind?"

"I'm afraid I can't tell you that . . ."

You mean you don't know—Joseph corrected mentally, feeling the tightness in his belly ease. David Mason had kept quiet as he had expected, and they were both safe now. He shook his head sorrowfully.

"I try to help the people who come to my prayer groups, but it takes time, and spirituality and mental stability are not always allied. It is possible that one or more of those people were taking some prescription which made them unable to deal with the levels of power we employ. It is even possible that someone might have taken something else in a misguided attempt to increase his sensitivity.

"I am sorry to hear it, as I feel in some part responsible for not having screened them more thoroughly before we began." Joseph spread his hands helplessly and bowed his head. "I will pray for them." He folded his hands again. Peripheral vision showed him confusion in the policeman's eyes.

The kitchen door swung open and the new girl—Ava, he remembered her name now—came in with the tray. Her heavy breasts swung out against the loose sweater as she set the tray down on the table, and Joseph felt another, more pleasureable tension begin to tingle along his veins. The tray held a pot of hot water, instant coffee, teabags and cream and sugar, with a plateful of doughnuts—the refreshments were calculated to be reassuring—and after a moment's hesitation the officer accepted coffee, though he let the sugar alone.

Joseph ostentatiously spooned sugar into his tea. Ava felt the intensity of his gaze and flushed self-consciously. The policeman finished his coffee and began to gather up his clipboard and cap, and Joseph forced his attention back to the man.

"Officer, the only thing I offered to the group was apples." His voice shook with sincerity. "And, at least in my hearing, drugs were not mentioned at any time. That is all that I can say!"

"If we need more information, I'll let you know." The officer stood up and Ava moved quickly past him to open the door.

"Thank you, my dear," said Joseph softly as the sound of the squad car faded. He could feel the throbbing of released pressure at his temples, and another throbbing elsewhere that grew as he looked at her. This craving for a woman's flesh came upon him sometimes, as acutely as any addict's need, especially when he had been under strain or in fear. It was a hunger which, despite the multitude of female bodies he had known, had never been completely fulfilled.

Ava blushed again, and tried to smile. "I was glad of the chance to help you."

"Were you?" Joseph sighed wearily. "We have nothing to hide, but those who follow an alternative Path are always vulnerable to misinterpretation by the Law. I confess, talking to the officer was a strain."

Instinctively, the girl took a step toward him. "I'm good at massaging backs," she said eagerly. "Would that help you?"

"I am sure it would—" he gave her his tenderest smile. The skin of his palms tingled, anticipating the sweet weight of those marvelous breasts between his hands.

As he had expected, Ava's technique was unsophisticated, but it was effective enough to ease the tension from Joseph's shoulders, leaving him acutely aware of his need for her. The little bitch had better come through for him—she must know what it did to a man to be touched this way.

When she stopped, he rolled over on the bed and looked up at her. Her eyes widened at the sight of his naked torso, lean and lightly muscled. It was not a bad body, he thought complacently, holding her gaze with his own, but was she awestruck at seeing *him* half-naked, or had she really never seen a man's body before? His breath came a little more quickly.

"Thank you," he said very softly. "That's hard work, I

know, especially when you have to bend over so far. Why don't you let me work on you a little now?'' He sat up and patted the bed beside him.

For a moment she hesitated, then the bed gave to her weight as she sat down. Not much—she was really a little bit of a thing, except for that wonderful frontage.

"Come on now, take off the sweater—'' he said with a smile. "I can't do you any good through all that wool!''

Ava turned a little away and pulled the sweater over her head. As it dropped to the floor she crossed her arms in a vain attempt to cover her breasts.

"I'm sorry, I don't wear a bra—I can't find one big enough—'' Blushing furiously, she stopped, staring at the floor.

"My little bird, my sweet child, what are you ashamed of?'' Joseph said caressingly. He reached over, turned her head, tipped up her chin so she had to meet his eyes. "Your breasts are the gift of God—see, they are beautiful!'' Very gently, he took first one wrist, then the other, and pulled her arms away.

And they were beautiful. Images both biblical and profane fluttered through Joseph's memory. He saw her shiver and fought to still his own trembling.

"You're cold—'' he put his arm around her and pulled her against him, and unbidden, his other hand went out to cup that cool, smooth flesh that presented itself so invitingly. She jumped at his touch, but he held her, and as she looked up, tightened his hold and kissed her, and still kissing her, pulled her down beside him on the bed, holding her gaze with his own.

"Please—'' she said weakly. "I don't know. I've never—''

"You have vowed to obey me as your teacher—lie still, and I will teach you now.'' She looked up at him with wide eyes, and he knew that he ruled her will entirely now.

And for a little while, then, Joseph Roman commanded all the power he hungered for, and the emptiness within him was almost filled.

Ruth looked once more at the piece of paper on the seat of the car beside her, and then at the address on the house across the street again. It was the announcement for the meeting of the Order of Paradise that she had taken from Ariel's car to give to the police. Only what she had given them had been a copy, because when she saw the return address in the corner, Ruth had known she would need it, not that day, but as soon as she had recovered. She wanted to ask Joseph Roman some questions of her own.

In the last dim daylight the house looked ordinary enough, its flaking paint exposed behind the bare branches of the sycamore in the yard. It was an old Victorian, the last survivor of a more gracious age in a west Berkeley neighborhood converted mostly to stuccoed apartment buildings, where black children shouted and chased each other in and out of the garages as they played. From the amount Ariel had said she was paying, Ruth would have expected something more imposing, but perhaps all the money had gone into the cream-colored Chrysler in the drive.

She glanced in the rear-view mirror and saw that the cop car that she had passed on Channing was still parked there. She wondered if they were interested in Master Joseph, too. She could not imagine what harm the man might do her, but it was nice to know that if she ran into trouble there were cops around. Some obscure need to armor herself against criticism made her fumble in the bottom of her handbag for her lipstick and then, still looking in the mirror, apply it. There was nothing she could do about the dark smudges that still shadowed the flesh beneath her eyes, but perhaps she could smooth her hair—

I'm delaying—Ruth realized, putting the lipstick away. *I really don't want to go in there!* She had delayed most of the week before coming here, and now she was holding back again. But now, having recognized her fear, Ruth could not allow it to govern her, so she straightened her jacket, opened the door and got out of the car.

The brown-haired girl who opened the door looked awfully young to be living in a house with someone of Joseph Roman's reputation. Her features were too irregular to be pretty, and her pink sweatshirt strained across breasts that made her look top-heavy, but she moved as if she were trying to keep from dancing.

"I'm from one of Master Joseph's classes," said Ruth neutrally. "Could I please talk to him?"

She could see the girl assessing her, and did not know whether to be relieved or piqued when she obviously decided that Ruth was not threatening, opened the door for her and went off to find Master Joseph. And Mr. Roman, when found, clearly could not quite remember who Ruth was.

He seemed sleeker, somehow, than he had been on Sunday, easing into the couch with the satisfied grace of a cat that has successfully made off with something succulent. The girl, who had introduced herself as Ava, stood behind him, leaning slightly forward as if she were presenting her heavy breasts to be plucked like fruit from a tree.

"No, you probably don't recall meeting me—" Ruth said quietly, still standing. "It was a rather eventful evening. I was at the Order of Paradise meeting."

With a certain bitter satisfaction she watched his face change, and it seemed to her that in the moments before his expression settled to a pained concern she had seen the flicker of fear. She found a straight chair and without invitation sat down.

"It was my fault—" Master Joseph said sorrowfully. "I had not anticipated the effect of so much power on those unprepared for it. I have been praying for all of you."

"Power, hell!" Ruth exclaimed, leaning forward. "Ariel tried to kill herself! You drugged us, and I want to know how, and why!"

Sternly he shook his head. "How indeed? You saw no drugs there! And can you swear that whatever vision came to you was only a drug-dream? Was there truth in your vision? Tell me!" Suddenly he was on his feet. A swift stride brought him to her chair, and Ruth's sight was trapped by the glitter of his dark eyes.

"Come now, my dear—" his voice had become a caress that compelled the ear as his gaze controlled the eye. "You are seeking the Truth, aren't you, and the Power to fulfill your dreams? You have always stood in shadow, unrecognized, despised—but you have that within you that could astound them all. You glimpsed that power in your vision, didn't you? Tell me, tell me . . ." He swung the silver cross he was wearing on its chain.

That smooth voice stilled thought as the flicker of light on metal focused sight, and the images that for three days Ruth had been trying to suppress sprang vividly to life—the wasteland of burning sand and tortured stone and the faces of the lost souls that wandered there. Yes—she had been powerful there.

Half caught in memory, she felt his hand move along her forearm, and the delicate seductive touch of his fingers on the sensitive spot at the center of her palm . . . And with the flicker of arousal came the horror of the rape that had released that power in her—with a cry of rage Ruth was on her feet, thrusting Joseph away with a force that sent him sprawling on the floor.

"How dare you attack the Chosen of God!" Ava screamed at Ruth, and scurried around the couch to help him. Slowly Joseph sat up, with a fury in his gaze that would have frightened Ruth, if she had not still been quivering with her own rage.

"Bitch!" The concentrated hatred in his voice struck a chill through Ruth's anger. "You frigid, scheming bitch! Are you trying to frame me?" he stared at her. "Or was it revenge you were after? You came to the meeting with that skinny Ashton woman, didn't you?" Suddenly he grinned, nastily. "You're jealous! Now I understand—just a rabid lesbian mad at me because her girlfriend's a silly twit who got out of her depth and couldn't handle it!"

Ruth felt the blood leave her face.

Stiffly, Joseph got to his feet. "Dyke! You don't know what you're giving up! Come on, dyke, and I'll show you what you've been missing—" He started toward her.

Bile rising in her throat gave Ruth the power of motion again. Choking, she ran for the door. Behind her, Joseph began laughing in harsh peals. She could still hear him as she got through it and retched painfully into the bushes outside, and the sound followed her as she stumbled down the steps and across the street to her car.

"You knew—you knew more than you were saying about him—" Ruth burst through the bookstore's door and saw Del Eden's eyes widen. "My friend tried to kill herself. She's in the Herrick psycho ward now. Why didn't you tell me what Joseph Roman was?"

Ruth's question, fueled by the anguish of her meeting with Joseph Roman, came out as a shout. Shaking, she fought to regain self-control, but at her twitching fingertips she could feel the talons that had been there in her vision, honed and ready to rend and tear. What he had said to her wasn't true—it *couldn't* be true. Ariel was only her friend. They were all in this together—this old woman before her and that slimy bastard who had destroyed Ariel's mind. They *deserved* to be destroyed.

She took a swift step toward Del Eden, and rocked back as if she had walked into an invisible wall.

The bookseller's blue gaze caught Ruth's and held it. For a moment Ruth stood, paralyzed, and then, as abruptly as if she had been splashed with cold water, her fury winked out.

But it seemed that rage was all that had been sustaining her. Dizzied, Ruth fell back against the counter and felt strong hands on her arms, holding her, guiding her to a wicker chair.

"Take a deep breath—yes—now another." A calm voice steadied her until her sight began to clear. Focusing, Ruth saw Del bending over her, deceptively ordinary in a gray skirt and sweater over a white knitted blouse.

"You came in the other day to ask about Joseph Roman— you were going to one of his meetings, weren't you? What happened there?" the older woman asked quietly. Embarrassed by having witnessed the outburst, the other customers turned back to their browsing, and the golden cat that had leaped toward them sat down abruptly and began to wash.

"Can't you tell?" Ruth said bitterly. "Or are you a fraud, too? Just a pusher, like him!" She shut her lips, unable to tell this woman the rest of it, as if repeating what Joseph Roman had said to her would make it real.

The blue eyes holding hers did not change. "Drugs?"

"I think so—" said Ruth. "It was either a drug, or Master Joseph is really as powerful as he wants everyone to believe he is. Everyone tripped out, anyway, and there were physical sensations."

"What did he give you?"

"The doctors can't analyze it, and Master Joseph didn't say. Master Joseph would swear on the Bible, the Koran and the Torah that he didn't give us anything at all . . ."

"He did this without *telling* you?" As Ruth nodded, Del Eden straightened and let out a long breath, her eyes clouding as if her attention had gone inward. Light from the front windows gathered in the crystal ball on the counter and flickered across her features as she moved.

"And what I want to know," Ruth went on after a moment had passed, "is why you didn't warn me what he was!"

"I didn't know . . ." the bookseller said slowly. "I had heard that he uses drugs, but he has never done anything like this before."

"Didn't you?" Ruth said wearily. An inner voice that belonged to the controlled, ordinary person she used to be protested that it was unfair to blame this woman for what had happened to her and Ariel, but the same part of Ruth's mind that still resonated to her vision sensed more than Del Eden's surface showed. Her voice sharpened.

"You must know some things, or how did you stop me just now? Don't you have a responsibility?"

Ruth could feel the pressure as Del Eden's full attention snapped back to her.

"Yes—" her voice, too low to be overheard, was tuned precisely to reach Ruth's ear. "It prevented me from judging Mr. Roman before he had sinned. I sensed a weakness in the inhibition that prevents abuse of power, but there are many of whom I could say the same. They mean well, mostly, and most of the time they do no harm. It is only when they are subjected to the wrong pressure, and exposed to the wrong temptation, that they fall. My responsibility prevents me from hastening the process by suspicion or fear."

Looking at the older woman's face, Ruth recognized a carven implacability, like the image of Justice above a court-room door. Backlit by the thin sunlight from the front windows, there was an edging of brightness around her cap of silver hair.

Ruth straightened, facing her. "And when someone has fallen? When he has dragged others with him down into the pit?" Vividly, she remembered the devastated cityscape of the mind in which she had nearly been lost.

"The sanctions shall be invoked against him," said Del Eden softly. "But I think that Joseph Roman will make his own punishment now. My first concern must be for those he harmed."

"For my friend—" said Ruth quickly.

Del Eden looked at her, and the grim features softened. "For her, and for you . . ."

That evening Ruth sought the computer as another woman might have headed for the liquor closet. Too much had happened—maybe the logical disciplines of programming would help to get her emotions under control. The computer wasn't always predictable, but it wasn't consciously inimical, either, and what she got out of it would bear at least some relation to what she had put in.

She pulled down the map from the game menu and considered it. Perhaps she could make the area analogous to West Berkeley a nest of mutant thingies. With a certain grim satisfaction, she found the spot where Joseph Roman's house was located and typed in the legend, "Monster's lair."

Ruth switched to graphics and began to sketch the building, but as she manipulated and edited she found that it was looking more and more like the fraternity house where Jeff had taken her . . .

I guess that's understandable, she thought grimly. *Jeff and his friends raped my body, but Master Joseph raped my soul!*

She could feel the sweat beading on her forehead, and fought to ignore the demons that were gathering—not in the Forbidden City, but in the dark recesses of her own memory. The picture was clumsy, but it would do for now. Biting her lip, she switched to the text editor, and started typing in code.

It's easy enough to invent enemies, Ruth thought as she moved the digitizing pen down the pad and watched the computer mutate the picture she had drawn, *but where am I going to find allies?*

Then she remembered Del Eden's promise, and steadying her breathing as the older woman had taught her, she felt obscurely comforted.

5.

*I bestow on you the powers of the male
and the female, and also those of heaven
and earth. The mysteries of my art must
be handled with courage and greatness of
mind if you would conquer me by the
power of fire, for already very many have
come to grief, their riches and labour lost.*

Beatus: "Aurelia Occulta" *Theatrum
Chemicum* IV

Rain beat and pattered against the hospital window, and Ruth
suppressed a shiver. Ariel had only the sheet and the thin
cotton blanket to cover her. Did she feel the cold? If so, she
showed no signs of it. This was the first time Ruth had been
allowed to visit her since the week before, and the nurse had
cranked the hospital bed half-up so that they could talk, but
for the past five minutes Ariel had been staring at the slick
gray moiré of the rain-streaked window, saying nothing at all.
At least her friend's eyes were not vacant, Ruth told herself,
as if that were some consolation. They were only focused on
something no one else could see.

Ruth realized that her fingers were clenched in the cabled
interlace of her camel-colored sweater, and forced them to lie
flat on her wool skirt. It was a pleasing weave of earth-toned
tweed. She had dresssed up in hopes of cheering Ariel, and
perhaps from a kind of defiant determination to act as if
Joseph Roman's accusations meant nothing to her. Realiza-

tion of how irrelevant her looks were now made her feel cold
again. She took a deep breath and let it out slowly in the way
Del Eden had taught her to control her fear. In for four beats
. . . and out . . . *Joseph Roman was wrong!* In . . . and out
. . . *I love her, but only as a friend!* And in . . . and out
again . . . Ruth repeated the litany.

"Ruth—"

The thread of sound divided two indrawn breaths. Startled,
Ruth lost the rhythm of her breathing and met Ariel's focused, frightened gaze. Suddenly neither Joseph's gibes nor
her own reaction to them meant anything. Even if they had
been lovers, Ruth could only have felt pity for Ariel now.

"Ruth, I've got to get out of here. I'm afraid!"

"You're safe here, Ariel—nothing can hurt you now!"
Ruth leaned forward, trying to sound reassuring. Dr. Henry
had asked her to come today, to help reinforce Ariel's hold on
reality by talking to her.

If she only knew, she wouldn't have asked me—Ruth
thought, remembering the vivid imagery of her dream the
night before. *I have enough trouble myself, deciding what's
real!* She had been climbing a mountain, but when she reached
its summit there was a great gulf on the other side, across
which she saw burning an infinitely beautiful silver star. At
least it had not been the blasted city of her vision.

"It's this place that's hurting me! All these crazy people!"
Ariel played nervously with the sheet. Her fingers had grown
thinner, thought Ruth, or perhaps they only looked that way
because the hospital had taken away her rings. "I wake up at
night, and it's so horrible! I can hear people crying and
muttering to themselves, the same obscenities over and over
again. I'm afraid when I'm out, but it's almost worse when
I'm awake, because I'm here . . ."

"Well, you know they're not going to let you go as long as
you keep drifting off like this. Isn't that what scared you
before?" Ruth said pragmatically. Ariel pushed her thin,
bandaged wrists beneath the blanket, as if she could deny
what she had tried to do by hiding them, and Ruth felt
something in her belly twist painfully.

I'm doing this all wrong, she thought desperately. *I don't
have the training to deal with it. What am I supposed to say?*
She closed her eyes, opened them, and blinked again, as for a
moment she seemed to see her friend through a haze of dark

gray. Ruth gripped the seat of her chair concentrating on its hard reality, then reopened her eyes. The grayness was gone, but, like an afterimage, she felt the impact of Ariel's despair.

"I know," Ariel said very softly after a moment had passed. "I only did it because—" she broke off, swallowing. "They've given me so many drugs I don't even remember what I saw that night, or maybe it's *who*, but it was terrible. Only now that I've thought about it, I realize that if I were dead I might be stuck there, so you don't have to be afraid that I'll try to kill myself again. But if I don't get better soon, they'll take me away to Napa, and the State Hospital is even worse than here. If they take me there it won't matter if I die or just let the darkness take me. I couldn't bear to live that way!"

Ariel's voice had risen, and she was shaking so hard that Ruth was afraid one of the nurses would see. The chair scraped as she leaned forward to put one arm around Ariel and the other on her wounded hands.

"I know, I know—" Ruth murmured instinctively. "But you've got to keep your head straight long enough for them to let you go! Have the psychiatrists been any help at all?"

Ariel let out her breath in a long, shuddering sigh and leaned against Ruth's shoulder. "They ask me questions about my parents and my sex life, and I answer them until it gets to be too much and I drift out again, just as if someone were calling me. My sex life isn't the problem—I didn't care much for all that sweaty groping when I was married, and I certainly don't miss it now. What's bothering me is out *there*, and I can't remember it when I'm *here*—" she gestured in frustration. "So how can I tell them about it?"

Holding her, Ruth felt the sense of darkness ease. Mechanically, she began to stroke Ariel's hair. It was a measure of her desperation that Ariel, who normally was too fastidious to tolerate much touching, should take comfort in this contact. Ariel's comment about her sex life had surprised Ruth—it had never occurred to her that maybe they were both "frigid bitches"—not homo-, but non-sexual. Ruth supposed her own experiences in college gave her a reason to dislike sex. But what was Ariel's problem? Wordless intuitions swirled in Ruth's awareness; she felt Ariel's turmoil in ways she could not define. Remembering her own experiences, she wondered if perhaps she had visited that place Ariel was talking about too.

"Just concentrate on all the things you do know—" Ruth said bracingly. "Remember who you are!"

"Who I am?" Ariel laughed weakly. "They won't give me a mirror, but I can see reflections in the windows—and the person I see isn't anyone I know! My memories are like a book I've read and don't remember very well. I try to look inside myself and there's no one there. Maybe there isn't anyone to remember, Ruth, have you considered that? Maybe I don't exist at all!"

"Then who have I been friends with for so long?" Ruth flinched from the word *love*. "Have I been talking to nothing all these years?"

"Perhaps you have been talking to a mask, Ruth," Ariel said sadly. "Maybe everyone is a mask, and they think I'm crazy because now I know . . ." She pulled away from Ruth's arms, her gaze focusing inward.

"No, damn it, Ariel, don't you go away from me!" exclaimed Ruth, panic fluttering in her belly. She gripped her friend's shoulders hard. "Look, if it's all masks anyway, why don't you put some up around you that will make you feel safe?" As Ariel's attention snapped back to her, shocked, pained, but *there;* something that Del had told her flashed into her memory.

"Don't all those mystics you've studied with say that the spirits of life are all around us? Think of them—think of Archangels surrounding you like bodyguards! Look, there's Raphael, wrapped in clouds, with a bow and arrows to defend you!" She pointed to the east, toward the hills. "And down to the south is Michael with wings like fire and a great sword; and Gabriel in the west, winged all in mother-of-pearl, sounding his battle horn!" She jerked Ariel around, and around again. "And Auriel in the north has a big shield to guard you! Do you see them?"

Pointing, Ruth felt her awareness split. One part stood back, astonished at such silliness, but with the other she could see great glowing forms that warded the space around Ariel's bed with mighty wings.

"But they're not real—not real!"

With a shiver, Ruth realized that Ariel was seeing them, too.

"Does it matter?" she said fiercely. "Aren't they beautiful? Wouldn't you rather look at them than anything else you've seen here? If you're not real you can make your own reality. If things bother you—summon the angels for protection. They're your own private astral security force—as long as you want them, they won't go away!''

That private part of Ruth's brain told her that this was as fanciful as any of Ariel's delusions. Perhaps she ought to be locked up, too. She looked over her shoulder, suddenly afraid that Dr. Henry or one of the nurses might have heard her. But this end of the ward was empty.

It was empty, that is, except for the glimmering figures of the Archangels that her inner vision still showed her standing at attention. She felt them even more vividly than she saw them, sensed balanced energies intensifying until the chill, processed air of the hospital was charged with power.

Ruth took a deep, energizing breath. *Did I really do that?* she asked herself. *I wonder how?*

Ariel lay back with a sigh, looking, despite the lack of make-up and her matted hair, more like herself than she had for some time. Ruth managed a crooked grin.

"There, isn't that better?"

"I guess so," Ariel said, her eyes closing. "But I don't have enough energy to tell. I think I could rest now. I think . . .''

"You think it would be nice if I left you alone—'' Ruth finished for her.

But Ariel was asleep by then, and only the Archangels in their corners watched Ruth go.

David Mason huddled on the bench in front of the Victorian cupola, which was all that remained of the University's original chemistry building. He ignored the rain that had soaked his fine hair and was now seeping through the water resistance of the jacket over his shoulders and working its way down his neck. Behind the textured terra-cotta tile of the chemistry library across the courtyard, students were studying, oblivious to their silent watcher. Hurrying passers-by glanced at him curiously from beneath dripping umbrellas, but with finals upon them they were all too busy worrying about their own problems to bother him.

After a morning spent on routine tasks that seemed steadily more meaningless as the day went on, David had started home, but suddenly even that seemed pointless. Legs that seemed to have lost their strength got him as far as the bench, and there he stayed. He could hear the muted roar as rain-swollen Strawberry Creek rushed beneath the bridge toward the center of the campus, but the shouting in David's head was louder.

Better living through Chemistry, hah! You were going to save the world, or at least yourself, and instead you've betrayed every tenet of scientific ethics! You're an asshole, David—you really are!

David had considered going to Dr. Langdon and telling him everything, but, even more than his own disgrace, he feared hurting the man who had believed in him. He had considered suicide—there were certainly plenty of poisons in the lab. He might even have been able to make it look like an accident. But safety habits, so ingrained as to be almost instinctive, could trip him up, and besides, he was afraid of pain. He might come to it yet, but not that way.

Yet other people had already been fucked up by what he had done—even if the accident he had seen when he was looking for Joseph was unrelated, the people at the house had clearly suffered. Even subjects in a double-blind experiment were told about the procedure and the risks. But these people had known nothing! How could he possibly make expiation?

From a long ago visit to Sunday School, a verse came to him, *"An eye for an eye, and a tooth for a tooth."* And from an operetta he had been forced to attend at boarding school, *"Let the punishment fit the crime."* David grinned sourly and wiped the rain from his eyes. In his pocket was an envelope with .5 milligrams of the stuff, which he had considered sending anonymously to the police. He had thought of a more appropriate use for it now.

Automatically, David observed his sensations—the stuff in powder form was almost tasteless; it was a little like eating dry gelatin. With a grimace of self-mockery he realized that he could renounce lab and lab book, but not his training. He had taken notes on his experience the other time, too, and he wondered if this more-than-doubled dose would be able to override that internal conditioning, whether even death could silence the invisible observer that even now was analyzing his pain.

He waited, awareness turned inward, and noted when his pulse rate began to quicken, his forehead to grow numb—when he had to open his mouth to the rain because his mucous membranes were becoming dry. After a time he noticed that he was hungry. Whether he was wet or dry had become irrelevant. David squelched inside to the candy machine and jammed coins into the slot, buying candy until his pockets would hold no more. Then he wandered out into the rain once more.

Now that he was walking, there seemed no reason not to continue. He moved toward the north side of campus, letting his feet take him where they willed. This was not so different from the last time, the internal observer told him. But that didn't matter either, for he was entranced by the sensory pleasure of walking in the rain.

Presently he came to the dome in the lawn of the Engineering Center and leaned over it, staring down at the students in the library below until someone noticed him, and their waving and pointing annoyed him into going away. The path of least resistance was downward and south, between the flaking, green-painted temporary bungalows that had housed one orphan program after another since the Second World War.

As he passed between the neo-Roman buildings that lined the way to Sather Gate like giant mausoleums in a cemetary, David stumbled and his inner observer informed him that he was becoming dizzy. Perhaps it would be a good idea to sit still for a little while.

Ornamented like a jewel box in bronze, the old library was before him. David stumbled up the marble stairs, past blank-eyed busts of dead scholars and into the still warmth of the reference room. He eased down into one of the hard chairs and contemplated the fretted ceiling until its painted beams began to writhe, and the carved bosses flowered like exotic blooms.

He became aware that someone was shaking him. Was he making his observations aloud? And if he was, well, they were all here for knowledge, weren't they—why should anyone object to it? He tried to explain about the biological transformations involved in creating that jungle in the ceiling, but the faces surrounding him grew flushed or fearful.

David felt their emotions like a mental shout. *Campus Security*—that thought came clearly—it was the desk clerk at the telephone. Suddenly, David was afraid, too. He lurched to his feet, sent the boy who grabbed at him sprawling and shoved past a girl toward the door.

Now he saw pursuers everywhere. He ran toward the anonymity of Telegraph Avenue, but officers were coming from the Student Union and he could not cross the bare expanse of Sproul Plaza unseen. He heard the hushed crackle of a walkie-talkie, saw a dark shape and doubled back past the trees edging Strawberry Creek and then down under Sather Gate Bridge as the police went by.

Sobbing, he worked his way upstream, hidden from his pursuers by the steep slope of the ravine. But now he felt the wet and the cold painfully. He had to find some place where no security guards would think to look for him.

The Campanile tolled the hour and, looking up, David saw its beacon already glimmering through the dissolving air. Moving furtively, he clambered up the bank and slipped through the garden around it. A dogged group of tourists were just going in. David eased in among them and huddled by the door of the elevator as it creaked upward, peering through the window at the anonymous shapes stored on the partial floors of the surrounding granite shell. And then, as the tourists made their obligatory effort to peer through the clouds, he opened the door to the emergency stairs and started down, seeking a place to hide.

"Thank you, Tom—I didn't look forward to making another trip out to the car in this!" Ruth dropped her umbrella into the stand by the door and thumped the bag of groceries down on the table. Raincoat dripping, Tom followed her through the door and set the other bag beside it.

"Happy to help. I've just been digging, preparing the flowerbeds, but this is the off-season for gardeners, you know, and I really don't have much to do. I guess I'm not as tuned to the natural cycle as I ought to be. Maybe I should learn to hibernate, like a bear."

"Yeah—I wouldn't want to put out any leaves and flowers in this weather, either. Maybe some coffee will warm me up—want some?"

Tom nodded, took off his slicker, and hung it carefully on the rack by the door. Ruth filled the coffee pot and put it on, still shivering with a chill that she knew came as much from seeing Ariel that morning as from the temperature in the room.

While the coffee was heating, she stuck a floppy in the

Mac and switched on the new "Sleeper" program that a friend had sent her the day before. Normally the computer was set to go blank if left for any amount of time, so that the image would not be burned into the screen. With the Sleeper, the blank screen was filled by an endlessly mutating arrangement of lines in rainbow colors. Another command activated the sound, so that the light show was accompanied by the sort of subtly shifting tones that made "space music" so popular. She stared at it for a moment before returning to the stove, but she was still thinking about Ariel.

"Is your friend any better?" Tom asked, as if he had been reading her thoughts.

"A little, maybe—I don't know. Being in the hospital may be making her worse, but she certainly isn't ready to go home." The swirl of steam from the coffee maker was mesmerizing. Still thinking about Ariel, Ruth only realized the coffee was done when Tom got two stoneware cups from the cupboard and held them out to her.

How can I stand here making coffee as if nothing were wrong? Why did this happen to Ariel and not to me? Ruth shuddered again, more violently.

Abruptly, Tom set down the cups and put his arms around her, and too surprised to draw away, Ruth let herself lean into his embrace. Tom's muscles had the wiry strength of maturity rather than the sleek firmness of a young man's body, but they were hard enough to uphold her. His scent was an unmistakably masculine composite of clean sweat and the smell of the moist earth and new grass he had been working with.

When her husband had embraced her, there had always been an element of need in his grip that gave Ruth the suspicion that she ought to be supporting *him*. Maybe that hint of weakness had kept her from feeling threatened; maybe that was why she had married him. But if Leonard's touch had not frightened her, it had not really aroused her, either.

Reactivated by her vision and her disastrous meeting with Joseph Roman, the memory of other male arms pinning her down flared vividly into awareness and Ruth stiffened. Tom's grip eased instantly, so that she stood lightly circled by his arms, breathing raggedly as she tried to banish the memories of those young men's bodies, heavy with muscle from college athletics, pounding painfully against her own.

"There's something wrong—" Tom said softly. "Not just your friend. Is it me? Do you want me to let go?"

"Yes. No—" Ruth was not sure which question she was answering. She thought she had dealt with what had happened to her in college long ago. But her vision had shown her that only her surfaces had healed, and that somewhere deep inside, her violated integrity still bled.

Tom stood very still, his embrace undemanding, until with a long, shuddering sigh, Ruth rested her head against his chest. His arms tightened only a little then, but some other sense recognized a current of awareness between their bodies. If she lifted her face now Tom would kiss her, and after that, very likely, his responses would be like those of any other man.

And whatever her sexual orientation, Ruth knew she was not ready for that. "It's not you. It's me—" she said into Tom's chest. "I know it's not fair to you, but I just need someone to be here, right now."

Determinedly, she pressed her face against the itchy wool of his navy sweater. After a few moments she felt his tension ease. He kneaded the rigid muscles of her shoulders, as gently as if she had been a child, until she also began to relax. Ruth felt tears prickle beneath her eyelids. How long had it been since anyone had offered her simple tenderness?

She realized then how little she really knew about Tom—he had been married, she knew, and his wife had died. After that he had left his job with one of the large corporations in San Francisco, built up enough business as a gardener to live on, and moved here. But those were only externals. She did not know what pain Tom kept locked inside him, just as he could know nothing of hers. But some wordless sensitivity had enabled him to set aside his own desires to comfort her.

The sense of wonder that realization had brought her remained even after Tom had gone.

David lay shivering in the dust of the Campanile's fourth floor while the storm raged around him, staging the slow journey of the drug through his system by the bone-deep ringing of the bells. The invisible observer, whose distant voice was now barely audible, noted that it was just as well he had found refuge when he did, for his connection with his body was increasingly tenuous.

Intermittently, David was aware of his surroundings. For a time he had stared out the narrow window, but when the knobbly coppiced branches of the plane trees in the garden began to writhe like hydras, he fell back against the boxes, shuddering. The lamps below cast a dim light into the building's interior, and after a long time his distorted vision identified the long white shapes leaning against the wall as dinosaur bones.

The observer tried to tell him they were extras, there because they were too big for any other storage, but he knew better. They were the bones of creatures he had bred in the lab, and even as he watched they grew monstrous bodies; or perhaps he had shrunk to a bacterial perspective, for he was in their world now, and they pursued him through the channels of consciousness until the observer's last, dispassionate whisper was outdistanced and David wandered alone in the Abyss, fleeing his fears.

It was still raining. As she changed from her skirt into an old pair of jeans, Ruth listened to the infinite variations in rhythm on the roof just overhead—from the roar of the cloudburst to a delicate pattering, punctuated by the musical gurgle of water overflowing the gutters outside, and the hollow plonk of water dripping into the coffee can she had set under the leak in the bathroom. From the needles of the pine tree outside the window, water dripped in necklaces of pearl.

She sat down in front of the computer. Despite her own inner turmoil, the contact with Tom had steadied her, and even if her world was falling to pieces around her, she still had to finish the Forbidden City game before July. She clicked the digitizing pen to bring the screen back to normal and the rainbow mysteries of the Sleeper configuration disappeared. As her concentration shifted, the symphony of sound outside faded from awareness.

Wishing she could write a program as easily as she had summoned up the Archangels, Ruth slipped in the game disc. The computer hummed faintly as it loaded, the icon appeared on the screen and she selected it, then moved quickly to the map where the quester in the game would be. The map was still fairly simple. She had tried to get away from the grid layout by extrapolating her structure from a map of the city of Berkeley, with the University as the citadel. The Claremont

Hotel was some kind of fortress, and the Rad. Lab. an abode of demons. The rest of it she was still working on. The portions for which she had finished the graphics were laid out in solid black, the rest of the map in gray. So far, there was a lot more gray than black.

Humming under her breath, Ruth switched to the graphics editor and began to construct the slopes of Strawberry Canyon, smoother than they were in reality, sculptured curves rising to overlook the town. Now she needed to plot the path down it, how the shadows would fall at different times of day, how the view of the city below it would change. She switched back to the text editor and began to type in the Cartesian coordinate triplets that would place this image on the grid.

Awareness moved from the level of visual imagery, itself already an extrapolation of reality, down to the deeper level of computer algorithms that would govern the manipulation of images. Lines of code flowed across the page—

When she finished the sequence, Ruth stared at it. It would work, probably, but it was going to take more memory than she could afford. There must be a more elegant way to do it. She typed and erased first one alternative, then another. What she needed was a way around all that—she bit her lip as almost without volition her fingers began to flicker across the keys. When she had finished, another block of code blinked at her from the screen.

As she hit the key to save her work and then in a habitual precaution set the printer to add another quarter-page of hard copy to the pile of printout in the box, Ruth felt the elegance of that solution as an almost physical sensation, the way her body felt after a massage, with every component balanced and at ease.

She was only vaguely aware that the rain had settled to a steady pounding. The gray sky outside had dimmed to velvet darkness, and the screen was the only source of light within the room. It had been hours since she had eaten anything. But more than food or rest, she needed to know whether her intuition had been correct, whether her programming would prove out at the next level of symbolic reality.

She moved to the map as if she were playing the game, selected her point of departure in the hills, clicked again, and suddenly the abstract she had just created was before her, a textured, earth-colored slope that rose toward a purple heaven, and beyond it, blue depths beneath a single star. She drew the light pencil up the winding path, entranced by the shifting terrain around her.

Compelled by color and pattern, perception was drawn upward and inward: the star, the slope, the shadowy city below. Too swiftly the sequence was completed. Briefly, Ruth dipped into the text editor again, made a small adjustment to slow it, and from the music editor added a whispery flute sound. Again sound and image played, drawing the awareness toward an unreachable goal. Back and forth Ruth switched applications programs, tapping in new commands to hold the image on the star, increasing its radiance, adjusting so that it pulsed in regular variations of light and sound.

Staring, entranced by that rhythmic vibration, Ruth lost consciousness of keyboard or computer. She was *standing* on the slope, gazing with longing on the star that twinkled mockingly so far away. And faint as a reflection, she saw a line of light arcing out over the city toward a distant peak—no, not a line, but an edge of hardness like the polished blade of a Japanese sword, taking on solidity as she looked at it, arching with a *katana*'s perfection over the depths below.

But as she wondered at it, the stones beneath her feet began to slip away. Ruth struggled for balance, but the solid earth was disintegrating all around her. She tried to go down the mountain, but the ground bucked as if it would fling her bodily onto the roofs of the City below. There was no way back, and only the most tenuous of connections with whatever lay beyond.

It was a choice of terrors.

Heart pounding, Ruth crawled out onto the sword-bridge. She felt the tremor as it took her weight, and a cold slap of wind. A swift glance back showed her that the hills had disappeared, but ahead of her she could see something—a darkness that veiled the terminus of the bridge and the far mountain. Grimly, she continued crawling.

Now she was near the middle, acutely conscious of the blue depths below her, the irregular grid of the City in which vague shapes surged and swirled. Looking down, she thought she saw Ariel reaching up to her, pleading, and then a young man who looked familiar, though she did not know from where. She stared downward, and realized that she was looking at the desolate cityscape through which she had wandered before.

The winds had grown stronger. Now from the left, now from the right they blew, so that in resisting the pressure from either side, she risked falling when it ceased or changed. The wind howled around her with many voices that she could not refuse to hear—

"You're going to fail—you can't finish the program on time!"

"You couldn't keep your husband! You abandoned your son!"

"Bitch-dyke, woman-lover, you don't even know what you are!"

Ruth took one hand off the bridge to cover her ear, felt herself slipping, and grabbed for the slender support again.

"Your best friend is going crazy, and you can't help her!"

Ruth shook her head frantically and tried to hunch her shoulders upward, as if like a turtle she could withdraw into her shell. If she fell she would become a monster as she had been before, and this time she did not think she could win free. But she could still hear them, spitefully repeating every self-accusation, all her hidden fears.

"You're not a real woman!"

"You don't know how to love!"

"Nobody loves you—"

The voices shrilled in her ears, in her heart, in her memory. And underlying them all, a deeper compulsion that beat at her awareness.

"I am the Lord of the Lost—come to Me, come to Me!"

"NO!" Ruth shrieked aloud. "I refuse! It's not TRUE!" She clapped both hands over her ears.

The bridge bounced beneath her; she felt herself flung outward. Howling gleefully, the winds whirled around her—in her awareness a confusion of images spun. Consciousness clutched at brightness, clung, and desperation clothed it with a radiance of wings.

Light and sound exploded around her, deafening, deadening sensation, and then, for a time, Ruth was aware of nothing at all.

Someone was hitting her on the head. Ruth stirred and groaned, trying to escape it, and realized dully that though her head hurt, the pounding was coming from the door.

"Ruth, are you all right?" It was a man's voice, harsh with concern.

In her awareness, images of the Abyss warred with the darkness of the room around her. She had been falling— she had fallen—she was on the floor, anyway, and her chair was overturned nearby.

She grunted and sat up, blinking, as the door burst open and a shape, which she recognized by some sense surer than sight as Tom, charged across the lower room. In a moment he was bending over her, checking her with swift, impersonal hands. Confused, she stared up at him.

"What happened?"

Tom sat back with a sigh and gestured toward the window. "Lightning hit the pine tree. But the rain has almost put the fire out now."

He helped her to her feet and she peered outside. He was right. Flickers of flame still edged a ragged, charred scar down the trunk, but even as she watched, more of the little lights winked out. Slowly, Ruth's brain began to function again.

"My God—the computer!"

She turned too quickly and Tom steadied her. The big screen was pulsing with multi-colored sparkles like an animated Jackson Pollock painting, matching the soft static from the speakers. She stumbled back to the computer, turned it off, and then, holding her breath, switched it on again. After a moment's pause the logo appeared on the small screen, and Ruth sighed.

"It looks like the program's okay—"

"But didn't you lose the piece you were working on?" asked Tom.

"Yes, but it doesn't matter. I was only testing something," she said absently. In the distance she could hear sirens wailing like lost souls. Abruptly she remembered the Abyss, and began to tremble.

"Do you want me to stay with you?" said Tom softly, holding her.

He must think she had been frightened by the lightning! Ruth opened her mouth to refuse him. It was the violence inside her own head that was making her shiver. She was still shaking, and abruptly she realized that she would rather have him think her a physical coward than try to explain what was really wrong. Nodding, she swallowed the words and her pride.

Solid and undemanding, Tom cuddled her against him until morning came. As Ruth drifted in and out of troubled dreams, she came to realize something of what Ariel was going through. But her friend had no one to hold her. Silently, Ruth began to weep, not for herself, but for Ariel and the others she had seen in the Abyss, who still wandered alone.

6.

There was a glass case of quartz crystals in the front window of Eden Books. Ruth stood behind it, half-tranced by the glitter of sunlight on outer facets and internal diffractions. As she moved her head, light shifted in a rainbow glimmer and focused to a point of brilliance like a tiny sun. Perhaps it *was* a sun—perhaps the crystal contained a miniature world as strange and varied as her own. Worlds within worlds within worlds—the mind strove to comprehend, and failing, was whirled away. Caught, consciousness followed the play of light within the stone past icy slopes and frozen waterfalls, seeking its source . . .

"The light goes on forever, but the journey cannot be completed all in a day. Rest now—return, breathe—yes, in . . . and out . . . in . . . and out again . . ."

Ruth felt the hand on her shoulder and blinked, still dazzled by universes of light. But the touch anchored her. After a moment her sight cleared and she realized that it was Del, solid and ordinary in a navy cable-knit sweater and well-worn jeans, whose voice had brought her back from wherever she had been.

"I wonder if that's what it's like when Ariel spaces out—" she said finally.

79

Del smiled and took her hand away. "Is she any better?"

Ruth sighed. "I don't know. The doctor tells me she's conscious more of the time, but still very depressed. She's seeing a psychiatrist, of course, but I don't think she can tell him what's really wrong."

"Did the visualizations of the Archangels help her?" Del moved back toward the counter. Despite the improvement in the weather there were no customers, for which Ruth was profoundly thankful. An Emerald Web tape, playing softly in the background, masked street sounds, and peace was almost palpable in the room.

Ruth turned quickly. "It's possible—they were certainly vivid!" Memory suddenly matched what she had imagined at the hospital with the chaotic images of her vision the night before. "I don't know if they helped Ariel, but I think one of them may have saved me!"

"Something else has happened to you—" Del Eden was standing very still, her eyes half-closed as if she were listening.

Ruth nodded. "That's why I came to you. When I woke up this morning it all seemed like a bad dream. Then I looked outside the window at the pine tree . . ." For a moment she stared, as if seeking inspiration, at the bulletin board with its announcements of neo-pagan festivals, workshops by psychic healers, shamanic drummers, and a witches' cauldron full of other activities, then plunged into a description of the nightmare that had nearly engulfed her soul.

"My mind is like a bug-filled program," she finished. "The image of the slope and the star was like executing a command with a hidden subroutine with an infinite loop that you can't interrupt. If the lightning hadn't struck just then I might have been worse off than Ariel by now!"

"Possibly," Del answered her. The electric teakettle in the niche behind the counter began to spout steam and she unplugged it, then poured an herbal mixture into two tea caddies, dropped them into the waiting cups, and poured. "Though I suspect that your mind is more disciplined and better trained in manipulating symbols than hers. I believe that was what saved you. The analogy is not exact, of course, but one might call the brain hardware, and language and archetypes, the patterns that link them, are the software of the mind."

"Jellyware—" said Ruth with a faint smile. Del lifted one eyebrow. "That's what they call the human component in a computer system these days. Do you really think being a programmer helped me?'' She took the cup Del held out to her and sipped carefully. There was mint in it, and something fragrant and soothing like the scent of a meadow on a hot summer day. It wasn't coffee, but it wasn't bad.

"When a program crashes, how do you deal with it?" Del asked in turn.

"Try things—" frowning, Ruth tried to analyze responses that had become automatic over the years. "Try new routines, alternate commands, and swear at the machine—if I really get stuck I look at the manual." She grinned up at Del. "Do you have a manual for the mind?"

Without answering, Del walked across the store and pulled several books from one of the shelves. *The Mystical Qabbalah, The Ladder of Lights*—Ruth read the titles as Del handed them to her. "The Kabbalah is Hebrew, isn't it?"

"Yes, originally. Today, there are really two Kabbalahs, the traditional Jewish and the Western occult versions—though you would never guess it from reading the works in metaphysical bookstores." Del smiled ruefully, sat down again and picked up her tea.

"In Hebrew, *Kabbalah* means 'The Tradition,' and consists of an extensive esoteric literature dealing with such matters as the creation of the universe and the mystical significance of the Hebrew alphabet. Since the Renaissance, non-Jews have been incorporating parts of it into their own systems. Most of the contemporary metaphysical uses derive from the material developed by the English Order of the Golden Dawn."

Ruth looked at the books more carefully, vague images of medieval rabbis and alchemists swirling in her memory, then blinked and turned back to Del.

"How does all this help me and Ariel?" she asked.

"Depending upon your point of view, this is a model of the unconscious mind of man, or of the Consciousness of God," said Del, opening the second book to a diagram of ten numbered circles linked by lines in a pattern that reminded her of a hopscotch design.

Ruth contemplated it. "It looks a bit like a decision tree."

Del smiled. "It is a tree, certainly—the Tree of Life." She traced a line like a lightning flash from the circle at the top to the bottom. "The first sphere is Kether, the Crown, the white light that is the source of all colors and all creation. From here the power descends from sphere to sphere until it reaches the world of manifestation. Each sphere is an aspect of the Divine, a constellation of images and archetypes.''

"It's sort of like a program menu, then," said Ruth, "and the circles are files."

Del smiled gently. "It wouldn't surprise me. They could be similar because both are the products of human minds, or because both correspond to some cosmic plan. It really doesn't matter which is true."

"But with a computer, at least I know how to get into the system," Ruth complained.

"This system is all around you, as it is within you. Once you understand its symbols, you can move from level to level at will." Del thought for a moment, then reached into the cupboard behind her and pulled out a poster which she unrolled across the counter. Ruth saw the diagram from the book in color, with astrological signs and Hebrew lettering around each sphere.

"We begin here with *Malkuth*, the Kingdom—" Del pointed to the lowest sphere, quartered in earth tones. "Above it is the Foundation, *Yesod*, the astral sea whence come all archetypes. This is the level that men reach in dreams—"

Abruptly, Ruth remembered the silver sea in which she had floated at Master Joseph's ritual, and the images that had come to her there.

"But you can't take the poster with you when you're dreaming," she answered.

"You must memorize the map with its paths and symbols and guardians—it is a means for enabling the conscious and unconscious components of the mind to talk to each other." The conviction in Del's voice was impressive.

Ruth stared at the glowing spheres. She found the pattern they made on the paper oddly satisfying, like an elegant sequence of computer code. But there was something wrong—between the top triangle and the next one was a gap where logic would have completed the pattern with another sphere. Frowning, she pointed to it.

"Tradition tells us that an invisible sphere is there—*Daath*, the sephira of Knowledge. According to one school of thought, our own world originally held that position, but after the Fall it was cast down, and now a great Abyss yawns between us and the higher spheres. It can only be crossed by a bridge as narrow as the blade of a sword.''

Ruth shivered. *The Abyss*—she had not imagined it! It was a real place in the country of the mind!

"That's what I saw in my dream—'' she whispered hoarsely. "I nearly fell in! What saved me, Del? I'm afraid to use the computer, or even go to sleep for fear it will happen again!''

"Call upon the Archangels for protection!'' said Del. "You and your friend both come from a standard Judaeo-Christian background, and the angels are powerful cultural archetypes. You can anthropomorphize them, or see them as forces. They have been pictured as all Eyes, or Wings, or Wheels. Visualize them and they will come to you!''

Ruth closed her eyes. Memory accessed the winged radiance she had seen in her vision, and then some faculty beyond memory multiplied it into whirling arcs of feathered splendor that were also Personalities, each potent with its own individual Power. Her spirit expanded painfully, glimpsing glory beyond glory; then perception failed and dropped her gasping back into her body.

"God, what's happening to me?'' she groaned, pressing the heels of her palms against her eyes as if she could rub her vision away. "I just start thinking about it and I go off again!''

She felt Del's arms around her, the comforting warmth of the older woman's body and the soothing murmur of the voice that had been so vibrant a moment ago.

"It *is* God that is happening to you—or the gods, if that is your belief—the call of the spirit and its power . . .'' said Del softly. "There are many who strain all their lives for even a glimpse of what you have seen. For you, taking the Paradise drug was like a pregnant woman taking castor oil to start labor. Your spirit labors now to be reborn . . .''

"If God had anything to do with this it was a rape, not a seduction!'' said Ruth bitterly, deliberately extending the metaphor. "The Holy Spirit has a lot to answer for . . .''

She had recalled the rape of her body in college in devastating detail in her first vision; but this invasion of the spirit was almost worse, because much as she resented it she could not reject it utterly. She realized that she *wanted* that winged brightness, she longed for that distant star.

"I know, my child, I do know . . .'' Del murmured against

her ear, still holding her. "People talk about religion as if it were aspirin, or a certificate of social respectability. But the shamans and the mystics in every age know that the Spirit seizes and shakes you loose from all certainty!"

"And if you refuse to be shaken?" asked Ruth stubbornly.

"It is worse than suicide, for you deny your soul. Despite the pain of bearing him, would you kill your child?"

Ruth shook her head. In her vision she had had to make that choice too.

"And what if you say *yes*? What comes afterward?" she asked finally.

There was a long silence. Wondering if the older woman had heard her, Ruth turned to look at her, and then as quickly shut her eyes, feeling as if she had invaded some unimagineable privacy. But in her mind's eye Del Eden's face, stamped suddenly with the imprint of ecstasy, still shone. And then, after an endless moment, the answer came.

"What comes after is Joy . . ."

Joseph Roman sat in silence in front of Inspector Stephenson's massive desk, dark with age and scarred from years of use, wondering if he had made a mistake and what was going to happen now. He cursed the bravado with which he had offered to come down to the Berkeley Police Station, never imagining they would take him up on it. From the next office he heard a phone ring, and a murmur of voices. He shifted uncomfortably in the hard wooden chair and tried to focus on the moving shadows of the budding sycamore branches against the pebbled window.

But the forked shadows made a net upon the glass. *I'm trapped!* Joseph swallowed panic. *They've found out about the drug somehow.*

The door opened on a wave of sound from the hall, then closed behind a big man in a sports jacket and worn corduroys—very big, very black, deceptively slow moving, thought Joseph as he half-rose to meet him.

"I'm Inspector Stephenson." The big man nodded and moved around the desk, put down the manila folder he had been carrying, and sat. "We'd like to thank you for coming down here to talk to us."

Joseph subsided back into his own chair, mumbling a meaningless acknowledgement. He was not aware that he had been offered a choice. Officer Zabrowski had shown up that morning with the request and a patrol car in which to carry it out. Joseph had had the distinct impression that meek compliance would be the better part of valor.

Inspector Stephenson opened the manila folder, glanced at its contents for a few moments, and closed it again. He looked up at Joseph.

"You've been arrested twice, I see—once for statutory rape, and once for fraud. Is that correct?" The dark eyes were impassive. Joseph felt as if he were facing some inhuman force that waited with inexhaustable patience for his reply.

"I was never convicted," said Joseph with what was intended to be equal imperturbability. His palms were damp, and he blotted them unobtrusively against the pale gray wool of his trousers.

"Yes, I see that the charges were dropped, both times, before the cases went to trial. You had good lawyers." His understanding smile suggested that they both knew how little the proceedings of the law sometimes had to do with justice.

"My lawyers had good cases—" Joseph Roman said blandly, beginning to understand the rules of this game. In fact, they *had* been good lawyers, with good money behind them from people who did not want to see Joseph Roman under oath on the stand.

"Like doctors and psychiatrists, religious leaders are unfortunately vulnerable to hysterical accusations, particularly when emotions run high and factions form," Joseph went on. "I am very sensitive to the needs of women, Inspector, and at times my concern has been misinterpreted."

It had been a woman who had paid his legal fees last time, thought Joseph as he waited to see the effect of this response, a woman who did not want her husband to know just how much money she had contributed to building a temple that was never more than a drawing on the wall. But that was not Joseph's fault—a temple where he could serve his gods properly was still his dearest dream. But there were so many expenses. Somehow, no matter how much he collected, the money misted away.

And who, he wondered then, was going to pay for his lawyers if things went wrong here? For a moment Joanna De Laurent Winslow's face glimmered in his memory, and he almost smiled.

"That's why we assumed you would want to cooperate with us—" the Inspector said gently, startling him back to awareness. "We know that several of the people at your last meeting were under the influence of some kind of hallucinogen. We would like to know what it was, and where it came from."

"Nothing illegal, I hope?" said Joseph helpfully.

"Not yet," corrected Stephenson. "If it had been a controlled substance we would not have had to 'request' your assistance, we would have pulled you in." The Inspector's face seemed somehow to have grown darker.

Joseph looked at him and swallowed nervously, wondering if they had analyzed the drug and were stringing him along, or whether the officer was subtly disguising the fact that he had no idea what it was. He knew that the idea of an unknown drug out on the street would drive them crazy. But Joseph found it hard to feel much sympathy. His answer, at any rate, was not hard to find. At all costs his story must maintain consistency.

He shrugged and tried to look sorry. "What can I say? I certainly didn't see any strange powders or pills—"

"I'm sure you didn't. No one else did either, by the way." Inspector Stephenson frowned. "But someone had something, and I don't want any more of it in this town. Maybe you're telling the truth and you don't know, but our only lead is through you. So you have to know we're going to be watching you like a cat watches her first kitten, and if you put a foot wrong we'll have a warrant out before you can sneeze!"

Joseph felt his hands grow cold. "But you don't have a warrant now," he said as steadily as he could. The Inspector gave a regretful shake of his head. "Then if you've finished this interrogation I will take my leave of you. I do have other things to do."

Other things to do! thought Joseph wildly as he pushed through the swinging door, passed the clerk's window for the city jail, and clattered down the broad curving stairs to the street. *Indeed I do!* And the first of them was going to be a call to Joanna de Laurent Winslow in Piedmont, on a pay phone chosen at random, because he was certain his own phone must be tapped by now.

They had not forbidden him to leave Berkeley, and if he

got out now, perhaps they would find something else to worry
about and leave him alone!

David Mason stood at the edge of the crowd that had
gathered at the corner of Telegraph and Channing to listen
to the hypnotic music of the cymbalom player, less from
interest in the performance than because he lacked the energy
to go around it and continue on.

That happened to him a lot lately—he would be stopped by
some simple obstacle until another force stirred him from his
inertia. Vaguely he wondered if his state could be expressed
by an equation. Fortunately, long training carried him through
his work at the lab, but he had never felt fully alive outside of
it anyway, and there seemed even less point to the daily
business of living now.

The music thrummed loudly and then sank to a murmur of
melody, punctuated by a silvery ripple of sound like plucked
harp strings. There was a little murmur of appreciation for the
musician's virtuosity, and even David felt a faint curiosity at
the variety of sounds the man was getting from a single
instrument. The crowd shifted, and for a moment he could see
the flicker of spoonshaped hammers striking the strings. There
were little bows at the ends of the hammers, and the musician
was wearing guitar picks on his thumbs.

That explained how the sounds were produced, but not
how they were affecting him. The music pulsed compellingly,
one melody transmuting into another in patterns whose rules
David did not understand. He thought that his visions on the
night of the storm had had some inner logic as well, but there
was no table of elements to refer to here. He had taken the
drug in some vague notion of expiation, and now he wandered in a wilderness of the spirit for which none of his
knowledge of the chemistry of the brain gave him any guide.

He tried to force himself to think. He had come down here
to . . . look in at Cody's for a book for his mother's birthday.
Just another block to go, he thought, he ought to go. But he
was still standing there when the musician resolved his melody at last and began to pull the hammers off his fingers for a
well-deserved breather.

Slowly, consciousness began to reconstitute itself. The movement of the people around him stirred David to motion like
waterweed in a current; he turned, someone gripped his arm,

and he found himself staring at a woman with reddish-dark hair, blocky in a maroon carcoat.

"It's *you*—I've got to talk to you!"

"What are you doing? I don't even know you!" Startled into full awareness, David tried to pull away, but the woman held on grimly, her eyes almost black in her pale face as she inspected him.

"You came to that house in the hills after Joseph Roman's class," she said more calmly. "I heard you arguing with him. What do you know? My name is Ruth Racusak—" her gaze held him more surely than her hand. "Some weird things happened to me that night, and I'm trying to understand why. Will you help me?"

Something in David's own face must have betrayed him, then, for abruptly she let go. *She knew! She knew*—the guilt that had ridden him ever since that night shattered David's defenses and he began to shake, still standing there.

"It looks like some weird things have happened to you, too—" the woman said softly. And then, suddenly, "How long has it been since you've eaten, anyway?"

Startled by the question, David tried to remember, and then shrugged. What did it matter? What was she going to do to him? As if she had read his mind, the woman smiled and slipped her arm through his in a grip that was just as sure as the first time, but friendlier.

"I'm hungry too—come with me to my favorite place along here. I'll feed you, and we can talk, okay?"

Too bewildered to resist her, David let Ruth lead him away.

"Have you ever had Ethiopian food before?"

David's fascinated gaze moved from the intricately embroidered hanging of crosses and interlaced knotwork behind her to Ruth's face. The walls of the restaurant were covered with palm mats and split bamboo screens and decorated with embroideries and bright, coiled baskets, and travel posters and paintings. He shook his head.

"No—I didn't even know this place existed. I usually settle for a hamburger in the garden at Reza's when I'm here."

"The Blue Nile has been one of my favorites for a while." Ruth smiled. "I don't cook much, but I like interesting food, so I collect restaurants. If you're into hot food, the chicken *tibs* is good, or one of the *wat* dishes, if you like things milder.''

David blinked. He had been expecting tears, accusations, anything but this banal conversation about food. He wondered if he had imagined what she had said to him on the street, but he *did* recognize her—she had been in the living room with a another woman when he got to the house in the hills.

"This was your idea. You order for me, and then tell me why!" he said abruptly.

Ruth nodded and spoke to the exquisite waitress who was waiting patiently, smoothing the embroidered white cotton dress that was so striking against the warm brown of her skin. When the girl had gone, Ruth leaned back with a sigh.

"I had a bad trip that night, and my friend is still in the hospital," she answered harshly. "I don't think Joseph Roman is enough of a magician to do that all by himself, but if there was a drug, the doctors couldn't identify it. I heard you arguing with him. Now, why don't you tell *me* why?"

David's looked as if for inspiration at a painting, almost medieval in its flat perspective and stylized drawing, of Solomon welcoming the Queen of Sheba, but the King's painted eyes stared at him accusingly.

"It was a new drug—" he said almost too softly to be heard. "I made it. Joseph conned me into giving it to him. I never meant him to use it that way!"

"What the hell was it?" Now it was Ruth's turn to stare at him.

"Joseph called it Paradise, but maybe it *was* Hell! I thought I had made 11 Hydroxy THC—" he saw her incomprehension and went on, gaining confidence from being on familiar ground, "the active ingredient in grass. But now I'm not so sure. I took a massive dose myself a few days ago—out of guilt, I guess, and I don't think that even pure THC could account for . . ." words failed him and his voice trailed away.

Ruth frowned. "A few days ago? The night of the lightning storm?" Her gaze seemed to go a little fuzzy as he nodded, as if she were remembering. The waitress came then with their order, and for a few moments he was distracted as she showed him how to use pieces of the thin *injera* pancakes to pick up the food.

"I saw you. What I mean about weird is that the experiences keep going on—" said Ruth. David's expression must have betrayed him then, for she laughed. "And that night I had the psychic equivalent of an aftershock. In my vision I saw you. Was it very bad for you? I wasn't sure I was going to make it out again."

David realized that he was trembling, took a long swallow of honey wine and set his glass down again. In the midst of the disaster that he thought had completed his alienation, suddenly a companion was holding out her hand. Tears stung his eyes and he made no effort to hide them. It didn't matter if this woman saw the weakness of his body. She had already seen the nakedness of his soul.

"Yes," David whispered. "It was bad. I'm a scientist—or I thought I was, anyway. We sneer at the social sciences a lot, you know, because they borrow our vocabulary and our methods and try to apply them to intangibles. The thing about real science is that you can measure everything you're working with; you can be precise and sure."

He took a deep breath. "But you're always on the outside, controlling the numbers, the models, the substances in the experiment. I was on the inside this time! I thought I was still wandering around the campus. I went into the chem building, but it was a maze. I took refuge in one of the labs, but this time I was inside the test tube—the experiment was happening to *me*! The life of a cell and my own life were the same; I was caught in the patterns; chemical reactions were irresistible forces I couldn't understand!"

Ruth put down the scrap of *injera* with which she had been mopping up gravy and looked at him. "A week ago I would have laughed at you," she said soberly. "Now I think you're lucky you haven't gone crazy."

"I haven't?" David asked unsteadily. "Since Joseph took the Paradise drug from me I'm not sure I've been sane—" Suddenly aware of his hunger, he tore off a piece of *injera* and scooped up some carrot and chicken.

"It took a lightning bolt to get me out of it, this last episode, and my friend Ariel is still having a pretty bad time," said Ruth. "How did you get free?"

David shrugged. "I did what I always do when I get confused. I started reciting the Table of Elements, over and over again. Finally, I guess, the drug wore off. Anyway, suddenly it was daylight, and I was still saying the Table, and feeling like sludge that's been through the centrifuge.''

Slowly Ruth began to smile. "It's not a bad litany for affirming an orderly universe. If the stuff affects you the way it does me, you may need it again.''

"I'd rather understand what's going on in my head so I can control it—'' David answered her, gathering up a generous dollop of rice, gravy and chicken and popping it down. Already his head felt clearer, whether because the food was bringing up his blood sugar, or from relief at being able to talk to this woman, he couldn't say.

"That's just what I said a day or two ago." Ruth looked at him curiously. "There's a woman named Del Eden who knows about these things. Will you go with me to see her? Maybe working together we can figure out what's going on with this and find a way to help my friend.''

David sat back with a sigh, fully aware of himself and his surroundings for the first time in days. But he was not back to normal, for he, to whom other humans had always been a mystery, realized that he could understand this woman whom he had met barely an hour ago as he understood the compounds he worked with—he could perceive her toughness of mind and the vulnerability behind it, and the sincerity of her concern for him.

He looked at Ruth in wonder, and saw the brightness of release glimmer in her eyes as well.

"Thank you—'' David Mason said then.

"Joanna, I must thank you for your hospitality—'' Joseph Roman shut the door of the Mercedes behind him as the chauffeur went around to the trunk to take out his luggage. She had sent the car for him so that the continued presence of the Chrysler in the driveway would mislead anyone watching the house. Remembering its peeling paint, he thought there could hardly have been a greater contrast.

He cast a quick, appraising glance at the building from which Mrs. Winslow had come out to meet him and mentally blessed the natural good taste that impelled him to buy quality clothing. His wardrobe was not extensive, but what he had brought with him was good.

Joanna de Laurent Winslow rustled toward him across the gravel of the drive in a trouser and tunic set of turquoise silk and held out her hand. He took the scented, cinnamon-tipped fingers gently and bent his head in a gesture somewhere between homage and benediction. She laughed, pulled her hand away and patted his cheek.

"Welcome to Templar Court. I should be insulted," she added playfully. "You have never been willing to accept my hospitality before."

"I was wrong—" said Joseph as he followed her up the broad stairs. They were carved of the same pale stone that faced the entry way. Above it, the house angled away in oddly faceted levels that followed the rise of the hill, as if it had been a sculpture rather than a dwelling. All the kingdoms of the world lay spread out below them, or at least most of Oakland and the luminous blue of the Bay. More trees hid the place completely from the road, but off to one side he could see gardens, and the pale gleam of a pool. "Such beauty deserves a pilgrimage."

She laughed again, as if the compliment had been for her, and led the way through the mahogany door down a tiled hallway to another double door. He smiled ruefully, remembering how he had wanted to preserve his status with her by retaining an element of mystery. All he really needed to do was pander to her vanity.

"My misfortune has been a blessing if it enables me to see you in a setting so worthy of you!" he went on.

"Well, we could not leave you to be persecuted by small-town policemen!" Over her shoulder, Joanna smiled. "Come in—it's time for cocktails, and there's someone—an old friend of my husband's—who would like to meet you."

Joseph paused a moment to straighten the jacket of his suit, a little rumpled by the ride, and followed her into the room.

His first impressions were of stark, polished surfaces and bold accents of greens and purples and oranges in unexpected combinations that challenged the senses, as the superb workmanship of every gleaming table and opulent cushion challenged self-esteem. It was a room whose expensive drama would overwhelm any who were not already secure in their own wealth and power, and Joseph felt his pulse quicken in response to it.

He moved forward across the thick creamy pile of the carpet, and as he did so, all the jarring shapes and colors rearranged themselves like a kaleidoscope into a backdrop for the man who was rising from the leather-covered couch at the far end of the room. Joseph's first confused impressions of an exquisitely tailored gray silk suit were submerged in awareness of the supple ease of movement in the blocky form it covered, and that, again, by a sudden, disorienting shock as he met the man's black eyes.

"Reverend Roman, I believe?" The voice had a resonance that sent a shiver through Joseph's skin even before he touched the man's hand. "I am Luciano Abaddon."

7.

The essence of science is to discover identity in difference.

F.S. Marvin, *Chemistry*

"Do I really have to learn Hebrew?" David grimaced as Ruth laughed at his third attempt to pronounce the God-names for the spheres on the Tree of Life. "Master Joseph taught us the general theory of the Tree, but we didn't go into the gory details!"

Pallid afternoon sunlight glowed on the colors of the poster they were studying. Del Eden had put it up for them when Ruth dragged David into the store after feeding him. He was still trying to figure out exactly why.

"You don't have to be able to make light conversation, just pronounce it!" exclaimed Ruth. "For a man who says *Escherichia coli* at the drop of a test tube, you're doing a lot of complaining!"

He looked at her a little doubtfully, and saw that she had accompanied the words with a grin. David realized that she was teasing him. His own sister had never paid enough attention to him to do that. It made him feel easier with her, somehow.

"How about *Xanthomonas oryzae*, or *Haemophilus haemolyticus*?" he replied.

"Aren't those the 'barbarous names of evocation' they use to summon spirits?" asked Ruth.

David straightened and stared at her. "You know, in a

94

way, they are—those are some of the microorganisms that produce restriction enzymes that break down DNA. And you had better call on the right one if you want your results to be predictable, or even safe, sometimes.''

"Men used to think the microorganisms that cause disease were demons, because they didn't have the tools to perceive them—" Del Eden came out from the back of the store and paused beside them. "Precise terminology and procedure is essential in any operation when the forces being manipulated are powerful, whether you call it science or magic.''

David turned quickly. This white-haired woman with the kind eyes still scared him. Ruth, he could almost understand. She was into computers, and she had shared his visions. But after his experience with Joseph Roman, David twitched nervously at the very name of Magic. The trouble was, Del Eden reminded him of his research professor more than anyone else he knew.

"But why bother with all the foreign terminology?"

"For the same reasons you use Latin in biology—" answered Del. "In ceremonial magic, Hebrew is a kind of international language, and many of the names are themselves composite words expressing specific divine functions and relationships. For instance, the syllable -el in the name of an angel means 'God.' And here," she pointed to the purple circle just above the base of the Tree, "the God-name for the sphere of Yesod is *Shaddai El Chai*—Powerful Lord of Life, specifically of physical life, for this sphere governs procreation by reflecting the Divine Plan into the world of manifestation.''

"I ought to be taking notes—" said Ruth ruefully. "I'll never remember it all.''

"The Pattern comes first, and then the numbers and colors." Del's finger moved from the white sphere at the top down the Tree. "The correspondences can be memorized later, and even when you think you know them all you will still find more to learn. The study of the Tree can fill a lifetime, and more than one lifetime, if you believe that way!''

Del sighed, and David wondered how many lifetimes *she* had been studying these things.

"I wish you would simply tell me what to do!" Ruth was still frowning.

"No!" Del's denial startled them all. "That is the temptation a teacher must battle constantly. That's where Joseph
Roman went wrong! There is a difference between sharing
knowledge and tools for learning and requiring the student to
give up his will! A well-known occult teacher wrote, 'Love
under will, that is the Law,' but it should be, 'Love under
free will.' I can try to share with you what I have learned
about the inner worlds, point out opportunities and dangers,
and guide you on your way, but you must decide where you
want to go!"

Del stood with arms crossed, the silver ankh she wore
glittering against her blue sweater as her breathing quickened.
David stared at her, comparing her warnings with Joseph's
proud dogmatism. He had been trained to believe that the true
scientist spoke with certainty only about results that had been
demonstrated repeatedly, and even then, with the qualifica-
tion that some new paradigm might force reevaluation one
day. It occurred to him now that perhaps it was not Joseph's
theories that were at fault, but his methodology.

"You've already told me how to use the symbolism of the
Tree to control my visions, but isn't there anything we can do
for Ariel?" Ruth asked softly.

Del took a deep breath and David could see the lines of her
body ease as she let her tension drain away.

"Nothing physical— It is her spirit that is wounded now,
and the work must be done on the inner planes. If you will
get her consent to it, we can do a healing ritual."

"We?" Ruth cast a swift glance at David and then looked
back at Del again.

"The format I use works best with five people. There are
two friends I have worked with before who might be willing,
and you should be there, with a picture or something belonging to your friend for us to use as a focus. We would need
two others—" She looked at Ruth inquiringly.

"There's a man who lives in my house that I might ask,"
Ruth said thoughtfully. "He's never done this sort of thing,
but he's very steady, and open-minded."

The bells on the door chimed as a late customer came in
and began to browse along the tables, but Del and Ruth were
both looking at David.

I can't, he thought desperately. *I don't even know these
people. I was no good at this in Joseph's class—they wouldn't*

want me if they knew. But beneath those surface protests a deeper awareness throbbed with the pain that had not left him since Joseph Roman took the drug away.

It's my fault if anyone has been harmed . . . Slowly, painfully, David nodded, and was rewarded by a sudden light in Del Eden's gray eyes.

Candlelight burned ruby in the crystal curve of the wineglass as Luciano Abaddon turned it back and forth between his powerful hands. Joseph watched its hypnotic flickering, hardly aware of his fascination; which was odd, since he had often used a similar technique to compel attention. But the perfection of the prime rib and the rest of the meal that the wine had accompanied had simultaneously satisfied his hunger for food and for luxury, lulling all other awareness. This was how life should be lived.

"You are a very interesting man, Reverend Roman," said Abaddon. "A man of cultivation and intelligence. Why have you wasted your talents trying to enlighten neurotic women and emasculated men?" He set down the wine glass and a soft-footed servant took it, and with it the bottle, which had been a 1983 Chateau Prieuré Lichine. Other servants were clearing away the porcelain and silverware.

Hearing his own thought echoed, Joseph cast a quick glance at Joanna, who was presiding over the table in a designer gown of misty lilac crepe, whose soft folds provided tantalizing glimpses of the blue baroque pearl suspended between her breasts. She smiled at him, obviously too secure in her own wealth and power to take Abaddon's remark personally.

"I can only serve those who come to me—" he said finally.

"No—" Luciano Abaddon shook his head gently. "You are a man of power. Those who come to you should serve *you* . . ." As Joseph stared at him, Abaddon pushed back the mahogany chair and got to his feet. "Let us continue this conversation in the library—they will bring our brandy there."

Joseph followed the silken sway of Joanna's hips into a room that managed to suggest the traditional luxury of a good club without clashing with the rest of the modern decor. The bookshelves and cabinets were of some oriental wood with a silvery sheen like the breast of a dove, the armchairs in taupe suede. The ceiling was papered with a marbled design in teal blues like the endpapers of some rare edition, and oriental carpets that picked up the rich tones of the book covers were scattered upon the waxed parquet of the floor. In addition to books, the shelves held objets d'art—a pigeon's-blood glazed Chinese vase, a small, contorted bronze. A Presidential citation framed in gold hung against the blue of one wall.

As Joanna turned to close the door, the soft material of her gown clung to the smooth line of hip and thigh and Joseph was abruptly certain she wore nothing beneath it. His own automatic response to the idea startled him—he had always considered Joanna off-limits, a rich woman whose value as a resource must not be compromised. Now, invited into this room as if he belonged there, he began to wonder.

He cast a swift look at Mr. Abaddon, who was telling the servant who had magically appeared in the other doorway where to set the silver tray with the brandy decanter. Joanna had introduced him as a businessman with many interests, a friend of her late husband's. Was she Abaddon's woman now?

The servant left. Abaddon selected one of the armchairs and gestured to Joseph to take the other one. Joanna poured brandy into snifters fragile as soap bubbles, served the two men, then poured for herself and eased down into a couch lushly upholstered in cordovan leather.

"I said you were a man of power—" said Abaddon. "What are you using that power for?" He drank delicately, then set the snifter back down, contemplating the amber liquid in the glass.

Joseph sipped at his own brandy, using the movement to cover his confusion as he sought for an answer not only for Abaddon, but for himself. It was a question he had not asked himself for some time. It had, always, been a matter of power, from the vision that had shown him his own abilities to the rush he got when others followed him. The brandy was as mellow as a summer day, and like summer, it warmed. Joseph took a deep breath, centering himself, feeling his *ki* like a fire that sent energy sparking down every nerve.

"I teach self-fulfillment, and freedom from fear of the conventions and conventional fears," he said carefully. "The Children of Light will inherit the Kingdom, and there is a spark in every man that can be nourished and grow—" Obviously Abaddon already had worldly power, but from what he had just said, he wanted something more. Controlling his breathing, Joseph fanned the inner flame in himself until he felt energy pulsing around him, then projected it toward the other man, seeking to link them within his field.

And then Abaddon lifted his head and looked at him.

Joseph jerked as the force he had projected shocked back upon him, but before he could recover he was transfixed by the flare of a power that overwhelmed his own as a lightbulb is made pale by the sun. Then it was gone.

Joseph blinked as vision returned to him. He saw Abaddon meditatively swirling the liquid in his glass, and for one moment wondered if he had imagined it. But perspiration was still beading on his brow. His breath caught as the other man's gaze came back to him and he felt the deliberately muted pressure of Abaddon's power.

He's the real thing . . . The thought came on a wave of mingled disbelief and fear. *It exists—it's real!*

"The powerful must rule the weak. It is their duty, and their destiny. Only thus can order be imposed upon the world. As I have said, you are a man of power—"Abaddon's voice was as smooth as the brandy. "Have you never dreamed of acting upon a broader sphere?"

Joseph's fingers tightened on the fragile glass, then he set it to his lips and gulped thirstily, welcoming the glow that helped distance his sense of the other man's presence. How could Abaddon speak to him as an equal—didn't he *know* what he had just done?

He cleared his throat. "What do you mean?"

"The wise act not on the objects but on the sources of power. The common people are ruled by their leaders—but who rules the rulers?"

Joseph strove for self-possession. "You do?" It was not quite a question. He tried to remember what he had heard about the secret workings of the great industrial complexes that dominated the world economy. At their first meeting, he had wondered if Abaddon's business might be something like the Mob. But he was no longer sure. Abaddon might well have international business interests at the highest levels, but that was not the kind of power he had demonstrated just now.

"Come now, why are you being so shy? We are in the same business, after all!" Abaddon smiled mockingly. "While the Elks and the Shriners play their games, have you not suspected that there are real ceremonial Orders at work behind the closed doors of power?''

Only an effort kept Joseph's mouth from opening in surprise. Of course he was familiar with the legend that secret societies were behind all the major events in history. He had always discounted them, but he wondered now.

Joanna rose from the couch in a single fluid movement and picked up the decanter. As she bent to refill his snifter, Joseph glimpsed the sweet curve of her breast and breathed in the subtle musk of the scent she wore. He tried to distract himself by thinking of Ava, but the girl seemed callow and disproportioned compared to this polished loveliness. Senses swimming, he settled back in his chair again.

"Are you saying that there is such an Order? Are you asking me to join you?" he said boldly.

"It exists—" said Luciano Abaddon. "But there are, naturally, certain requirements . . . Its name and nature can only be revealed to those who are accepted into it, and to be accepted, the aspirant must have a certain talent, and contribute something worthwhile."

"You say I have some ability, but you have also pointed out the deficiencies in the use I have made of it," said Joseph bitterly. "What do you suppose I can offer you?"

"Your abilities at the last meeting of the Order of Paradise appear to have been considerable—or was it more than your own abilities? I think the real story of what went on that night must be a step in the right direction, don't you?" Abaddon set down his glass and leaned forward. "It was a drug, wasn't it? No, don't flinch, I am not interested in legal technicalities. But if this is something new, it could be useful to us, and I think we could be useful to you . . ."

Joseph's mouth had gone dry. For a little while, lulled by the good food and the alcohol, he had actually forgotten why he was here. If he had the kind of lawyers these people could buy, his problems with the Berkeley Police Department would become technicalities, indeed. But the only coin he had to buy their help with was knowledge, and knowledge was power.

"Come now, Joseph, don't you think I could take the information from you if I desired?" Abaddon asked, very gently. "But I want *you* . . ." The black eyes held his.

Some inner voice, long stifled, whispered, *he wants your*

soul! But Joanna's scented fingers were massaging Joseph's neck, and he realized that without their help his knowledge would be no use to him.

Slowly he nodded. "It was a drug, a derivative of marijuana. I call it Paradise."

Joanna's laugh tinkled painfully. "A drug? That was the great secret you used to tempt me back to your Order?"

"A drug with my trance induction to focus its effects!" answered Joseph with returning pride. "The ritual use of psychedelics is one of the oldest traditions. You were more than stoned that night—you went where I sent you! If there was nothing more involved than getting high, then why did you invite me here?" He stifled the doubts the police interrogation had instilled in him. Using the drug had been an inspiration!

"That night we found out that Paradise induces a visionary state almost immediately," Joseph went on. "With the right dosage, and the right ceremonial preparation, I could give people whatever visions I willed!" He looked defiantly at Abaddon and saw in the other man's eyes a sudden glow.

"I was right, then!" said Abaddon. He rose from his chair and began to pace the carpets, soft-footed as some prowling jungle beast. Then he turned, and Joseph stopped himself from flinching as he felt the force of the man's personality again. "And this drug is yours? No—" Abaddon corrected himself. "You are not a chemist. But you know one, don't you! Give me his name!"

"No!" Joseph heard his own answer with a shock of surprise.

Abaddon stopped, considering him. "Now I wonder if that is some last vestige of honor, or simple self-interest? It does not matter. If you can get me an additional sample of the Paradise drug now you may keep your secret for a little while. If it proves as useful as it sounds, then I will want either the maker, or his name."

Joseph swallowed, returning Abaddon's gaze like a monkey to whom a cobra has just given a reprieve. "I can find the chemist," he said.

"Good. I assume he has good reason to keep silent. You will encourage him in that, and explain to him the desirability of selling me the formula . . ."

Abaddon leaned back against one of the cabinets, still watching him. Joseph nodded automatically.

"What about the rest of the group?" asked Joanna. "Some of them at least must suspect what happened to them. How are you going to keep them still?"

"I think the police have talked to most of them already," said Joseph. "But I took care to arrange things so that no one could be sure. I believe that most of them are loyal to me." Once more, he was beginning to recover his confidence.

"We will reinforce their loyalty—no, not by threatening violence, though if necessary, we have the means—" Abaddon responded to Joseph's look of alarm. "No, I think a ritual is called for—we will take advantage of the opportunity to show Master Joseph the kind of magic we do at the Elysian Lodge! The service of your disciples may be useful to us, but you must waste no more teaching on sheep! The hidden knowledge must be restricted to those who can use it best. Above all, we must take steps to prevent the common people from using occult powers."

"You are very sure of yourself!" A last defiance spoke through Joseph then. "You are very sure of *me!*"

Abaddon straightened where he stood and his dark gaze caught Joseph's and held it until those glowing eyes seemed to fill the world.

"Yes, I am sure of you, Joseph Roman," Abaddon said quietly. "I am your master, you know it now . . ."

That night Joseph Roman slept between sheets of the finest percale. But he slept badly, haunted by dreams in which he pursued a veiled woman who taunted and eluded him until, with a final effort, he seized her and swung her around. Only as he tore away the veil his captive roared with laughter, and he saw that it was not Joanna but Luciano Abaddon, and he whimpered in terror as Abaddon's feral strength forced him down.

Tom's strength maneuvered the battle-scarred black truck through the traffic on the Bay Bridge with a deceptive ease. Ruth felt Martin bouncing beside her on the broad seat and smiled. It was her weekend to take him, and trouble with the Honda's starter had nearly turned it into a disaster. She had been trying to explain to the boy that by the time they reached the Exploratorium by bus half the day would be gone, when Tom had volunteered to take them there. It was the first really clear day in weeks, but he said that the ground was still too wet for gardening. Ruth hoped that was true, but even if she had known he was only trying to salve her conscience, she would probably have been too grateful to refuse his offer.

"Look, you can see Angel Island!" Martin pointed across her.

"The truck lets us look over the railing. You can see everything—" Ruth answered him. "I didn't realize what I was missing by driving a little car!"

Tom, his eyes on the traffic ahead of him, gave her a peripheral grin. "Mehitabel is not the world's most comfortable ride, but she can go almost anywhere!"

Ruth braced herself against the dashboard as he changed lanes and laughed. But despite the rattle and sway of the truck, she felt more relaxed than she had in days. Certainly it helped to know what the drug was and where it had come from, but she thought that what she was learning about the inner world probably had more to do with it.

She blinked as they emerged from the tunnel through the naval base at Treasure Island and the silver cables of the suspension bridge looped up before her. Beyond it, San Francisco glittered in the sunlight like a celestial city. Dazzled, Ruth thought of the light of Kether, and felt that light flare through her and the tingling at the top of her head that meant her inner awareness had been activated. With double vision, she saw the steel and glass highrises of the town that columnists called "Bagdad by the Bay," and the enchanted towers of an eternal city.

For an endless moment she experienced the Idea of City, a harmonious interdependence of man and artifact existing as a separate organism. In Kabbalah, each sphere had its own magical image. If the Idea of San Francisco could be personified, what would it be? In her mind's eye she seemed to see a woman, past her first youth but still beautiful. The marks of experience around her painted eyes only added to her charm. It was a faintly exotic beauty, the breeding of many cultures tempered by a European education, contemporary as the latest designer fashion, ancient as a classic porcelain.

Then Martin giggled at something Tom had said to him, and Ruth fell back into ordinary consciousness with an almost physical jerk. They were going down Lombard now, almost to their destination. And yet the city still shone, as if she could see through its surface to some deeper reality. At that moment she thought that all the pain might be worth it for this expansion of perception, if only she could help Ariel.

Even to ordinary consciousness, the Palace of Fine Arts that housed the Exploratorium had the appearance of fantasy. It had been designed by Bernard Maybeck and built originally in papier mache for the 1915 Exposition, and the people of San Francisco had become so fond of the opulent Corinthian columns and capitals around the pool and the curved exhibition hall that they had raised money afterward to have them reconstituted in pink cement. Sunlight glittered on the water and glowed through the first white blossoms on the plum trees that edged it, and as they walked past, a single swan sailed majestically by.

Ruth put her hands over her ears as they entered the echoing cavern of the exhibition hall. Martin was off and running immediately, excitedly calling to them to come and see. He was normally a rather quiet boy, happy to amuse himself with books or gaming, but not here. For a moment, Ruth found the contrast of shadow and long rays of light slanting down from the eaves, and the rush and clatter of machines on the floor, overpowering. The Exploratorium was like an overgrown, professional, permanent science fair, offering hands-on experiments in infinite variety.

"Let's take things one at a time—" said Tom, and Ruth was not sure whether he was talking to Martin or to her. It was good advice, anyway.

They moved forward to an exhibit in which parabolic mirrors refracted light so that the car keys that appeared to be on top of the box were really inside. It was deceptive, as her visions had been. On the other hand, there really was a set of keys in the experiment, and there really had been a kernel of truth in her visions—identifying it was a matter of correct perception.

Martin pulled free and ducked under the plywood side of a triangular enclosure labeled The Kaleidoscope. She heard his muffled squeal of excitement; he called to her and with a sigh of resignation, she bent and straightened again inside. The walls of the triangle were lined with mirrors. From three sides Ruth saw herself reflected, and for a moment she was struck by surprise at how pretty her hair looked from the back and side. Then she realized that each mirror reflected not only her and Martin, but her images in each of the others, and each of those images was reflected in turn so that she saw the two of them repeated in endless sequence in multiples of three in all directions. Then Tom joined them, and now there were three of them, combined and recombining ad infinitum.

Were they all the same, or were these different selves, branching timelines of existence extending into uncounted dimensions? Dizzied, Ruth shut her eyes and held onto Tom's arm.

"Are you okay?" asked Tom as they emerged from the kaleidoscope.

"Yes—" Ruth took a deep breath. "Just a little over-whelmed by seeing so much of myself." And that was true on more levels than one. Ever since she had taken the Paradise drug, she had been forced to face her own inner realities.

"Did you see *me*, Mom?"

Ruth reached out to Martin and hugged him, for a moment acutely conscious of the energy contained in his firm child's body. "How could I miss you, love? You were all over the place!"

Martin giggled, then pulled at her arm to get her moving again. They paused briefly at the Low Frequency Light exhibit, which demonstrated how ultraviolet light could warm a spot on a heat-sensitive drum even when a filter blocked the visible spectrum; they passed the jet of air that kept a beach ball suspended, and turned back to it when Tom wanted to see what happened if you used your hand to deflect the air. It occurred to Ruth that producing visible effects by manipulating unseen forces this way was a magical metaphor, too.

As they continued onward, Ruth realized how many of the experiments were conducive to a metaphysical interpretation. She had not noticed that when she was here before, but obviously that kind of perception was conditioned by expectations, just as the assumption that all rooms were rectangular and all clocks round led the visitor to see the Distorted Room as normal when viewed from the outside.

After a while she found herself suffering from sensory overload. She sat down on the bench in front of the colored shadows where she could see the Enchanted Tree that lit up in sparkles of red, yellow and blue when the children clapped their hands. Tom took Martin up to see the holograms and light diffraction exhibit, but when they returned it turned out that both of them had spent most of their time trying to avoid crashing into the moon in the Lunar Lander video game.

"Mom, I landed it perfectly twice in a row!" Martin took her hand and she squeezed it.

"How did you do?" She looked up at Tom, who was grinning.

"Well, I did it right once. On the other hand, I didn't flame out completely as often as he did!" Tom strode along on her other side, hands thrust into the pockets of his corduroy jacket. They moved around the end of the hall past the rainbow whorls of the Sun Painting and back toward the entrance.

The big bell mounted against the wall clanged vigorously, a shockingly natural sound amidst all the buzzing, whistling and thumping of the experiments. Ruth was certain that she had once heard "pocketa-queep" coming from somewhere in the section on electricity, but she had never been able to identify the machine.

"I don't want to go home yet—I didn't get to ride the gyroscope chair, or do a gravity drawing, or—" Martin began.

"Next time you should head for those first." Ruth stopped him from continuing the catalogue. "It's almost five, and they're going to kick us out in a few minutes. Let's avoid the rush and go now!"

As they crossed the Bridge, Ruth let Tom and Martin recapitulate the day without her input. She had enjoyed herself as much as they had, but she had been very glad to leave. The combined assault on her physical and psychic senses had left her twitching. Even one of those experiments could have fueled a week's meditation. A whole hall full of them reminded her of the chaos of images she had encountered in her visions.

"Do you like spaghetti?" Ruth hung her jacket on the back of a chair and turned to Tom, who was still standing in the doorway.

"Sure—do you want some herbs for it?" He clattered back down the stairs and in a few minutes returned with several jars of fragrant home-dried leaves from last summer's garden—basil and oregano and thyme. Ruth drained the ground round and added it and the herbs to the base of sauce from the freezer that simmered on the stove, drained the spaghetti and set both on the table. She got Martin to turn off the TV and set places with less effort than she had expected, and soon they were all sitting down, Ruth and Tom at the head and foot of the table, and Martin in between.

Ruth saw Martin glance to either side as he picked up his milk glass. He drank deeply, and when he set it down again, a white moustache covered his upper lip, and he had a distinctly smug smile. *Just like a real family!* His thought was almost audible.

Ruth watched him with a mixture of exasperation and pain. Was it so lonely then, living with his father and Sissy and his step-sister? In the etiquette of divorce, that was a question one didn't ask. She listened to him talking to Tom about the experiments at the Exploratorium. Before Tom became a gardener he had worked in electronics, and he had enough technical background to explain some of the things Martin didn't understand. She supposed it was not fair to make Tom play tutor this way, but she also knew that she was going to take advantage of his willingness as long as she could.

When at last Martin went to bed, there was a moment of uncertainty, and then Tom picked up his jacket and moved toward the door.

"Thank you for coming with us today," said Ruth. She was aware of mingled relief and regret that he was leaving.

"I don't get to play very often. It was fun."

Seeing his tanned features crease into a smile, Ruth realized that he really had enjoyed it. His kindness to her son had not been a ploy to get her into bed, as had happened with men a few times before. Impulsively, she reached up and kissed him.

Something flickered in Tom's eyes. His hands came to her shoulders and for a moment he held her. Then he grinned and let her go.

When the door had closed behind him Ruth stood for a moment, listening to the sound as the refrigerator shifted gears, the suppressed giggle as Martin laughed at something in the comics he was reading in his room, the creak of wood as the house adjusted to the cooling air. She could read, or watch TV, but she knew that she really ought to do just a little more on the game.

David had given her a picture of Hildebrand Hall. Hardly aware that she was smiling, she replaced the ribbon in the printer with the cartridge, switched over to the scanner application, and fed the photograph through. When she had finished adjusting the contrast and intensity, she transferred the image into graphics and began to play with it. No longer would it look like a campus building—by the time she was done it would be the laboratory of an alchemist with mysterious corridors and pulsing sources of power. And it seemed to her as she worked that what she was doing was in its way as true a portrait of the place as the original photo had been.

It was nearly midnight by the time Ruth had reworked the image to her satisfaction. Martin was long asleep by now, and the house was still. She had done enough on the game, but an inner tension still kept her from her bed.

She turned off the computer, and then the lights in the loft. Then she went to the bracket on which she had set up a simple altar and lit the candle there. She sat down on a straightbacked chair facing the flame and, taking deep, regular breaths, felt the flutter in her solar plexus as she finally allowed the attraction she had been resisting all day to draw her awareness inward. And then, with the same careful fascination with which she had approached the exhibits at the Exploratorium, she continued her experimental journey into the worlds within.

8.

*It is a tree that grows on the tops of the
mountains, a young man born in Egypt, a
prince from Andalusia, who desires the
torments of the seekers ... I can see no
weapon against him save resignation, no
charger but knowledge, no buckler but
understanding.*

Book of Ostanes (Arabic)

For the rest of the week the weather held clear, and the fruit
trees with which some inspired city planner had edged
streets all over Berkeley burst into glorious bloom. Plums
blossomed in white radiance, attended by pink retinues of
flowering cherry, and an occasional quince tree added its
blush to the bridal splendor. As Ruth turned the corner onto
Benvenue, the beauty of the trees made it hard to concentrate
on her driving; but in the five years that Ariel had lived there,
Ruth's muscles had memorized the way.

Ariel's wedding had been in the springtime. The trees were
transformed by memory into bridesmaids in a rainbow of
pastels; lovely, but for once in no danger of outshining the
bride. Ruth had never yet found just the right words for
the way Ariel had looked that day, but she did not think
that anyone who had been to that wedding would ever
forget her. The papers had covered it lavishly—she still
had the clippings—but neither the glossy official portraits
nor the yellowing news photos had succeeded in capturing

a beauty that made plum blossoms look gross and snowflakes stiff.

On that day, Alexandra Ashton had transcended mortality, and it occurred to Ruth now that Ariel had been trying to recapture that moment of perfect beauty ever since.

Ruth pulled up in front of her friend's apartment, turned the key, and then sat, nerving herself to go in. Dr. Henry had called her that morning to say that they were moving Ariel to a nursing home, and Ariel wanted her to go by the apartment and get some things she would need.

A nursing home would be better than Napa, anyway, Ruth told herself as she climbed the stairs. Ariel's brother was willing to help pay for it, and it gave her a reprieve.

The air in the apartment had that flat smell of a place that had been shut up for some time, mingled with a memory of Ariel's lilac perfume. But the place was still in the same exquisite order in which Ariel had left it. Ruth yanked on the cord, and the off-white, open-weave curtains parted, letting a flood of light into the room.

Cream-colored carpeting reflected it upward, glowing on the white-painted woodwork and the pearly lavender of the walls. The couches were upholstered in pale shantung, with throw pillows covered in delicate shades of lilac and peach, aquamarine and rose and pale gold. Being in this room was like standing in the middle of a white opal, and it had always made Ruth, who tended to favor earth colors when she thought about decorating at all, feel clumsy and dull.

Only one note of color jarred. Someone had dropped a deeper blue throw rug from the bathroom on the floor. Ruth bent to pick it up and stopped, staring, with the rug still dangling from her hand. Where the throw rug had lain the whiteness of the carpet was marred by a spattering of brown stains. Reddish brown . . . bloodstains . . . Ariel's.

Ruth dropped the rug and stood back, biting her lip painfully. She had almost forgotten what had put Ariel in the hospital. In this temple of purity the bloodstains were a desecration, just as the gaunt creature she had just visited at Herrick was a travesty of the exquisite woman she had known for so long.

For a moment she stood still, on the edge of understanding. Then her watch beeped the hour, she recovered herself, and went on into the lacy perfection of the bedroom.

Feeling like an intruder, she opened drawers and packed clothing and cosmetics into a tapestry suitcase. Now what she needed to find was a photo of Ariel. Del had told her that a picture could provide a useful focus for visualization by those who were not familiar with the person needing healing, and a physical object which the patient had used could help establish a connection.

It sounded like superstition, but she knew that psychometrists used articles belonging to missing persons to make clairvoyant contact with them, so maybe there was something in it. Some of the procedures required for working with computers seemed ritualistic, too, until you understood the principles involved. In any case, now was no time to start getting skeptical.

Ruth vaguely remembered having seen a photo album in the apartment. Ariel had put the wedding pictures into a book, and she seemed to remember others, with pictures of Ariel at proms and parties. Leaving the suitcase open on the bed, she pulled open the door of the walk-in closet that occupied one side of the room.

She remembered that Ariel's wardrobe had been large enough to cause severe stress to the storage capacity of their little room at Mills, and only the fact that she herself had owned so little made it possible for Ariel to manage. This closet had the same exquisite orderliness that Ruth remembered, but it still held an awful lot of clothes. There were also drawers and neatly labeled boxes, however, and in one of them she found what she was looking for.

Like everything else, the photo albums were in order, stacked from childhood on—with a book for every two or three years through college, a big volume for the wedding and another for the first years after, and then only one, still half-empty, for all the years since then. Feeling uncomfortably as if she were going through the effects of someone who had died, Ruth spread them out on the rug.

The more recent pictures reminded her of fashion photos, as if they had been taken of the clothes, not of Ariel. She put the top two books aside with the wedding album and began to leaf through the earlier ones, looking for something that she could use as a link to the real Ariel—or at least the Ariel that she thought she knew. Maybe one of the college pictures . . .

But even at Mills, Ariel had already known how to show

the camera the face she wanted it to see. Somewhere, thought Ruth, there must be a picture of the face she had glimpsed during those days after the rape when she would not leave her room. The images flipped past as she turned the pages— backward through the years until they included Ariel's pudgy, preoccupied father and complacently fashionable step-mother, too. But in all of them, Ariel wore her beauty like a mask.

It was not until she came to the beginning of the oldest album that Ruth found what she was looking for. The picture showed a woman dressed in the height of fifties New Look fashion, holding a fair-haired child. The baby had the un-marked prettiness of any well-fed, well-cared-for child, but despite the elegant clothes, the face of the woman was full of a luminous concentration that outshone the superficial beauty of her features.

Ruth's throat ached as she realized that she was looking at a picture of Ariel with her real mother, who had died or disappeared—she had never dared to ask which—when Ariel was not quite three years old.

Ruth stood in the foyer of the nursing home, nostrils flaring at the sweet, decaying smell of old age and disinfectant, ears twitching at the squeak of wheeled trays and the unfocused babbling of those to whom no one would listen anymore. But the place was clean, its decor reasonably harmonious, and the staff looked friendly. Why was she more horrified by the idea that Ariel was staying here than she had been by the hospital?

While she waited for someone to show her the way to Ariel's room, Ruth thought about it. The hospital had been depressing, but at least its atmosphere of urgency implied that one way or another, the problems of the patients there would soon be solved. The nursing home was a limbo where hope was eroded into endurance or an apathetic despair. *There should be a sign over the door,* she thought as the nurse led the way down the corridor—*Abandon hope all ye who enter here.*

Ariel's room had a window that looked out into a little garden. The walls were painted a delicate pink, and in addi-tion to the hospital bed there was an imitation-walnut table and two chairs. Ariel was in the bed—Ruth hoped it was because all she had was nightgowns—but the two novels on the bed table were still stacked with undisturbed precision.

"I've brought you some shirts and pants and a couple of caftans—" Ruth knew she was babbling, but at least she had gotten Ariel to respond with a murmured reply. She finished hanging the clothes in the tiny closet, then pulled out a framed watercolor that was one of the lesser pieces Ariel owned, but still superior to the reproduction on the wall of the room, which it replaced. A linen cloth covered the plastic table, and in a porcelain vase she put a spray of plum blossom she had picked outside the apartment.

When she had finished, the room, though still far from imitating the elegance of Ariel's usual surroundings, had acquired a hint of personality.

"Thank you," said Ariel. "It is prettier now. I don't know why you've done all this for me . . ."

Ruth sat down in the chair by the window, suppressing a sigh. Ariel looked better than she had in the hospital. She was not quite so thin, and her hair had been shampooed and brushed out. But violet smudges like old bruises were still there beneath Ariel's eyes, and in the eyes themselves Ruth saw the lingering fear.

"I do it because I love you—" suddenly the words that had frightened Ruth came easily. Even if her motivation had been sexual, it would not have been possible to think that way about the woman Ariel was now. Perhaps that was what gave her the freedom to say it. Ruth was aware of an appalled recognition that for the first time in their relationship, Ariel's beauty was not a barrier. She could admit her love because for the first time she felt able to offer it as an equal.

"I don't deserve it." Ariel's eyes filled with tears and she looked away. "The person you thought you knew was an illusion. I'm ugly inside."

"Not to me," Ruth said earnestly. "You may not be what you thought you were, but who is? It doesn't matter, as long as the light is there and we can see it." She stopped, frustrated by the difficulty of saying what she meant without echoing Joseph Roman's hypocrisies.

Ariel looked at her with a wistful smile. "I never expected that *you* would be preaching metaphysics to *me*! If you can believe it, I'm glad, but I can't, not anymore." The smile faded. "When I look inward all I see is darkness."

Ruth stared at her helplessly, even now aware of radiance

like a distant music, and knowing that if she shifted her attention she would be there.

"There's a woman who runs a metaphysical bookstore here in town—Eden Books—do you know it?"

"I've been there," answered Ariel without interest.

"She's helped me a lot—can I bring her here to see you?"

"No!" Ariel shook her head with sudden vigor. "I don't want to see any more magicians! That's what did this to me!"

"Okay, but can we at least try to do a healing circle for you?"

Ariel laughed bitterly. "Why are you asking me? No one else has asked me what I wanted since this mess began!" She gestured around her.

"I know," said Ruth quietly, knowing also that it was not only the tyranny of the medical establishment but Ariel's own lack of will that was keeping her here. "That's why I'm asking now. Del wouldn't do it without your permission, and without your willingness it couldn't work anyway."

"Even if I don't believe anyone can help?" Ariel asked, shaking her head.

"You cared for me when I didn't think I was even worth wiping anyone's feet on." Ruth got to her feet. "I'm going to love you now, whether you deserve it or not! Will you at least let me try to help you?" She went to the bed and kissed Ariel on the brow.

The other woman stilled, and after a moment she managed a watery smile. "You always were stubborn," she whispered. "If it makes you feel better, I suppose I owe you the right to try . . ."

It was not exactly enthusiastic cooperation, but it was permission, and probably as much as could be expected just now. Ruth gave Ariel's hand a squeeze and, through the tears that blurred her own eyes, found her way to the door.

"Ruth's friend Ariel is wandering in the Abyss. Our purpose tonight is to contact her spirit and to invoke the forces that will protect and balance her sufficiently to accept healing. Is this in accordance with the will of all of you?" Del's voice seemed to deepen, and Ruth felt a tremor ripple down her spine. The renovated storeroom behind the bookstore in which they were sitting had the classic simplicity of a tea room, but already she felt an intensification of atmosphere, as if the barometer were dropping before a storm.

Murmuring their assent, the others settled into position, and Ruth felt a renewed wonder that they should all be here—a wonder that was not unmixed with anxiety. She trusted Del, but she could not help remembering the last time she had participated in a ceremony.

Ruth cast a quick look to her right, seeking reassurance from Tom's solid strength. After a few minutes of discussion about his work, Del had asked him to take the northern position and represent the element of Earth in the ritual. He had at first resisted putting on the green and brown robe that Del had given him, but it seemed to Ruth that it emphasized his personality. Ruth smoothed the silky sky blue of her own robe. She was sitting in the east, for Air—she supposed because her work with computers was mental and involved communication. David Mason, who wore the swirly blue-green Water robe, was watching with a kind of professional interest.

But the two who interested her most were the friends upon whom Del had called to complete their circle—Karen Holst, the magnificent blonde woman she had met the first time she had visited the bookstore, and her husband Michael, who had longish dark hair and a beard, and moved with the stealthy grace of one of the larger carnivores. He wore a patch over one eye.

Del had asked Karen, who was wearing a garment printed with green leaves and flames, to invoke the element of Fire. Del herself, in a robe of warm gold, sat by the central altar on which she had placed the picture of Ariel, surrounded by votive lights for each element and a tall, central candle of gold.

Michael was the only one of them who was not robed. He had no need of one to proclaim his function, for enameled pins of motorcycles adorned his leather jacket like medals, and as he sat on guard before the doorway, across his knees rested a short sword in a worn, wooden sheath.

"I am going to ask Michael to cast the circle, and then each one of you will invoke the appropriate Archangel and the protection of the element you serve, using your own words to affirm its qualities," Del went on. The golden ankh upon her breast gleamed as she shifted on the tatami mats that covered the floor, to make sure each one understood. "When we have done that, I will lead you into a light trance, in which we will envision our passage up the Paths to the Abyss, where I will seek to make contact with Ariel's spirit, and bring it back to the sphere of Tiphareth. This is not unlike the journey a traditional shaman makes to recover a separated soul, only our procedure is more controlled.

"As I do this, it is essential that each of you express the power of your element, holding it in balance with the others. Only thus can I make this journey in safety. But when I begin invoking the golden light of healing around Ariel, send me your strength, and I will go out upon the planes to carry it to her. Meanwhile, Michael will maintain the circle of protection, which prevents other influences from disturbing us here.

"When I go into deep trance, I will lie down. I will appear to be unconscious; I may mutter or moan, or there may possibly be some other phenomena. You must not touch me or attempt to rouse me—be patient and wait until I return. I know what I am doing. Your task is to maintain the visualization of your protecting Archangel, and keep the circle intact."

Del's voice was even, conversational, without any of the drama that had characterized Joseph Roman's delivery. But Ruth felt herself settling, steadying. Abruptly she realized that the ritual had already begun.

"Doorkeeper, I call you to watch and to ward us. Do your office now." Del nodded to Michael, who got to his feet in the same fluid motion with which he unsheathed his sword. Ruth drew in her breath as light flared from the wicked, wave-edged blade. It was a kris—she had heard of the Malayan weapons, but never seen one before. Then she forgot all speculation as he swept it up to guard and began his clockwise stalk around the room.

"With flaming sword this sphere I ward—" Michael's voice was deep, powerful, and the air tingled where he passed.

"From all harm, guard!"

Joseph Roman pushed back the heavy, crimson silk sleeves of his robe. It was just a little too big for him, but he welcomed the deep hood that shadowed his features, for he was not entirely certain of his self-control. They were all dressed alike, even Joanna, but the power that emanated from Luciano Abaddon would have identified him in pitch darkness, and Joseph was at the same time attracted and afraid.

He acknowledged that the setting was partially responsible for both feelings. This was the sort of temple he had always dreamed of building, even though it was only a room in a private house—but what a house! The room was not large, but it had marble columns and the signs of the zodiac painted upon the plastered walls. A circle and triangle were inlaid in pale stone into the polished black granite of the floor. Abaddon stood in the center with his hands upon an altar of black stone.

Joseph had seen a pile of red robes in the chest from which they had taken his, and wondered where the major rites of Abaddon's Order were held. The flickering candles multiplied the shadows of the five participants as if the spirits of the other members had come to observe them.

He suspected that Joanna's chauffeur was the man next to him now, and, even robed, the other two had a massive presence that suggested Abaddon's bodyguards. Joseph had thought they were simply hired muscle, but clearly they were something more as well!

"*Hekas, hekas, este bibeloi!* Be ye far from us, O ye profane!" Abaddon's voice reverberated from stone. "Run far and hide your faces, ye of lesser race and spirit, lest in seeing, you should be blasted, and in hearing, deafened by the manifestation of Power. All ye who have not taken the oath and made the sacrifice, flee far from this citadel, for it is death to the uninitiate to view the Mysteries."

Abaddon's words cracked and rolled like the crashing of thunder, and Joseph was still trying to comprehend them when someone pulled his hood down over his eyes and his arms were gripped suddenly from behind.

"Here is one who is uninitiate and profane—" growled a deep voice close behind his ear. "What shall we do with him?"

"Bring him to me—"

Joseph's pulse was pounding so furiously he could hardly hear. There was nothing to be afraid of—they knew him, he had come willingly—the shrill voice of reason gibbered against terrors that came leaping up from the dark. But it did not matter if he had understood the command. The same strong arms that imprisoned him frog-marched him forward.

"Mortal, do you know that it is death to stand where you stand now? Even to look upon our place of working is forbidden to those who are not sworn to the Order of Omega." Now Abaddon's voice seemed apallingly close, a hideously intimate speech of soul to soul.

No matter that he had been invited—no matter that he had not known—Joseph strained to control bowels loosened by fear.

"Are you of the true race, Joseph Roman? Are you strong in spirit to pursue the Path? Will you give worship to the One who is to come, and obedience to the Order in whose power you stand?" The pressure eased enough for Joseph to collect his wits again, and he recognized in those words an echo of something he had once used on his own group. He thought then that he had spoken truer than he knew, or perhaps he was simply in the hands of someone whose skills surpassed his as his had surpassed those of the poor stumbling souls who came to him.

But it did not matter which was the truth—Joseph was nodding already, struggling to make his voice carry the words—"I am, I will, I am!"

"So be it then. Prepare yourself now."

Joseph stood still, fighting to control his breathing. Delicately he extended his other senses, recognized the squeak of the chains and the whirl of displaced air as the great censer swung and clouds of incense began to swirl in choking concentration. Under his eyelids he was aware of an irregular flicker, and knew that candles had been lit in the room.

"Hear Me—*Ar Th'laf, Reheibet, Atheleberset*." Joseph jerked as the words of invocation were spoken, alternating murmured lines of text with the heavily intoned Names— "*A Belatha, Abeu, Ebeu, Phithetasoe, ib Th'laf!* Thou Shining Force of Breath! Thou that flowest, Thou that goest! Thou Saviour, save!" He recognized the invocation but could not place it—only that it was something by Crowley. Incense bellied around him and for a moment it was impossible to breathe.

"I invoke Thee, the Terrible and Invisible God who dwellest in the Void Place of the Spirit—*Arogogoruabrao!* Thou spiritual Sun! Satan, Thou Eye, Thou Lust!, Cry aloud!, Whirl the Wheel, O my Father, O Satan, O Sun!" Twitching at the Name even as he understood the function of its shock value,

Joseph felt a blast of heat and knew that the Guardians of the southern quarter were there.

"Hear Me—*Ruabra laf, Meriodom, Babalon Bal Bin Abaft*. Thou Woman of Whoredom! Lady of the Understanding of the Ways! *Aeoou Ischure*, Our Lady of the Western Gate of Heaven, Mighty art Thou!" This was a woman's voice, Joanna's, mellow and slightly mocking. A moist breath of air kissed his skin under the robe, and Joseph felt his flesh respond to the menace and the promise in those words.

"I invoke Thee, *Ma Barraio loel Kotha, Athore Balo, Abraft!* Thou Goddess of Beauty and Love, whom Satan, beholding, desireth! The Fathers, male-female, desire Thee!" A male voice picked up the refrain, grounding them, echoed almost immediately by all of the voices in chorus—

"Hear Me, and make all Spirits subject to Me, so that every Spirit of the Firmament, and of the Ether, upon the Earth and under the Earth, on dry land and in the Water, of Whirling Air and of rushing Fire, and every spell and scourge of God may be obedient unto Me!"

Joseph staggered as if the floor had shifted beneath him, or as if he had been buffeted by a blast of air. Then something snapped into place as if a great door had been slammed shut, and he felt the long fade of vibration to equilibrium.

The silence that followed was just long enough for Joseph to realize that there had been no physical basis for any of those perceptions, then Abaddon's voice rang out, and self-awareness was lost once more.

"My Lord, come forth to Me! My secret self beyond self, Hadith, All Father, thou Sun, Thou Life of Man, thou Five-fold Sword of Flame! Thou Goat exalted upon Earth in Lust, thou Snake extended upon Earth in Life! Spirit most Holy! Seed most Wise! Innocent Babe, inviolate Maid! Begetter of Being! Soul of all Souls! Word of all Worlds . . ."

This was all Crowley's, and Joseph felt some of his confidence returning, for he had taken the degree of *Philosophus* in an off-shoot of Crowley's Lodge many years ago. And this also was the secret deity whom Joseph himself had seen in vision once, and ever after worshipped.

"Come forth, oh Hidden One, oh Perfect One, Thou Lord of the Universe, next step in Creation, fulfillment of the past and promise of the future, oh Thou new man who dost transcend all earthly Law! Come down to this Citadel of the

West, where the servants of Thy Order await Thee—'' The deep voice rolled forth again, filling the heart with an almost unbearable weight of expectation. And these words were not Crowley's, though they stirred some deep response in Joseph's being, so that he shouted with the others,

''Come, Lord, come!''

''We are Thy toys, Thy creatures, Lord, we are Thy slaves to do Thy will! Bring forth Thy Day of Might! oh Great One, bring forth Thy Night of Power!''

The voice of the first of the invokers answered him—

''And I heard one of the four living creatures say, as with a voice of thunder, 'Come!' And behold, a white horse, and its rider had a bow; and a crown was given to him, and he went out conquering and to conquer.''

''When he opened the second seal, I heard the second living creature say, 'Come!' and out came another horse, bright red; its rider was permitted to take peace from the earth, and he was given a great sword.'' Thus spake the voice that had invoked the power of fire, and images of flame and darkness flowered in Joseph's vision at his words.

Then Joanna's husky voice took up the tale. ''When he opened the third seal, I heard the third living creature say, 'Come!' And behold a black horse, and its rider had a balance in his hand!''

''When he opened the fourth seal, I heard the voice of the fourth living creature say, 'Come!' and I saw, and behold, a pale horse, and its rider's name was Death, and Hades followed him; and they were given power over a fourth of the earth, to kill with sword and with famine and with pestilence and by wild beasts of the earth!'' The words of the invoker faded and Joseph waited with a painful intensity for the reply—

''Then the Dragon that was cast forth will arise and make ready the Kingdom, and the Son of Light will be restored to His throne. Those who have served Him will be rewarded, but those who opposed Him will serve them, for the power of the Adversary will avail for nothing in that day.'' Abaddon had taken up his part of the apocalyptic litany. His voice rang like a great bell, and like a lesser, Joseph felt his spirit resonate. Powerless, his power was still sufficient to perceive the energies that Luciano Abaddon had summoned here.

''But those who will conquer on that day must be sealed

to His service. Here is one unpurified and unconsecrate—speak, slave, and say what you seek within this citadel!''

Half-tranced by the invocations, it was not until the hard hands of his captor jerked him upright that Joseph realized that Abaddon meant *him!* Rusty as if he had not spoken for centuries, his voice came back to him with words half-remembered from another initiation.

''My soul wanders in darkness and seeks the hidden Light. I believe that in the Order of Omega knowledge of that Light may be obtained.''

In the red darkness behind his hood it seemed to Joseph that someone chuckled. ''Are you ready to take Oath to us?'' the voice went on.

''I am ready—'' Immediately his hands were freed and he was thrust to his knees. But before Joseph could react, his wrist was gripped and guided past a rustle of cloth to something warm and throbbing which a moment's shocked awareness identified as a man's phallus, already erect and pulsing with power.

''Place your right hand upon this holy symbol and take your left hand in mine. Bow your head, repeat your full name by which you are known on earth, and say after me:

''I, Joseph Henry Roman, in the presence of the officers of this Order and the Lord of Light, do solemnly promise to keep secret the Order of Omega, its name and its members, its purposes and its proceedings, and to obey its commands . . .''
Phrase by damning phrase, Joseph repeated the words Abaddon gave to him. His fingers quivered at the touch of the thing on which they had made him put his hand, afraid to flinch from it, even more afraid to grip the heat of that pole of power.

''If I fail in this, my Magical Obligation, may I be judged by the Divine Guardians of this Order, who journey upon the Winds, who strike where no man strikes, who slay where no man slays. And as I bow my neck under the Sword of the Conqueror, so do I commit myself into their hands for vengeance or reward.'' He jerked as something cold and sharp was laid against his throat, and in a whisper finished,

''So help me my Mighty and Secret Soul, and the Great God who reigns within!''

Abaddon stepped away, but the hand that had touched his phallus was still held stretched outward. In the same moment,

Joseph felt the blade leave his throat and a swift stinging in his arm, followed by a dull warmth there. Then the hood was dragged back from his eyes.

The first moment of disoriented vision showed him redness—red silk robes, red candlelight, and red dripping in a steady stream into a silver bowl from a deep gash in his arm. Joseph's nostrils flared at the sudden metallic tang. Abaddon reached down, dipped his finger into the dark liquid and marked Joseph's brow.

"Thus are you purified! Thus are you consecrate! By your own blood you are bound!"

Joseph's muscles bunched to pull away—he had given them his oath and his blood, it must be done now! But the muscle men held his arms, and the brilliant gaze of Luciano Abaddon held his soul.

"There is power in the blood," said Abaddon softly. "It must not be wasted! We had a purpose there tonight—don't you remember?"

Blinking, Joseph stared back at him. They had planned to put some binding upon those who knew about the Paradise drug.

"Yes, now you are remembering, but your spirit has knowledge beyond the senses, and your spirit will seek them on the inner planes. Of course we will bring you back—" Abaddon laughed at Joseph's struggles. "What do you take us for? But go you must, whether you will or no!"

In a rustle of silk, Joanna moved closer. She licked her lips, watching his blood flow; Joseph could not tell if fascination or design had brought her there.

"There are other ways of raising power." She touched her robe and the front fell open, revealing a body perfectly tanned and tended, nipples already pertly pointed even before she touched them. "I will show you some of them, one day." Her silky pubic bush was just at eye level; he smelled her musky female odor and his pulse speeded, and as his body was stimulated his blood flowed faster into the bowl.

Joseph tried to see her face, but her features swam in and out of focus. He looked in appeal to Abaddon, who smiled and leaned over him, almost whispering in his ear.

"Thus saith the voice of your secret soul—'Let me enter the Path of Darkness . . . I am the only Being in an Abyss of

Darkness; from an Abyss of Darkness came I forth ere my birth, from the Silence of a Primal Sleep . . ."

Sleep—came the undertones, whispering to his spirit, *sleep, and let your spirit go free!* He swayed, and now only the strength of the guards kept him kneeling there.

"In the name of Lilith, Queen of Demons, I conjure you, be you separated from your body; in the name of Samael, the Liar; and Gamalael, the Obscene; may your essence be sundered by Gharab Tzerek, the Ravens of Dispersion; by the Disputer, by the Burner, by the Breaker in Pieces, by the Concealer and the Hinderer may you be detached to roam the spheres; may body and spirit be sundered by him who splits the Throne of God!"

As the titles of the Tree's dark Angels rolled from the lips of Abaddon, Joseph felt the darkness rushing up around him. Over the basin of blood a mist was forming, within which distorted shapes swirled. He was cold, and his head was spinning; he felt the names of the Qlippoth plucking at his soul. And after a time even Abaddon's eyes disappeared in the chaos. He could no longer feel his body. Gibbering, the demons fell upon him, and Joseph let them carry him, unresisting, away.

9.

*The Neverland had always begun to look
a little dark and threatening by bedtime.
Then unexplored patches arose from it and
spread, black shadows moved about in
them, the roar of the beasts of prey was
quite different now, and above all, you
lost the certainty that you would win.*

J.M. Barrie, *Peter and Wendy*

Joseph floated aimlessly in the Void.

He did not feel bodiless, but the body he had there obeyed different rules than the one he had left behind. A thought could move him where he willed, and there was no visible connection with the material world. For a time he was preoccupied by the new sensations. He had attained this state briefly a few times on drugs, but fear had always snapped him back into his body before. Even the Paradise drug had not brought him here, for he had only eaten a small portion of the apple, and he had been in control of the meditation then.

Now he felt an irritating pressure that would not let him be still. He began to move away from it, and his surroundings grew more distinct. He was walking down a street somewhere in Berkeley, though he could not quite remember its name. A low fog had come in, and everything was a little indistinct around the edges; the farther houses growing more substantial as he approached them, while those he had passed gradually faded away. Perhaps because it was so dim, everything seemed leached of color. Only overhead did the mist appear to thin, and against the dim blue distances he glimpsed a bright line, as if a power wire were reflecting the light of the invisible sun.

There seemed to be very few people about. Sometimes he thought he saw a curtain move, but when he looked around there was no one there. One block led to another; tree-shaded streets of two-story, brown-shingled houses giving way to neat rows of stucco cottages with tiny gardens. Presently he came to a main street that reminded him of Telegraph Avenue, for in the distance he could see the beacon of the Campanile and a shadow behind it that must be the hills. There was a bus stop on the next corner. He thought he would sit for a while, but as he approached it he realized there was already someone there.

He sat down. The other turned, and Joseph jerked back. His father favored him with a sour grin.

"What are you doing here?"

His father stared at him for a moment without answering the question. "You still think a lot of yourself, I see," said the old man, eyeing the silk suit Joseph was wearing. He sniffed. "Some woman give you that, or did you come by it honestly?"

Joseph felt a hard knot growing in his belly. It had been years, but he recognized the reaction that talking to his father had always produced in him.

"After all I did for you—working myself into the grave so that you could go to school like a gentleman—you're still no better than a gigolo."

Joseph stiffened. "I'm a spiritual teacher! People pay good money—"

"You're a fraud! And a liar—always were! They'll find you out, and then where will you be?" The old man's head made a swift, vulturine turn. Joseph's gaze was held by glittering eyes.

He felt the world spin and clutched at the bench. Shadows thickened at the edges of vision; he saw his first wife, her features contorted in hatred, and other women whom he had had to leave when they started making impossible demands. He saw the policemen who had questioned him, the professors who had failed him, the apprentice who had taken the rap for him when he was accused of fraud, and hanged himself in jail. Beyond them surged faceless crowds whose murmur swelled—

Liar! Fraud! Murderer—you never had any powers! His silk suit began to unravel around him and a cold wind carried the threads away.

Joseph cringed and tried to cover his nakedness. "No, no!" he shouted. "I had to protect myself! I had to stay free to follow the Path my vision showed me!"

It was all in your imagination! the voices cried.

Joseph strained to recall the glory he had seen, that flowering of inner splendor that had inspired him, but the vision was fading like fairy gold. But without that, he was nothing—he couldn't be nothing! Had he deceived himself, or had he been deceived? For a moment, Joseph teetered on the edge of understanding the choices that had brought him here. Then, like a man drowning, he grasped at certainty. He remembered Luciano Abaddon.

"I have powerful friends!"

Abruptly, he felt the presence of Abaddon near him. His father and the spirits who had taunted him disappeared. Joseph took a deep, shuddering breath.

"My father's dead. Some of those others I saw are dead, too. Is this Hell? Has my body bled to death back there?" The thought of being condemned to this place forever terrified him.

From the Presence behind him he felt dark laughter. *"What do you think? This is the country of souls."*

"Can you get me back to my body?" asked Joseph desperately.

"I will. I have a use for you there. But first you have a job to do."

Abruptly, Joseph remembered what their purpose had been. He looked down at his nakedness. What he wanted to do was flee to his own house and visit Ava or Laurel in their dreams. Would they think they had had intercourse with an incubus? He was not likely to find out, however, for he was convinced that getting back to his body depended on the will of Luciano Abaddon.

"Give me my clothes back, then. I'm not going to face even a spirit like this!"

"That depends on the strength of your will—" came the

thought of Abaddon. *"Use your imagination. How do you wish to appear?"*

Shaken as he was, Joseph found it hard to concentrate on anything at all, but after a few moments he brought this training in visualization to bear and achieved the illusion of a garment not unlike the crimson robe he had been wearing before. Moving with more purpose now, he impelled himself toward the house in the hills where he had held the last meeting of the Order of Paradise.

He found George Makarios in his den, thinning hair awry and spreading paunch belted by the cord of his plush robe. He was trying to put together a jigsaw puzzle. The scene seemed to be of greenery, perhaps of a garden, but as he tried to fit a piece in place, the shapes and colors shifted unnervingly. With a whimper, the man threw it down and began to search through the pile again. Joseph realized with relief that George was still alive, and this was his dream, or maybe his nightmare. He drifted forward and lifted one hand commandingly.

"George, listen to me. I have come to help you!"

The man turned, scattering jigsaw fragments across the carpet. As he recognized Joseph, his face worked painfully. "Master Joseph! Master Joseph, I don't understand!"

"You don't have to understand, my son—only to follow me," said Joseph soothingly. Watching the man's face change, he felt power filling him once more.

"What . . . what do you want me to do?"

"Come with me and wait until I call the others here—" Joseph moved through the house to the front door and opened his arms.

"Members of the Order of Paradise, I summon you in the name of the Lord of Man who is to come! Waking or sleeping I speak to your spirits. Ye who would achieve true power, ye who have entrusted your souls to me, I call you to come to me here!" One by one he began to speak their names.

And as Abaddon had commanded the subjection of all spirits in the beginning of his ritual, one by one the souls that resonated to Joseph Roman's call began to come. Very soon perhaps half a dozen men and women stood before him—it was hard to tell, for their forms dimmed and solidified again as their focus varied.

"Members of the Order, hear me. As you have answered my call tonight, I command your obedience. Keep silence

regarding me and our Order to the police and to anyone who
may ask. Wait for my call and do whatever I require of you.
All will be well if you keep faith with me!'' Joseph let
certainty ring through his voice and felt the subtle glow of
approval that told him that Abaddon was with him still.

His students were still waiting. He realized that, like ele-
mentals, once summoned they must be formally dismissed
again. Again he lifted his hands, but when he had finished,
one form remained in the yard. He could tell it was a woman,
but she was veiled.

"Why are you still here?" he asked sharply.

"I am afraid—" Her voice was faint; he could see her
trembling. He motioned her closer.

"Why are you wearing a veil?"

"I am ugly. No one must see me . . ." As she answered,
she half turned, as if she feared he could see her even through
the fine cloth. Joseph took a quick step forward and pulled it
off. She put up her hands with a cry, but he held them,
looking at her.

Her features were less ugly than unformed, a half-finished
sketch of a face by a clumsy artist. Her body looked all right
under the clothes, but the clothes themselves kept changing—
always exquisite, in the height of fashion, but always new. It
was by the clothes, finally, that he recognized her.

"You are Ariel Ashton, aren't you?" he said in wonder,
realizing that just as imagination had clad him in the red robe,
this was the way she saw herself, here.

"Yes," she whispered. She glanced behind her as if she
feared someone would hear.

"It's all right, there's nothing to fear—" Joseph patted her
with a practiced hand. She gave a half-sob and clung to him,
quivering.

"But there is, there is—don't you see?" She looked fear-
fully around her. And as Ariel pressed against him, Joseph
did begin to see. Instead of blades of grass, the lawn sprouted
questing tentacles, and the trees reached down with bony
fingers. The house was watching with inimical blank eyes,
and every shadow stirred with sinister intention. Joseph shuddered in sympathy, then realized that he must control his
imagination or he would find himself in the same state as she.

"Look, it's only grass—green grass, needs cutting a little;
there's a bleached patch where a dog got into the yard, but

it's only grass . . ." Frowning, he forced himself to see it, gripping her arm until it must have hurt her. He revisioned the trees, and the house, and the street until he saw them as he had before, and Ariel gave a long, shuddering sigh and he knew that she saw it, too.

But she continued to hold on to him.

"Please let me stay with you! If you make me leave you, it will all get horrible again. I try to stay in the world, but I'm drawn back again, and it's more terrifying each time. Master Joseph, please—I'm afraid!" Need gave Ariel's features a semblance of beauty as she stared up at him.

"But I can't—" Joseph began, and then he felt Luciano Abaddon's presence strengthening. *You can,* came the silent voice. *We need someone with easy access to the inner planes. Bring her closer to me and I will bind her* . . . Though direction meant nothing here, Joseph took Ariel's arm and they moved down the street together.

"You may come with me if you will swear to serve *my* master," he told her. She almost stopped walking, looking at him.

"You never told us you had a chief! Is he greater than you?"

Unwillingly, Joseph nodded. "He serves the Lord of Light— the Sovereign of the Age that is to come. I am beginning to believe that all the world will serve his cause one day . . ." He had not believed it before he said it, but he realized it must be true, or how could Abaddon have compelled his obedience?

"Will you promise that?" he asked. He felt her gathering herself to answer when another sound distracted both of them. In the distance, a point of light was moving along the road, and from it came a sweet calling—

"Ariel . . Ariel . . ."

Where the light passed, the landscape sprang into color—a supranormal rainbow richness of hue that made it painfully clear how colorless the scene had been. Leaves shone as they do when the sun is setting behind them, and shingles and stucco had an inner glow. Even the streets glittered, as if it had just rained, and the sky was like a stained glass bowl.

Only the figure itself was too bright for its features to be seen.

As the light drew closer, they could see that it was clad in a headdress and cope of glittering gold, with a rosy cross blazoned on its breast, from which rays of brilliance shone. Then it was before them, its light enfolded them, and they were in the center of the rainbow sphere.

"Ariel, I have been seeking you—" the voice was deep and calm, with a resonance that reminded Joseph oddly of Abaddon's. But Joseph thought it belonged to a woman, though it was hard to be sure.

"Who are you?" Fractionally, Ariel's grip on Joseph's arm eased.

"I am a friend. I have come to take you home . . ."

"She is coming with me—" said Joseph. Perhaps his eyes had adjusted, for now he could make out the woman's features—strong features, transcending gender, with no make-up and the brilliant headdress hiding her hair. She looked directly at him and he blinked, for her eyes shone.

"Joseph, you may come too," she smiled, and suddenly he felt a warm wave of love wash over him.

Something that had been frozen within him for years trembled on the verge of opening. She was so strong—could she protect him from Abaddon? But his father's rejection had been too recent. Love was dangerous—it got you hurt—the only safety was in power. And Abaddon held Joseph's body as surety for his obedience now.

"It will be all right, Love welcomes both of you—come with me—" She held out her hand. Ariel let go of Joseph and took a step toward her. Joseph himself began to tremble despite his fear, for the light around her was like the light he had seen in his vision long ago.

Then a bolt of power flared between them, like lightning, like a laser—pure force striking the soul. Prisms splintered, rainbows shattered around him, and he was spun out of consciousness into the dark.

When the Dark Light struck, the Otherworld kaleidoscoped into a confusion of images. In instinctive response, Del Eden's shields flared around her while consciousness retreated to the single affirmation of identity. Swiftly, she sped back along the lifeline of energy the others were channeling to her, pursued by an invisible Power identified only by its ruthless arrogance. Unprepared and unknowing, Del could not oppose it, but she had enough control to slow her flight and formulate one Name of Protection—*"Mikael!"*

"MIKAEL!" The Name resonated through all the levels of the inner worlds. And suddenly she saw him exploding into manifestation, fiery cloak flaring, armor blazing gold, the incandescence of his sword yet less bright than his eyes. The sword flickered forward, the eyes of the Archangel flashed fury, and the deadly Power that followed her recoiled.

Then Del snapped back into her body and saw Michael's kris edged with an electric flicker that scattered brilliance around the room as he struck out at the darkness and returned to guard again. A chill wind rushed through the temple, blowing out every candle but the golden one in the center, and a silent thunderclap shook the air.

The silence that followed seemed deafening. Finally Michael's rigid stance relaxed a little, and Del found her voice again.

"Is it gone?"

Michael lowered his sword and half turned. "I think so. It wasn't expecting our warding." He turned the kris thoughtfully. "Now, I wonder—" with a swift flip he sheathed the blade. Karen raised one eyebrow, and he grinned. "This blade won't go back to rest without being blooded, you see," he explained. "So I think I hurt It—whatever It was . . ."

"But what *was* it?" asked David in exasperation.

"Evil . . ." said Del, remembering that sense of dark beauty and ruthless power. "It was tremendously strong!"

"Stronger than you?" asked Karen shaking her fair head in wonder.

"I'm good, but I'm not that good—" Del managed a wry smile. "At least not when I'm unprepared. And I've never encountered anything quite like that before. I wonder what Joseph Roman can possibly have gotten himself involved with now?"

"Joseph!" exclaimed David Mason and Ruth, almost as one. "Was he there?" asked David. "What about Ariel?" Ruth echoed him.

"They were both out there," Del answered. "Ariel was with Joseph, but I think I had almost convinced both of them to come to me when that other Power hit us. Now I have a question for you—" she straightened, and looked at Ruth and

David. "Did Joseph wear a red robe in the rituals you attended?" Both of them shook their heads.

"Oh dear," Del felt her fears begin to take a shape that frightened her, and these men and women for whom she had taken responsibility were all waiting for her to tell them what to do.

"Who wears red robes?" asked Michael harshly at last.

"The Order of Omega," Del answered him. "For years I've been hearing rumors, but I didn't want to believe them. According to the stories, there is supposed to be a powerful magical fraternity whose members wear crimson robes and meet at the Elysian Lodge."

"Are they a Black Lodge?" Again it was Michael who asked.

"Maybe. It depends on one's politics. Theoretically there is no reason why politician and captains of industry should not use ritual to invoke the help of higher powers. We do the same." Del thought of the flimsy evidence on which she was building this chain of reasoning—a chance conversation with a gardener, some odd references in a newspaper gossip column, the testimony of a few people who had come to her for help in psychic defense, whose problems were not all nerves.

"It depends on which powers . . ." said Ruth darkly. "I remember you told me once about the Black, the White, and the fatuous fraternities. Except for the drug, the Order of Paradise would have been pretty harmless, but anything that can scare Del must be serious."

Karen nodded her agreement. "What Del's saying does raise spectres of the Thule group and the Bavarian Illuminati, doesn't it?" She tried to laugh.

"The Thule group was real. The Illuminati may be a myth, but they are a myth with power. And any group with the right contacts or a charismatic leader who is bent that way can draw on that energy," said Del heavily.

"Well, whatever they're doing," said Michael, "someone there knows his stuff. I haven't felt anything that strong since—" Karen gave him a stricken look and he shut up suddenly. "It wasn't Loki," he added, "but it was just as powerful."

Del's anxiety crystallized suddenly. "What disturbs me is the idea that the Order of Omega is interested in Joseph Roman, because if he hasn't already told them, they will certainly find out about that drug of David's soon, and that will mean danger for him, and possibly for us all. If we know about them now, then they most certainly know about us as well." The flickering candle cast leaping shadows about the room, as if dark forces were already creeping up on them.

"But that must mean Ariel's in the worst danger of all," exclaimed Ruth. "She was out there with him!"

"She'll be threatened only if they have a use for her," answered Del. "You must go see her tomorrow, Ruth, and try to find out how much she remembers of what went on."

"What are you going to do about the Order of Omega?" David Mason found his voice suddenly.

Del sighed, looking from one to another. As she would have expected, Karen and Michael were concerned, but resolute, for they had fought this sort of battle before. Ruth Racusak was biting her fingernails without seeming to be aware of it; Del wished she could have had longer to train her and David, who was watching her with huge, haunted eyes. Only Ruth's friend Tom, who had scarcely said a word all evening, continued to project the same solid strength, tempered only by his concern.

"I had hoped that I would never have to do anything!" Del said finally. "But with reason or without it, they will fear us now. You should all put a new warding on your houses, and pay attention to your shielding. Let us hope it does not become necessary to take more explicit action. A full-scale magical battle is not something one gets involved in for fun."

"Is that all we can do to protect ourselves?" David's voice cracked and he swallowed suddenly.

"Not quite, for if there is a power behind the Order of Omega, there are also powers on which we can call. I have never had to do so, but I think that perhaps this is the time to call on what we know as the Occult Police. We cannot be certain what is wrong, or what to do, but Their judgement will be sure." Del took a deep breath, steadying her breathing, letting her awareness deepen to touch each of the others.

Ruth spoke first. "What must we do?"

"Regularize your breathing, renew your grounding, relax—" Del moved into the familiar litany. "Now close your eyes, and blank out all vision. Whatever images float into your mind, chase away. When you have an empty screen, visualize a red sphere. Let it glow brightly until the seeing is secure, then superimpose upon it a black Calvary cross. Do you have that image? Good, now hold it, and as you do so, project a plea for protection . . ."

Even as she spoke, Del saw the image flash into visibility like a slide projected upon a screen. She had been warned to use the signal only if matters were serious, but the memory of the force that had touched her still made her shiver, and she was not easily scared. If she had cried "wolf" too early, she was willing to pay the penalty, but senses for which she had no words told her that she was justified.

And if that was so, then she was in for a battle that would use all her skills. Del had hoped this task would fall to someone younger, stronger, of higher initiatory degree. But she was already involved, and now she must fight with whatever resources and allies came to hand.

Focusing her will and her intention, Del Eden concentrated on the image of the black cross until it pulsed with power, and focused all her fear and need into a long, wordless cry.

Ariel had put on make-up for the first time in weeks. Ruth told herself it ought to be a good sign, but the pink lipstick and the artfully applied blue shadow looked garish against Ariel's pallor, like a mask. Ariel had dressed with care for the first time since coming to the nursing home, in a cream-colored raw silk pantsuit with an applique of irises from White Duck workshops. The tailored lines made it only too apparent how much weight she had lost.

Ruth tried to focus on the flowers arranged on the table, afraid her face would reveal too much if she looked at Ariel anymore. It had been hard to pull herself out of bed that morning, haunted by images from the dreams in which her unconscious had tried to come to terms with the magical explosion of the night before. Her face in the mirror had not looked much better than her friend's, and she had been tempted to stay in bed. But Del had told her to check on Ariel.

"The doctor says that if I continue to improve I could be out of here by the end of the week," said Ariel brightly.

"That's wonderful—" Ruth answered her, and it was, so why was her gut cramping with anxiety? Perhaps Del had been able to help her, after all, but how could she ask? "I've been pulling for you, all along."

"Yes, I'm sure it will be a relief not to have to come see me all the time. Hospital visits are always so dreary."

Ruth stared at her. "I didn't mind. You would have done the same for me . . ." Outside, a bird was sounding its repetitive sweet call—*It's spring! It's spring! It's spring!* But what springtime would come for the tense, haunted woman in the other chair?"

"Would I?" Ariel gave a brittle laugh. "I don't know what the person I used to be would have done!"

"Why shouldn't you be the same person?" asked Ruth carefully. "Has something else happened—have you had any strange dreams?"

Ariel gave her a swift, almost guilty look, then shook her head. "I don't know. I told you, I don't remember anything. But I don't think I want to be the person I was before. What was she good for, anyway? She flitted through life like a butterfly, no use to anyone, including herself!" She got to her feet and began to move nervously about the room, straightening the bedspread, adjusting the position of the vase of flowers.

Ruth opened her mouth to deny it, then slowly shut it again, for to some degree, what Ariel had said was true. She tried to rub some of the fatigue from her eyes.

"We had some good times, though, during those years—" she said finally.

Ariel shrugged. "Right now I can't remember them. Don't try to force me back, Ruth. I want to get out of this hole!"

From down the hall they could hear a clatter of dishes. An opening door brought the undistinguished odor of institutional food.

"I'm not trying to force you into anything," Ruth swallowed. "I just don't want you to lose the good things. I want you still to be you!"

"Damn it, don't say that!" Ariel turned on her. "You'll drag me down to the pit again! You've clung to me like a leech ever since we left school—let me go! Let me be free!" Ariel stopped, chest heaving, looking at Ruth with a stranger's eyes.

The bright air dimmed. *But I've been trying to help you!* Ruth's heart cried, but her lips could not form the words. She got to her feet, blinking, refusing to let Ariel see her tears.

"All right—if that's the way you feel I won't bother you anymore!" Words came unwilled, honed and hurtful. "I have a job to do and a child to raise. You're right! I don't need to waste time here!''

Her eyes were blurring too badly to be sure what Ariel's face was saying behind the painted mask. She did not want to see it. She did not want confirmation of the death of love. *Whatever it was that I have felt for her,* thought Ruth, *she has killed it. At least I don't need to worry about my sexual orientation anymore.* Stiffly, she walked out the door.

It was not until she was halfway home that Ruth remembered that she had not warded Ariel's room, or reminded her to keep visualizing the Archangels. But she could not go back there—she could not! She was still crying when she pulled into her own drive.

Automatically, she made a new pot of coffee and went to the computer. The digitizing pen traced a way along one of the main routes of the Forbidden City and turned a corner. There ought to be some kind of a conflict here. Ruth switched applications, selected the Gothic font and began to type out a new scroll—

𝔜𝔬𝔲 𝔥𝔞𝔳𝔢 𝔧𝔲𝔰𝔱 𝔱𝔲𝔯𝔫𝔢𝔡 𝔱𝔥𝔢 𝔠𝔬𝔯𝔫𝔢𝔯 𝔦𝔫𝔱𝔬 𝔞 𝔰𝔦𝔡𝔢 𝔰𝔱𝔯𝔢𝔢𝔱, 𝔴𝔥𝔢𝔫 𝔶𝔬𝔲 𝔯𝔢𝔞𝔩𝔦𝔷𝔢 𝔱𝔥𝔞𝔱 one of your companions has disappeared. You call her name, but only the wind answers you. Cautiously, you go forward. Suddenly you hear a deep growl. You turn, and see a creature out of nightmare. You grab for your weapons as it comes toward you. And then you see, looking out from the monster's face, the eyes of your missing friend.

What will you do?

10.

It is not known precisely where angels dwell, whether in the air, in the void, or the planets. It has not been God's pleasure that we should be informed of their abode.

Voltaire, *Philosophical Dictionary*

Joseph Roman lay back in the deck chair, cocooned in a cotton blanket like a geriatric patient on a cruise, and closed his eyes, letting the warm spring sunshine sink into his bones. The scents from the garden were dizzying in their sweetness. Birds were singing, and water lapped peacefully against the sides of the swimming pool. Sounds came to his ears with hollow echoes, amplified by the water. The temperature had turned unexpectedly balmy, like a preview of summer, and the grounds of Templar Court were an enchantment. If only the pleasant lassitude he felt had been caused by the weather, he would have been quite content.

But the ache in his arm reminded him of the blood that he had lost. It was no more than one might donate at a blood bank, they had told him, but Joseph had always felt faint when anyone even suggested he might be a donor. The thought of it made him queasy even now, two days later.

Ice tinkled in a glass and a shift in the wind brought him a breath of musky perfume. But weak as he was, even the knowledge that Joanna de Laurent was sitting nearby, wearing only the briefest of tiger-print bikinis under her black velour robe, did not arouse him. *I have to get my strength back,* he told himself. *I have to get out of here . . .*

Joseph jerked at the hollow boom of a body striking the water, and felt a momentary rain of spray. Involuntarily, his eyes flew open and he glimpsed Luciano Abaddon churning across the pool like Leviathan. For a moment he saw that powerful progress as pure force applied to water, too focused for a human personality to be its cause. And the thought of trying to escape such a phenomenon seemed suddenly ridiculous.

After a time, Abaddon pulled himself out of the water, shaking himself like a dog. Joanna laughed and put up one arm to shield her hair from the spray, then handed him the blood-red towel that had been draped over a chair. Joseph watched as he toweled away the droplets that glistened on his brown skin, realizing that the line of the man's suits owed as much to the excellence of the shape beneath them as to their expensive tailoring. Abaddon's body was blocky, but firmly muscled—the body of a wealthy man who could afford health clubs and conditioning machines and extensive vacations where the sun shone.

For a moment it seemed absurd that he could be anything other than that. He was certainly a businessman, anyway, for Joseph had heard him talking about the stock market on the phone, and knew he had a computer in his room. But he operated at a level that no longer required his daily presence, and his skills were exercised not in the office, but behind the scenes in the club or the boardroom. He seemed to be involved in financial operations in a number of areas. For the past two days he had been in San Francisco, attending to some of them.

Then Joseph reached for his glass of juice, and the ache of his healing arm recalled his memory of Abaddon's other operations.

Abaddon finished drying himself, shrugged on a beachcoat whose crimson reminded Joseph uncomfortably of the Order of Omega's magical robes, and sat down next to Joanna. A servant came and set a pitcher of Margaritas and more orange juice on the glass-topped table.

"So, how are you doing?" Abaddon's black stare fixed Joseph suddenly.

"Pretty well," said Joseph warily, "it's a lovely day . . ."

"Indeed it is—" Abaddon grinned. "Fresh air and sunshine, you'll be back to normal in no time!"

Joseph was uncomfortably aware that this was an order. *And what will happen if I don't get better soon?* he wondered with a mixture of fear and rebellion. *Can he command my flesh to heal?* Healing, on the whole, was not something he would associate with Abaddon.

"So, what do you think of the Order of Omega?" Abaddon drained his glass, set it down, and leaned forward. Joseph was aware of his attention as if a light had been directed at his eyes. He framed his answer carefully.

"I was very impressed."

This time Abaddon exploded into laughter, and Joseph found this hilarity more disturbing than his quiet menace had been.

"Impressed! I'm sure you were, but you must have some questions, and now I can answer them."

Joseph allowed his memories of that night to flood through him in images of fear and splendor. He recalled Abaddon's invocation, but he could not remember what its purpose had been.

"Who were we worshipping?" he asked in a whisper. "Who is the Lord of Man?"

Luciano Abaddon straightened, and his robe looked more than ever like a ritual garment now. Perhaps it was a trick effect of light reflecting off the water of the pool, but it seemed to Joseph that his eyes glowed.

"The Beginning was Alpha, but at the End of All Things Omega shall be supreme. We worship Omega, who will be the Lord of All when the new age comes. He is the epitome and the archetype of the new race, the perfect Man that is emerging from the old. For millenia He has been traduced and denied, but He will come!"

"When?" whispered Joseph, enraptured in spite of himself by the grandeur of a concept so far beyond his own pallid gospel. "When will Omega come?"

"When mankind is ready for Him!" Abaddon's voice rang out in answer. "When the men of the new race rule the world."

"And how does the Order serve this goal?" Joseph's pulse raced with exultation. His earlier fears were forgotten; he realized now that he had finally made contact with the real powers behind events, and no one would ever be able to call him a failure again.

"The outer Order is ostensibly social, and its members are recruited from the leaders of government and industry," Abaddon answered him. "Human beings love secret societies— they love being part of an in-group that will define their superiority by excluding the weak and obscure. Once they are initiated, they are bound by the threat of exposure, and more surely, by the oaths that they have sworn . . ." He smiled very gently at Joseph, who remembered the penalties he had invoked upon himself and shivered.

"But that is not the only reason for gathering such men into a ceremonial lodge. Most of the men who founded this country were Freemasons, and they built their mystical symbols into the nation's soul, but they were infected by ideas of equality. That has weakened the country ever since. The people are sheep. We will be truly secure only when we are ruled by an elite that is adept in the use of both physical and spiritual power."

He paused, poured another Margarita, and drank appreciatively. "The social and financial network of the outer Order allows us to exercise power in the external world. And because these are people with drive and vitality, they can provide a great deal of energy to be channeled on the inner planes. That is where you will be useful to us—"

"I won't be bled again!" Joseph exclaimed, recoiling.

"No, that will not be necessary," Abaddon agreed blandly. "But you are a trained ritualist. You can be of great assistance in performing our ceremonies. And of course the Paradise drug could be a very useful tool."

Joseph's stomach, just settling after his last outburst, gave another lurch. He had *known* that must be coming! Why hadn't he been prepared?

"I want the chemist, Joseph, and the formula, and the drug itself—preferably all three. It will be much better for you, and for the chemist, if you can persuade him to work for me. I want that woman you were with on the astral, as well. Someone who slips in and out of other states of consciousness so easily will make an excellent messenger, while she lasts."

Joseph took a deep breath, trying to summon up strength from somewhere, since he knew that he had no choice but to obey.

"In another day or so you should be strong enough to travel. You will return to Berkeley, find them, and bring them here. Don't worry about the police—" he added, reading Joseph's expression. "They have been muzzled as far as you are concerned."

"And what about the other woman, the one we met on the inner planes?" Joseph asked, and saw Abaddon's black eyes go opaque, like those of a serpent he had surprised once in the grass. He ought to know who she was, but her radiance had disguised her. Fleetingly, he wondered if she could have freed him if Abaddon had not intervened, and suppressed the thought almost as soon as it had come.

"I know where to find *her*," said Abaddon coldly. "And I will know how to deal with her if she troubles us again."

The trouble with good weather, thought Ruth as she stared at the glowing leaves of the fern in front of the window, was that it made it so hard to sit inside and get your work done. The fern was only one of the plants that Tom had brought her, and the loft was beginning to look decidedly woodsy. She supposed that if you let a gardener into your life, things were bound to start growing—

—Except for the Forbidden City game, which she had hardly touched since Ariel's abortive healing ritual. Even the thought of her friend made her grimace as if she felt a physical pain. But it wasn't physical—it wasn't even really a pain. What she felt now was more like an emptiness where Ariel had been. The odd sense of relationship that was developing between her and Tom Halpern did nothing to make up for it, no more than it would have if she had lost Martin.

But Ariel rejected me! Ruth told herself. That was the hard thing—that after all she had suffered and done, her friend should turn on her. *Ungrateful bitch! It will be your own fault if the demons grab you and screw you blind!* For a moment, the image of Ariel held down and misused, as she herself had been, throbbed in her inner vision and Ruth's fingers stiffened into claws. But it was the old, exquisite, Ariel she was seeing rolled in the mire, not the already ravaged woman she had visited in the nursing home. Ruth cried out and ground the heels of her hands against her eyes until she saw red, as if she could wipe the vision away.

I can't afford to invoke perfect justice, or what will happen to me? Ruth thought in anguish. *Mercy—healing mercy is what we all need now*—An effort of will summoned the color blue to soothe her throbbing eyeballs, royal blue, the color of Chesed, the sphere of magnanimity.

I don't have a choice, Ruth realized suddenly. *Or rather, the choice has already been made. I won't make Ariel talk to me again, but I have to keep doing what I can for her—if I can figure out anything to do . . .*

At least there was something she could do about the game. After worrying about Ariel, the problems of programming seemed relatively straightforward. The computer didn't tell you to pick up your love and go away. Unless you did something *very* stupid, that is.

It had been so long since she had changed anything on the screen that the Mac had automatically switched to the Sleeper program. The colored lines shimmered across the monitor hypnotically, and Ruth swore and tapped the keyboard to bring up the game map again.

Her problem was no longer where to find conflict. Right after the ritual she had built into the game a mysterious leader, who promised the mutant horrors glory when their new race mastered the powers of the City and marched forth to conquer the world. Clearly, if the city held the Knowledge of the Ancients, then the villains had not found it either, or they wouldn't have to skulk through the shadows anymore. Unless, of course, they were simply incapable of recognizing it.

But meanwhile, they were still immensely powerful, and it seemed to Ruth that her poor players were going to be overwhelmed. There had to be some source of allies. But in real life you couldn't count on the cavalry coming over the hill, and in a metaphoric sort of way this game was becoming more and more real. A possibility, but not a certainty of help was what she needed now.

Ruth stared out the window again, this time without looking at it. Abruptly she remembered a maze game that had been popular among campus hackers awhile ago. You could get onto the BMUG computer net and announce that you were playing it, and anybody else who was free could log on and play against you. You never found out who your opponents were until the game was done.

Sometimes it seemed to Ruth as if her life was like that

already. But maybe she could program in a way for people to sign on as secret allies . . . Grinning, she switched applications and began to type in code.

The good weather held through Valentine's Day, and the research groups on the north side of the chemistry building scraped the rust off the portable barbecues on their balconies and invited the rest of the department for hamburgers and beer. David Mason smelled the roasting meat as he came up the stairs, and discovered that, with Pavlovian predictability, he was salivating.

"Hey, David, are you coming? Harvey's people have got a keg of Michelob, and Dr. Randel's donating a lot of ice cream!" One of the guys from the research group next to his waved cheerfully in the direction from which the delicious odors were coming. At the mention of the ice cream, David's stomach gave an anticipatory rumble. All his internal systems appeared ready to celebrate; he supposed he might as well indulge them.

A little shyly, he nodded, and then went on to his own office to set down his pack and jacket. A month ago, he thought, he would have stayed there, no matter how good the food smelled. But after getting to know Ruth Racusak and Del Eden, his chemistry colleagues seemed relatively comprehensible.

Someone had put a placard up on the door to the men's room in the hall, so that it now read, "Jeremy Rifkin Controlled Environment." Snickering somewhat guiltily at this tribute to the man who for years had been a sometimes necessary gadfly regarding safety standards for research into DNA, David followed the noise down the corridor to join the group outside.

It was a multi-level party, joyous with delight in the new season and the new semester. If it had been planned, it would have been held in the student lounge, but it had grown spontaneously, like a crystal in solution, adding clusters wherever space allowed.

David wandered onto one of the balconies, and in a few minutes found himself with a moderately well done hamburger on a paper plate, trying to get through the crowd around the card table with the condiments.

Conversations bubbled around him in the usual synthesis of shoptalk—someone was getting tenure, someone was getting a fellowship, someone else was about to move to another university with his graduate students trailing behind him like imprinted ducklings. Someone had gotten some unusual results in crystallography and was trying to repeat them now. There had been a flood on the fourth floor of Latimer Hall when a condenser valve had stuck. Somebody was about to get a giant grant from NIH. Two potentiometers had disappeared from the physical chemistry storeroom in Hildebrand, and Administration was arguing about whether they needed to improve security or record keeping.

"Those photographic ID cards they give us are silly anyway—anyone who knows how to pick a lock could get in without one, and the guards never ask you to show them once you're inside . . ." David recognized the voice of Bob Chovanian, who had the desk next to his, just as Bob gestured with the beaker he had filled with beer and foam spattered across David's arm.

"Oh—sorry about that—" Bob dabbed at it with a paper towel. "But don't you agree?"

"About the cards? I don't know. I do most of my work during the off-hours, and I guess all the security people know my face by now," David answered.

"That's true. If you didn't keep putting new stuff in the refrigerator, sometimes I'd hardly know you were there. What'sa matter—you studying to be a vampire?" Bob, whose sense of humor had not matured at the same rate as his intellect, began to laugh.

Flushing uncomfortably, David eased off through the crowd. The beer and soda were on another balcony. The group there had also brought a tape recorder, and the elegant transmutations of Vangelis competed over the babble of the party with hard rock coming from a radio a floor below. The beer tasted good, even to him, and David found himself talking to one of the few women in the department, a mass spectrometry analyst who worked over in Lewis.

From here he could see the slopes of Strawberry Canyon and the hilltops beyond them— vivid green, dusted now by the brilliant pale gold of wild mustard and the orange nuggets of California poppies. As the sun descended, the sky deepened from robin's-egg blue to a translucent sapphire, and the hillsides glowed. Imperceptibly, the beauty of the view and the girl's sympathetic conversation worked their alchemy on

David's spirit, and he realized that he was actually having a good time.

When full dusk fell and the party began to break up at last, he realized that this was the first such get-together he had stayed through in the three years he had been a research assistant at Cal. When he considered that he had been contemplating suicide just a few weeks ago, it was downright remarkable. He would have to tell Ruth and Del, he thought as he walked down the corridor toward his own lab. They would be pleased.

As David opened the door he heard the phone in the assistants' office ringing, and dashed to catch it, looking around for paper and pencil to take the inevitable message for Bob or Kim or Angelo.

"Hello, David? Good, I was hoping to find you in—"

In the moment of recognition, Joseph Roman's voice shattered David's euphoria, and the pencil slipped from his fingers and rattled unnoticed across the linoleum floor.

"I want to talk to you about Paradise . . ."

"No! Leave me alone!" David held the phone away from his ear.

"You must listen, David. It's your responsibility—" Joseph's voice came faint and tinny through the speaker, but still unfortunately clear, and he had said a word, *responsibility*, that David could not ignore.

"I don't think you realize how great a thing you've done . . ." The voice was smoother now, cajoling. David felt every hair bristle, but he kept on listening. What was the bastard getting at now?

"I want to apologize to you for the way I handled things. I was too enthusiastic and rushed ahead without the right preparation, but I want you to know the results of the experiment were successful beyond anything you might have dreamed."

They would have been golden words, if anyone else had been saying them.

"What are you talking about?" David said painfully. "People got screwed up that night. It was a disaster."

"Only because my methodology wasn't precise," countered Joseph. "But it did work, even so. People who had never had a trip were out on the astral. You were trying to produce the perfect high, but what you got was what mystics have been after since time began!"

David found that he was shivering. "If that's so, then the astral is Hell! I took the stuff again, just to see what I'd done to people, and it was like crawling through the city dump."

"But don't you understand?" said Joseph persuasively. "It needs more experimentation, with more subjects, under controlled conditions, to get the right effect every time!"

"You're full of shit, Joseph—just mouthing off a lot of pseudo-scientific terminology doesn't make it good science. What are you trying to get at, anyway?" David's shock was turning to anger now.

"I've got friends, David—powerful friends who could arrange for this thing to be tested properly, with no danger to you." Joseph's voice held an odd mixture of bravado and anxiety.

Powerful friends? thought David—had Joseph gotten mixed up with the Mob, somehow?

"There's money in it, if you play it right; and what's going to happen if you don't go in with me? You know there's no way you can develop this thing legally, and if you don't, some of the most brilliant work you'll ever do is going to go down the drain!"

"I know what I did, and how," said David determinedly. "And I learned a lot doing it. What happens to it doesn't matter anymore." He wasn't sure he believed that, but he had to try.

"Doesn't it?" The chill in Joseph's voice carried even through the wires. "It matters to these friends of mine—it matters a great deal. They're used to having what they want, David, and you'll be a lot happier giving it to them voluntarily."

"Oh yeah? And if I don't, what happens then?" David clung to his defiance.

"I don't know, David . . ." Joseph's voice trembled with a fear that did not sound feigned. "And I don't ever want to find out."

In desperation, David smashed the receiver back onto its cradle. Joseph Roman's voice was silenced, but in the stillness of the lab, David's own inner dialogue was frighteningly clear.

Joseph is not involved with organized crime—that I could deal with. His "friends" must be whatever it was that attacked our circle the other night. He's part of that Black Lodge Del was talking about, and if I don't watch out, they're all going to be coming after me!

                    *   *   *

Leonard came outside with Martin when Ruth picked the boy up the next Saturday, looking as if he had not slept well. Even sitting in the car, Ruth could hear a small child crying inside the house and winced, remembering what they had gone through with Martin at that age. Leonard came around to the driver's side to talk to her while Martin put his overnight bag in the back and climbed in.

"Martin had a cold earlier this week, and now he's given it to the baby—" Leonard sounded as if he thought Martin had done it on purpose, and the sympathy Ruth had been about to offer him evaporated. Leonard had already survived one child's infancy. It was his own fault that his second marriage had forced him to go through it all again.

"I'll make sure he gets plenty of sleep and some extra vitamin C," she said brightly. "Thank you for warning me."

She looked at Leonard critically, wondering if anything remained of the man she had thought she loved. He was losing hair on top, and gaining a little weight in the middle. She tried to remember what it had been like to live with this man, but he was a stranger. Abruptly, she realized that her experiences in the past few weeks had achieved what the five years since the divorce had not been able to do—they had broken the bond that had made her vulnerable to him.

Ruth started the car and startled Leonard with her most brilliant smile. "I'll bring Martin back Sunday evening, right after dinner. Have a nice weekend!"

Ruth was still grinning as she piloted the car onto the freeway toward the Bay Bridge. After a few minutes, she heard Martin sigh.

"Are you really feeling better? You know, we don't have to go anywhere today—" Ruth ventured a quick glance sideways. Martin looked a little tired, but he was brightening visibly.

"I'm all right, really," he answered her. "I'm just sick of living with Sissy and Dad!"

"I thought you were happy there," said Ruth after the silence had gone on for too long.

"It's okay, I guess, but there's nobody to talk to. I mean, when I make up a new character and try to tell them about it, they just sort of pat me on the head and change the subject."

"Well, don't think you would be allowed to spend all your time gaming if you lived with me!" Ruth said tartly, and Martin giggled.

"No way. But when I did talk about it, you would understand!"

Ruth blinked, and realized that the stinging in her eyes was tears. Leonard had been so certain that a conventional home and regular income would provide a better environment for Martin than her own somewhat haphazard existence, that it had never occurred to Ruth to question it. But suddenly she wondered if, now that Martin was getting older and developing his own quirky personality, her lifestyle might give him the kind of space he was going to need to grow.

Whether she could adjust to constant responsibility for him after almost five years of freedom was another question.

"Mama, is there any chance that I could live with you?" he said very quietly, and she knew that she could not delay answering this time.

"I think your father would be very sad to lose you—I don't know if he would even consider it." She took a quick breath. "But I'll see . . ."

"Okay. Where are we going today, anyway?"

The swift change of subject was deceptive. Out of the corner of her eye, Ruth could see the triumph in Martin's crooked smile. She took another breath, deeper and slower this time.

"Oh," she said lightly, "I thought we'd go take a look at some angels."

Tony Duquette's celebration environment for *La Reina de Los Angeles*—the Queen of Angels—had been created originally for the L.A. Bicentennial and housed in the Museum of Science and Industry in Exposition Park. After several years as a major tourist attraction, it had been moved to a church on Wilshire, and finally some Los Angeles chauvinist had put up the money to send the display on tour.

After a triumphant progress around the country, the Angels had taken up residence in the Cow Palace, which, in addition . to rodeos and dog and pony shows, had hosted a variety of non-agricultural events, including the Dickens Christmas Faire. Ruth supposed that putting San Francisco last on the tour list was a kind of insult, but she had been hearing rumors about this show for too long, and considering the way Del's ritual had ended, a roomful of angels might be just what she needed right now.

Standing in line for tickets, Ruth glimpsed a shimmer of gold from the tapestry suspended over the door. They inched forward, and she saw that it was an elaborate applique of an angel in armor. From his hands came two ribbons of flame, and for a moment memory superimposed the image of Michael Holst with his kris flaming in his hand. When they got close enough for her to read the placard, it was with a sense of inevitability that she saw that the tapestried angel was Mikael.

"The Queen of Angels is Catholic, isn't she?" asked Martin. Ruth could hear his unspoken question, *What are we doing here?*

"Well, she did start out life as a good Jewish girl," Ruth said with a smile, "and the angels are Jewish. In Hebrew, the name *Mikael*, for instance, translates to something like 'the Perfect One of God.' But the Queen of Angels is something more—she's sort of like the *Shekhinah*, the feminine presence of God who sticks around and helps people while Yahweh is hiding His face in anger. According to this poster, she's the old Earth Goddess, too."

Ruth was aware that this was an incomplete and probably heretical theology, whether you thought of yourself as Christian or Jew, but Del Eden had taught her to look for the spiritual identity behind all creeds. It stood to reason that if there was a Deity, His, Her, or Its nature would transcend the attempt of any single individual or group to define it.

Then they were moving under the archway, and Charlton Heston's magnificent voice rolled out Ray Bradbury's magnificent poetry in a narration that was at once an invocation and a spell.

The bare space of the exhibition hall had been transformed by banners and silken hangings that fluttered in an invisible breeze. Everywhere gold glittered, dazzling, triumphant, and figures of angels whose size was belied by their delicacy were supported by great wings. But everything led the eye to the image of the Lady in the center, crowned with jeweled flowers, robed with the seasons, whose face was a constantly changing hologram of all the races in the world.

Looking at Her, Ruth felt her throat tighten, and recognized the Beauty that had fascinated her in Ariel, and oddly, at times in the face of Del Eden as well. For a moment, she trembled on the edge of understanding the reason for the love that had linked her and Ariel for so long, a love that owed nothing to either psychological or sexual need. They were both part of something greater, something that could also be glimpsed in the serenely beautiful, ever-changing female Face she was looking at now.

After a time, sufficient self-awareness returned for Ruth to understand what she was seeing. Surrounding the lady were the figures of eight great Archangels, twenty-eight-foot high openwork collages of metal and color. There was another image of Mikael in flame and roses; Gabriel, studded with seashells over opalescent blue; Raphael, magnificent in crystal droplets and golden palm leaves; Uriel, Israfel, Zadkiel the Peacock Angel, Ariel in green malachite, Lord of the Winds and the Green Earth; and grim Azrael with a horned-skull headdress. Tapestries on the walls portrayed more angels, who in some cases were angelic forces from other cultures who bore the names of pagan deities.

As she moved around the room, Ruth came to the Lady altars for each element, guarding the sacred space just as she and the others had maintained the circle of power for Del. In the earth altar, gnarled graperoots supported a fantasia of neo-Gothic towers. The air altar consisted of draped pavilions suspended by birds, and the Madonna wore a feather robe. The fire altar was backed by a radiant sunburst, and the altar of water was encrusted with a glimmering profusion of seashell and coral and pearl.

There was a bench before the image of the Lady, and after a time Ruth sat down on it, not so much watching as experiencing the changing play of light and color and the music that followed the narration. This room was one artist's vision of the Court of Heaven, but seeing it, she remembered her own vision of splendor, and understood that though the images might be different, the reality they symbolized was the same.

With a deep breath, Ruth let her awareness shift inward and stilled, as the little lights around her flickered suddenly and then flamed forth as if Light had kindled Glory. For a moment, it seemed to her that every atom of her being was blazing; her spirit rushed upward with a beating of mighty wings, and all Creation resounded with a wordless paean of praise.

Then a warm hand on her own drew her back to ordinary reality. Ruth let out her breath in a long, shuddering sigh, put her arm around Martin and hugged him.

"They're neat, Mom!" he whispered. "I don't care if they are graven images. I'm going to put them into my next game!"

Ruth suppressed a laugh. "Well, I've read that there were statues of the Seraphim in the Temple at Jerusalem. Now we know why!"

And what about my game, she thought then. *Is there room for the Archangels there?*

As they left the chamber the narration was playing again—

"Gabriel! Zadkiel! Hadriel! Uriel! Michael, now . . .
*   and San Rafael . . .*
And Ariel, who sings . . .
Stand above the Queen of Angels,
And protect her with your wings!"

Abruptly, Ruth remembered the human Ariel, whom she had left without angelic protection. What would she think of this? Could she persuade her to come see it?

Angels of Mercy, watch over her, since she wants no help from me! Ruth's thought winged toward the angels behind her. *Grant her peace and protection, Mikael, our Defender, and Ariel, who sings . . .*

11.

But this rough magic I here adjure; ...
I'll break my staff, bury it certain fath-
oms in the earth, And deeper than did
ever plummet sound I'll drown my book ...

Shakespeare, Tempest V:i

Joseph Roman hung up the telephone, shivering. Luciano
Abaddon had not been pleased, and his displeasure had been
transmitted quite efficiently across the miles between Berkeley and San Francisco. Clearly, Joseph was not going to
persuade the inventor of the Paradise drug to work for
Abaddon, and having failed, he could not be allowed to
monopolize its secret.

And so, after two days of nightmares he had called the
number Joanna had given him, and in the end, he had told
Abaddon where he got the drug, and where its maker worked,
and his name. Abaddon had not explained how he intended to
assure David Mason's cooperation, and Joseph had not asked.
It was out of his hands now. But he could not help imagining
what would happen if David tried to resist Abaddon, and so
he was shivering.

Hearing the silence, Laurel came in with the snifter of
brandy Joseph had asked for, moist-eyed and billowing in a
faded orange caftan. He took the glass and drained it almost
at a swallow, coughed, and waited for its flame to warm him.
It was not very good brandy, nothing like the quality he had
become used to at Joanna's. He could feel it burning in his

belly, but he still felt cold. He motioned for another, and the woman scurried off to get it for him.

Darkness had fallen, but even by lamplight the room looked shabby. A certain standard of taste and luxury was another thing Joseph had gotten used to during the past few weeks. That was the lifestyle he had always aspired to, and he had fitted into it as easily as a custom-made shoe.

This time Ava brought the drink to him, and stood waiting while he sipped at it, gazing at him with hungry eyes. What an ugly bitch she was, thought Joseph as he felt the dull glow of the brandy begin to spread through him at last. Hadn't he seen before how her mousy hair straggled, or noticed her uneven features and bad skin? Neither she nor Laurel could seem other than gross and graceless to someone who had been living with Joanna de Laurent Winslow.

What had attracted him, Joseph remembered now, had been Ava's breasts, and they were still remarkable, round and firm as melons, straining the front of the T-shirt she wore. And, ugly or not, he thought as his gaze went to her face again, she was available, and that was something that Joanna de Laurent had never been.

Joseph felt the fire in his belly move lower, but he still felt weak from loss of blood. If he took Ava to bed, would he be able to function? He had the sudden sickening conviction that, without more expert attention than this semi-virgin could give him, he was not going to be able to achieve the release that was becoming an urgent psychological, if not physical, need.

Laurel, on the other hand, had been with him for years and understood his needs very well.

Without any other preamble, he set down the empty glass, walked over to Ava, and ran his hand up under her T-shirt. She jumped at the abruptness of his touch, but remained still as his knowing fingers tried to compass the firm flesh of her breast and tweaked the hard nubbin of her nipple. She sighed then, put her arms around him, and let part of her weight sag against him, looking up at him expectantly.

She wants me to court her now, Joseph thought in exasperation, moving his hand from one breast to the other. *But I don't have the time—I don't have the energy!*

"Laurel, come here—" he said aloud.

Ava blushed with embarrassment and started to pull away

as the other woman came into the room, but Joseph held onto her.

"Laurel, I need you to help me. I have been under a great deal of stress, and to do my work I must have release."

"With her?" asked Laurel softly. Her face showed in turn surprise, understanding, and a complacent satisfaction.

"With both of you—" there was no humor in his smile. He gripped Ava's hand and started toward the stairs.

"Joseph, what do you mean? You can't mean you want to do it with her there— Joseph I *couldn't* if someone were watching! I would be too ashamed! Master Joseph, *please!*" Ava tried to whisper into his ear and pull away at the same time.

Joseph ignored her babblings. He could hypnotize her into compliance, but he didn't have time for that, either. His awareness had narrowed into a driving urgency to exercise his power in the one area that was left to him. He yanked her toward the stairs and when she cried out, slapped her.

"Shut up, bitch! You swore you'd obey me and now you're going to do it, that's all. Stop making such a fuss and maybe you'll get some pleasure out of it, too!"

The high color came and went in Ava's face, and then suddenly all the fight went out of her. But she was weeping and shivering as they went up the stairs, Laurel close behind her.

It did not occur to Joseph, then or in the stimulating moments that followed, that in this, too, he was obeying the will of Abaddon.

David stood in the silent laboratory, screwing up his courage to destroy Paradise.

For two days he had come into the lab only during the day when other people were there, and gone home early, hoping their presence would protect him from Joseph Roman's powerful friends. But it bugged him to have to wait his turn to use equipment and find the words to trade small-talk with the other grads while he was doing so. With those limitations, there was no way he could put in enough time to get his scheduled work done for Dr. Langdon's project. And even with precautions, awareness of the falsely labeled flask in the refrigerator and the extra lab book in his desk drawer frazzled his nerves like a subsonic vibration in the air.

And that was the bottom line, David thought as he went to

the refrigerator. As long as the Paradise drug existed, it would be a temptation to people who wanted to control other people's minds. If he succeeded in keeping it from Joseph and his allies now, someone else would be after it later. As long as any analyzable physical products or notes on 11 THC existed, its creator was going to be in danger.

David could no longer deny the obvious conclusion. His work on the Paradise drug had to be destroyed.

But it tore at his gut, as if he had decided to murder his own child.

Lead-footed, he went to the refrigerator. Through the window next to it he could see the full moon, paling the stars in a cloudless sky. Inside and outside made an odd contrast—the lab was all hard edges and metal and glassware glittering in the harsh fluorescent light, everything labeled and defined; the world on the other side of the window was dappled with the uncertain glow and transparent shadows of moonlight, in whose glamour nothing was what it seemed. In the human psyche, thought David, it was the other way around.

The shadows seemed to waver as he stared at them, as if dark figures were slipping from one patch of shade to the next, from the trees bordering Strawberry Creek to the sheltered entrance to the Giauque Low Temperature Lab, then up the stairway, always keeping to the shadows, converging on Hildebrand Hall. It was an odd fancy, but the measured stride of the campus security guard passing beneath the lamp as he made his rounds gave the eye something solid to focus on, and when David looked back at the stairway, everything was still.

He unlocked the refrigerator and opened it. The beaker of *E. coli* was at the back, with the vial containing the rest of the extracted 11 THC next to it. He jammed the vial into the pocket of his jeans, and carefully carried the beaker to the nearest counter. The Lysol disinfectant was in its place by the sink. Feeling like a murderer, he poured some into the culture and watched the stuff turn white, then hastily emptied the contents of the beaker down the drain.

And it was gone—the triumphant achievement of so many lonely hours was gone as if it had never been, and there would never be a paper in *Nature* or *Cell*; no one would ever know what he had done, and what were the chances that he could make such a breakthrough again?

On the other hand, David was finally free from the fear that one of the other grad students might ask him what that odd beaker of stuff *was!* It had been a remarkable achievement, but it should never have been done—not like that, in secret, without authority. He had done penance for at least one of his sins against science, and in the midst of his regret he felt relief as well.

Now there remained only the lab book to get rid of, and he would be completely free.

David had turned on the coffee maker in the grad office when he came in. He filled his mug and set it on his desk. The bottom drawer opened with its usual metallic squeal of protest, which sounded tonight like a moan of anguish at what he was about to do to the precious papers it had guarded for so long, and the mug wobbled frantically.

David gulped down enough hot coffee to keep it from spilling again, and felt under the pile of Xeroxed articles from *The Proceedings of the National Academy of Science* for the familiar worn surface of the composition book. Then, leaving the drawer gaping behind him, he carried book and coffee mug back into the lab.

The warmth of the coffee made him aware of his senses, so David set it down. If he felt too much, he would not be able to go through with this. The blue flame of the bunsen burner he had lit glowed steadily. Steadying his own nerves with an effort of will, David ripped out the first page of the lab book and fed it to the flame.

The paper caught, flared yellow and a dirty orange that sent a little trail of dark smoke up the fume hood. David held it, watching the fire creep closer to his fingers until the pain became unbearable. Then he dropped it into the sink, where it sizzled until only charred curls with the residue of the writing shining against the black surface remained. With sudden violence, David smashed the fragments into powder, then turned on the faucet and flushed it down the drain.

Again he repeated the process, and again, while his coffee grew cold in the mug on the counter beside him. It would perhaps have been sufficient only to burn those pages where the notes for this experiment had been; there was nothing significant in the rest of the book. But he could not bear the mute accusation of those torn edges, and so, page after painful page, the innocent followed the guilty into the flames.

And then someone opened the door.

Hypnotized by the last flickers of the page he was burning, it took a moment for David to register the sound as unexpected. He was already wondering who in the research group would come in at that hour, and how he was going to explain what he was doing as he looked up. Then he stopped, staring.

"Are you David Mason?"

At first, shocked, glance, the neat three-piece suit of the man in the doorway suggested IBM or FBI—some kind of official abbreviation. But the eyes were wrong, the voice was wrong, the fluid, controlled way the man moved into the room was wrong, wrong, wrong! Warning buzzers resonated in David's skull.

"Who are you? How did you get in here?" His voice sounded squeaky, his questions inane, even in his own ears. The man in the gray suit laughed.

"You've got a lot of faith in your security system, kid. It might stop a sneak-thief, but not a professional."

A professional . . . David's brain began to function again. Police would have come for him in the daytime, with a warrant. The only professionals who would infiltrate the building at this hour just to get at him had to be enforcers sent by Joseph Roman's "powerful friends."

It would do no good to lie about who he was—a quick search would turn up the photographic cardkey they all had to carry for identification by security after hours. Where was the guard, anyway? He dared a quick glance at his watch—one a.m.—the man wouldn't be due along again for at least a half hour. This guy must have been waiting for a while, then, to learn his routine.

With a sudden lurch in the pit of his stomach, David remembered the shadows he had seen outside. What if they hadn't been a trick of his vision? There would be others then, back-ups in case this one failed.

But that seemed unlikely.

The intruder moved with the smooth efficiency of a well-oiled machine, while David puffed as if he had climbed the stairs up to the lab instead of using the elevator.

"What do you want?" he asked weakly. "There isn't anything valuable here—" The security system that this goon had penetrated so easily had been intended to protect the College of Chemistry against petty theft and vandalism.

"Oh, I haven't come to steal!" The enforcer sounded faintly affronted, but there was a glint of irony in his muddy brown eyes. "I'm just here to offer you an invitation . . ."

David's face must have reflected his reaction, because Gray-suit laughed again.

"From a friend of a friend of yours, you might say. You've got something he wants. If you give it to him, he'll pay very well."

David swallowed. *"A friend of a friend . . ."* He had been right, then. But what Joseph Roman had done with the Paradise drug had been bad enough. The thought of what the sort of power that had attacked their circle could do with it made cold sweat break out on his skin.

"I don't have it—" David scooped up the last of the ashes from the sink and let them float back again. "It was too dangerous. I burned all my notes and destroyed the bacteria." His heart pounded as he thought how close he had come to chickening out and keeping the stuff after all. "Just now, in fact. It's all gone—I can't make any more."

Gray-suit frowned. "But you know how you did it—"

"Not exactly," David answered hastily. "Not without my notes. It was hard enough to do it the first time!"

"It's no use making excuses to me." The man moved toward him, and David began to back away. "Maybe my boss will believe you and let you go, or maybe he'll find a way to help you remember . . ." he grinned nastily. "But he's got to make that decision, so you're coming with me!"

No. David was shaking his head silently, edging around the counter.

"Look, egghead, I don't think you understand—" Gray-suit's veneer of manners was wearing thin. "You can come easy, and stay in one piece, or you can make it hard for me, in which case I'll leave just enough of you to answer questions."

"I won't go with you!" said David hoarsely. His first betrayal of his vocation had nearly driven him crazy. If this man's boss coerced him into reinventing the Paradise drug for him, guilt would keep him in the Abyss forever.

David saw the enforcer's stance shift, and the sudden flicker of light as a knife appeared in his hand. He probably had a gun as well, but the noise would attract too much attention. He wouldn't want to use it if there was any other way.

David's heart was thumping heavily as he watched the other man come closer, and he could feel sweat beading on his brow. *If you give him too much trouble he'll kill you—* came the clear voice of his internal commentator. *You'll be as dead as those bacteria you destroyed!* And maybe he deserved it, thought David in answer, but suddenly he wanted very much to live to see the sun on the hills above Strawberry Canyon again.

He waited until he thought he would explode with the tension, gauging the distance as the man came around the counter, then launching himself with desperate energy along the other side toward the grad office. The phone was there—he skidded through the door and grabbed for it: *9-911*—David's finger was on the last digit when Gray-suit hurtled through the door after him; the knife flashed toward him and he dropped the phone and darted through the other door.

He heard the sound of the phone being ripped out as he slammed the door behind him, turned the latch, lunged for the first door, groped in his pocket for the key and struggled to lock it as well. Almost immediately it shivered as a heavy body struck it, but for the moment it would hold. He started toward the lab door, then stopped short. Were the others out there waiting for him? Those doors could only be locked from outside.

Gasping, David stared around him, searching walls and counters for some way to defend himself. The lab held plenty of potential for fire, flood or explosion, but if Gray-suit was hampered by the need for silence, David was inhibited by years of conditioning against doing anything that might damage the laboratory.

The office door shook again, and a sudden crack bisected its middle. David galloped to the storage shelves, grabbed a big plastic pipette and plunged it into the bottle of sulfuric acid. As he pulled it out again he heard wood smashing and the door went down. Brandishing the pipette in front of him, David straightened.

Gray-suit's jacket had split at the shoulder, and his face was flushed with fury. As David's hand came up, the enforcer, responding to the movement before he could have known what David held, drew back his arm. David saw a flicker of light in the air. The knife sliced across the tops of his fingers. The pipette clattered to the floor.

The enforcer was still coming. David grabbed an Erlemeyer flask from the counter and threw it awkwardly, then a beaker—threw anything he could reach to keep a shower of shattering glassware between him and the other man.

Glass clashed and tinkled all the way around the long counter. David caught his breath, glimpsed the light switch and swatted downward, leaving a bloody smear along the wall. Suddenly the only source of illumination was the moon, whose deceptive light glittered on the broken glass strewn across the floor.

The other man was stronger, but David knew the ground. If he could move very quietly . . .

Hardly breathing, David hunched below the level of the counter and began to creep back around toward the storage shelves. He could hear his enemy following. The enforcer would expect him to head for the door to the hallway, but he dared not go out into the light with the other man behind him. He had to stop him somehow.

His foot crunched on glass; a hiss told him that the enforcer had realized his error. David grabbed for the still unstoppered bottle from which he had filled the pipette, turned and tossed it just as his enemy leaped toward him.

Impetus carried the man forward. Certain he had missed, David rolled away through broken glass, but his hand came down on the hard plastic of the pipette and he gripped it as he came up again. Even as he fumbled to fit blood-slick fingers around the plunger, he saw the dark figure of his enemy rise to take him. And then the shadow screamed, and screamed again, as the sulfuric acid David had thrown at him ate through suit and skin.

Gotta get out of here . . .

David gulped air, trying to think through the sounds that the thing that had been his enemy was making on the floor. He had to get out past the others, he needed more defenses. From somewhere, a scene from a movie flickered into memory and he bent and grasped with his good hand for the jar of pump oil at the end of the shelf.

The enforcer's moans faded to an awful bubbling. Through the pounding in his head David heard the sound of running footsteps. Was it the security guard? He couldn't chance it.

Trying to move quietly, though it was becoming hard for him to make his abused muscles obey him, David slipped through the doorway to the lab next door.

After a short, clumsy search, he found the phone and dialed the number that Gray-suit had stopped him from completing before. The campus cop on duty sounded bored.

"No, this isn't a crank call—I'm a grad student in chemistry and some vandals have gotten into Hildebrand Hall!" David was speaking in a hoarse whisper. As he waited for the man to answer, he heard a sound in the hallway outside.

"Look, I think they may be armed. I'm not going to hang around and wait to be shot! Just come up here, okay? This is an emergency!"

Gently, he cradled the phone, crept to the lab door, and peered out just in time to see another gray-suited figure going into his own lab. David eased through the door without closing it and stumbled down the hall.

He heard a sharp exclamation behind him. He forced himself into a run as the second man burst back into the hallway and started after him, then stopped short in front of a storage closet as a third enforcer came up the stairs.

"Put them down—"

The voice was hard, the word clipped short. Both men had their guns out already, and David knew that the pipette could never squirt that far. Chest heaving, he bent to put jar and pipette on the floor. He straightened slowly, his strength at an end. But as he did so, his eye fixed on a design of black and yellow triangles, so familiar he rarely noticed it, on the closet door.

Could he do it? He remembered how Michael Holst had stood to repel the powers of darkness, and his heart resounded with the Archangel's name.

Mikael! Give me the strength!

And as if a door had opened, new energy flared through him. In almost a single motion David rose and swung round the door handle and pulled out the first thing he touched within. He had no idea what it was, except that nothing stored in an unlocked environment like this could be more than mildly radioactive. In fact, the cannister was so light he wasn't sure there was anything inside, which would explain why the closet had not been locked.

But the enforcers didn't know that.

David swung round with the cannister held in front of him as they were still aiming their weapons, trying to decide if what he had done was dangerous.

"Radioactive! Do you see that sign?" He jerked his head toward the closet door. "I've got nothing to lose—keep away from me!" Grinning insanely, David set the cannister on the floor and unscrewed the top. The two enforcers were backing away, but he was still covered by their guns.

Still bent over, he took the top off the jar of pump oil. Then he picked up the cannister again, kicked over the jar, and started down the hallway.

The eyes of the man he was heading for widened. "It's radiating already—" David said hoarsely. "You'll be sterile, your hair will fall out, you'll die!" He could hear the other enforcer advancing behind him, then the crack of a wild shot that buried itself in the wall beside him as the man slipped in the widening pool of extra-slippery pump oil.

"Get back, and it might not fry you too bad—that's right, I'm just going to ease past!"

The gunman seemed hypnotized by the dull gray metal of the thing David bore. David moved on by, turned so that he was walking backward, felt the edge of the first stair behind him, set the cannister down and ran.

He could hear the crackle of walkie-talkies behind him as he stumbled up the path toward Cowell Hospital. Vaguely, for the adrenaline that had fueled his last effort was draining with the blood that dripped from his hand, he wondered whether the enforcers were still there, and how the police were going to explain what they found.

Then he was leaning on the registration desk at the hospital. He had just strength enough to hand the clerk his student ID, then the walls began to whirl around him and David fell into blissful unconsciousness at last.

Joseph Roman paused at the door of the nursing home, nostrils wrinkling at the smell. Late the night before, clouds had begun rolling in from the sea. Now the sky was a dismal gray, and there was a dampness in the air that promised rain. His mood was as gloomy as the day. His little session with Ava and Laurel had eased the worst of his tension, but it had taken most of a day's patient sleuthing to find out where Ariel Ashton was living now, and for a moment he fervently wished that he had failed. He had never been able to abide these places.

To Joseph, death seemed far preferable than life surrounded by decaying bodies and disintegrating minds. And the only thing worse than being sentenced to spend your old age watching the slow erosion of your powers would be to come here while you were still young, and strong, and, as he remembered Ariel, beautiful.

But, of course, he had no choice. After his failure with David Mason, he had to deliver Ariel.

He took a quick breath, straightened the jacket of his pale-gray wool suit and centered the pendant silver cross on his white turtleneck, and strode through the door. The receptionist looked up curiously as he came in. She was young, black, wearing stylish, exaggerated lines and bright colors that jarred with the decor of the reception area, which was furnished in "instant motel."

"Good morning—I'm Miss Ashton's clergyman—" automatically he gave her his most gracious smile, and was rewarded by seeing her body shift from the slouch of boredom to attentiveness. This one might be a sharp dresser now, but he would guess she was from a good, church-going family. She certainly knew how to treat the clergy.

He let his voice ease into just the hint of a drawl. "Do you think I could see her now?"

"Oh yes, Reverend—you sure can. You just go down that hall there, Miz Ashton is in room number nine!" She gave him a broad smile, and something in Joseph quickened a little as he wondered about the sweet black flesh under those bright clothes. Would she have those wonderful steatopygous haunches like some black women he had seen? He was primarily a breast man, but he could appreciate a good piece of ass.

Seeing him hesitate, she waved him down the hall. With an effort, Joseph controlled his thoughts, gave her a benign smile of farewell, and followed her directions.

His first sight of Ariel shocked away all thoughts of the black girl. She was sitting by a table that was still set with her almost untouched breakfast, staring out into the garden. Her thin hands were clasped tightly in her lap, and he did not think she really saw the first rose-colored blooms of the azaleas, any more than she saw him until he coughed and came all the way into the room.

It took all of Joseph's skill in dissimulation to keep his face from showing what he was thinking. Ariel Ashton had always been a bit too skinny for his taste, but as a woman she had been an exquisite, elegant work of art, and now she was an emaciated caricature. *Ugly*— she had called herself ugly when he had met her on the inner planes. He saw now that she was willing her physical form to reflect that internal reality.

But, with a little flicker of wonder, Joseph remembered that on the astral he had been able to restore her beauty.

"Ariel—" he said softly.

She started, turned, and shrank away.

"What are you doing here? I'm ugly now—you did this to me!"

"No, Ariel, you *are* beautiful . . ." Joseph's voice was even softer now, caressing her. "Don't you remember?"

"Remember what? I remember going to your damned ritual and waking up in the hospital!" Ariel's clasped hands twisted to cover her wrists in a gesture that looked as if it had become habitual, but as she did so, Joseph saw that the white skin was marred by ugly purple scars.

He had a dim recollection of that woman friend of hers saying something about suicide. At the time, he had been too frightened and angry to pay attention. Now, seeing the evidence, he felt a lurch in his belly, as if he had run over something in the road. But he had no time to worry about that now. He had to make her trust him and get her out of here.

"Ariel, look at me!" He leaned over the table and held the chain of his pectoral cross so that he could turn it to catch the light. The flicker distracted her and he spoke again.

"Ariel, you have listened to me before . . . I have shown you light and love, Ariel, so listen to me now . . . Let your muscles ease, Ariel—let all your tension flow away—breathe deeply, regularly, in . . . and out . . . in . . . and out . . ." He extended his awareness to encompass her, and felt her resistance gradually fade away.

"Do you hear me now, Ariel?" She nodded, and Joseph took a deep breath. "Sink deeper, deeper, now the Gate opens . . . you are here in this room, but you can see the Otherworld around you—tell me, Ariel, do you see it now?"

"Yes—I see it. Everything is gray and horrible . . ."

Joseph felt a spark of exultation. What a wonderful trance subject! Abaddon had been right to want her—she had gone under with no trouble at all.

"But I can make it light for you—don't you remember? And I can make you beautiful . . . I see you as beautiful, Ariel—I see you as beautiful *now*!"

And with all the power of his trained imagination, Joseph superimposed on the ravaged face of the woman before him the exquisite features he remembered, and slowly, subtly as a sunrise illuminating dawn's gray clouds, muscles relaxed and her grimace became serenity, her head lifted, the light came back into her eyes. She was still too thin, and pale—her face was less elegant than ethereal, the face of one who lived at once in both the worlds.

"I remember . . ." Ariel said suddenly. "I was with you. Let me stay with you, Master Joseph, or I will be afraid again!"

"Yes," he said very gently, the triumph within him warring with something absurdly like tears. "Follow me, Ariel, and I will take care of you."

Awkwardly, as if her muscles had stiffened from lack of motion, Ariel stood up. She put her hands in his as trustfully as a child.

"Take me away from here, Master Joseph. I can't bear it anymore!"

Once more Joseph was aware of the sounds he had shut out while he was concentrating on Ariel—a man's querulous complaining next door, a soft continuous whimpering across the hall, and, from somewhere else on the corridor, an old woman calling for her Mama, again and again and again. For someone of Ariel's sensitivity, this environment must be literally Hell . . .

"Come on, Ariel," he said more roughly than he had intended, "we're getting out of here!"

He found her coat and they went down the corridor to the lobby. The receptionist looked a little surprised and started to protest, but Joseph gave her his most convincing smile.

"I'm just going to take Ms. Ashton for a little ride—I think the fresh air will do her good, don't you?"

"I want to go—"

Ariel smiled like a child who has just committed some

secret mischief. Joseph slipped his arm firmly through hers, and they walked out the door.

They were already getting into the car by the time it occurred to the receptionist to wonder why they wanted to go out when it looked like rain. And it had been raining hard and steadily for two hours before it occurred to her to tell her supervisor that Miz Ashton was gone.

12.

All you who are led by your religion to prophesy future events and to interpret the past and the present to people, you who see abroad and read hidden letters and sealed books, who seek in the earth and in walls for what is buried, you who learn great wisdom and art—bear in mind if you wish to apply all these things, that you take to yourself the religion of the Kabbalah and walk in its light, for the Kabbalah is well-founded.

Paracelsus, *De Religione Perpetua*

"Ruth is it all right for me to stay here? Tom let me in—"

Water from Ruth's open umbrella splattered across the floor as she turned and saw David Mason sitting on the futon. Shock held her motionless for a moment, the dripping umbrella still in her hand. Half-healed cuts scored his cheek and there was a big bandage around his right hand.

"What the hell happened to you?" Recollecting herself, she gave the umbrella a final shake and jammed it into the terra-cotta stand.

David gave her a rather crooked grin. "It almost was, you know. I'm kinda surprised to still be here . . ."

"Well, you look terrible!" Ruth hung up her jacket, stalked over to him and stood, waiting.

She had just gotten back from a frustrating hour with the people at the nursing home. They had no idea where Ms. Ashton was—she had the right to leave if she wanted to. That was all they would say. And here was David, looking like something the cat had dragged in. She could feel the knot in her belly tightening again.

"Those people Joseph Roman's gotten mixed up with sent gunmen after me—" he said abruptly. "They wanted me, and/or the Paradise drug . . ."

"Oh shit—" Ruth sat down rather suddenly on the futon beside him.

"Yeah, it was—" David agreed. Ruth sat in appalled silence while he told her what happened two nights before. "It was yesterday afternoon before I woke up in Cowell Hospital, and then the police had me answering questions until I was ready to pass out again."

"Did they really believe those guys were vandals?" Ruth asked in awe.

"Not when they saw they were wearing three-piece suits! I think the fuzz finally decided they were after the technical equipment, but one of them can't talk and the other two aren't saying anything. Even if they told the police why they had come, who would believe them? Like I said, I got rid of all the evidence. Except for this—" David added, pulling a small glass jar full of pale golden powder out of his pocket. "I was leaving it for last, but now I think I'll hang onto it for a while. It might come in handy."

Ruth shuddered. "What are you going to do now?"

"Well, I was pretty safe at the hospital, but they can access my school records easy if they want to, so I don't dare go back to my apartment or home. The only thing I could think of was to come to you . . ."

Ruth put her arm around him and gave him a hug, feeling the tension in his back and shoulders relax slightly as she held him.

"You did the right thing. Del says she's had some trouble on the psychic level, but nothing has bothered me. They know where Del is, and Joseph Roman told them about you, but he hardly knows I exist, much less that we know each other. They won't think to look for you here!

"Meanwhile, we've got another problem—" Ruth sighed

as the loss washed over her again. "My friend Ariel has disappeared from her nursing home, and nobody seems to have any idea where she's gone!"

In the week that followed, guilt drove Ruth to phone every emergency ward in the Bay Area and visit every police department and jail. None of them had seen anyone answering Ariel's description, nor were they inclined to put any effort into looking for her. The implication was that they had too many unsolved crimes on their books to spend time worrying about a missing person when there was no evidence of foul play.

There was no way Ruth could explain to them the kind of foul play she feared. And it was all her fault! If only she had warded Ariel's room as Del had told her to—if she had been more patient, more understanding! How could she have allowed herself to react to Ariel's words when she knew her friend wasn't well?

On the other hand, whoever the Order of Omega had sent searching for David Mason had been equally unsuccessful.

"Are you sure those guys at the nursing home told you everything?" David asked as Ruth handed him the toast she had just made.

"The supervisor was very cooperative. She showed me the notes she had taken when the receptionist told her Ariel was gone."

Ruth watched David chewing his toast and sighed. For the past week he had been sleeping in Martin's room. Really, it was just like having Martin there, except that instead of gaming magazines, David read all the scientific journals she had been able to find for him.

"But you didn't talk to the receptionist yourself?" David swallowed his toast with a gulp and stared at her, the cup of coffee halfway to his lips.

Del had given Ruth some herb teas, and drinking them in the evening did help her to sleep better, but both she and David still needed several cups of Mr. Peet's Blue Mountain in the morning before they could function. She supposed that shared need had made it easier for them to get along.

"I couldn't. She was off-duty, but surely the supervisor's report—"

"How do you know she told her super the whole story? I mean, did you always tell your boss everything?" David drank, set the coffee cup down, and began working on his scrambled eggs.

At least he was beginning to look healthy again, Ruth thought as she watched him eat. And he did have a point.

"Okay, maybe I should go back there and try to talk to her," she said finally, stabbing at the egg on her own plate.

"Do you want me to go with you?"

"You can't! David, the whole point is to keep anyone from seeing you, especially with me!" Ruth's fork scraped across the plate with a squeal that startled both of them.

"Look, it's no use staying safe if I go crazy here!" David's knuckles whitened as he gripped the mug. "Langdon told me to take some time off and recover—well, it was going to take them a while to put the lab back together anyway! But they'll be back at work by now, and I keep wondering what's happening. I've got to have something to do!"

Ruth stared at him helplessly, wishing she could order him as she did Martin. Enveloped in an old bathrobe of Tom's, he should have looked ridiculous. But he didn't, even with his hair sticking out wildly on all sides. Abruptly, she remembered that he had managed to outwit three of the Order of Omega's men. It occurred to her that after that, he was not likely to take arbitrary directions from anyone. And the rainstorm that had followed Ariel's disappearance had been succeeded by a succession of warm spring days—not weather to make one content to stay indoors.

"I know how you feel," she said quietly. "None of us can go on this way. But try to stick it out just a few days longer. If nothing has happened by then, I won't argue if you want to go . . ."

"Well, considering that I planted myself on you without any invitation, I guess that's fair."

David gave her a crooked grin that reminded her again of Martin. Her son was going to be with her again that weekend. If he didn't bore David stiff describing his gaming characters, the two of them might keep each other amused, and that would solve the problem for at least a little while.

*　　*　　*

Joseph Roman sipped at the pureé of fresh mushrooms which Joanna Winslow's *nouvelle cuisine* chef had served as the first course of their meal, and looked down the table, wondering why he was not enjoying himself more. He was not yet sufficiently accustomed to this lifestyle to be jaded by the exquisite food and expensive wine, and he could hardly criticize the company.

The mahogany table had room for six people, but there were only four of them there. Joanna, whose tanned shoulders rose smoothly above a strapless sheath of black moiré, sat at one end of the table. Instead of a necklace, the top of the drape was clasped by a circle of smoky black star sapphires and diamonds, and two large matching stones surrounded by diamond chips glowed from her ears.

Across from him on her right was Ariel, draped in a gown of white crepe, which Joanna had loaned her, with a string of pearls. The loose fit of the gown helped disguise the fact that it was too big for her, and Joanna had obviously helped her with make-up as well. Joseph had to admit that the improvement over the haggard woman he had spirited out of the nursing home was considerable, but Ariel still reminded him of a little girl who had dressed up in her mother's clothes.

It was, he supposed, a dinner worth dressing for. The servants had taken away their soup dishes and set down fine Spode plates laden with servings of poached salmon with cucumber dill sauce, fresh asparagus, baby carrots cooked to the edge of tenderness, and delicately seasoned rice pilaf. Joseph watched Ariel pick at her food. Joanna's chef had taken the need to tempt her appetite as a personal challenge, but she was still too thin. He wanted to coax her to eat more, but she was listening to Joanna's conversation with Abaddon. He toyed resentfully with his own salmon, from which the chef had managed to remove virtually all the bones, and listened to them.

"And how are the plans for the Mardi Gras ball progressing?" asked Abaddon.

Joanna set down her glass. "Quite well—we have the Gaslite and Empire Rooms reserved at the Claremont Hotel, and the invitations went out several days ago. People are beginning to respond already, and I think we'll have a good crowd. The Mayor will be there, and several members of the City Council. I've rented costumes for all of us, along with some extras in case anyone is unable to get outfitted in time.''

"And the special guests I requested you to ask?''

"Their invitations went out first of all,'' Joanna answered him.

"Good,'' said Abaddon. "The party will provide a perfect cover for us to deal with certain business regarding the Order.'' He consumed the remainder of his salmon in a few efficient bites, and turned to Ariel.

"Miss Ashton, I'm sorry I was out of town when you arrived, but I am delighted to meet you. You are exquisite, my dear—'' Abaddon's voice was as rich as the sauce on the salmon.

Joseph could see Ariel relaxing beneath its spell at the same time as she struggled to understand his meaning. Did she realize that it was Abaddon's power that had separated them on the inner planes?

The servants took the remains of the main course away and the chef tossed a radicchio salad with vinaigrette dressing, served portions onto glass plates, and handed them to the servers.

"I feel as if I had escaped from a nightmare, but it's hard to believe that any of this is real—'' She gestured at the twisted silver candlesticks, the panelling, the hand-woven tapestry on the wall.

Abruptly, Joseph realized one of the things that was bothering him. Ariel's make-up was perfect, but it was like a painted mask, hiding the beauty he had seen in her as well as the marks of illness her mirror showed. Made-up by Joanna's maid, wearing Joanna's clothes, she was like a mechanical doll. He took a long swallow of the *Chateau St. Jean Le Petite Étoile fumé blanc* he was drinking and held out his wine glass to be filled again.

"What is reality?'' asked Abaddon smoothly. "We shall make a brave new world for you to live in . . .''

"I think I should like that—'' said Ariel dreamily. Her gray eyes widened, became luminous as they caught the candlelight. "All I ever wanted was for things to be beautiful . . . But the world outside isn't like that, and the world inside—'' she stopped short, her face changing as she remembered.

"Ariel!'' Abaddon's voice compelled her attention as surely

as Joseph's had. "The Power I serve rules the inner world. I will protect you—you have only to do what I say—"

As he continued to speak to her, Joseph recognized the melodious flow of words that had seduced him, also, not so long ago. It was strange to be listening as that compulsion was laid upon someone else, while Joanna watched with the same feline smile. But *he* was the one who had brought Ariel here. Abaddon ought to have let him continue to handle her. The servants exchanged the salad for dessert plates and brought in a platter of fruit and Brie. Joseph drank more of the wine.

"But I don't want to go back there," Ariel whispered, and Abaddon's eyes narrowed. "Only if *he* goes with me—" she lifted her head and looked at Joseph, and for a moment the beauty he had seen in her before shone through her clear eyes.

A little blurrily, Joseph smiled back at her, hoping that the spurt of triumph that had flared through him had not been too obvious.

"She's fixated on him," murmured Joanna to Abaddon.

"Well, we expected that—" Now his gaze moved to Joseph as well, considering.

"He will be with you, then, wherever you go—" Abaddon nodded slowly, and Joseph was sobered abruptly by an odd, irrational breath of fear.

"Del, I know Joseph has got her—the receptionist at the nursing home described him down to the silver cross he wears! But where?"

Del Eden reached out to grip Ruth's shoulder, adjusted her own energy flow to drain off some of the tension that buzzed in the air around her, and felt her grow calmer. The mist that had followed the warmth of the day veiled the world outside the windows of the bookstore, giving them a sense of privacy that was not completely illusory. Her wardings surrounded the place with the psychic equivalent of a stone wall, and the mist should have made it hard for any physical watchers to recognize Ruth and David when they came in.

"They're not at his place?" she asked.

Ruth shook her head. "I talked to the police department. They've had a watch on his house and they said he was back for a few days last week and then left again. He didn't bring

anybody home with him, and the two women who live there
with him are the only ones in the place now.''

"You think they were telling you everything?" asked David from the other chair. It seemed to Del that the boy had
steadied, even grown solider, since she had seen him last, as
if his brush with death had finally made him care about his
body as much as his intellect.

"About that, yes," said Ruth slowly. "But I did pick up a
sense of constraint, almost of exasperation, as if they were
under orders to hold off, somehow."

"That could be." Several intuitions crystallized suddenly
in Del's awareness. "If the Order of Omega could send
enforcers after you, they can probably put some pressure on
the police department as well. They are not the Mob, but they
seem to be imitating it."

"Oh, wonderful!" said Ruth sarcastically. "That means
we won't get any help from the authorities even if we find out
what's going on?"

"Possibly. At least it means we must be very careful . . ."

"But what are we going to do about Ariel? You found her
on the astral before—can't you go looking again, and maybe
persuade her to come home?"

Ruth was pleading, and Del sighed, remembering the days
when she, too, had been new to the Path and certain that there
was no problem that couldn't be solved by the right ritual or
spell.

"It's true that Omega hasn't thrown anything at me lately,
but we don't have a full circle for protection. And the equinox is less than three weeks away," said Del.

"What does that have to do with it?" David asked.

"The equinoxes mark the changing of the astral tides, and
the six weeks before either one are a bad time for any kind of
magical operation. Occult groups are prone to quarrels; people feel their powers at an ebb. It's usually better to spend
that time in study and contemplation and wait for the power
to start flowing again before doing a ritual working." She had
proved that one through experience.

"But Ariel can't wait, even if we can!" protested Ruth.
"And won't the astral upsets affect them, too?" She looked
haunted. "Please?"

Del knew Ruth blamed herself for her friend's disappearance, and it was no use to tell her that without Ariel's full

cooperation there had really not been much they could do. But forewarned and prepared for the dangers, something might be possible now.

"A full circle is stronger, but there are some operations that can be performed by a triad. If you two will represent the masculine and feminine polarities and balance me, we can try to contact her."

The light in Ruth's face was Del's reward, but she still had misgivings. She did not tell her that every night that week she had lit a psychic beacon on the inner planes and stood watch behind it, but though she had sensed Ruth and David and the others and invoked for them the protection of the heavenly powers, there had been no awareness of Ariel.

Del could feel the charged atmosphere of her temple as they stepped into it. That was inevitable in any place that is dedicated and regularly used for ritual, but she could still sense the extra energy that Michael's defense had put into the permanent warding more than two weeks before. That would help them. Michael Holst had left the imprint of his unusual personality so vividly that anything testing the barriers would sense it and perhaps believe that he was still there. Nonetheless, Del put extra concentration into her visualization of the circle before she took her place betweeen Ruth and David before the altar on the floor.

"Let's synchronize our breathing and center down—" she said softly. Peripheral vision showed her Ruth's black robe to her right and the white of David on her left side, like the Pillars of Severity and Mercy that flanked the Tree of Life.

Del took a deep breath and let it slowly out again, letting the strains and tensions of the day's work drain away, then took another, felt the tingle at the top of her head as she activated the power of the Crown chakra and pulled it downward, energizing the rest. At her age she had less natural resilience than the other two, but constant practice had made this rebalancing of her energies almost instinctive.

They are the two poles of power and I am the equilibrium . . . Del repeated the affirmation, extending her awareness to encompass Ruth and David, feeling it strengthen as they sensed her touch. Energy flowed between them, creating the three-pointed figure whose balance is more secure than two or four.

"In front of us there is a black curtain, thick and velvety, hanging in heavy folds . . .'' Dual consciousness allowed her to speak the words while all other awareness focused on building up the visualization and maintaining the triad.

"Put out your hands and find the edge, draw the curtains aside and step through . . . On the other side is a faintly glowing pathway. It's a road, with buildings to either side . . .'' She gave them a few moments to focus, then went on. "Look around you—can you see anything like a beacon?'' Even as she said it, Del became aware of a point of light glowing off to her left, apparently uphill, but she waited to see if the three of them were beginning to develop a rapport.

"Yes, I see something . . .'' Ruth answered hesitantly. "It's burning up high, like a light in a tower . . .''

"The Campanile—can the Campanile be here?'' asked David suddenly.

"True symbols exist on all the planes,'' answered Del. "We'll need the tower for a point of reference in our shared reality, so get a good, clear, image. If you have any difficulty, or any sense of being separated, move to that light and I'll come back for you.

"Now, let's move along this road. David, position yourself behind me, and stay aware of our surroundings, and tell me if you sense anything else moving here. Ruth, move a little forward. You know Ariel best, so think of something that identifies her essence for you, and extend your awareness outward, seeking it . . .'' Del had a momentary impression of the scent of lilac, and sensed Ruth moving. Behind them, the unmistakable radiance of her own temple continued to glow.

"Good, we're all moving now, walking along the road . . .'' Del had lost all awareness of her physical body. Her lips and throat were producing audible words as if by remote control. But she could see David and Ruth clearly to either side of her, glowing faintly and looking somehow more like *themselves* than they appeared in physical reality.

Maintaining contact, they moved forward through streets that looked faintly familiar, as if they, too, reflected some manifest reality.

"I think there's something—'' said Ruth, "over there where the ground rises—'' She began to move faster, and Del saw the grid of glowing streets rippling irregularly up the hillsides. They approached them with the smoothness of dream, for here, to think a thing was to make it so.

"Ruth, slow down—" Del's extended awareness sensed something they had not imagined—not another light, but an absence of image before them in a fold of the hills. "Stop! Both of you!" she reached out to hold them.

"Now, look very carefully ahead of you and tell me what you see . . ." She waited, trying to probe that blankness with a touch as delicate as a butterfly wing.

"I think I feel Ariel, but it's all dull and fuzzy," Ruth whispered. "I'm no good at this—I can't really see—"

"You *can* see! See me!" Del hissed as she felt Ruth's presence waver, then steady again. "You are here, both of you, and what you perceive has meaning. Look again, and tell me what's there."

"Nothing's there," said David, "and there should be, shouldn't there?"

Very carefully, they moved forward again, instinctively keeping to the side of the road, visualizing trees and buildings so they could walk in their shadows. The darkness ahead of them grew clearer—not emptiness, but a sphere of something drawn in the opposite of the radiance that made everything else visible.

"Ruth," said Del in a low voice, "that's their warding, and we don't want them to know we're here . . ." She avoided even thinking the name of the Order whose stronghold this was, lest she give it power. "Just once, softly, call Ariel . . ." She sensed agreement from the others, and then Ruth's painful cry—

"Ariel, I love you . . ."

The words floated away like a song through the dim air. Then, abruptly, they saw a flicker of murky red suffuse the darkness.

"Back! Get back to the temple!" Del grabbed for Ruth's hand, pushed at David, *willed* them with all her strength to retrace the way they had come. Vision blurred around them, but she could feel the presence of dark power coming after them.

The radiance of her temple blazed, but would her wardings hold it? If only Michael—the disruptive energy behind her licked at her awareness. Del pushed the other two ahead of her through the curtain, started to turn, then was herself thrust through as a great winged form blazed up between her and the Shadow, fiery sword lifting to guard.

Del let herself fall back through the curtains and into her body, and heard with inner and outer hearing a great clap like thunder, or a slamming door. Returning consciousness rang with fear and wonder and gratitude as she realized that the identity she had sensed in the temple's warding had not been Michael, but *Mikael*!

The monitor screen glimmered with shades of rust and brown. Ruth pulled down the color pallet from the file, adjusted the hue downward, and began to shade in the pathway. A switch in applications let her write in the code that would generate irregularities as a game player moved along it. Then she moved back to the text for this part of the adventure.

One of your group has been taken prisoner. You think she is being held in an estate hidden in the wilderness behind the town, but the place is guarded. You find a secret path through the hills and start along it, hoping it will lead to your goal . . .

But there would have to be obstacles. Frowning, she programmed in a false fork that led to lost time in a dead end, unless the players remembered to check for footprints, and a landslip that took out the original path and required the players to analyze terrain well enough to locate a feasible detour. But that was really too tame. She needed more action.

Suppose the players who were providing the opposition had to remember to discover and watch all possible paths in? What could they do to prevent the other side from breaching their defenses? She already had two sets of instructions going, so that once sides were chosen, both groups could play independently. For a while Ruth was busy weighing options and percentages. Then she returned to the graphics.

She knew this dark path through the hills. It led through her own internal labyrinth, but she did not know what lay at the end of the road. It was so easy to get bogged down in the minutiae of getting from one place to another—and to lose sight of the goal.

But the goal was Ariel, wasn't it? Ariel, who, like a fairy-tale princess, was now held captive in the enemy citadel. But this princess had gone willingly. Ruth was reminded of the modern stories in which the maiden was perfectly happy with the dragon. What if Ariel didn't want to be rescued?

I can't leave her in his hands, no matter what she thinks now! said that anxious voice that had ruled her for so long. But what if it was this kind of solicitude that had driven Ariel away? *She said she wanted love, so I gave it to her!* her other self objected. The memory of how Ariel had turned away meshed suddenly with an image of the way she herself had retreated from the comfort of Tom's arms.

"The love I gave her was like the kind of love I wouldn't let Tom give to me!" she said aloud.

And he had let her do it, and now she was beginning to think that a day might come when she could accept him after all.

I must love Ariel not as I wish to, but in the way she needs! The conviction formed gradually. *I must make sure she is all right, and then I will let her go . . .*

Ruth walked down the flagstoned path through the garden, her awareness of the vivid green of moss on the gray stones, and the pink-and-rose masses of azalea bloom overlaid like a double-exposure her remembered images from the night before. It had seemed too silly to mention to Del, but she had found it surprisingly easy to visualize the Otherworld, because what she saw was the same as the images of the City she had been creating on her computer screen.

Or had she created them? Was it possible that her unconscious had already accessed the inner planes even before her involvement with Del and the Paradise drug had begun? The thought was disturbing, and Ruth zipped up her maroon sweatshirt even though the air was still relatively warm.

The light of the setting sun still glowed in shades of peach and rose, but now and again a breath of moisture in the air presaged the mist that would be rising soon. Ruth breathed in deeply, appreciating the delicate perfume of flowers and the richer smell of new-turned earth where Tom had been working in the garden. She could hear the scrape of his trowel ahead somewhere. From the open window above and behind her came Martin's triumphant spurt of laughter, and she knew he must have scored in the chess game he had persuaded David to play.

Ruth brushed past the shiny leaves of the rhododendron and almost bumped into Tom, who was taking advantage of the last daylight to plant the tulips that someone had given their downstairs neighbor, Lorraine, for Valentine's Day.

"I'm sorry—did I step on anything crucial?" She stood on one foot to inspect the sole of her running shoe.

Tom laughed and put up a hand to steady her. "No problem. I was just finishing up here anyway. Isn't the sunset fine?"

Ruth nodded. She put her foot down again, but did not move away. She could feel the warmth of his hand on her leg, and found it oddly comforting.

"From here, you can see the Bay through the gap in the trees." He spread out his blue jacket and patted it invitingly.

After a moment's hesitation, Ruth sat down beside him. For a little while neither of them said anything. Between the fringed silhouettes of the pines just below them and the dim gray of the flatlands, street and house lights twinkled through massed trees. But within the frame of pine branches the distant waters glimmered like mother-of-pearl, and the perfect shape of Mt. Tamalpais rose like a transparency behind them, watching over the Bay.

"Have you had any news about Ariel?" Tom said after a little while.

"Sort of—" Ruth frowned. "David and I did a ritual with Del and I sensed her over there somewhere—" she waved southward. "I think she's with Joseph Roman and those Order of Omega people Del told us about—at least something like that chased us back to our circle again."

"But you don't know exactly where?"

Ruth shook her head, then stilled as another thought came to her. "But I bet there's somebody who does! Joseph must have told those two women he lives with where he was going to be. Tomorrow I'll go see them—"

"—And if they tell you where to find him? What are you going to do then?"

There was some emotion in Tom's voice that she could not identify. As she turned to look at him, he put his arm around her, and for a moment she was vividly aware of its strength and the warmth of his body close to hers.

"I'll go there—I'll try to get inside and talk to Ariel, and if she wants to leave, I'll bring her back with me," Ruth said at last, staring out over the bay.

"Let me come with you—" Tom said immediately. She

gave him a quick look. The strong muscles along his jaw were tense and she could not see his eyes.

"Why? I know you helped with the ritual, but this is different—"

"More dangerous, you mean," he said dryly. "Why are you trying to rescue Ariel?"

"Because—" how could she explain the tangle of emotions that had bound her and Ariel for so many years? It went beyond gratitude to Ariel for helping her so long ago. It did not matter that it was Ariel who had gotten her into this mess in the first place. Their relationship was part of Ruth's own identity, and there was no way she could follow the shining path Del Eden had shown her until it was resolved. And even that was not the real answer.

"Because I love her—" Ruth said at last. Even if she did it badly, that was the reason behind it all.

"Well, maybe I love you . . ." His arm tightened around her, but he was still staring out at the bay.

"You want to get me in bed, you mean—" Ruth accused.

Tom made a small, exasperated noise, and then he did look at her, and what she saw in his face made the breath catch in her throat. The lines around his mouth were deep with remembered pain, but his eyes shone with a gardener's unending hope that what he has nurtured with such patience will one day burst into bloom.

It had never before occurred to Ruth to liken herself to a flower.

"Yes, I do want to make love to you, very much, but that's not the only reason I care. Have you been worrying yourself sleepless because you lust after Ariel?"

No, but I'm not a man . . . Ruth bit back the automatic rejoinder. Tom had certainly given her no reason to insult him, and as for wanting Ariel, it had been so long since she had felt passion that she really did not know.

Impulsively, she kissed Tom's cheek. He stilled, and she waited, feeling the pulse pound in her throat, as his hand came up to turn her face and he kissed her on the lips. Tom's fingers were rough from digging in the earth and calloused from gripping tools, but his lips were tender, brushing hers, exploring, questioning, until her taut mouth softened and she let him pull her all the way into his arms.

Ruth felt like a frozen river in a thaw; deep currents stirring with almost forgotten power, washing away the stains that rape and an unfulfilling marriage had left on her soul. When the ice melted entirely, everything in the river's path would be carried away. With an effort that cost more than she expected, she pulled away.

"Not now, not yet, please—" she said breathlessly. "I can't afford to find out what I feel for you until this thing with Ariel is done. Can you wait for me?"

His muscles hardened. She felt his heart beating heavily against her own. Then he gave a gusty sigh and the pressure eased.

"As I wait for the flowers to grow . . ." His whisper echoed Ruth's own perception.

She relaxed against him again, and they sat in silence while the sunset sky dimmed to a misty dusk. But within Ruth's awareness, another radiance was growing. The inner light that had come less often as the breakdown products of the Paradise drug left Ruth's system budded suddenly in her awareness, then flowered in a silent splendor that included herself, and Tom, and all the lovely world around them in its single, many-petaled bloom.

13.

This region is closed on all sides, its
interior made up of intercommunicating
labyrinths. The protection is so complete as
to turn back all that is devilish and
undesirable . . .

Wei Po-yang, "An Ancient
Chinese Treatise on Alchemy"

"What do you want?"

Eyes glittered from the shadows behind Joseph Roman's
front door. After the brightness outside, it was hard to
see who it was. Ruth swallowed, wishing the knots in her
gut would go away, and trying to remember why she had
come.

"Master Joseph's not here—" the girl added, and started
to close the door.

"No—I know—" blurted Ruth. "It's you I need to talk
to—Ava, isn't it? Can I come in?"

Grudgingly, the door eased open. Ruth recognized the girl
who had been with Joseph when she was here before, but
there was no spring in her step now. Ava's hair straggled
down over stooped shoulders; even her big breasts seemed to
be drooping now. Her sweatshirt was dirty, and she looked as
if she had been crying.

Ruth followed her into the living room, wondering just
how she was going to persuade Ava to talk to her. At least
she had let her in. The coffee table was littered with dirty

dishes and soft drink cans, and magazines lay scattered on the floor.

"Are you looking for Joseph?" Ava asked abruptly. The couch wheezed as she sat down. Ruth took the straight chair she had used when she was here before. "Why?"

"I think he's with a friend of mine," Ruth said carefully. "She hasn't been well, and I'd like to see how she is. I expect you'd like to have Master Joseph back, too—"

"I'm not sure, but I don't want *her* to have him!" said Ava viciously.

"Ariel?"

"Who? Oh, not your friend—unless he's screwing her, too. I mean Mrs. Winslow!" Ava sank further into the couch, legs crossed untidily.

Ruth's eyes widened as she realized there was more wrong here than simple jealousy.

"I don't think he wanted my friend for sex . . ." Ruth said slowly, thinking out loud. "But she is very psychic. They might want to use her for something, and if I can get her away maybe they won't need him anymore . . ."

"Use her! I'll bet he is, the bastard! That's all any of them do—use people, just like he used me!" Ava started crying noisily, and Ruth rummaged in her bag for some Kleenex.

"Where does Mrs. Winslow live?"

"Don't tell her, Ava!"

Ruth jumped as the woman who had assisted Master Joseph at the ritual hurried into the room. She looked a little worn, but not desolate. *Laurel*—with an effort, Ruth remembered her name.

Still snuffling, Ava turned and glared at her.

"Why not? When you asked what we should say to the police if they came back here, he just laughed!"

"Laurel, I have reason to believe that Master Joseph has gotten involved with some dangerous people," Ruth changed tack abruptly. "It will be better for him if he comes back to you . . ."

"He can handle himself—" Laurel began, but she looked uncertain.

"Are you sure?" Ruth leaned forward, surprised at her own sincerity. "I've felt the power of the people he's with now, and they're really bad. And anyway, if Master Joseph didn't mind the police knowing, what harm can it do to tell me?"

Ava heaved herself out of the sofa and began to shuffle through the loose papers beside the telephone.

"Here, it's Mrs. Winslow's address in Piedmont. He left it in case we needed to contact him there—" Words and paper were offered quickly, but Laurel made no move to stop her.

Ruth glanced at it and thrust it into her purse.

"Wait—" Laurel stopped her halfway to the door. "If you see Joseph, tell him we love him and want him to come home!"

Ava was beginning to cry again. Ruth stared at them both, wondering if Joseph Roman had simply hypnotized both of these women or if maybe he had some good in him after all. Then she shook her head and went out into the brightness of the day.

If this were only just another sequence in my game! thought Ruth as Tom's truck swayed and rattled up the hill. *Then I'd know what to look out for!* Her guts felt like the tracks on a circuit board, and she understood the message they were sending—*fear*.

Mehitabel's powerful headlights flashed across a velvet lawn as they rounded a curve, the gardening tools in the back of the truck rattling musically. Ruth caught the flicker of color from a garden, the ornate facade of an Elizabethan mansion, then a massive, dry-stone wall. Piedmont was the elite district of Oakland, an area of massive houses with Bay views, staffed by maids and chauffeurs and surrounded by manicured yards.

"You ever work for anybody up here?" David asked across her. Ruth could sense tension in him, but not fear. It was more like the energy that surrounded a football player before a big game.

"Once or twice," Tom answered. "Not much taste around here, but lots of money, that's for sure. Anyway, I got to know the area. That's why I volunteered to drive."

Ruth grimaced. Tom had insisted on driving, probably because he was afraid that otherwise she would sneak off and leave him behind. Ruth had not argued. After their conversation in the garden the preceding evening, she no longer knew whether to welcome his protection or worry about his safety. Every irregularity in the road jounced her against him, and the feel of his hard strength was bringing back distracting memories.

Another curve revealed the dark expanse of the Mountain View Cemetery immediately below them, and the fairy lights of the city beyond it, beginning to blur now as rising mist thickened the air. Here the lots were larger, edged by hedges or walls. One could only guess at the lines of the houses whose lights glimmered through the trees.

"And my tools may come in handy if we have trouble getting in," Tom added cheerfully as he downshifted and Mehitabel chugged up another hill.

Ruth shuddered. That was what she was afraid of. It seemed to her now that Tom had insisted on coming along not to protect her, but because he had some misguided idea it would be fun. They were probably all going to end up in jail. And though it would almost be worth it to see the look on Leonard's face when he came down to the police station to post bail for the mother of his son, she didn't really want to deal with that now.

David flicked on the penlight and peered at the map again. "We're on Templar Place, but I don't see any Templar Court marked here."

"It's probably a private road," said Tom. "Keep your eyes open—there will be a very discreet sign somewhere on what looks like a drive. When they have parties up here, they station a guard at the entrance to direct traffic. Otherwise, if you can't find an address it's because you're not supposed to know." He let the truck slow down.

Ruth sighed, knowing that by herself she wouldn't have gotten this far, and wondering if that might not have been better for them all. But at this rate, they were unlikely to get anywhere anyway. This was not a computer game in which she could have found the entrance by typing in the proper spell.

And what spell would I sing? Ruth wondered then. *Ariel . . . Ariel . . . Ariel . . .* But there was no response, not even the essence of lilac that had guided her on the inner planes two nights before.

"There . . ." said David suddenly. Tom took his foot off the gas pedal and Mehitabel rolled almost noiselessly to a stop in front of a pillar faced with marble, from whose top a lantern glittered mistily. Chiseled into the front of the pillar was the address they had been looking for.

Beyond the pillar, smooth stone walls curved inward to an iron gate that was tightly closed.

"Well, you weren't expecting to just walk up and ring the doorbell, were you?" asked Tom when Ruth came back from checking the lock.

She stared at him. *The entrance to the estate is shut against you—you must find another way . . .* She could not remember if she had already written that obstacle into Forbidden City. As the mist thickened, it was becoming harder to believe she was still living in ordinary reality. But who was writing the script for *her*, if this was a game?

Later, when Ruth thought about what happened then, it seemed to her that this sense of unreality had made it easier to do what they did that night, and afterward, to remain sane.

Running without lights or motor, Tom let Mehitabel roll downhill until he could park her in a pull-out under the trees. Then they moved cautiously along the boundary, looking for a gap in the hedge. Close to half an hour had passed before they found it, and when they did, Tom's penlight showed that the greenery had hidden a strong chain-link fence, the top of which was interlaced with barbs.

"They don't believe in leaving much to chance—" Tom peered upward. "The lighter wire that runs along the top is probably connected to an alarm."

"Well, that's why we hauled your toolkit along." Metal clunked as David set it down. "I did some electronics when I was an undergrad. With a little luck I should be able to short it out, and cut the barbed wire . . ." There was a short silence as the two men looked at Ruth.

Common sense told her to give up now, to go home. But the moist air brought her the breath of hidden gardens, and suddenly Ruth was back in her childhood, the only girl in a neighborhood of boys, who kept her place among them by never refusing a dare. There had been one night like this one, heady with the promise of spring, when they had carried off the laundry that the mean old lady on the corner had left out on her line, and arranged it ceremoniously on the Methodist Church lawn.

Giggling absurdly, Ruth waved at David to go ahead and cut the wire.

"Look, David, I really think you should stay here with the car—" Ruth said when he was done. "I mean, you've spent the week hiding from these people. It doesn't make much sense to walk into their arms now—''

David shrugged. ''I can't. This week nearly drove me crazy, and I can't hide forever. I'd just as soon let them capture me—maybe if I talk to this friend of Joseph's I can convince him I'm not gonna be any use to him.'' He grinned suddenly, and Ruth had the sudden irrational conviction that he had some kind of plan.

Clearly, whatever madness had infected Ruth had affected the two men as well. The perfumes of the garden were alluring; none of them could stop now. They came out from the shadow of a line of cypresses and saw the house rising above them, its pale stone ghostly in the misty air.

But, except for the light above the door, it was dark and very still. The sixth sense Ruth had been developing seemed to have deserted her. She had no feeling of Ariel's presence in the house ahead of her—only in the gazebo they had passed in the garden.

Then they stepped onto the terrace, and abruptly the enchantment of the garden was replaced by a clammy dread. Ruth tried to go forward, but her skin tingled unpleasantly; from the stone walls of the building, dark windows peered at her like the empty eyes of a skull.

David exclaimed under his breath and stopped, shivering. Tom stepped closer to Ruth and put his arm around her.

''What's wrong?'' he whispered.

''Don't you feel it?'' Ruth answered. ''But maybe you wouldn't,'' she went on, not entirely understanding what she meant herself. ''Your feet are on the ground.'' Supported by Tom's stability, Ruth extended her awareness toward the building again.

Again that chill that was more than physical crept through her, disorienting and demoralizing. Tom's steady strength helped her to bear it, and she thought that, with him to hold on to, she might even manage to continue. But with all her senses focused on that effort she would have no hope of locating Ariel.

''It's warded against us—'' she said softly. ''We should have expected that. I don't think we can go on.''

''Do you want to go back, then?'' asked Tom hopefully, and she realized that he must be picking up some of it, too.

"No," she said decisively. "I'm going to knock at the front door."

Both men stared at her.

"Well, at least they won't be able to accuse us of breaking and entering, although they may wonder how we got onto the grounds. I wasn't planning to carry Ariel off by force, anyway. Maybe they'll let me talk to her."

They turned and started around the building. The prickling sensation on Ruth's skin grew stronger. Then a dog snarled softly, and a blinding explosion of brilliance stopped them where they stood.

"That's it, stay right where you are—don't anybody even *try* to move!"

Footsteps grated on stone, and Ruth squinted beneath the arm with which she was shielding her eyes. She saw Tom spotlighted in his blue windbreaker and yellow rubber boots, and David, in his loose jacket with his hands over his eyes. And coming toward them she saw a burly man whose hair was clipped almost to the point of baldness, with an equally sleek Doberman straining at his side.

"If you're the doorman," Ruth said between her fingers, "please tell Miss Ashton that a friend has come to call!"

He gave a short bark of laughter, signaled, and abruptly the intensity of the lighting was dimmed so that it was possible to see. The guard slipped off his dark glasses, and David, whimpering, took his hands away from his eyes.

"It's *him!*" Swift footsteps brought another man into the light, pistol in hand. This one was slimmer, dressed in a gray suit and tie. "It's that hippie scientist that fucked up Max—"

The guard's hand snapped out and grabbed the speaker's wrist as the gun swung toward David, who was still blinking owlishly, trying to see. With sick understanding, Ruth realized that Max must have been the man on whom David had thrown the sulfuric acid when he was attacked at the lab.

"Not without orders! If this is the guy you went after, the Boss wants him, remember? If you touch him without orders you'll get burned worse than Max!" He plucked the weapon from the other man's hand.

"The Boss . . . yeah—" The man in the gray suit relaxed and grinned nastily. "He has his own ways of getting even, I've heard."

"Yes, you might say that," the guard said dryly. "All

right, you—hands up against the wall!'' He gestured toward the side of the house.

Unpleasantly aware of the gun, Ruth complied. More men came out of the house to surround them. One of them patted her up and down, hands squeezing her breast painfully as they went by. From the corner of her eye, Ruth could see that the two men were being searched as well.

''Well, well, what have we here?'' The man in the gray suit pulled a green plastic water pistol from the pocket of David's raincoat. ''More acid, is it?'' Before anyone could stop him he squeezed the trigger, and a stream of clear liquid squirted across David's cheek.

For a moment no one breathed.

David had jerked when the stuff struck him, but he did not scream, and in a few seconds the liquid began to dry, leaving his skin unmarred. The guard touched his finger to the tip of the squirt gun, sniffed for a moment, then laughed mockingly.

''Well, if it makes you feel more secure, little boy, I guess you can keep your gun!'' Still laughing, he jammed the water pistol into David's pocket again, jerked him around and snapped handcuffs on.

A water pistol! Clearly a week in her loft had turned David's brain. Or maybe he had caught the insanity from her. Ruth could not tell whether she was suffering worst from mortification or anxiety.

''What are you doing?'' The cold touch of metal on her own wrists took Ruth by surprise. ''Just let me make one phone call! My ex-husband is a lawyer—you can't hold us here!''

''What makes you think we intend to?'' asked the guard with the dog. A man came out of the house and for a moment they spoke in low tones. Ruth saw satisfaction, excitement, and an odd hint of pity mingle briefly in the man's eyes. ''You'll get your phone call, maybe, when you've told your story to Abaddon!''

The name rang in her ears with a terrifying splendor. And in the moment before they were hustled into a long gray car, Ruth identified the feeling in the pit of her stomach definitely as fear, and focused all her energy into a wordless mental call.

Del Eden was trying to reconcile the month's billings from the distributors with her sales, when she felt her skin chill and her grasp on the figures broken by a painful mental turmoil. She stiffened, listening, but the street outside the bookstore was still.

It had not been physical, then—of course not. Del closed her eyes and let her body relax, turning her attention simultaneously inward and outward as she focused on a sense for which most people have no words.

The reverberations of the cry she had perceived still troubled the inner planes, like ripples from a thrown stone in a quiet pond. But like the stone, the source of the disturbance had disappeared. Del could detect in it only the pattern of fear, and the faintest sense of identity.

Steadying her breathing to control her own anxiety, she reached for the telephone and began to dial.

"Hello?" It was the voice of a sleepy child, and for a moment Del thought she had the wrong number.

"Is this Martin? Is your mother home?"

"She went out with David and Uncle Tom, but it's okay, because the lady downstairs is home . . ." he said. And then, belatedly, "Who are you?"

"This is the lady from the bookstore with the crystals—you came in with your mother one day. Can you tell me how long they've been gone?"

"Oh . . ." there was a short silence. "Mom wanted to wait until my bedtime, but Tom said it might take them a while to find the place they were looking for. I guess it was about nine-thirty—" As he woke up, Martin's answers were getting clearer.

"Did Ruth tell you where they were going?"

"Not her, but David said something about going to see Aunt Ariel."

Why didn't she tell me! thought Del. But the answer was obvious—Ruth must have known that Del would try to stop her. The important question was, what was happening to her now? She managed to say good-bye to Martin without alarming him, and sat for a few moments thinking hard. Then she picked up the receiver again and called Michael and Karen Holst.

From the outside, the Claremont Hotel glowed like an illuminated wedding cake. Inside, it was more as if the frosted decorations had come to glittering life. Against the

warm beige and pink and rose colors of the decor, costumes
that ranged from exquisite to silly—but were all expensive—
bounced and swirled. As Joseph Roman followed Joanna
Winslow and Abaddon through the glass doors into the hotel,
the concerted sound of a dance band, a singer, and several
hundred people chattering like inmates of the zoo they resem-
bled smote his ears.

Ariel shrank against him and Joseph patted her arm reassuringly. The pre-party cocktail hour they had come from had
been quieter. He pulled uncomfortably at the gorilla suit that
Joanna had rented for him. The head was even more awk-
ward, and he was still carrying it under his arm. Ariel, on the
other hand, looked as lovely as he had ever seen her, her slim
legs covered by iridescent white tights, and the rest of her by
a gauzy creation in pearly white and pale grays and blues that
managed to suggest wings.

Obviously, she had been typecast as Ariel. But who did
that make him, Caliban? Joseph could not decide whether to
be amused or angry. It all depended, he supposed, on whether
the costumes were an expression of Joanna de Laurent's sense
of humor, or of some deep gamesmanship on the part of
Abaddon. In the meantime, however, he would have to do the
best he could with this ridiculous outfit. Perhaps Abaddon
was testing his social aplomb.

Certainly Abaddon himself was free of any such handicap.
He swept regally ahead of them, looking quite at home in the
crimson robes of Cardinal Richelieu. As Joseph watched him,
he realized that the other man had managed to suggest spiritual authority without committing the occult solecism of appearing in the robes of his Order. One could see the suppressed
impulse toward genuflection in some of those they passed,
and from a few others, a salutation of more than social
significance. Joseph noted the faces of those who were not
masked, wondering if one of these days he would see them
robed in crimson, too.

The four men who followed them wore the loose red
surcoats of the Cardinal's guard over suits of maroon velvet.
Lace collars and plumed hats seemed oddly incongruous above
their expressionless faces and perpetually watchful eyes, but
it was certainly clear to whom they belonged. A buzz of
appreciative comment followed as the entourage swept into

the Gaslite Room, bearing witness to the effectiveness of the outfits, or possibly to the personality of Abaddon.

A table had been reserved for them. Drinks appeared. Abaddon helped Joanna out of the ankle-length Ember mink coat she wore, and handed it to one of his men to be taken up to the Tower Suite, which they had rented for more private partying later on. Underneath it, she was wearing the net tights and spangled red corset of Lola from *Damn Yankees*, the role in which she had been most successful when she was on the stage.

In any other company their contrasts would have been comic, thought Joseph, but here were pirates and clowns, a lady in a Carmen Miranda hat with a man in a walking Smile face, two halves of a donkey, and several creations that could have appeared in the latest science-fiction epic. Joseph took a long swallow of scotch and soda, and began to relax.

Joanna took Ariel off to find the ladies' room, and a riverboat gambler and a kilted highlander eased into their empty chairs. Joseph came alert once more, for these men had the same well-kept efficiency about them as Luciano Abaddon. He felt their eyes resting on him questioningly.

"This is Joseph Roman—" Abaddon nodded in answer. "He has considerable experience in handling people and power. I'm training him for a management position in the firm."

Joseph responded with a brief, uninformative smile, and saw the others accept his presence and then forget it as they turned their attention back to Abaddon.

"Have you spoken with the Judge yet?"

"He'll go along." The riverboat gambler answered Abaddon with a nod. "He understands the stakes involved. The Forces that are moving here now will affect the entire country soon."

"Yes, the subtle forces behind the decisions—where to invest, who to appoint, how to vote—the time to influence them is before the alternatives become clear . . ." Abaddon agreed.

"We'll hafta force the Forces then—" The highlander laughed as if he had drunk a little too much, and the other two looked at him coldly.

"The Governor *must* be reelected," Abaddon went on. Crimson taffeta rustled as he set down his drink. "He is serving us already without knowing it. When he does know it, he will have no choice but to cooperate. His own ethnic background is barely acceptable. I don't think he'll care where we draw the line, so long as he is on the side with the power.''

"The power—" the gambler sighed. "That's what it's all about, isn't it? When we have it, we'll be secure.''

"Can he follow directions?''

"He will follow the script we write for him—he won't be the first to do it, after all!''

Joseph felt the hair rising on his neck as he realized what they were talking about. He kept his eyes determinedly on his drink, afraid of what they might reveal. Spiritual power had been his specialty, and though he had dreamed of influencing the rich and famous in the manner of Nostradamus or John Dee, he had never thought about the form effective influence would have to take today. Psychological coercion he understood, but these men were talking about control of the highest offices, and political and economic manipulations on a scale far beyond anything he had ever dared to dream.

But once one considered the current situation in the country dispassionately, it ought to be obvious that, to straighten things out, extraordinary measures would be required. Men had been trying to achieve the perfect society by means of force or legislation for centuries. But the real changes had to come from within. Changes in a nation's psyche could be effected haphazardly by encouraging new movements in the arts and be popular culture, or precisely, by the calculated manipulation of symbols and energies on the inner planes. If the idea bothered him, thought Joseph, it must be because he was playing out of his usual league.

But I'll get used to it— he told himself as he finished his drink and signaled for more. *If Abaddon thinks I'm worth training, then I'll damn well learn!* He really had no choice. If Abaddon had his way, independent practitioners such as he had been would be persecuted out of existence anyway.

"Our day will come, won't it?" asked the highlander wistfully. Abaddon looked at the man with a cold appraisal that made Joseph put his own drink down.

"At the Omega hour our hope will soar across the heavens on fiery wings—" Abaddon's voice was pitched low, but he had given it the cadence and resonance of ritual. Joseph saw the effects of long conditioning in the way the two men at the table straightened and stilled. "Those who have been diligent and faithful, He will reward with authority over all living things; but those who are foolish or treacherous will be cast into the Abyss!'' Abaddon's quiet voice snapped out the final words, and Joseph knew that however rich and powerful they might be, the other two men felt the same chill that pebbled his own skin.

How far, he wondered, would Abaddon go to enforce that fidelity?

A woman dressed as a dance hall girl undulated among the tables toward them, with Ariel in tow.

''I do hope you all are finished talking business—'' She leaned over the gambler and kissed him. ''Joanna's going to sing for us in a minute or two. I've brought Miss Ashton back so we can all sit down and hear!''

Abruptly, the sense of danger receded, and the evening became merely a social occasion once more.

The gambler stood up, smiling, and escorted his lady back to a table nearby, and the highlander followed him. Joseph pulled out the chair for Ariel, and she eased down beside him with a sigh.

''I'm not quite as strong yet as I thought I was—'' she whispered. ''All these people! But they have been very kind—''

Joseph pushed the glass dish of peanuts in front of her. ''Here—''

''Oh no, I'm not hungry, especially now!'' Smiling, she shook her head.

''Eat something!'' Joseph commanded. ''If you can't eat these, I'll order something you can. You'll never get through the evening if you don't ground yourself now, and food is one of the best ways.''

''Yes, I know—'' she picked up a peanut and looked at it distastefully. ''I never wanted to be earthbound. That's probably why I have such trouble eating.''

''But food and sex are the two things that make it worthwhile having bodies at all!'' Joseph grinned.

''Would you be shocked if I told you that I've always felt sex was overrated as well?'' Ariel looked up at him and Joseph recognized around her eyes the purple smudges of fatigue that Joanna's careful make-up could not hide.

He *was* shocked, though he did not show it, and almost for the first time he considered Ariel as a woman, and wondered what kind of patient expertise might be required to bring her

joy. Could he do it? She was not the type of female who
usually inspired him, but having observed her so closely over
the past days, Joseph had become aware of the classic bone
structure beneath her delicate skin. Ariel had a kind of blood-
less beauty already. What, he wondered once more, would
she be like if she were whole?

A clamor of appreciative applause brought his attention
back to the stage. The portly gentleman in the clown's suit
who was acting as master of ceremonies was announcing the
still-great star of stage and screen, Joanna de Laurent. The
house lights went out, the pianist struck up a few chords and,
when the dusty pink curtains opened, Joanna stood, spangles
glittering, in a rosy spot of light that took fifteen years off her
age.

> *"Whatever Lola wants, then Lola gets—*
> *and what she wants, little man, is you!"*

Somehow, she managed to project the song simultaneously
to every man in the room. Joseph strove for self-possession,
but he could not entirely control his reactions. He had never
seen Joanna de Laurent on the stage, but now he understood
that it was not lack of talent that had induced her to retire.

Joseph missed the song's ending as one of the Cardinal's
guards bent to whisper into Abaddon's ear. Even without
understanding, Joseph caught the note of tension and an
electric quality of anger in the man next to him. As the lights
in the room began to brighten, he and Ariel saw that Abaddon
was staring at the door, and followed his gaze.

In the entrance, still in street clothes, were three more of
Abaddon's men. Joseph realized in astonishment that the
people standing so stiffly between them were David Mason,
Ariel's friend Ruth, and another man.

14.

David Mason looked at himself in the mirror, giggled, and
realized that he was stoned. The sight of his own eyes blinking owlishly beneath a wizard's pointed hat, while the rest of
him was draped in a voluminous robe covered with moons
and stars, would probably have set him off anyway, but the
stars kept trying to turn into comets, and the moons pulsed
with a rainbow glow. The light fixture in the bathroom shimmered with rainbows, too.

This was different from the last time. David's sensory input
was distorted, but he was still functional. Some part of his
mind as yet unaffected noted that, and thought that it would
have been interesting to properly study the variations in subjective experience. Unfortunately, part of the last batch of the
Paradise drug was now circulating merrily through his system, while the rest of it, dissolved in DMSO, was still
contained in the water pistol in his pocket beneath the robe.
The toy gun had been a marvelous idea, after all. That thug
would have destroyed a chemist's pipette, but who could be

afraid of a squirt gun? The thought started David laughing again.

Through the bathroom door he could hear the babble of conversation from the party outside—the private party that Luciano Abaddon had invited up to the Tower Suite of the hotel. When David came out of here he would have to pretend he was drinking to keep anyone from suspecting what was really wrong.

He and Ruth and Tom were being treated as guests, for now, and it had been Joanna Winslow's idea to further the pretence by putting them into some of the extra costumes. David made a face at the mirror and pulled the hat down over his eyes. He wasn't a wizard, he thought fuzzily—he was a goddamn *alchemist!* Still grinning inanely, he opened the bathroom door.

Ruth smoothed the midnight blue panné velvet of her gown self-consciously, and the spangled veil that Mrs. Winslow had draped over her head slipped off. She was sure she looked ridiculous. Wearing a costume was a ridiculous idea— she didn't even know what she was supposed to be. She glanced at Ariel, who looked utterly natural in her sylph outfit, and grimaced.

"Well, nobody asked you to come—" Ariel answered the look. "I don't quite understand why you *did* come. I wouldn't have thought this was your kind of thing . . ."

"It's not," Ruth answered shortly, too embarrassed to explain how they had been caught, cuffed, and carried off. What had begun as a somewhat harebrained escapade was becoming positively surreal. She had been expecting threats or physical torture, not the mental martyrdom of a society costume ball. "I was worried when you disappeared. I wanted to talk to you."

"Well, as you can see, I'm doing very well—" said Ariel. A graceful shrug of her shoulder indicated the people around them.

"Are you?" Ruth sighed and sat down on the cream-colored couch nearby, and after a moment's hesitation, Ariel joined her. In some ways her friend did look better than she had in the nursing home—Ruth realized now that some of her problems had probably been *caused* by the nursing home. But it seemed to her that there was something feverish about

Ariel's present gaiety. She was like a butterfly that knows if it stops fluttering it will fall.

And why the hell do I care? she asked herself. It was not this silly costume that made her feel such a fool—it was having made a fool of herself for someone who didn't need rescuing after all. And she had dragged Tom into it, too! Ruth cast a quick glance around her and located him having a civilized conversation about houseplants with Joanna Winslow. He had been too big for anything in the costume collection, but Mrs. Winslow had made him wear a broad-brimmed hat with a blue plume, so that he looked like a larger version of Tom Bombadil.

Tom seemed disgustingly contented. David was snickering over some private joke by the bar. Neither of them seemed to notice Ruth glaring at them. For a moment she hated both men, and Ariel, and herself most of all. She half-rose to stalk out of the room, saw the man whom Abaddon had stationed at the doorway, and settled back into the couch again.

She had forgotten the guards.

"Look, Ariel—you don't have the resources to join the jet set, and you can't live off Mrs. Winslow forever. What are you going to do?" She was still angry, but she knew that at least some of her suspicion about Joseph and his friends were true.

"I think I'm going to stay with Joseph, and work for Mr. Abaddon . . ." Ariel said dreamily. Ruth's shock must have shown in her expression, because Ariel shook her head, and then smiled. "Everything is different now. Joseph didn't force me to go away with him—he came to that place and talked to me, and he made me feel beautiful."

Ruth glanced across the room to where Joseph Roman, typecast in an ape suit, was talking to the magnificent crimson figure who had been introduced as Luciano Abaddon. There was something unnerving about the combination of man and beast in company with that incarnation of ecclesiastical power. She looked quickly back at Ariel.

"Is that what you want, Ariel—to be beautiful?" she asked softly.

"I must be—" Ariel did not meet her eyes as she answered her. "It is all I have."

Ruth stared at her in shamed silence, suddenly aware that something within her had *liked* seeing Ariel as she had looked in the hospital, and resented the way she looked now. She could hardly tell her friend that she had loved her better when she was ugly.

"You're brilliant and creative—you stick to something until you understand it and then you take it and do something new—" Ariel went on. "I always envied that. All I can do is try to reflect what people want and make it beautiful, but it never lasts. Ruth—what do you want from me?"

The question echoed down all the corridors of memory. But she could not seek for the answers—not here, not now. Ruth hid her face in her hands, afraid to see her own face reflected in Ariel's eyes.

"We will have to recruit them," Abaddon nodded toward Ruth and David, then turned back to Joseph. "The other fools in that group of yours are under control, and you can obviously handle Ariel. But these two know too much now, and they are causing entirely too much trouble."

Joseph frowned dubiously. He knew quite well that David had only given him the drug in the first place because he was stoned, and that friend of Ariel's was a bitch and a man-hater. Even the slinky dress Joanna had put on her could only streamline the force he felt in her, not disguise it. She was talking to Ariel now, and if he had not been with Abaddon, he would have gone over and taken Ariel away from her.

Abaddon interpreted his expression and smiled, his face smooth and sculptured above the crimson taffeta of the Richelieu robe. "No, I don't expect you to handle them—not until I have finished training you. But I want you to come along and listen while I talk to Mr. Mason. For the moment I'll leave the woman to Joanna. This first stage is a matter of psychology and the proper application of a little power."

Joseph nodded as if he understood, but his imagination was whirling. The suggestion of shared secrets and future revelations was heady—not so long ago, Abaddon had been practicing that psychology on *him*. He lifted his head and looked around at the selected guests who had been invited upstairs—an advertising executive, the owner of a newspaper, the vice president of the western branch of one of the oil companies. They were rich and powerful. A month ago they would have despised him. Tonight they ignored him.

A year from now, perhaps they would fear him.

Ariel was looking at him questioningly. Joseph returned her smile. In the past week they had begun to find out how good a medium she was—she had the kind of talent that can be invaluable to a leader in ritual, linking him to the other world while allowing him to maintain control on the outer planes. Abaddon had great plans for her, but it was he, Joseph, who gave her the confidence to try her wings.

Joseph had a certain native force and knowledge, and control. But except for the vision of the god within which had begun his study of magic, and the journey that he had been forced to make by Abaddon, he had little experience of the inner planes. Ariel balanced him. Together, they might even find that source of rapture once again. Together, who could tell what they might be able to do?

"You don't like the dress?" asked Joanna Winslow. "But have you really looked at yourself? You mustn't let false preconceptions blind you to your own beauty!"

Ruth was too dumbfounded to resist as Joanna steered her toward the large mirror above the credenza. She was still not quite sure how she had been detached from Ariel, but she was aware of a shamed relief that it had happened, for she had no answers for the questions that her friend had begun to ask.

But that did not excuse—Ruth stopped short as Joanna held her in front of the mirror, unable to deny that the clinging gown revealed an archaic strength in the lines of a body whose shape was not conventionally beautiful, and the spangled veil shadowed her blunt features with mystery.

"You should wear midnight blue more often," said Joanna. "It brings out the warm highlights in your hair."

Ruth straightened, still looking at the woman she saw in the mirror.

"Was that why you dressed me this way?"

"Not entirely—" Joanna smiled. "It seemed to me it was the kind of thing that Morgan LeFay might have worn, and you are a sorceress, aren't you?"

Ruth turned to stare at her, remembering the work she had done with Del. "What do you mean?"

"Ariel told me you're a programmer. Isn't that a modern sort of sorcery? These days, computers are part of our lives, but how many people really understand them? I don't, certainly. You can't imagine how I admire you because you do—'' The spangles on her costume gleamed as she gestured to a waiter to bring the drink tray around.

Ruth found it hard to imagine this elegant creature admiring her for anything. She accepted a glass of Dubonnet from the tray and took a steadying swallow.

"Well, I enjoy my work—I suppose *that's* unusual . . ."

Joanna sipped a little of her Martini and laughed. "That's because you are creating. Ariel said you were developing an adventure game?"

A little surprised that Ariel had remembered, Ruth nodded. "I have a contract with an outfit called Star Wares."

"I hope it assures you a fair share of the profits—I've heard stories of computer firms that got rich while their programmers starved."

Ruth shrugged. "Maybe. But they're the ones who offered me money, and I'm stuck with them now." Somehow her empty glass had been replaced with a full one, and she drank. She was not normally very interested in alcohol, but at the moment getting drunk seemed to be the only possible way to deal with the stresses and stupidities of the evening.

"Not necessarily," said Joanna. "Good lawyers can break bad contracts, and with the right connections, you could handle your own distribution and keep everything you made."

"But I don't want to mess with distribution—" Ruth blinked to bring Joanna into focus again.

"Well, you wouldn't necessarily have to. With the proper support, you would have creative freedom as well as marketing control." Joanna glittered in the soft lighting like some kind of mirage.

Ruth frowned. "What exactly are you offering?"

Joanna smiled brilliantly. "What do you need?"

Ruth drank quickly, beginning to understand why Ariel found these people so beguiling. What could she do with money and influence behind her? With her own company and the right people, she could develop the kind of educational games she had dreamed of—a coordinated system of materials, with adequate testing and distribution. The Forbidden City game was only a means toward that end.

"And suppose I was interested," she said carefully, finishing her drink. "What would you want in return?"

"Mr. Abaddon is interested in psychology. He feels that the relationship between the structure of a good program and the structure of the mind has not been sufficiently explored. It is possible that you could assist us in some experiments . . .''

A stairway led from the Tower Suite up to the open platform of the Claremont tower. As David followed Luciano Abaddon up the steps with Joseph behind him, he drew in a deep breath of damp air, hoping it would clear his head. The visual distortions were becoming more vivid, and he tried to remember how long it had taken him last time to lose contact with the external world. Sensitized by the drug, he could already feel the force in the other man, and he couldn't tell yet if his condition was going to make it easier for him to deal with Abaddon, or make him more vulnerable.

They came out onto the platform, a neo-Edwardian wooden structure that was a little smaller than the top of the Campanile, with four large, arched windows open to the raw air. David blinked as a flicker of red light rippled past him, then realized that this effect, at least, was external—two turning mirror balls had been suspended from the ceiling, and as they turned, colored lights set into the upper corners sent rainbows shimmering into the fog. How the hell was he going to interpret his perceptions correctly with this going on?

Had Abaddon somehow sensed his state and brought him up here to disorient him?

David was dimly aware of Joseph Roman looming in the background like a figure from his own closet of anxieties. But Joseph was only a shadow, indeed, compared with the solid power of Abaddon. David leaned against the parapet, fixed his eyes determinedly on the wooden floor, and waited, wondering what Abaddon had brought him up here to say.

"I have always liked high places—" The deep voice seemed distilled from the fog. "Look—you can see the whole world—"

On a clear day, maybe, but in this misty darkness? David turned to refute him, and saw the lights of Oakland glimmering in faerie geometries. And not only lights, for where Abaddon gestured, the dense air seemed to clarify. The green-lit peak of the Tribune tower appeared before him, larger than it should be from here, as if the image had been somehow magnified. Abaddon's hand moved again, and now he saw the supertankers docked in the Alameda harbor, and the giant structures of the derricks standing over them like Trojan Horses. Abaddon gestured northward with a sweep of his scarlet sleeve, and David saw oil storage tanks colored like Easter eggs nestled into the Richmond hills; westward, and he glimpsed the glittering financial fortresses of San Francisco, with the transmission tower, its joints picked out in rubies, poised on its hill behind them like a huge preying mantis deciding where to spring.

Were these pictures from the drug? What Abaddon was showing him was certainly less threatening than the visions David's own unconscious could provide. He began to relax.

"That's really pretty—"

"That is the world," said Abaddon. "Do you desire it?"

"No." He suppressed an impulse to giggle again.

"What, I wonder, do you desire?"

David blinked as a strong hand gripped his chin and he was forced to meet Abaddon's eyes. They were blacker than the night around him, reflecting the colored lights with a surface glitter that was fascinating. The rest of the world blurred around him, and David fought for control as he felt Abaddon's will infiltrating the cracks in his soul.

"You are a scientist," Abaddon said softly. "But not a team player, perhaps? Do you find it hard to harness your genius to someone else's load? You have done something brilliant, you know, and as you are placed now you will never receive the recognition you deserve."

David stiffened as he heard his own thoughts echoed, and sat down on a bench against the wall, but though he shut his eyes, he could not close his ears as Abaddon went on.

"You don't enjoy departmental politics, do you? Or the endless paperwork involved when you are running on government funds?" Abaddon's tone warmed, as if he were inviting David to share his wry exasperation at such folly. "Have you ever considered working for private industry?"

David shrugged. "I don't have my degree yet, and at least at the University you can come up with your own projects—"

"Ah—but in the University or outside it, doesn't your freedom depend on who you're working for? Suppose we offered to build you a lab of your own, perhaps up in the hills so that you didn't even have to deal with the city?"

Abruptly, David saw the buildings, so vividly that the scene seemed to hang in the air before him. Surely Abaddon saw it too, or he had plucked it out of David's head—but he knew, somehow he *knew*.

"Facilities, equipment, a few assistants whom *you* would choose . . . and your own choice of projects as well. Genius is not so common that we can afford to waste it on the goals of lesser minds. The manipulation of DNA is the magic of the future. I am sure that we could find a use for anything that you might want to do . . ."

Visions flickered through David's awareness. He gripped the edge of the bench he sat on, hoping the pain would hold him to reality. The drug's augmentation of imagination was betraying him now, as vistas of untrammeled experimentation extended themselves before him—all the projects he had ever dreamed of, and more, unfolding in dizzying profusion.

But he must not—there was a catch to it, why couldn't he remember? David felt consciousness teetering on the brink of some crucial awareness, while the bright vision beckoned ever more strongly.

The Otherworld became ever clearer as Del Eden sank deeper into trance. She had not sensed Ruth since that first frantic call, but David Mason's presence flickered in and out disturbingly. Yet there was something odd about it—after their psychic expedition in search of Ariel, Del had thought she knew the flavor of his mind, and this ebullience was hard to understand.

It was especially hard to understand if David had gone with Ruth to the house where Ariel had been and run into the same danger. The little sense she had of him indicated that they had moved, or been moved. But where?

She extended her own awareness farther, upheld by the steady glow of energy that was Karen, and guarded by Michael's strength, suspended in stillness, waiting for some disturbance in the astral ocean to tell her where Ruth and David were now.

And then it came, blossoming into a confusion of images in which she sensed both of them, mixed with a corrupt sweetness that set every nerve twitching. She drew on Michael and Karen for energy, and got a sudden clear impression of a high place lit by spheres of rainbow light. Refocusing made it a beacon; Del strengthened the link until, abruptly, the channel was clear to both Ruth and David, and she could see what they saw, and hear what they heard.

*   *   *

Ruth's head was buzzing. Disorganized impressions of the rest of the party, even a breath of damp air and a dazzle of colored lights, which she identified for some reason with David, competed for her awareness. Around and around it swirled. Joanna stood surrounded by a rosy blur. Ruth was whirling down, down—why not agree and let it carry her away?

"You're crashing, Ruth!" came a thought that was not her own. "*Get out of the loop—break free!*"

Ruth met Joanna's eyes, struggling to clear the haze from perceptions as disorganized as the random bits on a computer screen. *Got to stop it,* she thought. Kinesthetic memory moved her arm toward the place where the interrupt switch would be. Automatically, Ruth's fingers flickered, and her tongue was freed. She met Joanna's glowing eyes.

"No . . ."

The physical world had disappeared. David sensed Abaddon's presence like a magnet, and farther away, that of Ruth, shaken by visions of her own. Consciousness became increasingly symbolic. David saw himself as a flat *heme* molecule, being embraced by the tubular *globin* that was Abaddon.

Change your symbolism! The thought came from somewhere outside him, familiar, but not Abaddon's. Yes—something incompatible—the image of cyclic AMP formed in David's awareness, and abruptly he was repelled by a force as strong as his earlier attraction.

The world came back into focus around him. With an effort, David met Abaddon's glittering eyes. His voice creaked out the one word necessary.

"No."

Negation cracked consciousness as Abaddon became aware of the power that had broken his spell. His furious response was a blast of darkness that sent Del hurtling back to Michael's protection and snapped her contact with his prisoners.

Ruth felt David flung to the floor of the tower, and herself rocked back against the wall, as Abaddon's anger reverberated across the inner and outer planes. For a few moments, shock stunned her physical senses; then with an internal effort she rallied, managed to separate her own awareness from David's, and opened her eyes.

Joanna was sprawled ungracefully on the couch, rubbing her forehead.

Of course, thought Ruth. *She's probably linked to him.* Ariel appeared to have fainted, and the others seemed stunned or confused in degrees, depending on their psychism or how close they were to Abaddon. Those who were recovering stiffened as heavy steps shook the Tower stairs.

"My brothers of the Order, we have a small job to do—"

Ruth blinked as Abaddon appeared in the stairwell. Though his face was still flushed and his eyes glittered, the anger that had shocked them was changing to something more like the look on Martin's face when he was about to squash a bug that had lit on his plate—a mingling of outrage and glee.

"There's a witch out there who thinks she can oppose us—she's tried it before, and now she's meddling again. These three are her spies—" his finger stabbed at Ruth and Tom, and upward toward David, still in the tower. "They shall watch us destroy her, and then they shall serve Omega's will!"

"In the Name of Omega!" came the murmur of assent. Men pulled themselves to their feet and saluted Abaddon.

Still too dazed to really understand, Ruth heard him snapping out swift orders, and people began to move. Besides the bodyguards in costume and plainclothes, perhaps a half-dozen men remained in the room. It was only when one of the Cardinal's guards took her arm and forced her toward the stairs that she recovered enough to protest. Most of these people were powers in their own right—weren't they even going to ask Abaddon what he meant to do?

Their glances slid away from her as she was dragged past. She could glimpse in some faces discomfort, or even a kind of shamed pity, and in some, an expression that was closer to lust. But no one offered aid. She heard the sound of a scuffle behind her and saw Tom struggling with two of the more muscular men, but in a moment an armlock immobilized him, and he, too, was being forced up the stairs.

They came out onto the platform, and Ruth coughed as she gulped in damp air. The fog that had been rising earlier had now completely swallowed the town; it swirled hungrily about the tower, and only an intermittent glimmer suggested that a city still existed below. But something about this was familiar— abruptly Ruth remembered the astral mist in which she had wandered after taking the Paradise drug at Joseph's ritual. She shivered, not entirely from the cold.

Her captors shoved her down next to a crouched form that she recognized as David, and pushed Tom after her. It was a little warmer below the parapet and, huddled together, their combined body heat began to counteract the cold. Ruth took a deep breath and tried to pull up energy from the earth as Del had taught her. But all she could feel was Tom's steady strength holding her.

"Can you still touch Del?" she murmured in David's ear.

It took too long for him to understand her question, and when his head turned, more than the glitter of the candles was reflected in his eyes. But finally he nodded.

"What are we going to do?"

If David answered, his words were lost in a soul-scratching squeak as Abaddon bent to inscribe a series of symbols in chalk on the wooden floor. He straightened, motioned people to their places around the circle, and stepped inside the triangle he had drawn. Votive lights borrowed from the bar flickered madly in their glasses at the points of the pentagram, and other things, taken from a leather case that must have been in one of the cars, were laid out on a hassock from downstairs.

Abaddon's arms lifted like blood-red wings, and even the candle flames grew still. He looked around the circle, and smiled.

"In the name of Omega I summon you to the Circle of Power! The Lord of the Latter Days calls you to witness the punishment of those who would dispute His sovereignty!"

Joseph listened to the words of invocation with an odd mixture of professional curiosity about how Abaddon was going to manage a ritual under such conditions, a touch of unreasoning fear as he remembered what had happened to him the last time he had heard them, and some of the vicarious tension men feel watching auto racing or any other dangerous game. This time he could appreciate the power in the words themselves, and the discipline required to deliver them. And he could sense the energies they were raising, locking each power into place with calculated skill.

Ariel clung to his arm, quivering at each charged phrase. He glanced at her face, saw her already half-tranced, and took her hand. She shuddered then, and turned to him.

"I can feel them, Joseph—" she whispered, "but these aren't the same powers you used to call. They don't like people. Joseph, I'm afraid."

He could feel her shivering, in long, regular pulses like sea waves, and once more wished his own psychic senses were stronger.

"The circle is cast and warded, the powers await our command." Abaddon's voice was blurred by the fog, so that it was hard to tell from which direction it came. "Now we must prepare the instrument to enforce our will— Come here—" He beckoned to Ariel.

She took an involuntary step forward, then stopped. "What do you want me to do?"

"Lie down on that folded blanket and be still. Let consciousness go and I will direct you. You are tired now, aren't you? Lie down and you can rest . . . Your legs and arms are heavy, yes—you want to sleep—that's right, ease down now, down and down . . ."

Like a sleepwalker, Ariel moved forward. Her shivering was visible now, and as she settled back on the blanket, candlelight glittered in eyes gone wide with fear. The four men who were still dressed as Cardinal's guards drew their rapiers and set them on the floor around her to form a square. She closed her eyes obediently, but every line in her body revealed her tension. Abaddon's voice droned on, and Joseph saw some of the others in the circle begin to sway, but Ariel was still twitching, still involuntarily resisting his will.

"She's not going under," said Joanna in a low voice after a time.

"I know—" The purring incantation ceased; for a moment there was a tense silence in the tower. "But she is still the best subject we have. If she cannot be led, perhaps the proper stimulation will push her across."

Abaddon's smile was reflected by the others, and Joseph knew that whatever was coming they had seen before, and enjoyed. The shifting light reflected from the mirror balls mocked now one color, now another in the costumes they wore, as if they were indeed the demons of Mardi Gras.

"The masters of Tantric yoga have taught us the use of sex in changing consciousness and raising power. You—" he pointed to two of the guards, "hold her and get her tights off. And you—" now the gloved hand stabbed at Joseph, and he jerked as if he had been stung, "prepare yourself to take her, now."

"*Babalon-bal-bin-abaft! Athor-e-Balo!*" cried Joanna, and the others echoed her, "*Abraft, Abraft, Abraft! The Fathers, male-female, desire Thee!*"

The call became a chant, regular and pulsing. And in his own body Joseph felt the first hot throb of response. But at the touch of alien hands, Ariel jerked and cried out. The men laughed and one held her wrists while the other fumbled under her draperies and then stripped off tights and panties. The other woman, Ruth, began to curse, but her words were cut off, too, as one of the other guards grabbed her.

When they were finished, Ariel lay as if stunned. Her pale, bared thighs gleamed in the flickering light, and Joseph started toward her. Then she whimpered and tugged at the bottom of her costume in a futile attempt to cover herself. Joseph stood at her feet, just outside the square of swords, and she looked up at him. Even Joseph could sense the terror that was building in her now.

"No—please don't! Not here!"

Someone else had said that to him, not long ago.

"Go on," said Abaddon. He sounded faintly surprised at the delay.

"She's afraid—" Joseph stood his ground as Abaddon came around the circle toward him. Ava had been ashamed, and her shame had aroused him. Why wasn't this the same?

"Yes . . . if we cannot use her lust, we will use her fear. It will not matter in the end."

Were they really the same? Joseph felt the pressure of the chanting and instinctively stiffened against it. He had never made love to a woman he did not desire. He had never taken a woman who was truly afraid of him.

"Joseph Roman, remember your oath to me!"

Abaddon was close enough for Joseph to feel the pressure of his presence now. His senses swam as the power that had seduced him before beat against his awareness.

"Joseph, please help me—I'm afraid of the dark!"

He remembered the terror of being thrust out into that darkness. He remembered the wonder of seeing Ariel's ugliness transformed into beauty. She did not look beautiful now. Somehow, Joseph understood that if he did this thing she would never be beautiful again.

That indefinable hunger, which the flesh of women helped him ease, would never be satisfied.

"Joseph—" Abaddon's hot breath hissed in his ear. "I am your master. In the Name of the Lord of Light, obey me now!"

Joseph had seen the Lord of Light in the other ritual, and known him for the same divinity that he had once seen reflected in his own, inmost soul. That divinity spoke through him now.

"No . . ."

At close quarters, the blast of Abaddon's fury seared consciousness. Through the roaring in his ears, Joseph could barely hear Abaddon's reply.

"You refuse life? Then your death will provide the power!"

Blinking, Joseph glimpsed a blur of crimson as Abaddon moved, and then the gleam of steel. He was just beginning to turn as Abaddon brought up the rapier and plunged it through the fur of the costume into his heart.

Joseph felt the shock without comprehending; then pain spasmed through him, the world wheeled crazily, and he fell.

"Joseph, Joseph, oh, my love, no!"

The desperate murmur was close to his ear. He was lying on the familiar softness of a woman's body. Soft arms cradled him. Confused, Joseph strained against her, and the movement brought the agony again. He convulsed, and felt his spirit pour out to her in the perfect release that he had never found before.

He tried to say her name, but darkness sucked him downward, inward, and out again.

When Joseph's perceptions steadied, he was floating near the ceiling of the tower. Below him, his body lay sprawled in its own blood across Ariel, and Abaddon was setting the crimsoned rapier back in its place to close the square.

Joseph cried out, but nobody seemed to hear.

Abaddon straightened and lifted his hands in invocation.

"*Thaumiel, Ghogiel, Agshekeloh, Satariel* . . ." As the names of the Qlippoth vibrated across inner and outer planes, evil began to thicken in the air.

15.

*Beneath the Tree of my Life, the final
stream encircles an island where a cube of
grey stone lifts above the mists; it is a
Fortress, the Capital of the Worlds.*

Noel Pierre, "Black Sun"

David felt Abaddon's blade sear through flesh, and could not tell if it were Joseph's or his own. Consciousness was doubled now. He fought to separate his awareness of Joseph's confusion from Ariel's scream and the shocked murmur that echoed around the circle after it.

"He's dead!"

As Ariel pulled herself from beneath the body, the spectrum of shifting light matched the dark stain that spread across the front of her draperies and revealed it as blood. For a moment she knelt, staring down at what looked now like the carcass of some slain animal, while Abaddon's voice rolled out a succession of sonorous syllables that congealed the air. With doubled vision David saw an image of Joseph hovering near the ceiling, and a disturbance in the air above the body that flickered with unhealthy sparkles of light.

"*Golohab! Tagiriron!*" cried Abaddon, and the little lights began a sluggish swirling. A shudder of movement ran around the circle as the first awareness of shock or terror started to erode discipline.

David felt his awareness being sucked into it and moaned. Ruth grabbed him and held his head against her breast, breaking the spell, but his inner vision showed him vast forms heaving in the mist. He shuddered, and tried to form words.

"The Qlippoth—yes, I recognized the names—" whispered Ruth, understanding. He felt her mind open to his, and for a moment both saw the same horror appearing in the center of the square of swords.

Ariel was on her feet now. She swayed away from the mist that was rising from the blood of the beast and rocked back again, as if she had bounced against an invisible wall.

She's trapped in there with THEM! David could not tell if the thought was Ruth's or his own.

Driven by fascination or pity, two of the men in the circle stumbled toward Ariel, and the guards left their places to stop them.

"Now, while they're distracted, we can make it to the door—" Tom's painful grip startled David into momentary physical awareness.

Ariel screamed again, the sound's intensity oddly muted by the fog. A guard slammed into the man nearest her and he lurched forward, knocking one of the swords askew.

Suddenly everyone was moving. The guard and the man he had tackled went down, entangling the others. Keening, Ariel fell through the opening, and Ruth darted forward to grab her. Abaddon lifted his hands and shrieked out the rest of his incantation, and the mist darkened and expanded, extruding exploring tendrils toward the limits of the breached square.

David fell back against the parapet, felt something hard dig into his ribs, and remembered with momentary clarity what it was. Tom was already sweeping both women toward the stair, a step ahead of the panicking members of the Order of Omega. David fumbled with the folds of his wizard's robe, and pulled out the water pistol.

Suddenly the two levels of awareness fused and he was moving instinctively. He aimed the gun at the struggling mass on the floor and squeezed. The guard who had roughed him up got a faceful, then the second one, and a third. He tried for Abaddon, but the mist was in the way and he could not tell if he touched him. The next squeeze produced only a drop of dissolved drug; David threw the pistol at Abaddon and sprang for the stairs. As he started down he glimpsed something pale above him and he saw the change in the spectral face of

Joseph Roman as the spirit realized that someone could see him at last.

"*Come with us or they'll get you!*" David sent the mental cry. Then he felt the demons explode up out of Abaddon's square behind him and he launched himself down the stairway.

He could hear Abaddon shouting, "After them! After them!" behind him, and he did not know whether the sorcerer was commanding his bodyguards or the chaos he had released into the night.

Ruth ran down the corridor with Tom half-carrying Ariel after her and David bringing up the rear. Feet thudded on carpeting behind them. They had been cut off from the elevator, but there had to be a staircase! She saw a blur of movement ahead, faltered, and realized that the crazy flutter of spangles and feathers and flowing robes she saw approaching was their own images in the mirror at the end of the hall.

Then red figures darted into the reflection. Metal spat, something sang past her ear and the image shattered as shards of mirror exploded in front of them.

As Ruth slid to a stop she felt flying glass sting the arm with which she had shielded her eyes.

"Over there—" shouted David hoarsely. They ducked to the right as another shot punched into the wall; then David had the metal fire door open and they plunged through.

But there were no stairs. Instead, a giant slide spiraled down into the darkness below. Ruth clutched at the cold metal of the railing, fighting vertigo. The door rattled and Tom let go of Ariel and set his back against it. They heard the muffled thud as something struck it from the other side.

"Go on!" he yelled. "I can't hold for long!"

Unreasoning panic froze Ruth as David shouldered past her, Ariel's limp form in his arms.

"When I'm in position . . . lower her . . . when I was a kid, my sister . . . used to take me down the slide that way . . ." With an unfamiliar fluidity, David set Ariel in her arms, eased down on the edge, and reached for her again.

As a child, Ruth had been too terrified of heights to even try the slides. Shaking, she lowered the other woman into David's lap. With a shout he pushed off, and gathering speed slowly, spun downward.

"Ruth, go after him!" Tom rocked forward at another

blow to the door and groaning, braced himself against it again. "I'll be right behind you!"

She cast a terrified glance around her, in one look imprinting the scene. The faint screams she heard could have come from any wild party, but the wavering lights of the tower glowed dully on dizzying swirls of something that was thicker than the fog.

Above was chaos and the Abyss was below and she was lost between. Ruth closed her eyes, and in her mind's darkness glimpsed a shining arc like the blade of a sword. And in that moment of freedom, she stepped forward and down.

The smooth walls of the slide held her, and her body flexed around the curves as it whirled her away. Around, and around—centrifugal force swung consciousness outward, encompassing Tom spinning after her down the slide, the pale form of Joseph Roman drifting through the air, the forces building above the tower, the fog-bound town, and the misty geography of the other world. Then a familiar presence steadied her.

"We're with you—head for the bookstore!"

For an instant Ruth glimpsed a star of light shining through the fog, then she shot out the bottom of the slide and landed in a heap on the hard asphalt below.

David's body was responding instinctively. When he spoke, it was as if someone else relayed the words. But his awareness had become acute on the inner planes. As they hurried around the corner of the building and down through the gardens, he saw not shrubs and trees but patterns of energy. He sensed the glow of lives in the hotel behind them, and he saw his companions outlined in light. But above the tower swirled something deeper than darkness, and he feared it more than Abaddon's guards, who he sensed had followed them down the slide and were coming after them now.

"Hide behind the hedge there—" He realized that Ruth was not speaking aloud. *"In a moment they'll see us and shoot, but we need a chance to breathe if we're going to run."* She was already pulling Ariel down behind an artistically pruned clump of bushes, and Tom and David followed her. Overhead, a pale glow settled lower in the air.

They heard voices nearing, and the crackle of a walkie-talkie. Someone said something about the cars. Then David felt them withdrawing. He forced his lips to move.

"Can't outrun them . . . Over there . . . are blocked streets . . . faster on foot . . ."

"But where are we going?" asked Tom—very nearly his first question of the evening.

"Del wants us . . . to head for her place . . ." Ruth's light pulsed with effort. "Can't take Ashby—too easy to follow . . . try the back streets . . ."

David nodded, and Tom stared at them both, but before he could object, Ariel began to shudder and moan.

"He's dead, Abaddon killed him—*I* killed him!" Her breath drew in for a scream, and Ruth grabbed her shoulders and shook her, hard. Ariel choked and collapsed, sobbing, and Ruth held her, patting her back and crooning wordlessly.

"I wouldn't sleep with him, but I loved him, and now I can never—"

David reached out to grasp Ariel's arm. "Tell him . . . he is still . . . here . . . Look and *see!*"

As Ariel straightened, the ghost drifted lower. Pale as an overexposed photograph, it was still unmistakably Joseph Roman. Yet not entirely. As David stared at it, he realized that the hint of sleazy charm that had always marked the man was gone. Ariel blinked, and then sank back against Ruth with a little sigh, staring upward. Tom was still looking around in confusion, but David heard as well as Ruth and Ariel when the pale figure replied:

"I can't get back into my body. Am I dead? I don't understand . . ."

"Your body is dead," said Ruth gently. "It is time for you to go on now."

The ghost lifted a little, then settled again. *"THEY will take me if I try now. I will come with you, and help if I can—"* He turned toward Ariel, and she straightened and smiled.

"If everyone's rested, we should move on—" Tom said finally, and the four of them pulled themselves together and slipped through gardens as ghostly as the presence that followed them, past the tennis courts and through the gate to the road.

They were moving past the Julia Morgan Palazzo on Claremont, when Ruth heard the hissing of tires in the mist and felt the sudden certainty that their pursuers were near. She tried to remember the streets in the Elmwood area, but it was her computer map that flashed into memory.

"This way—" she whispered, and began to run. She had done her share of swearing at the ubiquitous Berkeley traffic barriers, but they might come in handy now! The sounds of hard breathing and fog-dulled footsteps behind her told her that the others were following. She glanced back, straining to see, but glimpsed only veiled shapes of trees and houses and anonymous forms moving through a gray mist more opaque than the Otherworld. She closed her eyes, and saw glowing shapes speeding along a path still faintly luminous with impressions of all those who had used it during the preceding day.

Lamplight showed a street sign labeled "Avalon" as they turned. On her map, this was an area of ruined palaces. They dashed down the street and around the corner and heard wheels squeal on asphalt as their enemies followed. A gun barked, and they knew they had been seen. Gasping, Ruth led the way across the grass in the traffic circle.

The car screeched to a stop and a door opened.

"Halt—we've got you trapped!" came a hoarse shout. "Hold it right there if you want to live!"

For a moment they froze.

"There's no exit!" exclaimed Tom, peering at the circle of houses around them. Ariel was sobbing with exhaustion and fear.

"Not for a car, but for us—" Ruth gathered her strength to run.

"I can't—leave me—" gasped Ariel.

"There is a path this way, follow me!" Ruth heard Joseph's words, and as Ariel stiffened, knew that she had, too. Running half-crouched, they slipped past a parked car and followed the dead-end street up the hill through the unlit mist, until they reached the footpath that led down the steep slope beyond.

As they hurried down Stuart the fog grew thicker, and as the physical world became less and less distinct, Ruth's perception of the Otherworld grew sharper. She could not feel their pursuers near, but the roiling darkness over the hotel behind them was growing deeper. As they crossed College Avenue she realized that there was some positive power ahead of them. By the time they reached Benvenue she could see it—a glowing pathway of light running beneath the houses parallel to the road.

"*What's that?*" came David's thought in her mind.

"*It goes toward the campus,*" Joseph answered him. "*Four lines of light cross there, above the Campanile.*"

"*That's the beacon we saw before, when we were looking for Ariel!*" thought Ruth. It drew her now, but Del was waiting for them. They had to cross it and go on.

As they passed the concrete traffic barrier that stood at the junction of Stuart and Hillegass like a truncated market cross, Ruth sensed a moving focus of danger coming toward them just as they all heard a car turn up from Telegraph.

How had their pursuers found them?

"They're between us and the bookstore! There's a park behind the school—quickly!" Tom led them in a sharp right turn, but in moments they could hear their enemies swinging around the barrier and coming after them.

"*Del! They've cut us off, but we're close to you!*" David's mental shout startled Ruth off stride, then she added her own power to the call.

A half-block, and they were running across grass. A car door slammed. Shots spat past Ruth's ear as if the gunman shared her ability to sense life-force. They ran through a damp gray cloud.

Then a deep thuttering vibrated like a drum roll through the heavy air. Something swept like a comet across the park toward them.

"Here—one of you get up behind me—Karen and Del are waiting on Telegraph with the car!"

The words echoed on both levels of consciousness, and vision showed her simultaneously the Warrior on his supernatural steed and Michael on his gleaming, gunmetal-gray Harley. David was closest; as he clambered on behind Michael, Ruth followed Tom and Ariel in a final dash. Behind them, Michael gunned the bike and thundered toward the foe, sent somebody sprawling, and wheeled across the grass in a swift arc after them.

Karen's battered, yellow Volkswagen was waiting. Breathless, they piled into it, but as Karen pulled up to the next cross street and started to make a U-turn, a long dark shape shot into the road behind her, and they could only go forward, up Telegraph toward the University. Michael circled again to follow, roaring past the other car and dodging bullets as he tried to drive it off the road. Ruth could hear tires screeching as it swerved.

Sparks flew as the car behind them scraped some obstacle, righted itself and wove erratically after them with Michael buzzing around it like an X-wing against an Imperial Destroyer. But surely more than Michael's harassment was disorienting their pursuers now.

As the Volkswagen lurched past the dim shapes of the shops on Telegraph, Ruth felt the ley lines that led to the University blazing with increasing power. At this hour, in this weather, the street was as empty as a scene from her game.

Karen was trying to turn the car. Ruth leaned forward, shouting—

"No, keep going! We can hole up in the beacon tower!" Even through the fog she could see it now, shining like a lighthouse in a dark sea.

From the front seat Del murmured some kind of agreement, and Karen floored the accelerator and sent the little car bouncing up the last block; in one heart-stopping moment she ran the light at Bancroft and lurched over the curb, then came to a screeching halt in front of the pillars that barred the entrance. Wheels screamed as the other car followed them. They scrambled out of the car, and as they sped across Sproul Plaza and through Sather Gate toward the Campanile, they heard the crash as their pursuer smashed into the barrier.

Ruth could feel the converging ley lines like a thrumming in her blood as they ran toward the low steps below the Campanile. Michael roared past them, leaped the machine over the stairs, and sped to the door of the tower.

When they reached it, Michael was fumbling at the lock with something from his toolkit. Shouts came from the slope behind them; they saw shapes wavering through the fog, shooting wildly. But none of the shots were directed toward the Campanile.

"Did the crash knock them silly?" asked Tom.

David laughed suddenly. "The drug . . . from my squirt gun . . . it's hit them finally!"

Ruth nodded. "They feel the power here, too—" She felt abruptly drained. Why was Michael still struggling with the door to the tower? Surely they were safe now . . .

But Del had moved around the side of the building and was

staring southward. Where the sky had been a featureless gray, now something was moving. Ruth's gut clenched as she remembered the sick writhing in the air above Joseph Roman's body, and at the thought, Joseph's astral form was beside her.

"It is the Qlippoth—Abaddon has mastered them and is sending them against us now . . ."

Ruth shuddered as a wave of chill air washed over her, and with it the almost tangible touch of fear. Then Michael called out in triumph, and Ruth and Del scrambled after the others through the open door of the tower.

On a clear day, you could see half of Berkeley from the top of the Campanile. Now, the tower thrust like a beacon through dense clouds, and all David could make out was the pattern of lights underlighting them from below, and southeastward, at their own level, a contorted rainbow glimmer from the Claremont tower. The perceptual distortions of the Paradise drug were wearing off now, and he strove to recapture the double vision that would show him the flow of power.

He shuddered as another wave of fear struck at them, and heard Ariel cry out and slump to the floor.

"We've got to set up a warding!" Michael's voice cracked through the mists that were curling around David's own mind, dragging him down.

"Use the ley lines!" cried Ruth. "Look, you can see the blaze just uphill from here where all the lines cross!"

David turned, and blinked as his perception adjusted. "We're on one of the lines, aren't we . . . it goes toward the hills past Hildebrand Hall . . ."

"Yes, and there's another, almost at right angles—" Ruth answered. "We crossed it just past Benvenue."

"I think I see one now," said Karen. "It runs from the Greek Theater down toward the Bay—"

"Toward Herrick hospital!" exclaimed Ariel, reviving as the pressure from their enemies faded. "That must be why everyone on the ward got so crazy the night they had the rock concert up there!"

"And the line that crosses it passes a little to the east of the Claremont tower . . ." added Del.

As each one spoke, the line described seemed to leap into visibility. Now all of them could see the eight pointed star radiating from a spot midway between the Campanile and Hildebrand Hall. This was like the trance David had shared with Del and Ruth before, and he surrendered to it gladly.

"There are eight of us," Del's voice resonated from the stone of the Tower. "Let our circle reflect the Pattern of Power."

Moving instinctively, David sat down with his back to Hildebrand Hall, and found himself facing Karen. Michael had taken up position to his left with his back to the Claremont, with Del Eden opposite him, facing it. To Michael's left, Tom balanced Ruth, and next to him Ariel, facing the apparently empty space where double vision showed him Joseph Roman's ghostly form. Living and dead, they were united, and as Ariel settled into her place, David felt the shift in perception as an almost physical sensation, and the Pattern grew brighter, or perhaps his awareness passed through the walls of the tower.

Interesting, he thought with that part of his mind that persisted in taking notes no matter what the danger might be. He hoped he would remember how they had done this later. If there *was* any later . . . if they survived.

"Feel the earth power beneath you," said Del. "Draw it up through your spine and let it flow clockwise around."

In the silence, David could hear her regular breathing. Automatically he matched his own to it, and felt physical sensations recede as awareness deepened on the inner planes. Now he was sensing the others, first as simple presences, then in fragments of thought as they settled into trance as well. As he breathed out, he let his awareness flow downward from his flesh through the floor of the tower to the earth in which it was founded. As he breathed in he felt a tingle rising along his spine and spreading through every limb. He could not tell if Del's command to link hands was mental or verbal, but he obeyed, and in moments began to feel the flow of power. This was similar to the procedure they had used when Del had gone out on the inner planes to seek Ariel, except that there was no one in the center, and David began to relax.

The next attack was so subtle that he hardly noticed it begin. Only he shivered with a cold that was not of the flesh, and remembered suddenly the other night that he had spent here, deluded and raving.

"You're no scientist—you gullible, drugged fool! You've

burned out your brain like those other poor fuckers you destroyed. You'll always be alone!'' As he tried to find words to deny it, David became aware of other accusations, and realized in horror that in the telepathic unity of the circle the others had all heard his deepest shame, and he knew theirs as well . . .

"You betrayed your best friend!"

"The man who loved you died for you!"

David felt Michael and Karen's pain.

"You cannot love!"

"You'll never find love again!"

Now it was Ruth and Tom who writhed under the lash of guilt and fear.

"Your beauty is gone, your flesh will decay, you killed the man who loved you!" Ariel's consciousness wavered at the words.

"Your flesh is decaying already—you will wander powerless forever, you are damned!" The spirit of Joseph Roman flickered like a blown flame.

"You thought you could oppose Me, and your pride has betrayed these souls to destruction! Old woman, you have outlived your power!" Even Del Eden winced at the derisive lash of those words, and David saw her suddenly as a senile old lady—saw them all as creatures utterly vile, and himself as the most despicable of all.

Despair and self-loathing smote them all. Their fires faded, their link to the earth thinned, the mists of the Abyss swirled in, seeking to set their spirits adrift on a limitless, dark sea . . .

David felt Del's pain as she fought against that dreadful tide. Then her voice came, cracked and desperate: "Earth spirit! Land soul! *Genus Loci,* help us! They will destroy you, too—come to us now!"

David's spirit struggled as the darkness closed over him. Then suddenly, patterns of light like a shorted circuit sparked in his awareness. They steadied; he sensed the star, the circle, and beyond them an outer ring of points of light where the ley lines touched the borders of the campus, linking even as he became aware of them in a flare of power from point to point to form a perimeter.

At the same time something pulsed in the center of the tower—first a glowing pattern like the astrological sign for Mercury based on the Aries sign, and then a bright, dark figure that turned, inspected them curiously, and then faced the Claremont tower.

Who are you? How did you know about me? they heard the spirit ask. *I've been so lonely—nobody's called me for such a long time—and now it's only because you're frightened. I should be insulted, but I can feel it, too. What is going on out there? It's shaking my Patterns already—*

The spirit's gabble was interrupted by another blast, like the chill wind before an approaching storm front, or an avalanche, or a tidal wave. They all stilled, their personal horrors forgotten as the sense of some great power about to crash down on them extinguished all emotions except the simple desperate determination to survive . . .

The blood pounded in Del's head as she struggled for serenity. The Tempter had come too close, voicing the fear that shook her confidence every time someone came to her for counsel or she led a ritual— *They trust me! What if I lead them wrong?* She fought to steady her breathing, let awareness deepen as she sought the still point in the center of her soul.

Not my will but Thine—oh Thou who Art the Source of All, lead us now!

The circle of light that surrounded them seemed too fragile to resist the weight of the horror that was approaching, as if they had put up a picket fence to hold back the sea.

"*Behold the Angels of Destruction who shall end your world. I am Abaddon, Lord of the Lost, and you are all my prey!*" The deep voice resonated across the planes.

The stone walls of the tower had become transparent, and distant but clear, as if she saw him through the wrong end of a telescope, Del perceived Luciano Abaddon and knew that the physical form she saw was only a shell, which had been filled now by something never meant to be made manifest in this world. He stood in the midst of his shattered circle on the top of his tower, urging on the forces that boiled in the air above the city like a hunter his hounds.

"*Lilith, I command thee! Night Walker, Demon Queen! Summon thy minions! Speed to destroy those who would oppose My will!*"

A form shaped itself from the mists, womanlike, voluptuous, with Joanna de Laurent's eyes. But her feet were clawed like a vulture's, and she swept toward them on mighty wings.

"Gamalael, I summon thee! Pollute all love and lust with obscenity!"

A second figure took shape above them, hideously combining the features of Man and Ass. Its braying trumpeted discordantly across the skies, and all over the city sleepers woke screaming.

"Samael, Father of Lies! Poison all words!"

Another form swept across the heavens on dark pinions, upending a bottle that spattered a searing venom over the world.

"Gharab Tserek, summon thy Ravens! May Death's dark wings descend to rend my enemies!"

Abaddon called, and suddenly a storm of black wings thundered, and an infernal screeching scored their souls.

Del swayed, struggling to maintain some link with the others, but their warding had never been intended to withstand the Angels of the Abyss. She might have been able to face Luciano Abaddon in a duel of mortals, but she could not stand against the Power that possessed him now.

When his warding shattered, Abaddon's will had been seized by *his* Master—even if the weight of Glory crushed her, Del Eden had no choice but to invoke the aid of the Power *she* served. Abandoning her vain attempt to hold onto the circle, Del focused her will on the white light of Kether, seeking to draw it downward, to let her Self fade away.

But still the voice of Abaddon rang across the worlds, and *Tagiriron,* the Disputer and Despoiler of Beauty, appeared beside his fellows. The dull clouds glowed with *Golohab's* evil fires. *Agshekeloh* came after, destroying all order, and *Satariel's* dark pall blotted out all light. Where *Ghogiel* passed, all movement was frozen. Last came double *Thaumiel,* whose contending forces began to split apart the world.

Del felt the disintegration in every atom of her being. She fought, but it was stronger. Her destruction was certain, there was only one moment left to choose . . . Focusing all her powers into one final act of will, she screamed—

"Ain Soph Aur! Thou Limitless Light! Thou who art and art not all Things, I give up my being to Thee!"

Her body fell forward and lay motionless as her mortal cry was swallowed up by the chaos that sounded around them, yet silence followed it, sudden and terrible, as if even Abaddon were waiting for the reply.

But no words split the air, no blinding light smote the heavens. Only, as if from a great distance, came the whisper of sandaled feet striding across the world.

"Sandalphon, High One—"

It was as if the name had been spoken by the stones of the tower. But above the eastern hills the others saw the first flush of a light more beautiful than dawn, and heard the first faint harmonies as the Archangels came. Rank upon rank of them, Angels, Shining Ones, Devas, they distilled into vision; and a rainbow of glory flooded the waiting world.

Head brushing heaven, Sandalphon came striding, and where his feet touched the hills of earth the ground began to glow. Lilith tried to flee him, but he caught and embraced her, and suddenly he became more solid and her dull wings shone.

"Gabriel, Thou Strength of God, sound the note of Creation!"

The air dazzled purple and gold, and the braying of the Ass was turned to sharp sweetness by the long, strong summons of a horn.

"Raphael, Heal the poisoned world!"

Blue and orange flared in the feathered clouds, and the ionized air tingled. Everywhere men breathed more easily, and the dull ache of despair began to fade away.

Haniel came then, in a flutter of green leaves and white doves that swirled among the Ravens of Destruction until both winked away. Light blazed suddenly on the highest hilltop as if the sun had risen, but it was *Mikael*, marshaling the Hosts of Heaven with his spear. Where he pointed it, brightness shimmered; Light poured through the windows of the Campanile, and the faces of those within were illuminated; light shafted toward the Claremont tower, and the Angel of Disputation became a shadow.

Heat swirled like a red cloak around the Presence that came after, and in the incandescence of *Khamael*, the dark fires of The Burner were purified. Then blue light cooled the air, and all that The Breaker in Pieces had disordered, *Tsadkiel's* golden crozier made whole. All that The Concealer had hidden was revealed by the Eye that shone from the midnight robes of *Tsaphkiel*, and the stasis into which the Hinderer had plunged the world was broken by the Word spoken by *Ratziel*, the starclad Herald of God.

And as each great Power of Heaven met and matched its opposite, the sundering forces of *Thaumiel* faltered. For an endless moment there was no movement. And then even the rainbowed glory of the Angels themselves was reabsorbed into a pillar of undifferentiated white radiance that moved from tower to tower until it faced the Angel of Contention, and Division itself was rebalanced in one blinding instant of Unity.

Light, and Love, and Life unending were there . . . and spinning spirals of creation. Wheels of flame and eyes of lightning, radiant spirits, gods and angels . . . Leaves of grass and grains of soil, drops of water, sheen of oil, fish in water, birds in flight, the wind that whispered in the night, loping wolf and leaping deer, human laughter, joy and fear, child and mother, man and wife, all things danced the dance of life! And they who watched were nothing, they were none, and at the same time, they were All and they were One!

And all around them came the rejoicing of invisible voices, singing through every cell and molecule—

> *"Holy, Holy, Holy, Maker of All—*
> *Heaven and Earth are full of Thy Glory—*
> *Glory be to Thee, oh Thou Most High!"*

And then the glory shimmered and gently misted away.

Ruth straightened, stifling a gasp as stiffened muscles were forced to move again, and stared, blinking. The pale, featureless light of true dawn filled the tower, but in the center of the circle where the *Genus Loci* had been, a shimmer of radiance waited now.

Around her, the others were muttering as they tried to rise from the positions in which they had lain. The Radiance moved among them, and where it passed, pain eased, and energy flooded lifted faces until they shone. Ruth felt its touch tingle through every vein, and drew in a deep breath that tasted like the morning of the world.

Del Eden still lay motionless. But as Ruth summoned her strength to go to Del, the pillar of Light moved above her, and for a moment her entire body shone. Then she stirred, and the Presence separated itself; but when she sat up again, its radiance still glowed in her eyes, and Ruth had to look away.

"Someone's going to notice the cars soon and start wondering," said Michael hoarsely. "We should get out of here."

"But what about Joseph?" Ariel was staring across the circle where the wraithlike form of Joseph Roman was still faintly visible against the stone.

Slowly, as if she had forgotten how to use her body, Del Eden turned to look at him.

"My son, our enemies are departed. It is time for you to go on . . ."

"I am afraid . . ."

They were all still sufficiently linked for Ruth to hear Joseph's reply.

"You have won your battle—there is nothing to fear—" said Del gently, and then, with a sudden intensity that made something twist in Ruth's gut, "You are free now! Don't you understand how I wish I could come, too?"

Joseph's figure brightened, but he looked at Ariel.

"I cannot go. Her pain binds me!"

Now they were all looking at Ariel, who had covered her face with her hands. "Joseph—don't leave me—" she sobbed through her fingers. "Everyone leaves me! I've tried so hard to be good enough, but they always find out what I really am!"

Ruth got awkwardly to her feet and stumbled across the circle to her friend. "Ariel—I love you—you have made my life beautiful—Ariel, *please!*" She looked desperately over at Del.

"My child, he will not leave you forever, but if you love him, you must release him now!" Del answered softly.

Ariel reached out blindly and Ruth took her hand, feeling it tighten painfully on her own. Then Ariel lifted her head, and living and dead looked at each other with the same intensity.

"Master Joseph, do you want to go?"

"They are calling me . . ."

"Then I release you, but you must promise to come back for me!"

The pale image of Joseph Roman nodded. Then, slowly, he drifted toward the pillar of light that still pulsed through the center of the floor. There was a moment of hesitation, and he darted suddenly into the Radiance. They saw him limned in light then, with all shadow seared away. Shining as the Angels had shone, he moved toward Ariel, and as Ruth looked up at him she saw revealed in him the terrible beauty that he himself had seen once in a mirrored vision, and tried ever after to find again.

And now he had regained it, and the soul who had called himself Master Joseph gave the blessing he had parodied in his ritual to Ariel. For one moment her face burned with the same beauty as his, then her eyes closed, and she sank back against Ruth with the warm trust of a sleeping child.

The pillar of radiance seemed to shoot upward then, or perhaps it was a greater brilliance from above that came down to receive it. When light-blinded eyes could focus again, it was gone, and through the eastern windows of the Campanile they saw the golden glow of the rising sun.

16.

The heady scent of wisteria drifted through the open windows of Del's temple from the yard behind the store. It had been almost three weeks since the Angels of Light and Darkness had battled above Berkeley, and the grip of winter was broken at last. It was full noon, and they had come finally to the hour of the equinox, when all things stand in equilibrium.

Sitting cross-legged on the straw mat, Ruth fancied she could feel it, and something that had been still since the night of the astral battle began to stir in her. Her spirit was not dead, then, but only in need of recharging. Looking at Ariel and the others, she wondered if anyone else found their memories of that night unreal.

"My brothers and my sisters, we have come to the Cross-roads of Spring! We have seen how Light and Dark are balanced in the world of the Archetypes. Now it is time to seek the same balance within," said Del. Her golden robes gathered the light of the sun as she gestured, and they all stood while Michael drew his kris and cast the circle of protection around them.

"Behold, we stand between the worlds! What is between the worlds transcends the world!" Their voices rang out in unison— Ruth and Ariel and David, Tom, Michael and Karen Holst.

Del invoked the powers of the elements and the directions. Ruth heard Ariel sigh as they all sat down again, and thought then that perhaps it was not entirely over for her. Ariel had been very docile since they had taken her back to her own apartment, but she was not eating. It was all very well to have saved the world, but what she had wanted to do was save Ariel. Only, she understood now that no one can force salvation on another. In the end, Ariel herself would have to choose. At least she had come with them to the ritual.

"Between the three middle spheres and the three supernals a great gulf is fixed—" said Del. "This is *Masak Mavdil*, the Place of the Failures. We wait now at the edge of the Abyss in the soul's greatest darkness. The depths draw you, dizzying, dreadful—what demons dwell there? Take a moment now to look into your own darkness. What faults and fears have you cast into it? Are they exhausted and outworn, or do they still have power? Recognize them, name them and say silently—I am not this . . ."

Ruth felt her flesh chill at the words, and sent a horrified glance at Del. How could she remind them, knowing what they had been through? And then she looked at Del's stern features again and realized that she knew precisely what she was doing, that they all had to come to terms with what had happened before they could go on.

And suddenly she was seeing the Abyss as she had seen it in her vision, and she heard once more the voices of the demons taunting her.

"You're a failure, you're irresponsible, you're a cold bitch, you're unloving and unloved . . ." The litany echoed in memory, and more out of hope than belief, Ruth responded—
That isn't me!

Del tapped three times on the temple bell, and Ruth came back to external awareness. Ariel had made no sound, but her eyes were unfocused, and her cheeks glistened with tears. Ruth looked at her and felt her stomach tighten. The rest of them might be able to stand this, but what about Ariel? She glared at Del, but the older woman continued with unmarred serenity.

"The demons are banished, but still the Abyss yawns for you, and *Ridya*, the Veiler of God, conceals the other side. There is a bridge, but it is impossibly narrow. You must find your inner balance to get across . . ."

Dispassionate as a surgeon, Del led them through the Middle Pillar exercise, and as Ruth felt the tingle of energy move from the crown of her head down her spine, she forgot her fears again.

"This is the Middle Pillar of Equilibrium," said Del. "As you vibrate with this energy you link earth and heaven. Maintaining your awareness of your perfect balance, cross now the bridge that will bring you to Knowledge."

Ruth got to her feet, straightening her black robe. Across from her David was doing the same, robed in white as he had been the night the two of them had worked with Del. But they had to balance all the others now. One by one, they escorted each member of the circle to the balance beam on the floor. Supported by the polarities—black and white, yang and yin and every other dichotomy—each one walked the beam toward the round mirror above the altar.

Above the vibration of the chanting came Del's clear instructions—

"Behold the sphere of Daath before you. As you gaze into it, you will see the Angel who guards your soul . . ."

Ariel was still crying when they came to her. Ruth tensed.

"I can't do it—"

"Of course you can do it, we'll be supporting you!" Ruth held out her hand.

"I'll fall off!"

Ariel was shaking now, and Ruth understood that she feared more than a physical fall. But that was just why she had to try. She reached down and, before Ariel could resist, pulled her to her feet.

As they led her to the beam, Ruth felt her quivering like a strung bow.

"I don't want to balance my body—I hate this body—I only want to be free! Why are you doing this to me? Why couldn't you let me go?"

The soft whimpering went on and on as they moved Ariel

along the beam, and Ruth's heart wrenched with pity. But she felt Del's implacable gaze and kept going. Del's affirmation rang in her ears—

"You are balanced! You will not fall! I am not going to let you destroy yourself now!"

They were almost to the mirror. Ariel glimpsed it and began to struggle. Ruth felt David trying to hold her, braced herself as Ariel's energy swung like a pendulum between them, and in desperation projected her awareness *through* Ariel to David, straining for equilibrium.

"I can't look! I'm ugly! I'm afraid!"

"Gaze into the mirror and look upon the Goddess within!" Del's voice cracked softly across Ariel's pleading.

She stiffened and looked up, and in that moment Ruth and David found their balance and held her facing the mirror and whatever it was that she would see. Ruth's heart was pounding heavily. The tension was almost unbearable, but the balanced forces they were channeling held her just as surely as they did Ariel.

And then Ariel's face changed.

At first it was almost imperceptible, like the first illusory moment of dawn. But the transfiguration continued, as if it reflected some transformation in the glass. And still her radiance grew, surpassing her old, well-kept elegance, surpassing her beauty as a bride, looking suddenly like the picture of her mother in the old photograph, and bringing into focus all that was potential in her, until Ruth saw Ariel's true self shining through, as Joseph's had at the last.

And then, finally, the tension eased. The terrible beauty faded from Ariel's features, leaving her with the look of a newly awakened child. Ruth and David found they could move again, and guided her back to the end of the beam and then to her seat again.

Del came around to help Ruth assist David through the ceremony, and then it was her own turn.

If Ariel can get through this, I can— Ruth teetered on the beam and bit her lip. She could feel Del's steady support to her left and David's to her right. She took a deep breath, trying to center herself, but her sensitivity to the other two increased, as if they were not people, but forces, holding her up, drawing her down.

She cast a quick look at David and involuntarily tried to

pull free, seeing Leonard—no it was Jeff, it was the men who had raped her, who had betrayed her, who had tried to use her body or soul! But now she was overbalanced on the other side, and Del's power drew her toward a womb of sensation in whose darkness all self-awareness would disappear. Ruth shuddered, feeling herself a battlefield where the powers of the intellect and the flesh fought for supremacy.

I am not this mind! I am not this body! Something that was neither struggled for balance as she inched along the beam. *I am not this fear!*

But what am I?

Uncertainty fluttered breathless in Ruth's throat as she lifted her eyes to the mirror on the wall. Dazzled vision showed her dark and light reversed like the negative of a picture. A mask looked back at her.

And then, as her vision adjusted, it began to alter—flowing through a multitude of changes in which her own features were only one face in an endless stream. It was the universal Face of the Queen of Angels that was looking back at her, Her voice that answered—

"You are Love, the balance of all things . . ."

Ruth had no idea how she had gotten back to her seat. When self-awareness returned to her, Del was blessing a tray of apples.

"The Tree of Knowledge is planted in Daath, which is the unfallen Eden. Let us therefore share its fruit."

With an odd tremor, Ruth realized that these were uncut apples, and knew that Del had put them into the ceremony deliberately to heal their memories. But still it took some resolution to take one from the platter and bite into it.

But no vision followed, unless it was a heightened awareness of all the others—Tom's nurturing solidity, Ariel's luminous grace, Michael's strength and Karen's passion and David's integrity. And most of all, she felt the presence of Del Eden burning like a flame, and wondered again how Del had learned the Word of Power to summon the Archangels to their aid.

"Our ritual is almost over, and then it will be time to close the temple," said Del. "But while we are still in this sacred space I have something to say." She paused, seeking words, and for a moment the only sound was that of people trying to eat apples quietly. Ruth sensed expectation building in the room.

"The physical vehicle of the man who called himself Luciano Abaddon is destroyed, but the power that filled it, and the rest of the organization that followed him, remain. We have healed the wounds he gave us, and now we must consider whether there is anything else we should do." Del looked down at her folded hands, marked with the prominent veins and translucent skin of maturity. Even at rest in her lap, to Ruth they seemed strong.

"For many years I have tried to help those who came to me. But I'm afraid that is not enough anymore. Do you remember the question Glynda asked Dorothy in *The Wizard of Oz?*" Del looked up with a glint of humor that transformed her own face suddenly to that of the little girl who had watched that film long ago.

Ruth remembered watching it on TV with Martin. "Are you a good witch, or a bad witch?" she asked.

Del grinned back at her, and then her features sobered again. "That's the question, isn't it? There are those who fear evil in anyone who uses power, and Joseph Roman is an example of what can happen when the vision is lost. So what do we do?"

"We don't just sit around waiting for them to hit us again—" said Michael from his guard post at the door. "We have to prepare."

"But if you raise an army, you've got to find something for it to do in peacetime," objected David. "And the people who lead it are likely to get too fond of command."

"That is what *I'm* afraid of . . ." said Del. Suddenly she looked her age. "I don't want to pick up where Joseph Roman left off."

"Then we live with that fear—" Ruth found herself answering, "and we use it to keep ourselves in line. If someone had helped Joseph a long time ago, there might not have been any damage to repair. If the good guys are afraid to use power, then who can deal with the bad guys when they use it?" It was the choice she had made already, refusing to abandon Ariel.

"You are the leader, Del—" said Karen quietly. "You have to decide."

"Yes, I know I am," Del sighed. "For now. I am only too

aware that it's not the Wiccan covens and the other little
magical circles that send the *National Enquirer* into hysterics
that should worry people, but the cults that are run for
the rich and powerful. When such organizations begin to
corrode a nation's heart, only the independent occultists can
hope to oppose them." Afternoon light slanted through the
window and glistened on her silver hair as she drew breath to
go on.

"But I can't fight this battle forever, and I can't do it
alone. Every one of you has abilities I lack. We will have to
dare this together, or not at all."

Michael brought up his sword in salute, his good eye
sparkling. One by one the others nodded, even Ariel. Ruth
took a deep breath, feeling the same flutter beneath her
ribs that she did when she ran a new program for the first
time.

"Okay, count me in, too—"

What have I got myself into? thought David as he walked
up the slope in front of Wheeler Hall. He was still high from
the ritual, and his senses were functioning with an almost
painful intensity, as if he were missing the top layer of skin.
He passed students heading for the library to study or home to
dinner, but the hush of the evening weighted the warm air,
and the rush of water down Strawberry Creek sounded louder
than it did during the day.

The last of the sunlight enriched the green of the spring
grass on the hills and gilded the stone sides of the Campanile.
It was just past six, and the carillon was ringing out its
nightly concert, mellow as memory, showing no signs of
what had happened there. The magic was finished—their
ritual that afternoon had concluded it. Whatever crises the
future might hold, things were ordinary now. David walked
more slowly as he continued on toward Hildebrand, suddenly
unwilling to leave this threshold between day and night at the
balance point of the year.

The shadows beneath the trees drew him into their mystery.
Involuntarily, he found himself turning down the path where
a granite archway guarded the bridge across the creek to the
Faculty Club, and stopped short as he realized someone was
waiting there. He blinked, saw only shadows, and then, as he
turned, saw the figure once more.

If he tried to focus, he lost it. Peripheral vision showed him only a sweep of shade like a dark cloak, and the gleam of bright eyes. But David recognized it now as the spirit who had appeared in their circle in the tower, and realized he must be very close to the place where the ley lines crossed.

"Thank you for helping us—" he whispered, not sure if this was a product of his own imagination or something external that could hear.

"I was protecting myself, too—" the answer came immediately. *"Even for this place, that was a strange night . . ."*

David laughed, "We didn't do it on purpose, I promise you!" He took an involuntary step backward, up the hill.

"Don't go away! Nobody ever talks to me!"

"I have to go now, but I'll come back again, okay?" David turned again to face the *Genus Loci*, and saw only shadows. A shiver ran through the flesh of his bare arms, and he did not know if it was because the air was turning cooler, or because he had a friend in the Otherworld, and the magic would never go away now.

The cheerful chuckle of the creek below the bridge was his only answer, but he did not mind. He was whistling as he went up the stairs to Hildebrand Hall.

As David came from the grad office into the lab, he heard a soft hum and saw Bob Chovanian perched next to the Vortex genie, holding down the test tubes while the machine's gentle vibration mixed their contents. As David put down his coffee, Bob turned around and grinned.

"I was hoping you'd come in. I heard you were back, keeping night-owl hours again."

David shrugged uncomfortably. He had gone back to work two days after the battle in the tower, but only in the evenings. The THC project was drawing to a close. Dr. Langdon had told him to take it easy, and somehow he hadn't been able to get started on anything of his own. And he hadn't felt up to facing anybody, until now.

"I saw this place the next morning, you know, after those hoodlums had trashed it. Shit, what a mess! I thought we were never going to get all the glass out of the corners. At least it didn't delay the project. You were damn lucky to make it out alive. Are you okay now?" Bob went on.

Lucky—yes, he had been lucky, but his escape from Abaddon's men had been the least of it.

"Yeah, I'm fine—raring to go!" David grinned, realizing suddenly that it was true. The sense of balance he had found in the ritual was still with him, and the commitment as well. Whatever happened after this, he was sure of himself now.

"How's it been going for you?" he asked.

"Pretty good, now that the warm weather is here. I guess Langdon told you that NIH has accepted our report on the THC project?"

David nodded. "Are they actually going to do something with it?"

"They'll do more human testing, I expect, but that's not our problem now." The machine stopped, and Bob plucked out the tubes and set them in the rack. David eyed the other man suspiciously. Was Bob trying to tell him that the research group was finished? Surely he would have never looked so cheerful if that were true.

"We've got something new?" David felt an involuntary flutter of excitement as he asked.

Bob laughed. "Well, somebody over at U.C.S.F. has got some y-interferon that they think might work on AIDS, and they want us to test host-vector systems for synthesizing it. You interested?"

David nodded vigorously. He was more than interested. This was something important enough to occupy him entirely— the chance that he had almost forfeited, to do what he loved best.

"The specifications are on my desk in the office, if you want to look at them," Bob went on. "And while you're up, could you get a cup of coffee for me, too?"

Ruth took a long swallow of coffee and set it down. It was her second cup of the morning, and she felt almost human again. She had slept like the dead the night before—or perhaps not like the dead, who seemed to have a more intense existence than the living, but like a healthy child, and had awakened feeling more herself than she had in years.

The telephone rang.

"Ruth, is that you?"

Gooseflesh prickled up and down Ruth's arms as memory

looped through the past three months and back to the present again.

"Yes, of course. How are you, Ariel?" she asked carefully.

"Better . . . actually, I feel pretty well, though not quite up to driving. That's why I called you. I've lost so much weight that nothing fits right. Would you like to go shopping today?"

Back to normal— thought Ruth, or maybe not. Ariel sounded a little more subdued than she remembered, not so ready to make assumptions about what other people would like to do.

By the time they had visited a few shops, Ruth knew there had been a change. Ariel had chosen simple pants and tunics in shades of blue and dove gray, smoky lavender and sage. The dragon was dead, and the princess was in mourning.

"And what about you?" asked Ariel as she finished trying on the third outfit. "Are you planning to wear jeans for the rest of your life?"

Ruth shrugged. "What did you have in mind? I would feel silly in princess pastels, or even those subtle colors you've got there."

"No, you're not a princess, you're a sorceress—Mrs. Winslow was right about that. You should wear flowing lines and rich jewel tones. Here—"

Ariel pulled a loose silk shirt in deep teal blue off the rack and held it out to Ruth, hunted through the skirts and came up with something in a dusty rose jersey. Ruth looked at them dubiously, but she tried them on; and somehow, before they were done, she had another blouse in garnet, a flowing black gown with brilliant applique, and a pair of black pants in velveteen.

Ruth looked critically at her image in the mirror, and suddenly she saw Ariel next to her—the muted shades of the dreamer and the bold contrasts of the doer side by side. Again, memory was keyed by similarity—she had seen something like this before; abruptly their two faces became the single, ever-changing Face of the Queen of Angels . . .

Ruth shifted her footing as if the floor had moved beneath her, then realized it was an inner balance that had changed. They had passed through the equinox and now the tide was sweeping them out again, but where?

She helped Ariel carry her packages up to the apartment, and found herself sitting on the little balcony drinking jasmine tea, as she had so many times before. Nothing had changed, but everything was different somehow.

"Now that you've got some new clothes, what are you going to do, redecorate your apartment?" Ruth asked.

"Actually, I was thinking of that—" Ariel answered. From the balcony they could see across the backyards of South Berkeley toward the blue glimmer of the bay.

"Maybe I could study design and do decorating for other people, too . . ." Ariel added hesitantly. "What do you think?"

Ruth gave her a quick glance. "I think that's a wonderful idea! If I had more room in the loft I'd commission you, but at the rate Tom is bringing new plants in, I'm not sure there's going to be room for me!"

As another swallow of tea went down, Ruth felt the fragrant heat relaxing the tension that had been there since Ariel had phoned. Was she really healed at last? Ruth looked at her friend as if she had never seen her before. That porcelain skin was marked by the lines of humanity, but her eyes glowed with the serenity of someone who has gone down into the Pit and come out the other side.

"Why are you looking at me?" Ariel asked quietly.

Ruth felt herself blushing. "I'm trying to replace all my old images of you with the reality."

Ariel smiled. "I think we both need to do that now."

"In the mirror at the ritual, what did you see?" Ruth asked suddenly.

"My mother—" said Ariel. "She left, you know, when I was three years old. I never saw her again. She was always dressing me up and playing with me. I was in high school before I found out that she had died, but for years I thought I had done something wrong, or gotten too big and ugly and driven her away."

Watching her, Ruth wondered what scars the divorce might have left on Martin in places she could not see. At least she had remained a part of his life, however intermittently.

"You thought you were ugly, and I thought it was wrong to be a girl," Ruth said aloud. "How could we live this long without really understanding who we are?"

"Who are we, then?" asked Ariel.

Ruth thought of a line from the ritual—*Thou art Goddess, Thou art God.*

"We are the allies of the Angels . . ."

"It's going to be different now," said Ariel. "Joseph might have reverted to his old ways if he had lived, but he did choose to die rather than to hurt me. If someone, even Joseph, could do that, I guess I must be worth saving after all. I have to do something to justify it now."

Ruth realized that their shopping spree had been a symbolic act, like wearing robes for ritual.

"We both do—" she said quietly.

Ariel was crying, silent tears of release from strain. Ruth felt a suspicious stinging beneath her eyelids, and stopped trying to hold her own emotions in. And then, amazingly, Ariel reached out and hugged her.

"You are Love . . ." the Queen of Angels had said, and now this simple human contact released a spring of love in her that swept all her own fears away. Whatever they did or did not do with their bodies, what she had longed for was this union of the soul. She held Ariel against her and through her closed eyelids sensed the air glowing around them with a blaze of bright wings.

"Ruth, I do love you . . ." whispered Ariel.

Sunset was feathering the skies with a shimmer of rose and gold. Ruth slipped one of Masley's cymbalom cassettes into the player and flipped the switch to connect it to the computer, then activated the colored Sleeper program and switched it to the big remote screen. As the lines of light appeared they began to pulse to the throbbing music, altering speed and color and position like an extension of the sunset, according to the permutations of melody.

Tom stood by the stove, cutting up scallions and mushrooms and tossing them into the frying pan to join the thinly sliced beef that was already sizzling there. Ruth called out the window, detached Martin from the game he was trying to teach Lorraine's children downstairs, and got him to finish setting the table by the time the rice and spring greens were ready to put on.

Ruth suspected that Martin was afraid that she and his father would change their decision to have him live with her, and was on his best behavior. Watching him shovel in the food, she wondered how long it would last. She suspected that there would be times when both of them would regret the change, but at least she didn't have to feel guilty anymore.

"Do you think Ariel was serious about wanting to go back to school?" asked Tom.

Ruth set down her coffee cup. "I hope so. Half her problem before was having nothing to do. Studying design might be just the thing—she's always had exquisite taste, goodness knows."

"Well, if she gets some commissions, maybe she'll invite me to do the landscaping." He grinned, and Ruth was suddenly almost painfully aware of the strong column of his throat and the kindness in his eyes.

He's helped me get through all this mess and never asked for anything, she thought then. *But he does want something. Do I have it to give?*

"What did you think of the ritual?" she asked aloud.

"I liked it—" He was looking out the window now, watching the last of the sunset fade. "It was like the feeling I get in the garden, sometimes, when the earth and the plants and I are all part of one whole . . ."

Impulsively, Ruth stretched out her hand, and although she didn't think Tom had been watching her, he covered it with his own. Martin asked about watching TV then, and she answered without knowing what she said. Something odd had happened to her heartbeat, and she understood that the gift of love was for her. She did not need Tom to make her complete; she had needed to be complete in order to accept him.

We have fought beside the Hosts of Heaven and challenged the powers of Hell— she thought then. *Why am I so afraid?*

They all watched TV together, but afterward Ruth had no idea of what she had seen. She was too conscious of Tom beside her—suddenly she felt the warmth of his body like the heat of a flame. Her eyes followed the movements of his long, flexible fingers with a fascination that left her blushing whenever he looked at her.

And then, finally, Martin went to bed, and if he noticed his mother's abstraction he had the sense not to ask what was wrong with her. The silence deepened, and Ruth looked down at her jeans and shirt in despair. Ariel would have handled this so much better—she would have managed to put on a silky caftan by this time, or maybe some kind of negligee. But their shopping spree had not extended to lingerie. At the

thought of herself all dolled up in peach silk and lace, Ruth
began to laugh.

"Share the joke with me?"

Startled, she looked up. Tom was standing beside her, but
his face was in shadow. She wanted desperately to see his
eyes . . .

"I feel like a virgin," she blurted helplessly. "I don't
know what to do. I wish I could be beautiful for you—"

"I could tell you that you *are* beautiful, but I have never
yet met a woman who believed it. Look at Ariel! I have a
better idea—" His hand brushed her hair and she began to
tremble.

Ruth stood still as he fumbled with the clasp of her barette,
and then felt her hair spill over her back. With his hand still
tangled in her hair, Tom kissed her. She felt the first knot in
her belly loosen, and a silken heat began to pulse beneath her
skin.

"You are my garden, and I am going to cultivate you until
you bloom!" His hand moved down her neck and he began to
unbutton her shirt, and after a few moments Ruth recovered
the power of motion and started to help him. They were still
kicking free from the last of their garments as they fell onto
the bed.

As if he had been following a map of the Forbidden City,
Tom explored all of her secret places, and something that had
been locked forever opened to his gentleness. With strength
and sweetness and the skill of the husbandman he ploughed
her, and as he had promised, Ruth received his seed, and
flowered.

In that moment, she found a joy that transcended the
body's ecstacies. She sensed David's satisfaction as he worked
in the lab, Del's contemplation, Ariel's peaceful dreams, and
projected her passion out to them in a blaze of blessing that
could warm the world.

It was past midnight when Ruth woke, her body langorous
with love-making and her mind poised in a peace that made
more rest unnecessary. Outside, the almost-full moon rode
high, spilling light through the windows over the computer
table and painting a path across the floor. It was light enough
to see the keyboard. With the sure touch of a sleepwalker,

Ruth sat down and flicked it on. But she was not asleep, only totally at ease for the first time in years.

The computer pinged gently in greeting, and Ruth looked a little anxiously toward the bed. Tom turned and flung out one arm across the space where she had lain, but he did not wake. Smiling, she turned down the volume and slipped the game disc into the drive, and Tom was forgotten. Here she was most truly herself. Nothing else mattered here.

A flicker of her fingers brought up the graphics editor. The problem all along had not been expertise but application. Ruth had understood *how* but not *what* she was trying to do, and so the focus and development of the plot lines had remained confused.

She sat with the digitizing pen gripped in her hand, staring at the blank screen. What was the game about, after all? Solving problems, gaining skills and experience, acquiring knowledge? She glimpsed now a way in which all the tangled plot lines might be interlaced so that anything that one player did would affect the choices offered to all the others. It would be a truly elegant series of branchings, and there could be a progression in the kinds of challenges offered, as well.

Brows knitted in concentration, Ruth began to sketch out a bridge with a Gateway at its farther end. New code governed how the Gate would grow as the player approached it, and more work with the graphics showed the grain of the wood, the ornate handle on the door.

Eventually she would want to edit what came after, but now she needed to find out what was on the other side. Ruth switched to text again and began to type in—

You and your companions have solved the maze and reached the heart of the Forbidden City. You open a gate, and find before you a Garden. As you walk through it, greenery springs up around you, glowing with energy. The garden hums with life, bright birds play, and animal eyes glow like gems among the leaves. Beyond the fountain grows a single Tree, straight trunked, lavishly leaved, splendid in majesty. Fruit hangs in jeweled clusters from its boughs, and every fruit and every leaf it bears seems to be outlined in a glow of gold. Twined about its trunk, a serpent watches you.

You hesitate, but a voice speaks in your ear, "This is the Tree of Knowledge. Those who wander here may eat its fruit, for Love has conquered fear."

What will you do?

CAPTIVATING TALES OF FANTASY WORLDS BY TODAY'S BRIGHTEST YOUNG AUTHORS

PATRICIA McKILLIP

____ 0-425-09452-9   The Forgotten Beasts of Eld $2.95
____ 0-425-09206-2   The Moon and the Face $2.95
____ 0-425-08457-4   Moon-Flash $2.75

ROBIN McKINLEY

____ 0-425-08840-5   The Blue Sword $2.95
____ 0-441-10149-5   The Hero and The Crown $2.95

PATRICIA C. WREDE

____ 0-441-13897-7   Daughter of Witches $2.95
____ 0-441-31759-6   The Harp of Imach Thyssel $2.95
____ 0-441-75976-9   The Seven Towers $2.95
____ 0-441-76014-7   Shadow Magic $2.95
____ 0-441-79591-9   Talking to Dragons $2.25
____ 0-441-76006-6   Caught in Crystal $2.95

JANE YOLEN

____ 0-441-09167-9   Cards of Grief $2.75
____ 0-441-51563-0   The Magic Three of Solatia $2.75
____ 0-441-52552-0   Merlin's Booke $2.95